A RECKLESS WAGER

He continued to regard the ring steadily until Elizabeth startled him by saying: "I have not taken it off, not since the night you put it there."

He drew her roughly into his arms, bringing his lips down on hers in a kiss that was hot and hungry and demanding. . . . For so many months she had felt desolate and alone. She'd yearned to have him hold her, dreamed of having him want her, and now, in his arms, she knew she had come home. . . .

AT DAGGERS DRAWN

"I must be quite mad," she whispered to herself, realizing she was sitting in a man's bedroom, willfully touching his bare chest. She had begun to redo the buttons of his nightshirt when he startled her by bringing up a hand to clasp her wrist. . . .

Then, acting not at all like a sick man, he moved his other hand behind her neck and drew her face to his, meeting her lips with his own. . . .

By Lois Menzel
Published by Fawcett Books:

RULED BY PASSION
IN THE SHADOW OF ARABELLA
CELIA
A RECKLESS WAGER/AT DAGGERS DRAWN

A Fawcett Crest Book
Published by Ballantine Books
A Reckless Wager Copyright © 1987 by Lois J. Menzel
At Daggers Drawn Copyright © 1989 by Lois J. Menzel

http://www.randomhouse.com

Library of Congress Catalog Card Number: 95-96178

ISBN 0-449-22505-4

Manufactured in the United States of America

First Edition: July 1996

0 9 8 7 6 5 4 3 2 1

A RECKLES
WAGER

AT DAGGER
DRAWN

Lois Menzel

FAWCETT CREST • NEW YORK

Contents

A
Reckless
Wager

Chapter 1

JULIAN FERRIS, VISCOUNT Stanton, tooled his high-perch phaeton expertly through the narrow space between an old-fashioned landaulet and a hackney carriage and swept into Grosvenor Square without appearing to even slightly check his pair. His perfectly matched bays were well known in London, and today he was counting on them to rescue him from what he knew would be a long and tedious conversation with his godmother.

This formidable lady, the Dowager Duchess of Kern, would be incensed to find that he had driven himself in answer to her summons, but even she would not expect him to keep his horses standing long in the high wind of a chill September day.

Lord Stanton leaped gracefully down from the carriage as his groom ran to the horses' heads.

"I do not plan to be long, Jenkins, but if I am above fifteen minutes, walk 'em." He spoke over his shoulder as he sounded the knocker and a moment later was admitted to the house by a portly and disheveled butler. Stanton gave his caped driving coat into this worthy's hands, along with his high-crowned beaver and gloves, and found himself wondering if his godmother kept any servants under the age of sixty. If there were some younger ones, he mused, they would appear sadly out of place, for the whole musty heap spoke of a bygone era.

Twenty-five years ago the London town house of the Duke and Duchess of Kern had been a showplace for the aristocracy, and invitations to any function there were jealously coveted by the haut ton. Everyone who was anyone could be seen strolling the gracious rooms, conversing with only the cream of London society. But it had been many years since any strain of music rumbled through the formal reception rooms, and longer still since the ballroom had been closed for the last time. Even in those rooms the duchess now used there were unmistakable signs that time marches relentlessly on, leaving nothing untouched. Once bright carpets and window hangings were dulled by exposure and age. Vaulting molded ceilings showed peeling gilded paint, and on many of the high walls priceless portraits hung in dusty frames, too high and too numerous for the hands of elderly servants to tend.

The viscount knew his way well and did not stand upon ceremony with his godmother, but he permitted the butler to lead him upstairs to the drawing room and announce him properly.

"Lord Stanton, Your Grace."

The dowager raised her head as the viscount entered the room, and a smile lit her heavily wrinkled face. "Well, Julian, you have been prompt! I sent my note only yesterday."

Stanton eyed the frail, white-haired lady with patient indulgence. She vexed him with her efforts to direct his life, yet he held her in considerable affection. "I fancied that your need to see me was urgent, ma'am, and I had no desire to keep you waiting."

He crossed the room to her as he spoke, and she noted with approval his claret-colored cutaway coat and dove gray skin-tight pantaloons. As he seated himself in a chair she indicated near the fire, a reflection of the flames danced in the polish of his Hessian boots. He was a strikingly handsome young man, but the duchess realized he would not consider himself so, for vanity was not one of Julian's vices.

"It is fitting that you should call today, Julian. You have given me an opportunity to offer my felicitations." As his brows drew together in inquiry, she knew she had guessed correctly, and he had forgotten. "You are eight-and-twenty today, Julian! Never tell me that you have forgotten your own birthday!"

"I am afraid that I have," he admitted ruefully. "But it is not at all surprising. Such milestones mean little to me."

"Well, you may believe me when I say they are not so meaningless to others of your family."

"Yes, I know, Godmother. Eight-and-twenty and still unmarried! At my age my father and grandfather both had children in leading strings. How remiss of me."

"Sarcasm ill becomes you, Julian, and I cannot believe that

4

you are as indifferent to this subject as you pretend. You must have some thought for what is due your family and your noble ancestors. For over two hundred years, the title you bear has passed from father to eldest son in an unbroken chain. Is it your intention to destroy such a proud heritage?"

"I have never understood why so much attention is paid to that accident of history," Stanton replied. "Sooner or later, one of the Viscounts Stanton will die in a war, or sire only girls, and then the chain will of necessity be broken."

"Nonsense, Julian! The Ferrises always produce sons—strong sons. And so also will you, if you will convince yourself that it is time to take a wife."

This was not the first time the viscount and his godmother had had this conversation. Since his return to England in the spring, she had taken every opportunity to introduce the subject. The theme was always the same; only the characters changed. She was relentless in urging him to marry and never met an eligible debutante without considering the girl as a possible candidate for the future Viscountess Stanton.

"I know your feelings in this matter, Godmother. You have made them plain enough. But I cannot think that marriage is the answer for me. Henry would make a much better husband than I, or even Giles, when he is older."

"That may well be, Julian, but your brothers are not the head of this family. You are. And the responsibility is yours."

"I would not wish to see any wife of mine trapped in the existence my mother had to bear," he responded.

"Your mother had too much sensibility for her own good, which was undoubtedly the result of her being a Frenchwoman. But I agree that she received very shabby treatment from your father, very shabby indeed. He did not comprehend the meaning of the word *discretion*, a fault that you, my dear Julian, have not inherited. He married on a whim and for love—or call it passion if you will—and he found that passion soon dies. If you wish for a sensible marriage that you can be comfortable with, then you must carefully choose the proper woman. You insist that you are not a romantic. Very well. Choose a woman who is not desirous of having your heart at her feet. You must find a girl who is willing to fill the position of wife and mother and accept the fact that you would not be constantly dancing attendance upon her."

The duchess paused for a moment, and when he did not speak, she continued cautiously. "My niece by marriage, Louise Sherwood, has two charming daughters. The elder, Charlotte, is an exceptional girl. She is just twenty-one and has had several seasons. An excellent family, good connections, and the girl is handsomely dowered."

"I believe I have met Miss Sherwood, Godmother, but I assure you, the thought of making her an offer has never crossed my mind."

"Then let it cross your mind!" she snapped. "You cannot remain a bachelor forever! Marry you must, sooner or later. Now that the war is over and you are finished with soldiering, the time is ripe. Charlotte Sherwood is a sensible girl, with no silly romantic notions in her head. She is also remarkably lovely. It would be no penance to take such a girl to wife."

Stanton turned away impatiently, walked to the brandy decanter, and poured himself a liberal portion. He had every right to be annoyed with his godmother for this meddling in his private affairs, but he found that he couldn't blame her. Her feelings were, after all, in harmony with those of most of his family and friends, and indeed with those of society in general. A man of his age and social standing was expected to marry and produce an heir to secure the direct line. But even though he accepted these things, he still found the idea repellent.

Stanton had been to his share of weddings, and he knew the vows as well as any man, but regardless of his godmother's wishes, he had no intention of taking them. Perhaps he was a romantic after all, for he could see no sense in promising faithfulness and then breaking faith at the first convenient moment. His strong innate sense of fairness rebelled at the unwritten social ethic that expected wives to remain faithful while husbands could philander at will, provided, of course, that they were discreet. He had watched his mother suffer endless humiliation as his father had flaunted one mistress after another before the ton. Better not to marry at all than to involve oneself in a situation where pledges were made to be broken and honor sacrificed to desire.

His godmother had implied that Miss Sherwood, if he married her, would be sensible. In other words, she would be willing to accept his behavior even if she was disapproving or resentful.

Is that what he wanted for his life? Marriage to a woman who would not be particularly concerned if he shared another woman's bed? Such a marriage was a sham—meaningless promises, empty vows, hollow honor. He wanted no part of it. He had known his share of women, and he would be content to continue as before. When an interlude ended, when interest flagged and attraction faltered, he would just walk away—no commitment, no ties, no disillusionment, and, most importantly, no guilt.

The dowager duchess was beginning to lose hope that her godson would ever marry, and she was distressed for more than one reason. She wanted the family name protected, it was true, but she also wished to leave her not inconsiderable personal fortune to Julian and had convinced herself that she would not change her will in his favor until he should be safely wed. She had not previously mentioned this subject to him, but she had decided that today she would put her last card on the table and hope that it would be enough to force his hand.

"I am an old woman, my boy, and not in the best of health," she continued. "It would please me to see you comfortably settled."

The viscount smiled tenderly at the old lady and took her frail hand in his. "I have always thought that you would outlive us all, my dear."

"Don't speak nonsense, Julian! Only a fool would wish to live forever. But you change the subject. I wish not to speak of me, but of you, and of those who will come after you."

"But I am a ramshackle fellow, Godmother. We both know I would make the deuce of a bad husband."

"I am not convinced of that, Julian," she argued. "A wife and family could have a steadying effect on you, bring some sense of purpose to your life. I am a wealthy woman, Julian, as you know. I am willing to settle my entire estate on you if you will please me in this matter."

The smile instantly disappeared from Stanton's lips, and he dropped her hand as his brows drew together sharply. "A bribe, ma'am? This is not in your style, surely?"

She could not miss the clipped resentment in his words. "Not a bribe, Julian, rather an inducement. I know you have no need of my money, but few prudent people would refuse a large inheritance out of hand. I ask only that you choose a suitable girl and marry; I place no other condition on the bequest."

Stanton turned away and crossed to the windows overlooking the square below. The dowager maintained a prudent silence. She knew he was not pleased, but she had said all she intended and was now willing to allow the matter to rest. She could see that he was eager to be off, but she had not dismissed him, and his manners were too pretty to allow him to offer her any slight. She knew that he cared for her in his way, and for herself, she had loved him all his life.

The duchess had never borne her husband any sons, but Julian was a perfect example of the son she would have liked to have had. He was of moderate height with a quick, athletic figure. He had fine shoulders and a good leg, and the tight-fitting styles of the day suited him well. His handsome features were topped by a head of thick, medium brown hair that curled slightly. His slate gray eyes were fathomless to most, but the dowager had discovered over the years that they were always her best means to discover what he was thinking. He had a fine, passionate mouth, which, unfortunately, rarely smiled.

As he turned now to face her, she focused her eyes on the grim lines of that mouth as she forced her own into a smile. "Will you be attending Lady Selfridge's ball tomorrow night, Julian?"

"Yes, ma'am, I had planned to go."

"Then, no doubt I shall see you there."

Recognizing his dismissal, Stanton made the proper farewells and took himself off. He saw no sign of his carriage in the street and knew that he had taken longer than the prescribed fifteen minutes. His groom, walking the horses as instructed, soon reappeared, and as the viscount mounted onto the driver's seat, Jenkins handed over the reins.

The dowager stood at the window overlooking the square and watched her godson drive away. Lord Stanton was a nonpareil with the ribbons, and seldom a week went by when he was not challenged by one man or another to race one of his teams or pairs. His name was often to be seen in the betting books, for he could never resist the opportunity to race his bloodstock. This partiality for racing did not concern his godmother, for his wagers were never outrageous, and he seldom lost.

The dowager sighed and turned from the window as Stanton disappeared in the direction of St. James. He had grudgingly given her less than half an hour of his time but now would go on to White's and amuse himself for hours on end. If Stanton was to be at Caro Selfridge's tomorrow, the dowager had every intention of making a push at least to see that he and Miss Charlotte Sherwood should become better acquainted.

Chapter 2

LORD STANTON AND Sir Hugh Broughton sat silently as the last course of their dinner was cleared and the port decanter placed upon the table. Stanton dismissed his footman with a nod and then reached to pour wine for his friend. Sir Hugh was a taller man than the viscount, slimmer, and fair. Both were attired in strict evening dress, for they were to proceed shortly to Lady Selfridge's grand ball.

Earlier in the evening, the viscount had made his friend privy to the previous day's conversation with his godmother, and now he eyed Sir Hugh speculatively.

"What do you know of the Sherwood family, Hugh?"

"No more than the next man, I suppose. Lord Sherwood is in his early fifties; came into the title about two years ago. There are the two girls, a younger son in the army, and of course, Richard."

"Richard?"

"Yes. Richard Sherwood."

"Good Lord! Are you telling me this is the same family?"

"Yes. Of course. I thought you knew."

"No. I hadn't made the connection. If I recall Miss Sherwood, she is dark and slight."

"Yes. And Richard is a blond giant. I agree there is little resemblance, but they are brother and sister nevertheless."

Stanton smiled reminiscently. "Remember how much we missed him when he sold out?"

"I lost count of the times he rescued you from one of your harebrained schemes, Julian. When I look back now, I can see that some of your plans for our entertainment were really quite mad."

"One must have something to occupy one's time between battles," Stanton said defensively. "Even forced marches were preferable to sitting bivouacked in one spot for days on end. London is starting to bore me, too. There is a sameness about each day that makes one long for a change."

"You felt that way about Oxford."

"So did you, and we never knew a happier time than those days when we shook the dust of those august halls from our boots, bought our colors, and shipped off to Portugal. Now that the war is over, how do we occupy ourselves, Hugh? Have you given it any thought?"

"I plan to look about me for a wife. I'm the last of the line, after all, and I am not as opposed to the idea of marriage as you are, Julian. You might be wise to at least consider your godmother's advice."

"What! Are you taking her side in this?"

"No. Of course not. But as long as I've known you, Julian, you've had the habit of selling yourself short. I think you would make a fine husband."

"Your confidence is gratifying, Hugh, but I will stand by my decision. I must admit, however, to some little curiosity about Miss Sherwood. My godmother seems convinced that this girl would be the perfect wife for me."

Lady Selfridge's ball was an intolerable squeeze and no doubt would therefore be put down as one of the highlights of the Little Season. As Lord Stanton and Sir Hugh Broughton made their way through the press of people, they estimated that there were nearly four hundred persons present.

"I should have talked you out of coming here, Julian," Sir Hugh protested. "We will most likely be suffocated in this crowd."

"I promised my godmother that I would be here, Hugh, and

I will bet you a monkey, and even offer you odds, that she will have Miss Sherwood at her side."

"I won't take that bet," his friend replied. "You have been too damnably lucky all week. But I don't see how you can be so certain that she will have the girl in tow. She did no more than mention Miss Sherwood to you yesterday. Surely she won't *thrust* the girl into your arms."

"Oh, I would place no assurance on that, my dear Hugh. My godmother has no scruples when it comes to the matter of my marriage. If she could arrange to have me compromise a young lady—a lady of unquestionable suitability, of course—she would do it without a moment's hesitation. She is mad to have me married."

"And you are equally determined not to be leg-shackled. Although how you can turn your back on nearly eighty thousand, just to preserve your solitude, is something I cannot fathom!"

"I don't need my godmother's money, Hugh."

"Then marry the girl and give Her Grace's money to me," Sir Hugh suggested, "for I could certainly find a use for it."

"You know that I would do almost anything to oblige you, Hugh—but marry to improve your fortune?—no, my friend, I am afraid that there I must draw the line."

The two gentlemen made uneven progress through the reception rooms, full to bursting with elegant ladies in gowns of every color and description and equally elegant gentlemen in more sober darker hues. They were greeted by dozens of friends and acquaintances but managed slowly to gain the ballroom. Stanton methodically scanned the walls certain that he would find his godmother there.

Stanton laid a hand on Sir Hugh's arm to claim his companion's attention. "You were wise to refuse my wager earlier, Hugh, for if you will look ahead, against the far wall and to the left of that green urn, you will see my godmother, and, unless I miss my guess, the matron to her left is Lady Sherwood."

Sir Hugh followed the direction of his friend's gaze but only mumbled, "Very handsome woman. And the two young ladies?"

"The Misses Sherwood, of course. Charlotte, the elder, we

have met. She is in the rose gown. And her younger sister, very properly, in debutante white."

Stanton had paid little attention to Charlotte Sherwood on first meeting her, and if she had not been with his godmother tonight, he doubted that he could have recognized her again. But now, with his godmother's praise of her person ringing in his memory, he took a moment to observe her. She was a brunette, her dark hair cropped short in the latest fashion and curling about her face attractively. Her rose gown was simple but elegant and set off her excellent figure to advantage. She stood speaking quietly with her sister, a gentle smile hovering on her lips. Her complexion was flawless, her features feminine and harmonious. For one fantastic moment he tried to imagine her as his wife. If her personality matched her physical attractions, she would certainly be a woman of whom a man could be proud.

In the next moment, Lord Stanton and Sir Hugh stood before the duchess and she beamed happily upon her godson and his tall, fair friend. "Julian, and Sir Hugh, how good of you to seek me out. Allow me to introduce my niece, Lady Sherwood . . . This is my godson, Louise—Viscount Stanton, and his friend, Sir Hugh Broughton."

Both gentlemen took Lady Sherwood's hand briefly in theirs, and then she made them known to her daughters. Stanton had time only to note that Charlotte's voice was low and pleasant and her eyes a rich brown, and then he turned from her placid and serene face to make the acquaintance of her younger sister. He had to drop his gaze an inch or two, for Miss Elizabeth was shorter and slighter than Charlotte. The first thing he noticed about Elizabeth Sherwood was her smile, for it was warm and welcoming, and an indication of her extreme youth and innocence, he thought. Women better versed in the social graces did not bestow smiles so generously upon strangers. Elizabeth's hair, a shade darker than her sister's, was piled high on her head with only a few long curls permitted to escape onto her shoulder. As he took her hand, she sank into a curtsy deep enough for royalty, and as she rose, he found her staring boldly into his eyes. He was accustomed to having chits of this age stammer and blush and cast their eyes down upon meeting him. But Miss Elizabeth met his gaze directly, her brown eyes twinkling and mischievous, and despite himself, his rare smile appeared.

A moment later he turned to Charlotte again and solicited her hand for the next dance. Sir Hugh invited Miss Elizabeth to stand up with him for the same set, and the couples moved off to join the other dancers. The dowager smiled approvingly, even though she realized that her godson had asked Miss Sherwood more from a desire to satisfy an old woman's whim than from any desire to please himself.

Both the Misses Sherwood had been popular since their arrival upon the social scene. Their father had come into the title quite unexpectedly when his father and elder brother had drowned together in a yachting accident. Jarvis Sherwood had been, all his adult life, a seagoing man, rising on his own merits to the rank of captain under Lord Nelson. He was proud of his career and proud of the years he had spent serving his country. But overnight, at the age of fifty, he had become a peer of the realm, and the transformation had been overpowering. He had inherited not only the title but a large fortune as well, and considerable property in Surrey. His elder son, Richard, was now heir to a barony, and his daughters were expected to be presented at the Queen's Drawing Room and make their debut in Society.

The Sherwood family had moved from their modest home in Sussex to the handsome manor house at Sherwood Park. Lord Sherwood had, of course, lived there as a youth and was not unaccustomed to it. His children, however, found it very grand and were delighted that their fortunes had taken such a turn. The girls were both eager to enter Society, and their father generously settled twenty-thousand pounds on each of them. They could marry, or if they preferred, they could remain single, assured of independence through their own income.

Lady Sherwood watched her daughters move gracefully about the room. Elizabeth was smiling at something Sir Hugh had said to her but never faltered in the intricate steps of the dance.

"If you were brought out last year, Miss Elizabeth, how is it that we have never met?" Sir Hugh asked.

"I was not presented at court until this year, sir, so I did not attend such grand parties last year. Also, I don't think that you, or Lord Stanton, for that matter, often attend functions of this sort."

He smiled broadly. "It is true that we enjoy rather less crowded gatherings as a rule. But I am glad we came tonight."

On the opposite side of the room, Lord Stanton and Charlotte were having an equally pleasant conversation. "It seems you have a very military family, Miss Sherwood. Your father was in the navy, was he not?"

"Indeed, my lord. His last command was captain of the frigate *Valiant*."

"Then he was with Nelson at Trafalgar?"

"Yes, he was. He says it was the most glorious action of his career."

"I can well believe it. I served with your brother Richard in the Peninsula, and I think you have yet another brother in the army."

"My brother Jonathan is with the 1st Guards"—she nodded, smiling—"though he complains that it is dreadfully dull since the peace was signed."

"So you are Richard Sherwood's little sister," the viscount said thoughtfully. "I would never have guessed it. You are not very like him."

Charlotte smiled again but could not answer, for the dance was ending. Stanton returned her to her mother's side, thanked her politely, and begged her to convey his regards to her brother.

Lord Stanton and Sir Hugh stood for a few moments in conversation and then parted company as Sir Hugh asked another young lady to dance and the viscount strolled toward the library, which he expected would be a male stronghold tonight, where he could sit and enjoy a glass of brandy and some masculine conversation.

Even though he managed to find congenial company, Stanton's thoughts strayed more than once to Miss Charlotte Sherwood. His godmother was right. Miss Sherwood was a beauty. She was also intelligent, modest, and unassuming—altogether a very comfortable female. He found himself thinking that a man might search long and hard before finding another such paragon. And yet, if he were to allow such a woman into his life, he would be in many ways answerable to her. Simple civility demanded that, at least. For most of his life he had been answerable only to himself. A wife would drastically alter his life-style, placing upon him responsibilities that he did not desire.

Nearly an hour later, Stanton quit the library, determined to search out Sir Hugh and, if necessary, drag him bodily from the ball. The library was some distance removed from the public reception rooms, and Stanton stepped out into the quiet, empty hallway, closing the door behind him. He turned toward the ballroom and had just reached a spot where two corridors converged, when he suddenly collided with a young woman hurrying heedlessly from the other direction. She was nearly running down the hallway, yet her face was turned back, watching behind, as if she feared pursuit.

The sudden collision brought a startled exclamation from the young lady as she stumbled and lost her balance. Stanton reached quickly to steady her and for the briefest moment held her close against him, but in an instant his hands were at her waist as he set her away, holding her only long enough to be certain that she had regained her balance. It was then that he realized the young lady was not unknown to him, for he was staring into the startled dark brown eyes of Elizabeth Sherwood. Earlier in the evening he had written her off as an attractive child, but as she tumbled against him he was brought to realize his mistake. Young, she might be—but a child, definitely not.

"My Lord Stanton! Excuse me!" As she realized her hands had come to rest against his chest, she drew them quickly away and busied them in smoothing the front of her gown. "How foolish of me not to watch where I was going. Pray forgive me."

She glanced over her shoulder again as the viscount murmured, "Think nothing of it, Miss Sherwood." Her heightened color and obvious agitation were hard to ignore, yet the viscount was hesitant to intrude into what was clearly none of his concern. "Surely you are not alone in this part of the house, ma'am. What brings you here?"

"Lord Granbrooke offered to show me the picture gallery. It is said to be very fine, and I was eager to see it." She paused, glancing down at her hands in confusion.

"But . . .?" he coaxed.

"But I did not enjoy it . . . Lord Granbrooke . . . he . . ."

"You need say no more, Miss Sherwood. I am acquainted with Granbrooke. Sometimes he enjoys his wine too much."

Her face brightened perceptively at this possible explanation for the excess civility Lord Granbrooke had treated her to. "Yes, of course. It must have been the wine. Gentlemen sometimes do tend to overdo, don't they?"

"Some certainly do. May I escort you to the ballroom? I am sure that the duchess and Lady Sherwood will be wondering what has become of you."

"Yes, thank you, my lord. You are very kind."

She took the arm he offered, and they returned slowly to the ballroom. They did not encounter Lord Granbrooke, but Stanton sensed the young lady's anxiety and guessed that she was making a supreme effort to keep from turning to look behind them. There was no doubt in his mind that Granbrooke had taken her to the gallery to make some sort of improper advance. Granbrooke was a fool. If he really wanted to win this girl, he would never do so using such tactics. A young and inexperienced miss could only be frightened by that kind of behavior. Stanton considered dropping a word in his godmother's ear about warning Lady Sherwood but then decided that a word to Miss Sherwood herself would not come amiss and would possibly be better taken from him.

"If you wish to avoid such confrontations in the future, ma'am, you need only direct your admirers to a place where others are present. A crowd of people will generally dampen the ardor of the most passionate cavalier."

As he offered this advice in the most conversational tone, and accompanied by a gentle smile, Elizabeth could not take it amiss. She smiled in return, and he thought again how warm and lovely a smile it was, turning up the corners of a generous mouth to show a row of perfect teeth, denting both cheeks with tempting dimples, and lighting her eyes with a rich, warm glow.

"I thank you for the advice, my lord, and I promise that I will heed it." She wondered if he included himself in that advice and then chided herself for thinking that she could inspire any passion in the lofty Viscount Stanton. Even though she had never met him before tonight, she had heard a great deal about him. People said he was a confirmed bachelor, and his tastes ran to older, experienced ladies.

Elizabeth found herself thinking that the man at her side was not what she had expected. He seemed more friendly than aloof, and genuinely concerned for her welfare. He need not have inquired into her distress, nor was he obliged to escort her back to her mother or offer her friendly advice. Charlotte had said after her dance with Stanton that he had admitted knowing Richard. Perhaps he had been kind to her for her brother's sake, or perhaps because of the distant relationship they shared through his godmother. Whatever his reasons, she was pleased with him and disposed to like him.

Shortly after Viscount Stanton had returned Miss Sherwood to her mother, he encountered Sir Hugh again, and together they quit Lady Selfridge's ball. When Sir Hugh suggested they go on to Watier's, the viscount demurred, insisting he felt more reckless than Watier's. They went instead to Victor's, off St. James, a house that had lately been enjoying a spate of popularity. Victor's was most certainly a gaming hell, but it was a cut above some of the more disreputable places. Its owner kept an excellent cellar, admission was by private invitation only, and although the play was deep, it was fair. The gentlemen settled down to a friendly game of macao and a bottle of excellent cognac.

Lord Stanton and Sir Hugh had arrived at the club sometime after midnight. By three o'clock they were well into their second bottle of brandy, and both feeling a trifle above par. They were tiring of their game when Robert, Lord Granbrooke, approached their table. His flushed complexion indicated that he, too, had been imbibing freely, and he addressed the viscount jovially.

"Well met, Stanton. I have wanted to speak with you anytime these past several days. I have bought myself a new pair, and I think I may have found some cattle at last that will take the shine out of your grays."

Sir Hugh laughed rather loudly, but it was a sound totally devoid of humor. "Will you never learn, Granbrooke? How many times is it now that Julian has beaten your unbeatable horses? Is it three or four?"

"It has been four times," the viscount replied solemnly, "but I am not opposed to taking your money for the fifth time,

17

Granbrooke. Name the day and the distance, and my horses and I shall be at your disposal."

"Don't you care to see my animals first?" Granbrooke asked.

"Not at all. I am sure they are everything you say they are, and we will have a fine race. What should you care to chance on your pair this time?"

They mutually agreed upon a wager of one thousand pounds, although Stanton was certain that Granbrooke could ill afford it. It was generally known about town that his lordship was under the hatches, and the fact that he had been dangling after several heiresses indicated to most observers that he intended to mend his fortunes by making an advantageous match. The knowledge that he was a gazetted fortune hunter would not deter certain ambitious mamas from attempting to secure a title for their daughters.

Lord Granbrooke moved away and soon afterward left the club. Mr. Duffney, one of a group of gentlemen who had been standing nearby, offered his opinion on the proposed race. "I don't see why you bother to race him, Stanton. The fellow is a damned loose screw."

"I bother to race him because he is an excellent whip, and he provides me with good sport. It is no concern of mine how he chooses to conduct himself in his private life."

"Lately," Duffney continued, "he has been most marked in his attentions to the younger of the Sherwood girls—Elizabeth, I believe her name is. I feel sorry for the young lady who accepts him, for in a very short time he will gamble away whatever money she has brought him, and she will then find herself sharing his poverty."

Sir Hugh's interest was immediately caught. "I do not think you need concern yourself over Miss Sherwood's falling into his trap, Duffney," he replied. "I only met her for the first time tonight, but I assure you, she is quite above his touch."

Stanton added in support of his friend's statement, "Miss Elizabeth Sherwood also has a father and two brothers who will waste little time in taking Granbrooke's measure. My godmother assures me that it is a most unexceptionable family. Miss Elizabeth can look much higher than Granbrooke."

As Stanton turned from Duffney back to Sir Hugh, his attention was caught by a man across the room. In his present inebriated state the viscount found the strange gentleman's puce coat to be of a most offensive hue. "Who the devil is that purple popinjay?" he demanded. "That coat of his fairly pains my eyes!"

Sir Hugh turned to see to whom Stanton was referring, and his face lit with sudden pleasure. "That, my dear Julian, is Reginald Fielding!" he exclaimed. "The fellow I have been telling you about."

"The marksman?"

"The same. I swear I have never seen anything like it. I watched him for more than an hour at Manton's and never once saw him miss his mark."

"Invite the fellow over here, Hugh. I will try to suffer his coat, for I would very much like to meet the man who can shoot so well."

Sir Hugh soon brought Mr. Fielding to the table, and introductions were made. "I have heard a great deal about your talent with a pistol, Fielding," the viscount said. "I will look forward to seeing you in action sometime soon."

"Your lordship's own skill with pistols is not unheralded," Fielding returned.

"I am accounted, I believe, to be tolerably accurate. Would you care to make a match between us, Fielding?"

"Certainly, my lord. Anytime you like."

"Why not now?" the viscount asked.

"Now, my lord? You cannot be serious!"

"I assure you that I am," Stanton continued. "It won't be the first time pistols have been fired in this place. Sir Hugh tells me that you can shoot the spots from a playing card across the room. Shall we try such a contest?"

"I will be more than happy to oblige you, my lord, but not tonight. You have, as you know, been drinking. I, on the other hand, have not. Such a contest would be unfair."

Sir Hugh saw that Stanton was about to expostulate strongly, and he hastened to intervene. "He's right, you know, Julian. You wouldn't care to race your horses against a man who wasn't cold sober. Same thing holds true for shooting. You'll have your fairest match if you wait until you can meet on an equal footing."

This logic was inescapable, and the viscount lapsed into a brooding silence, but even after Fielding had departed, he still could think only of how much he would like to shoot the spots from a playing card. "I am certain I could do it, Hugh."

His friend smiled at him. "Perhaps, if you were sober, you could. But in your cups, I doubt if you could hit the card, let alone the spots."

Lord Stanton rose unsteadily to his feet. "Drunk or sober, my dear Hugh," he said defiantly, "I will wager you that I can shoot the spots from a five of spades across this very room."

"You are hopeless, Julian." His friend laughed. "Is there nothing you will not bet upon?"

"Find me a pistol, name your stakes, and we will see just how steady this brandy-soaked hand of mine really is. What shall it be, Hugh? I am weary of the same hundred-pound wager. Let this be one with some teeth in it. We shall each pledge something we would truly be loath to part with."

"Very well," Sir Hugh replied, considering. "I am so sure that you cannot do it, that I will wager my brown hack, the one I bought from Sorington."

"I thought it likely that sooner or later I could get you to put him up," Stanton said. "But what have I of equal value?"

There was silence for a moment while they both pondered this question, and finally Sir Hugh spoke. "There is only one thing that you have, Julian, that you truly value."

"And what would that be, my friend?"

"Your freedom."

"My freedom? What do you mean?"

"If you are so certain that you can accomplish this amazing feat of marksmanship, then wager your freedom against my horse. If you succeed in hitting all five spots, then the horse is yours; but if you miss any of them, you will follow your godmother's advice before the week is out and try your luck with the young lady."

The viscount's eyes opened in astonishment at the stakes his friend suggested. There were several men gathering about their table now that news of a possible contest had spread through the various rooms of the club. Stanton knew that Sir Hugh was referring to his offering for Miss Sherwood, but he would not, of course, mention her name in public and in connection with a wager.

"Those are very high stakes indeed, Hugh," he said,

meeting the challenge in his friend's eyes. "But I accept them."

This conversation was lost on the men listening, but they did glean from it that the viscount had decided to try his luck at the target and several of them set about preparations. It was found that the proprietor had an accurate pistol that he was willing to lend to the contest. Several tables were dragged against the far wall and multibranched candelabra placed on each to provide the best possible lighting. Duffney shuffled through a deck of cards to extract the five of spades. One of the waiters had been sent to procure a target board that was kept on hand for just such occasions as this, when young gentlemen who frequented the establishment insisted on such sport.

Stanton was permitted several practice shots to familiarize himself with the pistol, and then the playing card was placed upon the board. Total silence reigned as he raised his arm to fire the first round; the report was deafening in such a confined space. While the viscount carefully reloaded the pistol, the target was examined and found to have one of its spots removed, quite neatly, through the center. Many of the onlookers were amazed, for even those who knew the viscount to be a dead shot could hardly credit his accuracy after the amount of brandy they had seen him consume.

The second spot, and the third, were removed just as neatly, and Stanton was reloading for the fourth try. Sir Hugh was surprised to see that small beads of perspiration had appeared on Stanton's forehead, for Julian's was the coolest head under pressure he had ever known. Watching the steadiness of his friend's arm as he raised it for the fourth time, Sir Hugh was nearly ready to admit that he had lost his favorite hack. The trigger was pulled, the report sounded, and once again the target was checked. The ball had gone wide! It had touched no portion of the card's spot.

Some conversation broke out then, and several of the men wandered away, the entertainment being over. But the viscount continued methodically to reload the pistol. "I shall try for the fifth spot, Hugh," he said, "and if I hit it, I shall have four of five. Then the next time I try, I shall endeavor to improve my score."

Sir Hugh watched his friend in silence, suddenly feeling

very sober indeed. He had won his wager and kept his horse, but he was beginning to believe that the stakes he had insisted upon were too dear.

The fifth round was fired, and although the hit was not dead center, it had definitely struck the spot. "Damned fine shooting, Stanton!" Duffney exclaimed. "You must let me know when you plan to meet Fielding. That is one match I must see!"

Soon afterward, as the dawn was breaking, Lord Stanton and Sir Hugh walked slowly toward Sir Hugh's rooms in Ryder Street. The morning air was cold, and the more sober Sir Hugh became, the more he regretted the night's events.

"You know, Julian," he said finally, "tonight's wager was private between us, and no one would be any the wiser if we simply forgot the whole thing."

Stanton stopped abruptly and turned to his friend in surprise. "You know me better than that, Hugh! A wager is a wager, whether two people or two hundred are involved. You have won fairly, and when I play, I pay. Miss Charlotte Sherwood will receive my offer before the week is out."

Sir Hugh shook his head sadly. "If you end up in a miserable marriage, you will blame me for pitching you into it. I would not lose our friendship over this, Julian, even to satisfy your honor."

The viscount laughed aloud at his friend's concern. "There is no danger of that, Hugh. You and I have been through too much together to allow a mere exchange of marriage vows to come between us. And besides, you are forgetting one thing. My godmother has merely suggested that I make an offer for Miss Sherwood. Who knows? My luck may yet be in! The lady may refuse me!"

Chapter 3

In the book room of his London residence in Mount Street, Lord Jarvis Sherwood sat at a large desk liberally spread with papers of every description and found himself wishing for perhaps the tenth time that his son Richard had not been detained in Surrey. Lord Sherwood had no head for business and was the first to admit it. His naval career had satisfied him, and he had never wished to step into his father's shoes. Born the third son of a baron, he had been sent to Eton, and eventually to Cambridge, but he had never settled there. From his earliest recollections, he had wanted only to be a sailor, for the open sea to him was a magical, mystical place. He had badgered his father relentlessly, until finally, when he had come down from his second year, his father had capitulated. For the next thirty years the sea had been his life, and he had never regretted it. He had married well, settled his wife in a comfortable home on the outskirts of Portsmouth, and fathered four hopeful children. All in all, life had dealt him, he thought, a very fair hand.

As a young man with two older brothers, it had never occurred to the present Lord Sherwood that he would ever succeed to the title. His eldest brother, John, had never married, and when he had succumbed to a heart condition ten years ago, any thought of inheriting still had not crossed Jarvis's mind, for his brother Rupert already had two daughters and would no doubt have sons as well. But Rupert never did produce sons, and when he and his father were lost together in the yachting accident, Captain Sherwood became the new Lord Sherwood. Lord Sherwood found himself master of a large estate, a situation for which he had little training and even less inclination.

In addition to his two daughters, Lord Sherwood had two

sons: Richard, the elder, now twenty-seven, and Jonathan, aged twenty-two. Lord Sherwood had always hoped that his sons would embrace a military career. Richard had finished at Oxford and gone on to the Peninsula to join the army there, and although he had served well for more than four years, he was not enamored of the military. When informed of the fatal accident to his grandfather and uncle, he had resigned his commission and returned home. Jonathan, on the other hand, was eager to join the army, and no sooner had he finished school than he was off to the war. He was understandably disappointed when the hostilities ended within a year of his joining, for as he complained to his sister Charlotte, there was little opportunity for a man to advance himself during peacetime. Jonathan's regiment was part of the Army of Occupation in the Low Countries, but Jonathan himself had just arrived in London for a month's furlough.

Lord Sherwood had turned to Richard for help at the time of his succession and had found his elder son to be an excellent manager. He had dealt admirably with the lawyers, made sense of the mountains of documents, and taken over the reins of the estate as if he had been born to it. Lord Sherwood once apologized to Richard for thrusting so much work onto his shoulders and was more than a little surprised at his son's reply.

"Don't mention it, sir. I like the work. It gives me something constructive to do with my time, and I enjoy it that much more because I know you find it irksome."

Irksome was a much milder word than Lord Sherwood would have chosen to use. Farmers and tenants, cows and sheep, fodder and wool were all matters that he preferred never to think of at all. So from that time forward, Richard handled all the affairs of the estate, and his father enjoyed the first true leisure he had known in his adult life.

England had been at war for more than twenty years, and Lord Sherwood had spent the large majority of that time away from his country, family, and home. He was proud of his sons and daughters and very much in love with his wife, and he was determined to enjoy the good fortune that had come his way. He retired from active military duty, a decision made easier for him by the peace with France, but he still held a post in the government as adviser to the Admiralty. This position required that he spend a great deal of time in London, which he was able to do so long as Richard was willing to take responsibility for the Surrey property.

Lord Sherwood looked once again at the mass of work that had accumulated on his desk during the weeks of Richard's absence. "Thank God the boy will be back in town soon," he said to himself.

He was interrupted at that moment by the entrance of his butler. "Excuse me, my lord, but Lord Granbrooke has called and wishes an audience with you."

"Give me a few moments, Williams, and then show the gentleman in."

"Very good, my lord."

As the butler disappeared, Lord Sherwood opened a large drawer at the side of his desk and slid all the offending papers into it. They filled it nearly to the top. He shoved in the last pages and closed the drawer as Lord Granbrooke was announced.

Usually when a gentleman with whom Lord Sherwood was barely acquainted made a request to speak with him in private, he expected to receive an application for permission to address one or the other of his daughters. And, indeed, he had correctly guessed the reason for Lord Granbrooke's visit. Today the lady in question was Elizabeth, and Lord Granbrooke had called to make a very proper offer for her hand in marriage.

On the first floor at the back of the Sherwoods' town house was a small sitting room where the Sherwood ladies habitually gathered when they wished to be private. Miss Charlotte Sherwood entered this room now, and both her mother and sister looked up as she announced with a voice of doom, "Lord Granbrooke is with Papa in the book room."

Elizabeth looked imploringly at her mother. "Oh, Mama, what shall I do?"

"Come now, Lizzie, there is no need for such distress. This visit is, after all, no more than you expected."

"But, Mama, I did everything I could to discourage him. I even hinted that I had developed a *tendre* for someone else."

"Well, it clearly didn't serve," Charlotte said dampingly. "But I don't see why you should be in such a taking. You have only to politely refuse him. Or, better yet, have Papa do it for you."

This idea had not previously occurred to Elizabeth, and she grasped at it now. "Do you think he would do so, Mama?"

"I am sure your father would willingly do so should you ask it of him, Lizzie. But do you not think that Lord Granbrooke deserves, at the very least, the courtesy of a direct answer from you? It is not every day, after all, that a man asks a woman to be his wife."

"I'm sure you are right," Elizabeth said, "but I must admit that I am rather afraid of him."

"Afraid of whom?" This question from the doorway caused all three women to turn their heads as Jonathan Sherwood entered the room, resplendent in his Guardsmen's uniform of scarlet and gold. He was a well-made young man of above average height, with an open, smiling countenance. His hair, like that of his sisters, was dark brown, but his eyes, unlike theirs, were gray.

"Lord Granbrooke is with Papa and has come to make an offer for Lizzie," Charlotte explained.

Ensign Sherwood flung himself down on the sofa beside his youngest sister and offered gallantly, "Shall I go down and send him to the rightabout?"

"I wish you would," Elizabeth returned with feeling, "but Mama feels that his lordship deserves to have my answer personally, however much I may dread giving it."

"Do you think so, Mama?" Jonathan asked. "I would agree with you if I thought for one moment that Granbrooke's affections were involved. But we are all agreed, are we not, that it is Lizzie's fortune and not her admirable person that has taken Lord Granbrooke's fancy? I see no reason for her to meet him if she has an aversion to the task."

Elizabeth's hopes rose at her brother's words but fell quickly as her mother spoke again. "We may think that we understand his lordship's motives, Jon, but it would be folly to pretend that we are certain of them. If Elizabeth has engendered those feelings in a man that would lead him to offer for her, for whatever reasons, then it is her responsibility to explain to the gentleman why she cannot, or will not, accept him."

Hearing the finality in her mother's voice, and realizing that she was undoubtedly right, Elizabeth rose from the sofa resolutely. "Well, I must go then. Wish me courage."

Jonathan laughed outright. "That you have never lacked, little sister! When you have finished making Granbrooke the unhappiest of men, hurry back, and bring my father with you, for I have some news of my own to impart."

Elizabeth went quickly down the stairs to the ground floor and there encountered Williams, preparing to come in search of her. "Lord Sherwood would like you to wait on him in the book room, Miss Elizabeth."

"I suspected as much, Williams. Thank you." She glanced at her image in the hall mirror, pushed one stray curl back from her forehead, and made sure that her blue sash was neat. Then she followed the butler to the book room door.

Lord Sherwood, who had perforce spent months and sometimes years away from his family, had missed a great deal of his children's adolescent years. But during the past two years, he had taken advantage of the opportunity to know them better, and he could see now that his Lizzie was not looking forward to this interview. He walked forward to meet her and took her hand firmly in his. Elizabeth was not shy in company, but this was the first offer she had received, so the situation was unusual and therefore uncomfortable for her.

"Lord Granbrooke would like a few moments of private conversation with you, Elizabeth," her father said simply. "You may use this room. I will see that you are not disturbed."

He left on the words, and Elizabeth found herself nervously confronting Lord Granbrooke. If she was dispassionate about his lordship, she had to admit that he was an attractive man. He was not above medium height, but he had a strong-looking, muscular figure. She had heard that he was a noted Corinthian, and she could readily believe it. She had also heard that he was addicted to the gaming tables, and although this predilection did not exhibit itself upon his person, she was nevertheless convinced of its veracity. His interest in her hand, she felt, had always been feigned, and she had not the slightest doubt that were her dowry to vanish overnight, her suitor would vanish just as quickly.

She had not met him since their misadventure in Lady Selfridge's picture gallery, and she wished now that she had confided that incident to her mother. She had hesitated to do so, knowing that she had been foolish to accompany him there and that her mother would be displeased.

It had seemed harmless enough at the time. She had wished to view the paintings and had enjoyed the early part of their stroll down the long, narrow gallery. A full-length portrait of the present countess was exquisite, and Elizabeth had stopped to admire it, even though the cut of the crimson gown the countess wore revealed enough of her ample bosom to make Elizabeth blush.

"The countess is a lovely woman, is she not?" her companion had asked, noting her heightened color.

"Her gown is stunning," Elizabeth had answered.

". . . if a bit revealing."

Elizabeth had returned no answer, and Granbrooke had continued smoothly. "Married women have a great deal of license in the matter of dress. You would look enchanting yourself in such a gown, Elizabeth, and I would willingly buy you a dozen."

Elizabeth had turned startled eyes to him, shocked as much by his use of her name as by the meaning of his words. In the next instant he had taken her shoulders in his hands and bent his mouth to hers, but as she had instinctively pulled from his touch, his lips had never reached their goal.

"Please, my lord . . . you . . . I . . . please, excuse me." And with only that, she had fled, unable to voice the anger she felt, unable to command a glib rejoinder to gloss over the moment, unable to remain one instant longer in his presence, wanting only the busy ballroom and the security it provided. Moments later she had collided with Viscount Stanton outside the library.

Now as Lord Granbrooke stood before her she felt the unease of that evening returning as she slowly crossed the room and held out her hand to him, more from unconscious habit than from any desire to touch him. He took it and held it longer than she would have liked.

"My dear Miss Elizabeth, it is good of you to see me," he said very formally. "I am sure you must have guessed the reason for my visit. I think that you cannot be unaware of my sentiments upon this occasion." He paused briefly, and Elizabeth felt that she should say something, but not a single word would come to her lips. His lordship seemed undaunted by her silence, no doubt attributing it to maidenly modesty, and he continued smoothly. "I have spoken with your father, and he has given me permission to address you. It is my most earnest wish that you would consent to become my wife."

He is persistent, she thought, but still she said nothing, and after a moment, he continued. "Please allow me to apologize for my precipitate behavior the other evening. I frightened you, and you must believe me, I had no intention of doing so. I was swept away by your loveliness—"

Disliking the direction his thoughts were taking, Elizabeth finally found her voice. "My Lord Granbrooke," she interrupted, "I am honored by your proposal, but I am afraid that it is impossible for me to accept it." She had planned to say that she could not return his regard, but the words would not come. Instead, she heard herself saying, "I had tried to hint to you that such a declaration would not be welcomed by me." To her credit, Elizabeth was steadily regarding him as she uttered her totally fabricated refusal. She watched as the hope slowly died from his eyes, and then she dealt it the final, fatal blow. "The fact is, my lord, that my affections are otherwise engaged."

"I see," he said rather tightly. "I had no idea. Well, of course, if such is the case, then I perfectly understand. I am sorry if I have caused you any embarrassment, Miss Elizabeth."

"No. None at all, my lord."

It only remained for Lord Granbrooke to take his leave, which he promptly did, begging Elizabeth to convey his compliments to her parents. He then made her a stiff, formal bow and left the house. Elizabeth decided that his lordship had not expected to meet with a rejection and was having some difficulty in believing that he had. She did not regret the impulse that had made her mislead him, for she was certain that had she given him any other answer, he would have continued his pursuit of her.

The interview was disquieting for Elizabeth, but once relieved of her suitor, her spirits rebounded, and remembering that Jonathan had bade her hurry back, she returned at once to the sitting room.

"Back so soon, Lizzie?" Jonathan teased.

"It does not take a great deal of time to say no, after all," Charlotte said practically.

"Did you refuse him, then, Lizzie?" her father asked.

"Yes, Papa. I did. I have not the slightest wish to marry Lord Granbrooke."

"Lizzie is determined to marry only for love," Charlotte added scornfully.

"There is no fault to be found with that," Lady Sherwood said. "Your father and I made a love match, and it has served us well. But, come. Jonathan has some news that he wishes to share with us, and I am sure we are all most anxious to hear it."

"Yes, well, I do have an announcement to make," Jon said, "and although I daresay I should wait until Richard returns, I am bursting to tell someone. I have asked Harriet Putnam to marry me, and she has accepted!"

This communication had the effect of causing the Sherwood family to all suddenly begin speaking at once, and then just as suddenly to stop in midsentence, as they heard their voices mingling in confusion.

Jonathan laughed. "I can see that I have not surprised you!"

"Certainly not," Elizabeth said. "We have been expecting you to offer for Harriet forever."

Lord Sherwood crossed the room to his son and reached to take his hand. "Allow us to wish you happy, Jonathan. You know, of course, that we all hold Harriet in affection and esteem."

Jonathan did know this to be true, and indeed, it would have been difficult to find someone who did not like Harriet. She was a quiet, handsome girl, possessed of both pleasing manners and excellent sense. The Sherwoods had known her all her life, for she was the only child of their nearest neighbor in Sussex. As boys, both Jonathan and Richard had admired Harriet, and had even gone so far as to vie for her attention when they were home from school over the long vacations; but their interest had been neighborly amicability, with nothing of the romantic in it.

Squire Putnam, always ambitious for his daughter, had sent her at nineteen to spend a season with his sister in London. With the signing of the peace that spring, Jonathan's regiment had been billeted outside London, and he had been granted the opportunity to see his young neighbor in all her London finery. Harriet was much admired but seemed to smile more often upon her childhood playmate than upon any of her London beaux. It was not many weeks before Jonathan had become most marked in his attentions, but before anything could be decided between them, he had received orders to sail for Belgium with the occupational army and had not been back to England since. Now on furlough, he was determined to make good use of his time. He had been home only two days and was already engaged to be married.

"Have you spoken to Squire Putnam, Jonathan?" his father asked.

"Yes. I stopped at Portsmouth on my way home."

"And what did he say?"

"I think he had hoped Harriet would make a great match and not settle for a younger son," he said ruefully. "But he was a brick about it. He said that if I was Harriet's choice, he would do nothing to throw a rub in the way."

"Have you chosen a date for the wedding, Jonathan?" Lady Sherwood asked.

"Yes, Mama, we have. Three weeks from today—if you think we can manage it."

Chapter 4

SHERWOOD MANOR STOOD in a deep wooded valley, under the shadow of the Surrey Downs. The barony of Sherwood had existed from Saxon times, but the present manor house was of a much later date. During the reign of Charles II a previous Baron Sherwood, considering his medieval home to be anything but comfortable, had had the entire building razed, with the exception of the chapel, and had had the present house constructed in its place. It was a two-and-a-half-story-red brick structure, handsome and symmetrical, weathered by the passage of time. The house faced east, and the large leaded, mullioned windows of the breakfast parlor sparkled in the early morning sunshine.

Richard Sherwood sat in solitary state at the breakfast table, finishing a hearty meal. He was a tall man with very broad, square shoulders and a strong, athletic figure. He was the only one of the Sherwood offspring to have inherited his mother's coloring, for in striking contrast to his dark-haired brother and sisters, Richard's hair was bronzed gold and his eyes were blue.

From where he sat, Richard could see a groom leading his mare, Sultry, to the front of the house. He rose, and pausing only to take an apple from a bowl on the sideboard, he passed through the entry hall and down the shallow steps to the drive. He was promised in London tomorrow, but now, as he mounted his horse and set off, he considered how he would spend his last day in the country.

There were several tenants to see this morning, but with any luck he would finish by midday and beg a luncheon somewhere along the way, perhaps at the vicarage, where he planned to call and say good-bye. Then he would make one final stop at the receiving office, in the event there was any last-minute correspondence awaiting him. He should be home again in good time to spend a few hours with his father's agent before dinner. The following morning he would be off at first light, and with little more than thirty miles to travel, he could be in town by midday.

The majority of the park at Sherwood Manor lay before the house, to the east, wedged between two upstanding hills that ran parallel for a distance of half a mile. A pair of wrought-iron gates marked the entrance to the drive, and beyond them a winding country lane crossed at right angles. A left-handed turning led northward over several tree-covered ridges and gradually diminished into a cart track and finally a sheep walk as it rose over the grassy chalk country of the Downs. A right-handed turning, which Richard now took, led down to the fertile valley of the Tillingbourne, with neat fields at the foot of the hills and lush pastures stretching to the banks of the gentle river.

By the time Richard had finished with his tenants, the sky was clouding over, and what had begun as a bright late-summer day now held the promise of rain. Turning his horse still farther south, he crossed the Tillingbourne at the ford below the village and made his way toward the church steeple at the far end of the street. Dismounting, he tied his mare to the picket fence surrounding the vicarage. As he had suspected, he was invited for luncheon. The vicar and his wife begged him to carry their good wishes to his family in London, and he promised to do so, but it was almost two o'clock before he managed to get away. One look at the darkening sky told him that he must hurry if he wished to avoid a soaking. He made a quick stop at the receiving office and then turned Sultry toward home.

Richard had nearly reached the gates of Sherwood Manor when, coming round a corner at a canter, he saw a small boy and dog in the road and had to pull Sultry up sharply to avoid running them down. Richard thought the lad could be no more than eight or nine, and he was struggling to lift a large sheep dog that was clearly too heavy for him. The boy looked up apologetically as Sultry tossed her head in response to the unexpected pull on her tender mouth.

"I'm so sorry, sir," he said. "I could hear you coming, but I couldn't move her out of the way in time."

Richard dismounted, noting as he did so that this was no village boy, as he had at first suspected. His speech alone declared him to be gently born, and Richard saw that his short coat and breeches were well made, even though covered with large quantities of both dust and dog hair. "What ails your dog, lad?" he asked.

"Sheba has injured her paw and can't walk on it, and she is too heavy for me to carry. Aren't you Captain Sherwood, sir? From the Manor?"

"I am. And who might you be, young man?"

"Jimmy Ellis, sir. From Ellis End."

"I have met Sir Winston Ellis," Richard replied. "A relative of yours?"

Jimmy nodded. "He is my grandfather."

"Well, Jimmy Ellis, you happen to be in luck, for Sultry here has no objection to dogs, and I am sure she would be more than willing to help you carry your dog home. We will put Sheba up first, and then I shall mount and pull you up behind me."

Jimmy hesitated. "I must not trouble you, sir. I can manage myself."

"How will you get her home without my help?" Richard

challenged. When the boy didn't answer, he continued. "You should not hesitate to accept help when you truly need it, Master Ellis. When a helping hand is offered honestly and willingly, it can be accepted honorably and without obligation. Come now, for if we don't hurry, we are both likely to get a soaking." Even as he spoke several drops of rain fell, while to the north over the Downs, heavy black clouds were bearing down upon them.

Sultry turned an inquisitive muzzle round to her master as he hoisted the injured dog over the saddlebow but made no objection. Young Master Ellis held the dog steadily in place while Richard mounted, and then, reaching down, Richard took Jimmy's hand and pulled him easily up behind the saddle.

"Your home is to the north, Jimmy, is it not?"

"Yes, sir. Follow this road to the end of the wood and then eastward along the Downs."

They had covered only a short distance before the rain began to fall in earnest. "You would have been safely home by now, sir," Jimmy said, "if you had not stopped for us."

"Indeed I would, but don't let it trouble you. This will not be the first time I have been caught in a storm."

A little farther on, the trees ended abruptly as the lonely ridge of the Downs rose before them. The rain was being driven now in sheets before the wind, and Richard was thankful to be able to turn his horse eastward, putting the wind at their backs. They came at length to Ellis End, and although the house itself was not prepossessing, Richard thought the situation charming, with the stark, forbidding commons rising on the one hand and the gentle protection of a tree-covered ridge on the other.

As the house came into sight, Jimmy spoke suddenly. "If you would leave me here, Captain Sherwood, I'm sure I could manage myself."

Richard could not see the boy's face, but he could hear the uneasiness in his voice. "Something is troubling you, Jimmy. What is it?"

"Well, sir, the thing is that my mother isn't likely to be pleased to see me bringing Sheba home."

"No? Why not?"

"She told me I was not to go looking for the dog. Actually, what she said was that I should leave it to the servants. But she didn't make me promise that I wouldn't go, so I haven't really disobeyed her, have I?"

"Yes, young man, I am afraid you have. But I think I understand. When you have lost something that you care for, you are convinced that no other efforts at searching can be nearly as effective as your own."

"Yes, sir, that's exactly right! But the thing is, I'm sure my mother won't see it that way. And if she finds that I've troubled you, and gotten you wet into the bargain, she will be more angry still."

Richard considered the boy's request but finally shook his head as he replied, "I see your problem, truly I do, but I don't think I would be doing you or your parents any service by leaving you here in such weather." Jimmy made no reply, and in a moment Richard continued. "Where shall we take Sheba? To the stables?"

"Yes, sir, for Victor, our groom, will tend the paw, and we can shut Sheba into one of the loose boxes, to keep her from wandering off again."

They rode past the house and on to the stables beyond. Richard gave Jimmy a hand down, and then Jimmy led the big hunter while Richard carried the wet dog inside. There they discovered Victor and were just beginning to examine the wounded paw when Mrs. Ellis swept through the stable door.

She had seen their approach from the front windows of the house, where she had been anxiously waiting since the moment she learned that her son was out in the storm. When they did not stop at the house, she had donned a hooded cloak and hurried to the stables in their wake.

Throwing the hood back, she directed a stern look at her son, but when she spoke, Richard thought there was more concern than anger in her voice. "James William! I might have known that you would disobey me and go searching for that wretched animal. You will answer to me later. For now, leave that dog to Victor, and go to the house immediately and remove those wet things."

Richard had intended to give the boy an encouraging smile, but as Jimmy turned to leave, Richard had no thought to spare for him, for his complete attention was captured by Mrs. Ellis. He saw a tall, elegant woman of striking beauty, with an abundance of auburn hair, braided intricately and piled high upon her head. Her features were fine-drawn and delicate, her complexion extremely fair, with just a touch of color in her high cheekbones. In contrast to her pale skin, her brows were dark, and her lashes long and thick. Her cloak lay open to reveal a simple country gown of dark green wool, finely molded to a figure with full, rounded bosom and neat, trim waist. As she turned her direct gaze upon Richard, he realized he should have guessed that her eyes would be green and magnificent.

Victor walked away with the injured bitch, and Mrs. Ellis held out her hand to Richard. "I must thank you, sir. You have clearly aided my son, and at no small cost to yourself."

He took her hand briefly as he said, "Allow me to introduce myself, ma'am. I am Richard Sherwood, from the Manor."

She smiled. "I am pleased to make your acquaintance, Captain Sherwood. I have heard my father-in-law speak of you. It is unfortunate that we must meet under such circumstances."

"You make too much of it, Mrs. Ellis. I assure you, a little rain doesn't concern me."

"A little rain, sir! You are quite soaked to the skin, and I dare you to deny it."

His ready smile appeared as he said ruefully, "Very well, I admit it, but believe me, I was more than willing to help Jimmy. He was in quite a fix, for the dog was too heavy for him, and he was determined not to leave her when he knew she needed help." He considered that this view of the escapade may not have occurred to her, and he was determined to soften her displeasure if he could. "It hasn't been so many years since my younger brother Jonathan was getting into scrapes of this sort, but he always seemed to land on his feet."

"I can see that you think I am being overly protective, Captain Sherwood, but Jimmy has been gone for hours and has just recently recovered from pneumonia. When it started raining so heavily, I was frantic, and I am most obliged to you for bringing him safely home."

"I am happy to have been of service, ma'am. And now, if you will excuse me, I must be going. I leave for London in the morning and have still some business to attend to today." He moved to where Sultry stood waiting but then turned once more to speak. "Mrs. Ellis, there was one more thing. I know Jimmy expects to be punished for his disobedience today, and that, of course, is between the two of you. But he expressed a concern that you would be angry with him for involving me in his adventure. You must know that he tried to refuse my help, but that I . . . insisted. I would not like to think that any insistence on my part resulted in a harsher punishment for him."

"Very well, Captain, if that is what you wish, I will not tax him with it."

He thanked her briefly and then led his horse out into the stable yard and mounted. Raising a hand in farewell, he turned the mare and set off once again into the storm.

Mrs. Ellis stood at the stable door and watched until he disappeared into the grayness of the falling rain. She said a silent prayer of thanks that he had come upon Jimmy when he had, and that he had been disposed to help. Then suddenly she realized that she should have offered him shelter until the storm had passed or, at the very least, a coach to carry him back to his home. She chided herself for her bad manners, but recalling how the captain had shrugged off the storm, she thought it more than likely that he would have refused any offer she might have made, for he had said he was in a hurry and did not seem the type of man to pamper himself.

Chapter 5

RICHARD DINED EARLY, as was the country custom, but it was a simple meal and soon finished. When the family was not in residence, he insisted upon austerity in the household. Of all things, he disliked being fussed over, something the servants were apt to do when the family was in London and the captain in solitary residence.

Upon his return to the Manor earlier, he had endured a full twenty minutes of his valet's sullen silence after he had removed each piece of his ravaged clothing. Henchly knew better than to voice his disapproval, but the unspoken reproach was thick enough to cut with a knife. Richard always took particular care in his dress and appearance, but tonight he was preoccupied and refused to concern himself over a wet coat and a few dog hairs.

The meeting with his father's agent had been brief and fruitful, and now as he sat overlong at his port, he had leisure to reflect upon his meeting earlier in the day with Mrs. Ellis. What was her given name? he wondered. Why had they never met before? What manner of man was her husband? He had a partial answer for the second question. The Sherwood family had spent very little time in the country during the past two years. As long as the war with France had continued, it was necessary for Lord Sherwood to remain in London. When Richard came to Surrey alone, he came to work, and, residing as a bachelor, he was not expected to entertain. He wondered briefly why he had never been invited to dine with Sir Winston and his family at Ellis End, for they were the closest neighbors of his own class. Perhaps the Ellises, like his own family, were not often to be found in the country.

His reverie was interrupted by the entrance of Jepson, his butler. "Sir Winston Ellis has called, Captain. I told him you were still at dinner."

"Show him in here, Jepson, and bring another glass."

Moments later, Sir Winston was shown into the room. He was a burly man in his late fifties, with a ruddy complexion, overly long curling gray hair, and a heavy, unkempt beard. Richard rose to greet his guest, and Sir Winston replied with bluff informality, "Evening, Sherwood. Sorry to interrupt your dinner. Good of you to see me."

"You do not interrupt, Sir Winston. As you can see, I am merely lingering over my port. Please, share a glass with me."

"Don't mind if I do," Sir Winston replied, seating himself at the table. "Sarah tells me that you came to Jimmy's rescue this afternoon."

Sarah, Richard thought. It fits her. But he said, "If you have come to thank me for that small service, Sir Winston, let me assure you that both young James and your daughter-in-law have already done so."

"I did wish to add my thanks to theirs, but that was not the primary reason for my visit, Captain. Sarah mentioned in passing that you are traveling to London tomorrow, and you could do me a favor, if you would be so inclined."

"If I can, I will be more than happy to do so," Richard replied amiably.

"The thing is," Sir Winston continued, "Mrs. Ellis is traveling up to London herself, taking my daughter, Virginia, to spend some time doing the social whirl during the Little Season. Sarah insists upon traveling with only the servants. She says she doesn't need any other escort when she has her maid with her and a coachman and footman to do for her. And perhaps she's in the right of it. But I don't mind telling you, sir, that I can't be comfortable with the arrangement, especially when she will have Virginia with her, and young Jimmy as well. Sarah's forever coming the staid matron with me, but she's fair and far off if she thinks her widowhood lends her any protection, for she's a damned handsome woman withal, make no mistake about that!"

Richard found himself extremely interested in Sir Winston's disclosures, but his tone was carefully bland as he replied, "I will be more than happy to lend my support to the ladies' journey, Sir Winston. When did they plan to travel?"

"Sarah said you are leaving tomorrow, Captain Sherwood, and we have no intention of detaining you. I am sure they could be ready to leave by noon, if that would be convenient?"

It would make him half a day later than planned, but Richard made no objection to this proposal. Within several minutes, the gentlemen had settled all the details of the journey between them, and then Richard refilled his guest's glass and spent the next thirty minutes learning what he could about Sir Winston's intriguing family. Sir Winston was easily led to volunteer the information that his only son, James, had been dead for almost five years, and young Jimmy was now his heir. His only other child, Virginia, now aged twenty, had enjoyed her London debut the previous spring. His wife he did not mention, but Richard had gathered from the vicar that Lady Ellis had been dead for many years.

Sir Winston returned home that evening shortly before eight o'clock and threw his household into turmoil by announcing that the departure date for London had been moved forward two full days. "Captain Sherwood has agreed to escort you to town, and you must leave by noon tomorrow so as not to inconvenience him."

Mrs. Ellis, who under normal circumstances would not consider contradicting her father-in-law, was moved to expostulate. "But, Sir Winston, how can we possibly be ready in such a short time? We have only just begun packing."

"Nonsense. The servants do most of the work. Pack tonight what you will need for the first few days of your stay, and take it with you in the post chaise. The rest of your gear can follow in a few days' time."

Sarah had to admit that this plan was workable, although she was mortified that Sir Winston had foisted them upon Captain Sherwood. She already owed him a debt of gratitude, and now she was forced into being under further obligation to him. She blamed herself for mentioning the captain's plans at dinner. She should have known that Sir Winston would seize the opportunity to have his own way. She was well accustomed to her father-in-law's autocratic nature, and more than aware that she was no match for him, but as a rule he tended to display his high-handed tactics within the privacy of his own home. To consult Sarah concerning any plans he wished to make would never occur to Sir Winston. Any time she made the slightest bid for independence, as she had in suggesting that she travel to London on her own, he took umbrage, overset her wishes regardless of their suitability, and, more often than not, succeeded in having his own way in the end. This time his weapon had been Captain Sherwood.

Sarah wondered if the captain knew that their plans were being changed to accommodate him. It would not have surprised her in the least! Men were so pompous! Why should they care if she should be up half the night hurrying to be ready on time? What concern of theirs if she arrived two days early in London? What was it to them if her hostess, Sir Winston's sister, should be inconvenienced? The questions could go on endlessly, but to what purpose? It was a man's world, plain and simple, and no man of her acquaintance had ever missed an opportunity to drive the point home.

London, at least, would offer some peace from Sir Winston's tyranny, for their host, Lord Kemp, did not hold women in contempt. Rather, he chose to ignore them entirely, which suited Sarah well enough. Better to be ignored than oppressed.

Mrs. Ellis managed to find her bed shortly before midnight but slept fitfully and awoke with the headache. When she descended the steps to the drive some twenty minutes before twelve, it was to find the captain already arrived and her son gazing in awe at the four matched chestnuts harnessed to his curricle. The day was fine, the storm of yesterday having passed off as quickly as it had come. Thin white clouds riding high in a blue-gray sky promised a pleasant day for travel.

The captain turned to Mrs. Ellis immediately and smiled as he greeted her. "Good morning, ma'am. We are to have good weather for our journey it seems."

Sarah, embarrassed that her father-in-law had maneuvered the captain into his present role of escort, was prepared to offer him an apology. They were, after all, relative strangers, and she had no right to make demands upon his time or good will. But his ready smile and good-natured civility made an apology seem inappropriate, so she merely smiled and said, "It is good of you to accompany us, Captain Sherwood."

"Not at all, ma'am ... My pleasure. Your coachman has been telling me that Jimmy is an indifferent traveler. Do you think he would feel less queasy if he were to ride in the open carriage with me?"

Sarah glanced toward the captain's curricle, where Jimmy was in earnest conversation with Captain Sherwood's groom. "I appreciate the offer, Captain, but we should not inconvenience you."

"It would be no inconvenience, Mrs. Ellis. I would enjoy his company." When he thought he saw a trace of anxiety in her eyes, he added, "He will come to no harm with me, I promise. And we will be close behind your coach at all times."

It was clear to Sarah that he would press her until she gave her permission, and indeed, this did not surprise her. The captain was clearly, like her father-in-law, a man accustomed to having his own way—and she was a woman accustomed to relenting. So more from habit than inclination she said, "I do not fear for his safety, Captain Sherwood." She wanted to add: But I would rather not be under any further obligation to you. Impossible to say that, of course.

Richard was quick to pick up the note of restraint in her voice, and his next words surprised her considerably. "I have said nothing to Jimmy about taking him up, so there can be no question of disappointment for him if you refuse your permission. If you feel so strongly about his not traveling with me, then you need only say so and there will be an end to it. I will not press you to agree to anything you would not like."

She was convinced that that was precisely what he had intended to do. With his last words he had dropped his guard, but it was she who was completely disarmed. Left in full possession of the field, with the choice totally hers, she chose in her son's interest. "I have no objection to his going with you, Captain, if he wishes it."

Jimmy was therefore applied to, and finding him eager to take a seat in the curricle, Richard dismissed his groom, instructing him to travel with the valet in the baggage chaise. Jimmy climbed into the curricle, and Richard stepped back to take his leave of Sir Winston, who had just come out of the house with his daughter, Virginia. She was a diminutive brunette, quite dwarfed by both her father and sister-in-law. Richard was introduced to Miss Ellis and then the ladies were handed into the coach. Within a few moments the traveling-chaise rumbled off down the uneven drive.

Mounting into the curricle, Richard set his restive horses in motion. Thanks to yesterday's rain, there was no dust, and they would be able to follow as closely as they liked. Their progress for the first several miles was of necessity slow, for the country lanes and roads were not well maintained for coach travel. As Richard had suspected, the motion of the open carriage had less negative effect on Jimmy than the sway of a closed one, and although Richard watched the boy surreptitiously, he saw no sign of nausea. Even when they reached a better surface, Sir Winston's coachman did not push his horses unduly, and Richard was pleased to note it, for although the chaise horses would be changed as soon as they reached the London Road, Richard intended his curricle team to cover two stages. He didn't plan to make a change before Croydon, if he could avoid it.

Chapter 6

ELIZABETH SHERWOOD SAT in the window seat of the front salon, a worn copy of *The Taming of the Shrew* open on her lap. Lady Sherwood sat at her embroidery. There had been no conversation for some time, as both ladies were content in their separate occupations.

Elizabeth glanced up as her sister, Charlotte, entered the room. "Is Richard not yet arrived? I thought he wrote that he would be leaving early, Mama?"

"Indeed, he did, my dear, but it is only twelve thirty, after all, and he may have started later than he planned. And then, you know, one can never foresee the condition of the roads or the traffic one may encounter."

"Mama is right, Lizzie. Don't you remember the last time we journeyed from Brighton? We were stuck behind that plodding farm cart for miles and could not pass for the vehicles coming in the opposite direction."

"Yes. It was most vexing." A movement in the street below caught Elizabeth's eye, and she gazed down curiously. "We have a visitor, Mama, a gentleman, driving a curricle."

"Not Richard?"

"No, Mama. There is only a pair, and the driver is certainly not Richard, although I cannot tell who it might be from this angle, for his hat is hiding his face."

The visitor was admitted to the house, but some time passed and he was not shown up to the salon. "Perhaps the gentleman called to see your father," Lady Sherwood suggested. She meant the words innocently enough, but Elizabeth and Charlotte looked at each other and smiled. They were both remembering Lord Granbrooke's offer for Lizzie only yesterday and wondering if perhaps someone else had called on a similar errand.

Laying down her book, Elizabeth slipped quietly from the room. She tripped lightly down the stairs and found the butler lingering outside the door to the book room. "Is there a gentleman with my father, Williams?"

"Yes, Miss Elizabeth. Viscount Stanton."

"Viscount Stanton?"

"Yes, miss. Arrived just a short time ago and asked to speak with his lordship."

Elizabeth spun around without another word and walked back up the stairs at a decorous pace. The moment she knew herself to be out of sight of the hall below, she broke into a run and dashed the remaining distance to the salon, throwing herself through the door.

"Lord Stanton is with Papa," she said without preamble, "and I will be willing to bet you a monkey that he has come to offer for Charlotte."

"Elizabeth!" her ladyship admonished. "As much as you admire your brothers, I must beg you not to speak like them. Such language is hardly becoming."

"I beg your pardon, Mama. But don't you think it's possible—about Lord Stanton, I mean? What other reason could he have for calling here? He has never done so before."

"But, Lizzie," Charlotte complained, "I am barely acquainted with Lord Stanton."

"What has that to say to anything? You are forever saying that marriage should be a civilized, well-planned *arrangement*, with nothing so vulgar as love to taint it. Well, just such a marriage would appeal to Lord Stanton, I daresay. You are well suited, and the duchess, *his godmother*, did say just the other night that she had reason to think he was considering marriage."

"That is true, Charlotte," her mother agreed. "And there is no denying it would be a magnificent match for you."

Charlotte looked thoughtful, but Elizabeth jumped up, clapping her hands. "A viscountess, by all that's wonderful! And he's so handsome, *and* wealthy, and his *horses* . . ." She paused, enraptured. ". . . His horses are spectacular, and they say he has no equal in handling the ribbons."

"I think he is also quite a ladies' man," Charlotte said dampingly.

"Well, I daresay he may be," Elizabeth returned, "but it can not signify! His wife would be quite another matter, and I am sure he is much too aware of his own consequence to offer her any slight."

"Honestly, Lizzie," Lady Sherwood complained. "How you talk. Such topics should not be discussed by young unmarried girls."

"You always tell us to be realists, Mama," Elizabeth countered. "We know you and Papa have a love match, and personally I think it's wonderful and will not marry myself unless it is for love. But Charlotte is not romantic, and if she enters into marriage with a man of Lord Stanton's stamp, she must be willing to look the other way when he appears to have *another interest*."

Lady Sherwood shook her head resignedly. It was unfortunate that Elizabeth was so outspoken, and yet, she thought, her very outspokenness was one of her most endearing qualities. When other members of the family were all aflutter, Lizzie would utter some totally inappropriate banality that would bring them quickly to earth. And if someone happened to be in the sulks, just let Lizzie tell them they were dull as ditch water, and they would be well on the road to recovery. Lord Sherwood had been heard to say on more than one occasion that his little Lizzie had enough ballast to keep the whole family on an even keel.

Elizabeth felt that the truth, plain spoken, was the only truth worth listening to, and this was a maxim she lived by. She had no patience with pretense or artifice and was appalled to find herself using such tactics, when all her life she had abhorred them. Take for instance Lord Granbrooke's offer of the previous day. She had employed every pretense she could think of to put him off, and when that didn't answer, she was actually forced to *lie* to him, first saying that she was honored by his proposal and then telling him that her affections were otherwise engaged. How odious the man was to force her into compromising her principles just because he was too proud (or too thick-headed) to see that she wasn't interested in his presumptuous proposal!

The door opened at that moment to admit Williams. All three women looked up expectantly as Lady Sherwood asked, "Yes, Williams?"

"His lordship desires Miss Charlotte to wait upon him in the book room, my lady."

"Aha!" exclaimed Elizabeth. "You see, I was right! Hurry downstairs, Charlotte. You are about to receive the offer of every girl's dream."

Elizabeth's tone was mocking, but Charlotte knew that she was being teased to give her courage, a commodity that she often lacked, which Lizzie possessed in abundance.

Charlotte rose calmly and faced her mother. "What do you think, Mama?"

"The choice, as always, is yours, Charlotte, but your father and I would be pleased to see you so well established. You are old enough to make your own decision, and you alone can decide whether Lord Stanton will suit you, and whether or not you think you can build a life with him."

"Thank you, Mama." Charlotte kissed her briefly on the cheek, and then with a fleeting smile at Elizabeth, turned and followed Williams downstairs.

Charlotte entered the book room to find her father on the point of leaving. "Ah, here you are, my dear. Lord Stanton would speak with you privately, Charlotte."

"Yes, Papa, thank you." He winked broadly as he passed her, and she smiled in return. The viscount, standing near the middle of the room, was struck by the sweetness of that smile and by the gentle beauty of Miss Sherwood as she advanced and extended her hand to him. He had meant only to take it briefly in his but suddenly changed his mind, carrying it to his lips instead. She blushed slightly but spoke calmly. "How do you do, Lord Stanton?"

He inclined his head. "Your servant, ma'am." Charlotte was certain she should ask him to be seated, but he continued almost immediately. "I think you know the reason for my visit, Miss Sherwood."

"Yes, my lord."

"I have spoken with your father, and he has given me his permission to address you. He has also told me that in the matter of your marriage, you shall make your own decision, and whatever course you choose shall have his blessing."

"That is quite true, my lord."

He took her hand again and held it gently. "I think you are aware of my circumstances, Miss Sherwood, so we need not discuss them. Suffice it to say that I am twenty-eight years old and have decided that I should marry. I believe that we would suit admirably and would feel both honored and privileged if you would consent to become my wife."

Charlotte had been unable to look at him as he spoke, but now she forced herself to raise her head until her eyes met his. "I am equally honored and privileged to accept your gracious offer, my lord."

He found himself smiling down at her. Only yesterday he would have found it impossible to believe that making an offer of marriage and having it accepted could be so pleasant an experience. "Thank you, ma'am. You have made me most happy." He bent his head and kissed her briefly on the lips and then, straightening, said, "I will leave you now. With your permission I will see that the proper notices are made, and I will call on your father again tomorrow. Good day, Miss Sherwood."

"Good day, my lord."

Then, with a formal bow, he was gone, and Charlotte stood rooted to the book room floor, totally incapable of motion of any kind.

Chapter 7

SIR WINSTON ELLIS'S strong coach team reached the London Road without mishap, and the first change was made. Jimmy confided shyly to Captain Sherwood that he had never been driven in a curricle before, and this served as a basis for much of their conversation. He was full of questions about a four-in-hand, and Richard was more than happy to be his tutor.

"You are not too young to learn to drive, Jimmy, but you should begin with a single horse, and a less sporting carriage, perhaps a tilbury. I have one in London. If I took you up in it sometime, would you care to try your hand with one horse?"

Jimmy responded enthusiastically, and Richard realized belatedly that he should have spoken first with Mrs. Ellis. Remembering her reticence at the beginning of the journey, he thought it likely that she would be vexed with him, so he added, to cover his blunder, "We must, of course, check first with your mother. She may consider you too young."

"Did you learn at my age?" Jimmy asked.

"No. But I should have liked to. When I was your age, my father was at sea, and I was at Eton. My uncle let me drive his pony cart when I was eleven. I did very well," he said reminiscently.

"I was to start Harrow this year," Jimmy replied, "but then I became ill, and Grandfather decided to hire a tutor instead. I was disappointed, for I had looked forward to starting school."

Interspersed with their talk of horses and schooling were Jimmy's questions and Richard's answers concerning the countryside and the villages through which they passed. All in all, Richard considered it the most pleasant journey he had ever made along this road. His groom could never be credited with conversation as ingenuous or as diverting as Jimmy's.

Richard immediately perceived that traveling with Jimmy would give him a rare opportunity to learn more about the entrancing Mrs. Ellis. But almost as quickly as he entertained the thought, he rejected it. It would be unchivalrous to extract from a young boy information concerning his mother. If he was to discover more about Mrs. Ellis, then he must set about it for himself—a not altogether unpleasant prospect.

Within the traveling-carriage, Mrs. Ellis was occupied from time to time with her own thoughts about Captain Sherwood. Miss Virginia Ellis said she thought the captain handsome, and Mrs. Ellis agreed that he was indeed a well-looking man. It was his manner, however, and not his appearance that most interested Mrs. Ellis. For some reason she felt a need to get the man's measure, and just as she thought she was making some progress in that direction, he had deferred to her in that unsettling way. He had been compelled, politely, of course, to accompany them. But there was no clear reason why he should put himself out for Jimmy. She voiced this last thought to her sister-in-law, for even though there was little sympathy between them, they were wont to confide in each other, for in their situation neither of them had any freedom in choosing a confidante. They had each other or no one.

"Perhaps the captain has a naturally agreeable personality," Virginia mused.

Sarah grimaced. "Has any man?" They laughed together at the thought and decided that the majority of the men of their acquaintance were most disagreeable.

"Perhaps he shows an interest in Jimmy to advance his own interest with Jimmy's mother," Virginia suggested.

Sarah frowned. It was entirely possible, for it had happened before. During the past five years since her husband's death, Sarah had not gone unnoticed—women of her beauty rarely did. She did not encourage men to dangle after her; rather, she discouraged them, but several of her more determined suitors had attempted to reach her through her son. Needless to say, such tactics did nothing to advance their cause. Sarah had been inclined to like the captain at their first meeting, but his present behavior seemed to be falling into a pattern that she knew only too well, a pattern not at all to her liking.

Both carriages changed horses at Croydon, and at this point Richard thought it best that Jimmy leave the curricle and finish the journey with his mother. The handling of a strange team would demand his attention, especially once the town was reached and the traffic grew heavier. Even though Richard had no lack of confidence in his own ability, he felt that Mrs. Ellis might and would be more comfortable having the boy with her.

Having arrived in London, Richard escorted the ladies to their destination in Upper Berkeley Street, took civil leave of them, and turned his curricle toward his own home in Mount Street. Traveling without a groom, he drove around to the mews himself and moments later entered his father's house through a service door at the rear. He encountered Charlotte on the first-floor landing, and she hurried him to the sitting room, where he was surprised to find the entire family gathered.

There was a general outcry at his lateness. They had expected him hours earlier. He delivered kisses and handshakes about the room, explaining the while that he had been detained and unable to leave until midday. Everyone seemed in excellent spirits, and the reasons were soon revealed.

"Jonathan and Charlotte both engaged!" Richard exclaimed.

"How can so much happen so quickly? I have been gone only four weeks."

"You need only have been gone two days, Richard," Elizabeth chimed in, "for Charlotte became engaged today, and Jon only yesterday!"

"Well, who are the lucky spouses to be?" he asked, and then, looking at his younger brother, answered half of his own question. "No need to ask you, Jon . . . Harriet, of course, and a lucky devil you are! You don't deserve a woman half as good." Looking his brother over critically, he added, "You've gained weight since last I saw you, and it looks well on you. Army life must agree with you."

Richard moved to take Charlotte's hand in his own. "Don't tell me, Charlotte, that you have finally met a man who can measure up to the high standards you demand in a husband."

"Charlotte has received and accepted an offer from Viscount Stanton," Lady Sherwood said proudly.

A slight frown crossed Richard's brow. "Really? You surprise me."

"You are acquainted with Lord Stanton, are you not?" Charlotte asked.

"Yes. I know him well. We served together in the Peninsula." Richard refrained from saying more, simply wishing his sister joy, and leading the conversation to other topics. He soon went away to wash after his journey and change for dinner.

Elizabeth waited half an hour and then slipped out of the sitting room, up a second flight of stairs, and down the hall to Richard's bedchamber. Her gentle knock on the door was answered by Pull, Lord Sherwood's valet, summoned to wait upon Richard until his own Henchly should arrive. Pull ushered Elizabeth into the room and then busied himself tidying the remnants of Richard's bath. Richard sat before his dressing table, wholly absorbed in the delicate operation of tying his cravat. He was completely dressed for dinner, with the exception of his coat, which lay over a nearby chair.

Elizabeth knew better than to speak while he was concentrating on his neckcloth, so she kept a prudent silence, idly toying with one of his silver-handled brushes while she waited. Elizabeth stood directly behind her brother, and as he finished he glanced up at her image in the mirror. She was staring down at the top of his head with what amounted to a look of resentment on her pretty face. "You know, Richard, it's a terrible waste for a man to be blessed with hair of this color." She ran her fingers through it, noting that it was still slightly damp from washing. "Such beautiful, golden richness," she continued. "I would I had Mama's coloring as you do."

He reached up to take her hand and turned to meet her eyes directly. "Your own coloring does you no disservice, Lizzie, and well you know it. But you have not come to pay me compliments on my hair. You have something on your mind. Is it that you have no beau of your own, with all this talk of love and marriage?"

She shook her head. "No. Nothing like that. It's about Charlotte and Lord Stanton. I could see that you didn't like it above half."

He grimaced. "Little Miss Perspicacity. Let us hope that my feelings were not so transparent to everyone else. I should have guarded my reaction better, but I was taken by surprise."

"You think Charlotte and Lord Stanton will not suit, don't you?"

"I think Charlotte is a fool to seek a marriage of convenience, and I cannot think that any woman could be happy for long married to Stanton."

"You are very harsh, Richard. Do you dislike him so much?"

"No. You misunderstand me, Lizzie. I do not dislike him at all. In fact, I like him. He was a good officer, and is a fine man, and I will always be proud to call him my friend, but I can't think marriage will suit him."

"Perhaps not. But if he wants an heir, surely he must marry."

"That's true enough. But in that case I would prefer that he didn't marry *my* sister. Charlotte pretends to be tough and independent, but underneath she has the same fears we all have and the same need to be loved and cherished. She doesn't like to admit it, but I know it to be true, as do you."

"What will you do?"

"I will do nothing until I have taken time to consider the matter more carefully. And in the end, there may be nothing I can do, Lizzie. After all, if Father and Mother have both given this match their blessing, and Charlotte wishes it as well, it would be inappropriate for *me* to raise any objection."

"Even if you thought Charlotte would be made unhappy?"

He rose and reached for his coat. "Yes," he said resignedly, "even if I thought she would be made unhappy."

The entire family was home to dinner that evening, with the exception of Jonathan, who was dining with his betrothed. Many topics presented themselves for discussion, including the Sherwoods' ball, an event that was to be held in four days' time. Lady Sherwood had initially planned the evening as a grand entertainment for their friends and acquaintances, to coincide with Jonathan's furlough. But now it had begun to take on the form of a lavish engagement party.

"The girls and I have worked very hard planning it," Lady Sherwood said. "It should be quite a lovely evening."

Lord Sherwood smiled lovingly at his wife. "My dear, your parties are always exceptional, and with two engagements to announce, this one will no doubt be the grandest yet."

"If it's not too late, Mother," Richard put in, "there is someone I should like you to invite." She raised her brows inquiringly as he continued. "The reason I made a late start this morning was because I waited to escort some of our neighbors to town."

"Which neighbors?" Charlotte asked.

"The Ellises. Sir Winston's daughter-in-law, Mrs. Ellis, and her young son, and Sir Winston's daughter, Miss Virginia Ellis."

"I would be more than happy to invite them, Richard," his mother said. "I had been hoping to make their acquaintance and was planning to invite them to the Manor during our next stay in the country. If you will give me their direction, I will call upon them in the morning and invite them personally."

"I will accompany you, if you like," Richard returned. "They are staying with Lord and Lady Kemp, and you should issue the invitation to Mrs. Sarah Ellis and Miss Virginia Ellis only, for Mrs. Ellis is a widow, and Sir Winston has not come to town."

The following morning the proposed call was duly made. Richard, Charlotte, and their mother presented themselves in Upper Berkeley Street and found the Ellis ladies and their hostess at home. Lady Sherwood and Lady Kemp were not acquainted, so it was necessary for both Richard and Sarah to take part in the introductions. Lady Sherwood then issued her invitation, which was graciously accepted. With the two older ladies conversing amicably, and Charlotte and Virginia becoming acquainted, Richard took the opportunity to speak with Mrs. Ellis.

"I hope you were not fatigued by yesterday's journey, ma'am?"

"Not at all. I am a good traveler, Captain Sherwood."

"And Jimmy? Did he manage the last stage well enough?"

"Yes, quite well, but then the roads are so much better closer to town. I'm sure it was the pleasantest journey he has ever made. You must know that he talked of little else all evening. He so enjoyed your taking him up. I must thank you again."

"You will not perhaps be so quick to thank me, ma'am, after I have made a small confession. Did Jimmy tell you that I offered to take him driving with me while he was in town?"

"No, he didn't mention it."

"Well, I did tell him that you might not approve, so perhaps he thought it best to say nothing. I was carried away by his enthusiasm and made the offer without thinking. I know I should have said nothing without consulting you first. I have a tilbury in town and a very well-behaved older horse, and I thought Jimmy might like to try his hand at driving him. Perhaps early in the morning, in the park, when there is little traffic."

Why did this man insist upon insinuating himself into her life? she thought, but she said, "I am afraid I don't think that would be a very good idea, Captain Sherwood."

"No? You think he is too young? I think he has an aptitude."

"No. I do not think him too young, Captain," she answered hesitantly.

Richard regarded her critically. "Then you must question my skill. I assure you—"

She interrupted him irritably. "I do not question your skill, sir. I question your motive." How could she have said that? Surely she meant only to think it!

"My motive?" He was dismayed. "My motive is to teach

53

the boy something of handling the ribbons. What other motive could I have? I thought that since he seemed so keen to learn, and has no father, I could be in some part a substitute. . . ."

"And you do not consider this substitution to be an intrusion into my affairs, Captain?"

He stood silent for a few moments as she stared frostily at him, and finally he spoke. "I must beg you to forgive me, ma'am. You're right. I am intruding, and I apologize. I will not mention the subject again." He took a step back and bowed. "If you will excuse me?" He turned and crossed the room to join his mother and sister, and within a few moments they took their leave, but neither he nor Mrs. Ellis was to forget their conversation for some time to come.

Chapter 8

ON THE EVENING of the Sherwoods' ball, they sat down ten to dinner. In addition to the six members of the Sherwood family, Jonathan's betrothed, Harriet Putnam, and her aunt, Mrs. Satterly, were present, as well as Lord Stanton. To keep her numbers even, Lady Sherwood had invited a friend of Richard's, the Honorable Charles Warmington. Richard and Charles had been at Oxford together, and, finishing there, had joined the same regiment and continued their friendship abroad. Little more than a year into his military career, Charles had suffered a severe shoulder injury that had left him disabled and unfit for active service. He was a handsome young man with black hair and dark blue eyes, and although Lady Sherwood thought him too staid and serious, he could always be counted on as a perfect dinner companion whether he was seated beside a lively debutante or a half-deaf dowager. He was also a younger son of the Earl of Haigh, and a first cousin to Lord Stanton, and would soon be related to the Sherwoods through Charlotte's marriage.

They dined formally but at a table small enough to make some general conversation possible. Elizabeth had ample opportunity to observe her sister and Lord Stanton and saw nothing in their behavior to cause alarm. She thought Richard was studying them as well, although she had noticed that he seemed preoccupied for the last several days. The meal passed pleasantly, and presently they adjourned to the reception rooms to await the arrival of the first guests for the ball.

Charles Warmington stood near Jonathan at the side of the room. His eyes rested on Charlotte and Elizabeth with undisguised admiration. "Your sisters are looking lovely this evening, Jon."

"You must tell *them* so, Charles, not me," Jonathan answered, but knew his brother's friend to be right.

Handsome girls to begin with, they sparkled in their ball dresses. Charlotte was in pale yellow crepe worn over a slip of white sarcenet. A sash of darker yellow marked the high waistline, and a matching yellow ribbon was wound skillfully through her dark curls. Elizabeth wore white, a color her mother preferred for her at her age, but her gown was finely embroidered in a silver floral pattern. Silver dancing slippers peeped from beneath the hem, and a sparkling silver sash set off her trim figure to perfection.

Elizabeth glanced up at that moment to see Jon and Charles regarding her. She crossed the room to join them, and the conversation turned to a subject she was to hear mentioned many times throughout the coming evening.

"Have you heard of my cousin's exploit this morning, Miss Elizabeth?"

"No, Mr. Warmington. What exploit?"

"He and a fellow by the name of Reginald Fielding had a match at Manton's Shooting Gallery. Fielding is some kind of a marvel, it seems. They say he never misses."

Jonathan confirmed this last statement. "I have watched him at practice myself and have never seen a more accurate aim. Is it true, Charles, that Stanton matched him shot for shot?"

"I had it from Sir Hugh Broughton, who was present," Charles confirmed. "They continued the contest for over an hour, with neither of them ever missing the mark. Finally they agreed to call a halt and declared the match a stalemate. There was a huge amount of money wagered on the outcome, but it was all for naught, for no winner was declared."

Elizabeth left the gentlemen when her mother beckoned her, for within a very short time the rooms had become quite full. The orchestra had finished tuning, and the dancing was about to begin. Elizabeth turned to find Lord Stanton at her elbow. "Miss Elizabeth, my brother wishes to be made known to you. Miss Elizabeth Sherwood . . . Mr. Henry Ferris."

"How do you do, Mr. Ferris? I am pleased to make your acquaintance."

"I was hoping you would honor me with this dance, Miss Elizabeth."

"Thank you, sir. I would be delighted!" She went off with him and soon discovered that he was an excellent dancer. Mr. Henry Ferris could not be many years younger than the viscount, Elizabeth decided. He was a man of medium build, like his brother, and although she would describe him as being rather more striking than handsome, she decided almost immediately that she liked him very well.

"How well you dance, Mr. Ferris!" she exclaimed.

"Certainly I should be saying that, Miss Elizabeth," he expostulated.

"Only if you think to say it first, sir. I didn't know Lord Stanton had a brother. Have you a large family?"

"We have another brother, Giles. He is just twenty, and at Oxford at present."

"No sisters, then?"

"No. No sisters, ma'am. My father didn't believe in 'em."

She smiled, and he thought her smile enchanting. When the dance ended, he led her to where Charlotte stood with his brother. Mr. Ferris thanked Elizabeth for the dance, expressed his hope that she would honor him again later, and moved off through the throng.

Elizabeth had been instructed to stay with Charlotte or Harriet or one of her brothers until Lady Sherwood had finished greeting her guests, so when Charlotte's hand was solicited for the next set, Elizabeth looked about for Jon or Richard and found her elder brother only a short distance away. As she moved to his side she saw him staring fixedly toward the top of the stairway where their parents stood. She followed his gaze and immediately understood why he was staring. A tall, red-haired woman had just entered the room. She was wearing a gown of emerald green, cut low over her full bosom; even from this distance, it was plain to see that she was exquisitely handsome.

"Do you know her, Richard?"

Startled from his reverie, Richard looked down at her. "Yes. She is our neighbor from Surrey."

"Mrs. Ellis?"

"Yes, Lizzie, Mrs. Ellis."

"When you were describing her to us the day you arrived home, you failed to mention that she was beautiful."

"Did I?"

Elizabeth stared at her brother in disbelief. Could it be that Richard had been smitten at last? And by a widow who must be his own age or older? Elizabeth certainly saw admiration in his eyes, and there was something else as well, but exactly what, she couldn't tell.

"Will you introduce me?" she asked.

Richard seemed to be pulling his thoughts back from a great distance as he answered her. "Yes, certainly, if you wish it."

Together they made their way across the room, and Richard made the proper introductions, although to Elizabeth's ear his manner seemed more formal than usual.

"I am happy to meet you, Mrs. Ellis. Richard tells us you have a son and have brought him along to town."

Elizabeth was only making polite conversation, but Richard stiffened perceptibly at her side as he said, "If you will excuse me, I must speak with Lord Stanton." They nodded their dismissal, and as he turned away, he heard Mrs. Ellis respond to Elizabeth's last comment.

Richard could not deny that he was strongly attracted to Mrs. Ellis, but it was clear that the lady had not the slightest interest in him, so there was an end to it. He soon joined Lord Stanton, and they stood together watching the dancers.

"I have heard of your meeting with Fielding this morning, Julian," Richard remarked. "The whole town is talking of it."

"Yes. I am aware," the viscount answered. "I am beginning to regret that I met the man at all. Such an uproar over a mere shooting contest."

"I always knew you to be a fine shot, Julian, but I had no idea you were a nonpareil."

"I have improved."

"You are to be congratulated."

"On my marksmanship?"

"Yes, certainly on that, and also on your engagement to my sister."

"I was wondering when you would find time to offer your felicitations."

"There has been little opportunity for us to speak privately."

"True enough, yet I have the unmistakable impression that you don't approve of this engagement."

"Nor do I precisely disapprove. I would say rather that I am *concerned*."

"I thought we were friends, Richard."

"And so we are. But I love my sister. Is it so surprising that I should wish to see her happy?"

"You have some considerable influence with Charlotte, I think. You could use it to protect her interest, if you feel she needs protection."

"I could. But I will not. Charlotte has made her decision, and it is not my place to interfere. The advisability of such an engagement must be a matter for her conscience—and, of course, for yours."

Mrs. Sarah Ellis was favorably impressed with Elizabeth Sherwood. She thought her a very prettily behaved young lady, with forthright and friendly manners. Sarah glanced at Elizabeth now, where she stood speaking with Lord Granbrooke at the side of the ballroom. As Sarah watched, she was surprised to see Lord Granbrooke take Elizabeth's hand and Elizabeth quickly pull it away, a flush mounting to her cheeks. Elizabeth then turned abruptly and walked away, and Sarah watched in dismay as Lord Granbrooke followed in her wake.

Instinctively Sarah crossed the room in their direction, but the crowd impeded her progress. She finally reached the doorway through which they had passed but saw no sign of them in the next room. She moved quickly into the hall and approached one of the Sherwood footmen on duty there.

"Have you seen Miss Elizabeth?" she asked.

"Yes, madam," he said. "She went on down the hall just a few moments ago."

Sarah thanked him and moved in the direction he indicated.

The rooms in this part of the house had not been opened for the ball, and she had proceeded some little way along the corridor, wondering where Miss Elizabeth had gone, when she heard raised voices in the room directly to her right. She was sure Elizabeth was being confronted by Lord Granbrooke, and she felt just as sure that Elizabeth would welcome her intervention.

Without a moment's hesitation, she knocked, called Elizabeth's name, and then opened the door and entered. As she had suspected, Lord Granbrooke was with Elizabeth. They stood very close, and although he was not touching her, it was obvious that he had just put her from him as they were interrupted. Elizabeth was shaking, and there were tears in her eyes. She either could not or would not speak.

"I think your presence is not wanted here, my lord," Sarah said steadily. "You will please leave us." She made no effort to be civil, contempt sounding clearly in her voice.

More than aware that there was nothing he could say to defend himself, Granbrooke glared angrily at her and, without a word, turned and left the room. Sarah closed the door behind him and went to Elizabeth but after a few moments realized that she would not be much help. The girl was considerably shaken, and Sarah knew that a relative stranger was not the person needed in the present situation.

"Please wait here, Miss Elizabeth," she said. "I will be right back. Do you promise you will wait?"

Elizabeth didn't answer, but she nodded her head, and Sarah quickly returned to the ballroom. Her eyes swept the room for some member of the Sherwood family, and she was relieved to see Captain Sherwood standing nearby. Momentarily forgetting the recent awkwardness between them, she hurried to his side, and when she placed her hand on his sleeve and spoke his name, he started and looked down at her in some surprise. Light as her touch was, she communicated her anxiety with it, and he instinctively laid his own hand over hers.

"Ma'am?"

"Please, sir, come with me." The words were spoken lowly and urgently, and Richard did not question the appeal but accompanied her without comment. Once free of the crowded rooms, she said, "Your sister Elizabeth needs your assistance,

Captain. I am afraid she has had a rather unpleasant scene with Lord Granbrooke."

He followed her into what was known in the family as the yellow salon and found Elizabeth there, struggling to regain her composure. He moved immediately to the sofa where she was seated and sat beside her, taking her hands in his. "Lizzie, what has been happening here?"

"Oh, Richard . . . He is such a horrible man!"

"Who? Granbrooke? What were you thinking to come here with him?"

"I didn't come here with him," she objected. "I came alone. Partly to get away from him, and partly to be on my own for a while. But he followed me, and he . . ."

"Lizzie, tell me what happened," Richard demanded. "How long were you here with him?"

"It was only a few minutes, Captain Sherwood," Sarah offered. "I saw them leave the ballroom and followed immediately. It didn't take me long to find them."

She had remained standing nearby, and he looked up at her as she spoke. "I am obliged to you, ma'am." There was no doubting the sincerity in his voice as he turned his attention to his sister once again. "You must tell me what took place here, Lizzie. Did Granbrooke force his attentions upon you?"

"I'm not sure what you mean by that, Richard," she said in a small voice.

"Did he kiss you? Or touch you?" he asked impatiently.

"No, he didn't try to kiss me, but he backed me against that table and pressed his body against mine in the most disgusting way."

"Damn!" Richard muttered wrathfully.

"But it was what he said that frightened me," Elizabeth continued.

"What did he say?"

"I couldn't begin to repeat the words he used, Richard, but I know no gentleman would speak so. And his tone . . . his tone terrified me."

Richard rose suddenly to his feet. "Damn him! He shall answer to me for this!" He turned to Sarah. "I would appreciate it, Mrs. Ellis, if you could stay with my sister until she has composed herself and then see her back to the ballroom and into my mother's care. It will cause comment if she is too long absent."

As he turned to leave, Elizabeth asked quietly, "What do you plan to do?"

"I plan to see that Lord Granbrooke offers no further insults to ladies!"

His tone was grim, and as Elizabeth was assailed by a new thought, she sprang to her feet and, hurrying to her brother, took hold of his arm. "You will not call him out, Richard? You must not do so!"

"You need not concern yourself, Lizzie. I will deal with his lordship."

"Yes, I see that you must deal with him, of course, but not in such a way as that!"

He tried to disengage her hand, but she only held on more tightly. "Lizzie, it is not your concern, believe me."

"You're wrong! It is my concern. *I* am the one he insulted. Throw him out in the street, or knock him down, or anything else you like, but not a duel, Richard, *please*, I beg of you. *Swear* to me that you will not consider it!"

He took her chin in his hand. "Always the sensible, level-headed Lizzie. Don't you think your honor worth protecting, little one?"

"Nothing I have is worth protecting at the risk of any harm coming to you. If you love me, Richard, you will not endanger yourself just because Lord Granbrooke is a sore loser and a complete fool."

Richard gazed down at his sister with a great deal of tenderness, and Sarah realized that she was witnessing an excellent example of how a woman could bring a man round her finger if there was a strong bond of love between them.

"Very well, Lizzie, you win," he said finally. "I will not demand that he meet me."

"You swear it?"

"I swear." Bending, he kissed her gently on the cheek, and then, turning to Sarah, he said, "I am in your debt, Mrs. Ellis, and I will not forget it." Then before she could answer, he passed through the door and was gone.

Sarah turned to Elizabeth and smiled. "Well, Miss Sherwood . . . may I call you Elizabeth?"

"Yes, please do. And I would like to thank you, too, Mrs.

Ellis, for noticing that I was in trouble and for coming to help me."

"You're very welcome, Elizabeth. But if we are to be friends, then you must call me Sarah. Shall we go up to your bedchamber and ring for your maid so that she can repair the damage Lord Granbrooke has done to your hair? Then we shall return to the ball and find you a suitable partner for the next set, for I have noticed, Elizabeth, that you love to dance."

When they finally returned to the ballroom, Charlotte wondered aloud where Elizabeth had been, but Sarah fobbed her off with a tale of how one of Elizabeth's partners had trod upon the hem of her gown and they had retired upstairs to pin it. Henry Ferris claimed Elizabeth for the next dance, and she was soon restored to spirits, for he was unquestionably one of the best dancers in the room.

As the dance ended, Mr. Ferris led Elizabeth to where Lord Stanton stood in conversation with his future father-in-law. "Julian, dear fellow," Henry said to his brother, "the next dance is a waltz, and you really must stand up with Miss Elizabeth. She is as light on her feet as a rose petal!"

Elizabeth blushed at the compliment, but her father supported Mr. Ferris. "That's true enough, Stanton. My Lizzie is the best dancer in the family."

Stanton inclined his head and held out his arm to Elizabeth. "Will you honor me, ma'am?"

"Certainly, my lord, but it cannot be pleasant to have a partner foisted upon you." With a withering look at both her father and Mr. Ferris, she went with the viscount to join the other dancers.

"How can it be that we have never stood up together, Miss Elizabeth?"

"I only made your acquaintance early last week, my lord, and I think you don't grace the dance floor as often as you could."

"I don't dislike dancing, Miss Elizabeth."

"Then the explanation must be that you find your partners insipid."

He raised a brow at her insight and started to enjoy the conversation. "Perhaps I do, ma'am. Present company excluded. And Henry was right. You dance delightfully."

"Thank you, my lord. So do you. I have not yet congratulated you on your engagement. I suppose I should do so."

He looked at her quizzically. "You *suppose* you should? Are you opposed to the engagement, Miss Elizabeth?"

"No, sir. I am not opposed to the engagement. I am opposed to marriages of convenience."

"And you think that is what your sister and I are planning—a marriage of convenience?"

"Well, of course, my lord. It could scarcely be anything else, when you have only recently met and were barely acquainted when you proposed."

"I take it that you don't believe in love at first sight, then, Miss Elizabeth?"

"No, certainly not! I am sure there can be *attraction* at first sight, but love is not something that *is*, it is something that *grows*, and it cannot grow in an instant. Anyone can see that."

"I am sure you must be right," he agreed. "Your logic is irrefutable. But haven't you considered that four, or shall we say five, days would be adequate time for love to grow, given the proper circumstances?"

Elizabeth had not considered this option. Could it be that Stanton had offered for Charlotte as a matter of convenience, and then proceeded to fall in love with her? It was not impossible, and the very idea struck her as so romantic that she blurted out without thinking, "Have you fallen in love with Charlotte, my lord?"

He smiled down at her indulgently but did not answer and then was truly amused as the inappropriateness of her question struck her. She blushed scarlet and stammered incoherently, "Oh, my lord . . . I'm so sorry . . . I beg your pardon . . . How rude of me . . . How could I be so impertinent?"

"I don't know," he answered. "How *could* you be so impertinent?" He still seemed amused, and she felt enormously relieved that he didn't snub her.

"It is my besetting sin," she confided.

"What is?"

"My outspokenness. Mama is always warning me, and I try, I do really, but my tongue seems so often to have a mind of its own and will say just what it pleases. Please say that you will forgive me, my lord. I truly did not mean to be insinuating."

"No forgiveness is necessary, Miss Elizabeth, I assure you. I was not offended, and I would never consider you insinuating. I would much rather describe you as 'a breath of fresh air.' "

Chapter 9

PERHAPS THIRTY MINUTES later, Mrs. Ellis noticed Captain Sherwood speaking with his brother Jonathan on the far side of the room. She had seen nothing more of Lord Granbrooke and knew not whether he had departed after his encounter with her or whether Captain Sherwood had shown him the door. If the latter were true, the captain's immaculate person showed no signs of a struggle. His dark silk coat was still set straight across his broad shoulders; his smallclothes and elaborately tied cravat seemed not to have been disturbed. She allowed her gaze to travel down his entire person and then slowly up again, and when she brought her eyes to his face, she found to her dismay that he was fixedly regarding her. She felt a hot flush rise to her cheeks but would not now look away and continued to hold his gaze as he moved across the room to her side and said softly, "Such steadfast regard, ma'am. I was beginning to think that I had forgotten to finish dressing."

"I was only searching for some evidence of—"

"Of a mill, ma'am? And, as you see, there is none. So sorry to disappoint you."

"I am not disappointed, Captain. I only wish you to understand that I had no ulterior motive in staring."

"No need to convince me of that," he replied, his eyes roving out over the dancers. "I have it from Sir Winston himself that you consider yourself a 'staid matron,' and I am sure I need not worry that you may have designs upon my person."

She smiled. "How ridiculous you are, Captain Sherwood! But certainly my father-in-law never said such of me."

He turned his intense blue gaze upon her. "On my honor, ma'am. Those were his exact words."

"Then, I shudder to think what else he may have said."

"Nothing to your discredit," Richard replied, smiling, "I assure you. Shall we dance, Mrs. Ellis?" He held out his hand, and she put her own into it, and then, drawing her arm through his, he led her onto the floor.

The dance was a waltz, and Sarah could not repress a feeling of exhilaration as the captain's arm encircled her waist and he turned her onto the dance floor. She kept her eyes downcast, studying the pattern of his watered-silk waistcoat. A few moments later she happened to glance at her right hand, held firmly in his left one, and after a moment's scrutiny said, "Your knuckles are bleeding, Captain Sherwood."

His gaze idly followed hers, and he agreed dryly, "So they are, Mrs. Ellis. It cannot signify."

"Perhaps not to you, Captain. But if you should brush against some lady's ball gown, which has cost her two hundred guineas, believe me, she would not consider it insignificant. As you can see, your glove is quite soaked through."

"What would you have me do, Mrs. Ellis?"

"I would have you direct me to the edge of the floor, sir, and thence to some place where we could procure water and a cloth."

"You would treat my wounds, ma'am?" he asked, a smile lurking at the corners of his mouth.

"Certainly, Captain, if you will permit me."

She soon found herself at the side of the room. Disassociating themselves from the dancers, they made their way through several adjoining rooms, and as the crowd thinned, Richard spoke again. "Where shall we go?" he asked provocatively, "my bedchamber?"

She gave him a quelling look. "Your levity is not amusing, Captain. Show me the way to the kitchen."

"The kitchen! Surely you must be joking!"

"I assure you I'm not. I assume you *know* your way to the kitchen?"

"Of course I know my way to the—why the kitchen?"

"Because I am sure we will be able to find what we need there."

They soon made their way to the kitchen, which was in a

great bustle with preparations for supper. One of the maids fetched them a cloth and a basin of cold water with ice, and they retired into the servants' dining hall, which was deserted and relatively quiet. Sarah noticed that Richard left the door standing wide, despite the fact that closing it would have offered them considerable relief from the din of the kitchen beyond.

"Concerned for my reputation, Captain Sherwood?" she teased.

"No, ma'am, for my own," he answered glibly.

As they seated themselves at the table, she stripped off her gloves and held out her hand imperatively. He put his own in it, saying, "This really isn't necessary, you know."

She silenced him with a look and surveyed the damaged hand critically. Three of the knuckles were actually split and bleeding, and the fourth was scraped. The fingers were rapidly turning black and blue, and, to her eye, looked very painful. She started carefully to soak the blood away and apply ice to the swelling.

Richard winced, and she looked up apologetically. "I'm sorry," she said. "I'm sure it must hurt dreadfully."

There was so much sympathy in her voice that he laughed aloud. "If you think that, ma'am, you can know nothing of wounds. Compared to a saber cut or a bullet hole, this is child's play, believe me!"

He was smiling, and she knew he intended the comment to lighten her mood, but in fact it had the opposite effect. She stared at the hand she held. It was nearly twice the size of her own, strong and shapely. She paused in her work to look across at him. "You were wounded, then, during the war, Captain?"

"A few times," he admitted, and then grinned. "More than I care to remember."

"I had hoped that Lord Granbrooke would be gone by the time you returned to the ballroom."

"No. He was still there, and mighty cool, too. Tell me, Mrs. Ellis, is Miss Virginia Ellis an heiress?"

Sarah looked puzzled at the question but answered it readily. "Jimmy is Sir Winston's heir, but as his only surviving child, Virginia will have a very handsome portion, yes. Why do you ask?"

"I found Granbrooke ingratiating himself to her. You have been in town only a few days and he is already aware of her circumstances. The man is a damned loose fish."

"You have not told me how you came by this hand, Captain."

"I had intended only to show him the door, although an exposé on his personality in general, and his manners in particular, would have been much more to my liking. I politely informed him that I would see him to his coach. We were just descending the steps outside when he tried to excuse his behavior by informing me that my flirt of a sister had been encouraging him, and she had received no more from him than she deserved. If he had more to say, I will never know, for it was at that moment that my hand came to grief. He fell like a stone. Didn't even give me the pleasure of hitting him a second time. I would I had my promise back from Lizzie. I would willingly rid the world of scum such as he."

"You don't mean that, Captain. Surely such a man should be beneath our contempt. If you had insisted on making more of it, then Elizabeth would have done so as well. As it is, she has almost forgotten the incident and is upstairs dancing and enjoying herself, as she should be."

She finished with his hand and used a towel to dry it. "There," she said, "it should feel somewhat better. If you are careful, I think it will not start bleeding again."

He looked at her consideringly. "Thank you. You never did mention why you involved yourself in this affair, Mrs. Ellis."

"I happened to be watching your sister and Lord Granbrooke just before they left the ballroom. I could see that Elizabeth was angry, and I suppose I sensed that his lordship might cause trouble."

"But that does not explain *why* you followed them."

"I don't understand you, Captain."

"I am trying to discover your *motive*, ma'am." He had no sooner uttered the word than he regretted it, for she flushed and rose suddenly from the table. "I'm sorry," he said quickly. "I didn't mean to distress you."

"No. You meant to expose my bad manners," she replied, "and you are perfectly within your rights to do so. I followed your sister to offer her my help if need be. And you offered the same to Jimmy, and through him to me. *Your* intentions were both innocent and honorable, Captain, and *my* behavior was disgraceful. I beg your pardon."

He had risen to his feet as she did, and, taking her arm once again, they left the kitchen and made their way upstairs. As they came along the ground floor past the door to the book room, Richard paused and turned to face her. The corridor in which they stood and the hall beyond were both deserted.

He spoke quietly. "I was startled more than angered by your behavior the other day, and once I had time to consider the conversation, it didn't take me long to understand what you must have been thinking. I am not an advocate of oblique tactics, Mrs. Ellis. When I want something, more often than not I prefer the direct approach. If I had any intention of trying to fix my interest with you, I would not employ your son as a stepping-stone. I hope you can believe that, because it's the truth."

"I do believe you, Captain."

"Good," he said, taking her arm again and strolling on. "Then, if you have no objection, I will call for Jimmy tomorrow morning. Shall we say—nine o'clock?"

"Nine o'clock will be fine, Captain Sherwood."

Despite the fact that Richard had not retired until three-thirty on the morning of the ball, he was up at eight o'clock, ate a quick breakfast, ordered his tilbury brought round, and presented himself in Upper Berkeley Street promptly at nine. He found Jimmy eagerly awaiting him, and they set off together for the park.

Richard soon saw that he was not mistaken in thinking Jimmy would have an aptitude for driving. He listened carefully to Richard's instructions, and when Richard finally handed him the reins, he was pleased to see that the boy had light, even hands.

They stayed out only an hour and made plans to meet another day. Dropping Jimmy in the street outside Lord Kemp's house, Richard bade him carry his compliments to his mother and, turning his horse, set off again for home.

As he entered the house, Williams stepped forward to relieve him of his hat and driving coat. "His lordship is in the book room, Captain, and said he would like a word with you when you returned."

Richard crossed the hall to the book room, stripping off his gloves as he went, and entered to find his father puzzling over some papers on the desk before him. Lord Sherwood looked up as his son entered and spoke to the footman who was moving to close the door behind him. "Wait outside, Matthews, and please see that we are not disturbed."

There was no mistaking the seriousness of his lordship's tone. Richard glanced at the footman as he left the room, assured himself that the door was properly closed, and then advanced to stand near his father's desk. "Something is worrying you, sir. What is it?"

Lord Sherwood motioned his son to a chair. "Please, Richard, sit down. I have been doing some work this morning, and I have found something that troubles me greatly. As you know, I have little patience with accounts and estate matters. But you also know that when it comes to the matter of my position within the present government, I cannot bear disorder."

"Yes, sir, I do know it."

"Then you will understand my concern when I tell you that this file I hold before me is not as I left it yesterday. The pages are out of order, several have been turned upside down, and I suspect . . . no . . . I know, that it has been tampered with!"

Richard frowned. "Does it contain vital information, sir?"

"The contents would not be considered highly confidential, otherwise I would not leave them unguarded as they are. But they must be considered delicate, as they deal with such things as sailing orders, fleet movements, and various troop strength. We may be at peace with France, but we have no cause to relax our vigilance."

"I assume you think that one of our guests last night was responsible for this . . . encroachment."

"Yes, I think it highly likely," his lordship replied, "but every person present last night pretends to be a loyal British subject. What we seem to be discussing here, Richard, is not encroachment or trespass—but treason."

The word hung for a few tense moments between them, and finally Richard spoke. "Do you have any suspicions, sir, as to who this traitor might be?"

"No. I have asked your mother for a list of those who accepted her invitation, without arousing her suspicions, of course, and will have it compared to a list of those who have been suspected in the past. And then, of course, one always thinks first of those who have French blood."

"That will get us nowhere, sir, for surely dozens of our guests last night can claim a French progenitor or two. Your own grandmother was a full-blooded Frenchwoman. And think of Stanton—his mother is French, yet I have fought side by side with both Julian and Henry Ferris and would not doubt their loyalty any more than I would my own."

"Nevertheless, those persons with French blood must stand high on the list. On the other hand, we could find that the perpetrator is no more than a poor misguided Englishman who sees the offer of gold in return for services rendered as a thing of greater value than his, or her, own honor."

"Have you mentioned this incident to anyone else in the family, Father?"

"No. I have not. Nor do I intend to."

"Well, of one thing at least we can be certain. If this person hopes to collect additional information from you, it will be necessary for him to attach himself through some member of the family. Not a very pleasant thought."

"No. Not pleasant at all," his father agreed. "But if he is to be encouraged to find this house an easy mark, then we must make no mention of anything being amiss with my papers. We will not change any of the household routine. We will continue to leave this room unlocked and accessible as always. But you and I, Richard, shall keep our eyes open, and if in the natural course of things an opportunity should present itself, perhaps we will make an effort to capture this . . . person."

Chapter 10

IF THERE HAD been an uproar in the Sherwood house in the days preceding the ball, it was as nothing compared to the activity that now reigned. In little more than two weeks Lady

Sherwood would see her younger son married, and even though he had given her very little notice, she was determined to make the day memorable.

There would be a small, private ceremony at St. George's, Hanover Square, followed by a lavish wedding breakfast at Sherwood House. Jonathan and Harriet planned to leave early and travel the same day to Sherwood Manor, where they would spend the remaining days of Jonathan's furlough together. Afterward, Harriet intended to return to her aunt's house in London until her husband could make arrangements for her to join him in Belgium.

On the day of the wedding all the public rooms on the first floor were thrown open for the use of the wedding guests, including the yellow salon where Lord Granbrooke had detained Elizabeth. There was a pianoforte there, and Elizabeth had been coaxed into playing for them while Charles Warmington turned the music for her. Elizabeth's singing voice was low and pleasant, and she played well. She sang a Highland love song, and the words were both tender and touching.

Everyone seemed to be enjoying the day with the exception of Lord Stanton. The more lighthearted and gay the wedding guests became, the more his spirits suffered, until finally Charlotte spoke to him in rare confidence, bringing his growing unrest to a head and making him feel that if he did not escape the house immediately, he would be suffocated by high spirits and goodwill.

Seated beside the viscount at the side of the room, Charlotte stared down at the engagement ring on her hand and said impulsively, "What did you think of the wedding ceremony, my lord?"

He had almost said that he found it much like any other wedding he had ever attended but fortunately realized in time how inappropriate such a comment would be and said instead, "It was quite exceptional ... very moving."

"Yes," she agreed. "So I thought. My lord, we have not spoken about our own marriage." She continued to look down at her hands, and he turned to study her profile as she continued. "When I accepted your proposal, I did so because I, like you, thought we were well suited. During the past weeks I have come to know you better, and I wish you to know that

I think you an admirable person, and I will do everything in my power to be a proper wife."

Stanton was stunned into silence. I wonder how admirable you would think me, Miss Sherwood, he thought, if you knew I had offered for you as the result of a drunken wager and for the promise of eighty thousand pounds from my godmother?

He reached to take her hand, and she raised her eyes to his. He could think of nothing to say but managed to smile. It was enough for her. She returned his smile and relapsed into silence.

Stanton realized that Charlotte would not normally have spoken so to him. She was caught up in the elation of her brother's wedding day. She was relaxed, confident, and secure among her family, and he knew these feelings had prompted her pretty speech. But he wished she had not made it, for it brought home to him the enormous impropriety of offering for her in the way he had. This girl was both young and lovely. She was possessed of a gentleness and sweetness of nature that any man would find hard to resist. But just as clearly as he assessed Charlotte's character did he know his own. He did not love her and thought he never would. His nature was not constant, and even though he was attracted to her now, he knew that in less than a year he would undoubtedly make her miserable.

Somehow he managed to get through the remainder of that interminable day, and that evening, alone in the library of his home, he finally admitted to himself that he could not continue the farce. Richard had been right. It had been a matter for conscience—and conscience had been victorious.

The following morning Sir Hugh Broughton and Lord Stanton were riding in Hyde Park when the viscount startled his friend by saying suddenly, "I cannot marry Miss Sherwood, Hugh."

"Eh?" his friend replied, not sure he had heard aright.

"I said that I cannot marry Miss Sherwood. It wouldn't serve. I never should have asked her."

"You had to ask her. Swore you wouldn't renege on your wager, remember?"

"Yes. I remember only too well, and I am afraid I will have to settle with you some other way, Hugh, for I find I must go back on my word. I cannot continue with this engagement."

"Well, as to that, there is no question of going back on your word," Sir Hugh said reasonably. "The wager was that you should *offer* for the lady, which you have done, and the debt is satisfied. Whether you ever marry the girl is beside the point."

Stanton smiled at his friend's fine understanding of the gambling ethic. "Well, I will not marry her, of that much I am certain."

"Thing is, Julian, I don't rightly see how you can avoid it now. A gentleman can't cry off from an engagement."

"No," Stanton agreed. "But the lady can."

"True enough, but why should she wish to? She accepted you readily and seems well disposed toward you. Don't seem to me that she would be likely to cry off."

"Under normal circumstances I would agree with you. But I have been thinking that perhaps the lady could be *induced* to do so."

"Induced?"

"Yes, my dear Hugh," his lordship answered grimly. "Induced."

Having determined to end his engagement to Miss Sherwood and having decided upon the method that would best achieve this end, Lord Stanton waited only for the opportunity to put his method to the test. He met Charlotte several times during the days immediately following Jonathan's wedding and on each occasion his manner toward her was reserved, almost austere. On the fourth day, when they were both invited to the Suttons' ball, he knew his opportunity was at hand.

One entire side of the ballroom was lined with tall windows hung with golden brocade draperies. With the hangings closed as they were this evening, each window provided a small enclosure, large enough for a couple to stand in with ease and be, for all intents and purposes, hidden from the eyes of the assembly. Young girls were traditionally warned to avoid such window embrasures, for it was not unheard of for a gentleman to steal a kiss after whisking a girl into this secluded place. No one seemed to notice, however, if on occasion a married or betrothed couple disappeared for a few moments for a tête-à-tête.

Lord Stanton and Charlotte were dancing, and as the music

ended they found themselves near the ballroom windows. Taking her hand, Stanton drew Charlotte quickly through the draperies and pulled her to him, his arms about her waist.

"I have had no opportunity to be alone with you for three full days," he said. "Nor have I found opportunity to tell you how lovely you are tonight." His eyes dropped boldly to her low-cut gown, and she blushed and wished she had worn something less décolleté. He touched her face gently, and she looked up to meet his eyes in the dim light.

Surprised by this abrupt change in his recent manner toward her, Charlotte stood stiffly, vividly aware that his fingers were tracing the fine line of her jaw, then the side of her neck, and then down onto her shoulder. His fingers hesitated briefly as they came to rest against the neckline of her gown, and then very deliberately began to move again, following the neckline of her dress across her breast.

She gasped audibly and pulled away sharply. "My lord . . . please! You have been drinking, I think, and I also think—"

"And you also think I should not be permitted to sample the wares before the wedding night," he interrupted. "But I don't agree, dear Charlotte." He pulled her roughly into his arms and brought his mouth down on hers. Her lips were rigid and unresponsive, and for one fleeting moment he thought it would be amusing to coax her into yielding herself to him. But remembering that his purpose was to repel and disgust, he pressed his kiss ruthlessly upon her, bruising her mouth with his own.

Charlotte was profoundly shocked by his actions but felt that impassive behavior on her part would be the most effective way to damp his ardor. But when after a few moments he showed no inclination to desist, she struggled to free herself. He released her instantly, an amused chuckle escaping as he held her at arm's length.

"I see that there is a great deal I must teach you about love-making, my dear. I think I shall enjoy the task," he said consideringly.

Charlotte did not speak but wrenched herself free from his hold. He gave her a slight mocking bow and then held the drapery aside for her to step back into the ballroom. Conscious of the fact that someone might be watching them, she turned to face him and forced herself to say, "Thank you for the dance, my lord." He noted the tears in her eyes with regret, but only bowed formally and then turned and strolled away.

Charlotte did not see Lord Stanton again that evening and concluded that he had either left the ball immediately following their encounter or given up dancing in favor of the card room. Her evening was ruined. She forced herself to behave as normally as possible, and although her act may have convinced others, Elizabeth wasn't deceived. She saw at once that something was wrong, but Charlotte refused to discuss it. By the time they arrived home in the early hours of the morning, Charlotte pled fatigue and retired to bed, leaving her sister in suspense.

During his habitual early morning ride in the park, Viscount Stanton pondered the possible repercussions of his behavior on the previous evening. As he considered the matter dispassionately, he concluded that he could expect one of three possible responses.

The first and most desirable of these would be for Charlotte herself to call, or perhaps her father, to inform him that she no longer wished for the match. If Charlotte employed her father, Stanton was relatively certain that she would not disclose her reasons but simply inform him of her wishes.

The second alternative was that Charlotte would choose to ignore the incident and take no action of any kind. Perhaps she would be willing to forgive what she considered behavior resulting from the influence of wine. Or, if she confided in another female, she would perhaps be assured that such behavior was normal and must be expected and tolerated. If this proved to be the case, then he would be forced to employ even stronger measures to repel her, and the idea was repugnant to him. Therefore he sincerely hoped that Charlotte would *not* choose to forgive him.

Finally, he considered that Charlotte may have gone to her brother. There was some safety in the fact that he and Charlotte were actually engaged, for within the engagement he was permitted intimacies that outside that agreement would be considered gross impropriety. If Charlotte went to Richard, Stanton could only hope that Richard's fine intuition would see and understand that although the viscount's method may have been a bit reprehensible, his motive had been pure.

Charlotte would be safely out of the engagement, pride intact, and none the worse for a stolen caress.

Returning from his ride, Stanton settled himself in his library, intending to spend the day there. If any member of the Sherwood family wished to call upon him, he preferred that they find him at home.

When Elizabeth and Charlotte descended to breakfast at ten o'clock, they found Richard and their father already finished and their mother not yet down. Elizabeth barely waited for the footman who had served them to close the door before she blurted out, "All right, Charlotte, I won't wait a moment longer for an explanation of what happened between you and Lord Stanton last night. One minute you were dancing with him, happy as a grig, and the next time I saw you, you were regularly blue-deviled, for all you tried to hide it. What's going on?"

"I have decided that Lord Stanton and I should not suit after all, Lizzie," Charlotte replied.

"Why ever not?"

"I think his nature is too passionate."

"Most men are passionate. Mama told us that!"

"Yes, perhaps. But Lizzie . . . I am afraid of him!"

"I daresay you feel that way because you are not in love with him," Elizabeth said sensibly. "I think passion would be much easier to deal with if there were some love to accompany it."

"But men and women frequently marry without love," Charlotte said irritably.

"Of course they do. And so shall you and Lord Stanton. And I am sure you will deal admirably together," Elizabeth replied bracingly.

"Well, you're wrong," Charlotte contradicted, "for I will not marry Lord Stanton, not after his behavior last night!"

"For heaven's sake, Charlotte, what did he do?"

"He took me into one of the window embrasures, and he held me, and kissed me, and he . . . he . . . oh, Lizzie, I can't tell you!"

"Charlotte!" Elizabeth exclaimed. "Never tell me that his lordship compromised you! I don't know precisely what that is," she added thoughtfully, "but surely it cannot happen in a window embrasure!"

Charlotte smiled and turned watery eyes upon her sister. "Oh, Lizzie, you goose! Of course he has not compromised me, but I am beginning to think that you are right after all, and that I should not marry where I do not love, or at least feel some affection."

"You will not tell me what he did to distress you?"

"He had been drinking," Charlotte said, "and behaved, I am convinced, as no true gentleman would." Tears came at the memory, and Elizabeth impulsively took her sister's hand as Charlotte continued. "I can only regret that I did not have enough presence of mind to give him the set-down he so richly deserved! I am disappointed in him, Lizzie, and afraid of him, and I will not marry him! I had all night to consider my decision, and I will not change my mind." She looked down at the engagement ring on her finger and in one swift movement pulled it over the knuckle and dropped it on the table. "I am going to the drawing room this instant to write him a letter. I will enclose his ring with it, and I will politely but firmly inform his lordship that our engagement is at an end."

Shortly after midday Lord Stanton received a note and a small package, brought round by hand from Mount Street. He opened the package first, and his engagement ring dropped onto the desk. No more than he expected, after all. The note was also as expected: *I think we will not suit. . . . I am returning your ring. . . . I will not change my mind. . . . I am sorry for any inconvenience. . . . Please send the proper notices. . . . Yours, etc.* He wished she hadn't apologized, for the fault was entirely his.

He sat for some time in contemplation of Charlotte's note and then crumpled it into a ball and pitched it into the fire. He opened a drawer of his desk and dropped the ring inside. What did one do with *used* engagement rings, he wondered. How could he have been mad enough to involve himself in this whole business? It was so sordid. Mentally consigning his godmother's eighty thousand pounds and her matchmaking schemes to perdition, he rose from the desk, deciding to go to White's and find some diversion there to take his mind from his broken engagement, but at that moment the library door opened and his butler appeared.

"Miss Sherwood has called to see you, my lord."

"That would be my fiancée, Woodly," he said, with a fine disregard for the truth. "You may show her in."

"Very good, my lord."

Stanton turned and walked irritably to the fireplace. No escape quite yet, he thought, and, ignoring the damage to his gleaming Hessians, viciously kicked the end of a log protruding onto the hearthstones, thereby sending a shower of sparks up the chimney.

The door opened behind him, and he turned as the butler announced: "Miss Sherwood, my lord."

Stanton started and then stared when he saw that it was not Charlotte but Elizabeth who entered the room. She stopped just inside the door, and he remained standing before the fire until they were alone. He made no attempt to greet her.

"You misled my butler in the matter of your name, Miss Elizabeth."

"Yes, my lord. I was afraid you would deny me if I gave the correct name."

"And so I would have," he said grimly. "Why have you come here, ma'am? You must know that it is most improper for you to do so."

"I have brought my maid along. She is waiting in the hall. And you are engaged to my sister," she offered.

"I *was* engaged to your sister. That engagement is now at an end."

"You have had Charlotte's letter, then?"

"Yes, I have had her letter. But what is all this to you?"

"I watched Charlotte write that letter, Lord Stanton. You have made her very unhappy, and I don't understand why you should wish to do so. She would make you a good wife, if you would not press her and give her more time to become accustomed to you."

Oh, my God, he thought. The little sister has come to help us mend our fences. We cannot have this!

"Your sister is much too good to be saddled with a husband such as I would be," he said. "You may consider her well out of any connection with me."

"That's what Richard thinks, but I am not sure that I agree."

"You should, for he probably understands me better than I understand myself. What exactly did he say, if you don't think he would mind your repeating it?"

"He said he couldn't think that any woman would be happy for long married to you."

"And he's exactly right," he approved. "And do you know why? Because I am not long content with one woman. I estimate that a month of your lovely sister would be enough for me, and then I would be looking elsewhere."

"I don't believe you, sir," she answered quietly.

"Don't you, Miss Elizabeth?" he asked mockingly, advancing toward her. "Do you desire proof? Very well, you shall have it. My engagement to your sister has been broken for perhaps half an hour, and already I am prepared to take an interest in the woman at hand—and a very attractive woman she is!"

Elizabeth felt her color rising. "I don't understand you, my lord."

"Oh, I think you do. Any female bold enough to call at a bachelor establishment and demand a private interview cannot be ignorant of the consequences she may expect."

"I am convinced that you would not offer me any insult, Lord Stanton," she said boldly, believing her words as she spoke them and then doubting as she saw the gleam in his eyes.

"Your confidence is misplaced, ma'am," he said grimly. Then, before she could think or move, one of his hands went around her waist and pulled her to him, while the other cupped her chin and turned her face up to his. Even as she contemplated escape his lips found hers, and she was startled into complete immobility, for she had never been kissed before, and a barrage of totally new and strangely stimulating sensations swept over her. Elizabeth stood surprisingly relaxed in his arms, and although she did not actually respond to his kiss, her lips were soft and receptive.

Stanton had intended to deal her the same treatment he had dealt her sister, but when he met with no resistance and only the tenderness and innocence of inexperience, he found he had no wish to hurt her. His lips moved gently on hers, seeking a response.

Recovering, albeit belatedly, from her initial shock, the impropriety of the situation rushed in upon Elizabeth, and she pushed herself free from Stanton's embrace. Elizabeth did not have the slightest inclination to flee as had Charlotte. Instead she was outraged and allowed this feeling to manifest itself in a resounding slap, dealt to his lordship with the full force of her arm behind it.

He smiled at her attack, resisting an impulse to rub his smarting cheek. "I suppose I deserved that."

"You may consider it payment from both my sister and myself," she snapped.

He pretended to give the matter some thought and then said, "From your sister, I will accept it, but from you, no, I don't think I shall, for I have the impression that you enjoyed the moment quite as much as I."

Her eyes flashed with indignation at his suggestion, and she drew back her hand to slap him again, but he caught her wrist and held it tightly.

"No, no, my little tiger," he said. "I will not let you hit me again. You have revenged your sister admirably with the first blow."

"You are the most despicable, detestable man!" she hissed. "Richard was right. You would have made Charlotte miserable. You will be made to pay for this behavior, my lord, I promise you!"

"Intending to run to big brother with the tale of your woes, Miss Elizabeth?" he mocked.

"You are contemptible, sir! First you insult me, and then say you expect me to encourage Richard to meet a man who has proven himself to be unsurpassed in the use of pistols."

"Richard will not meet me, Miss Elizabeth, but not for the reasons you suppose."

"No. He certainly will not, for I have no intention of mentioning this incident to him. I am perfectly capable of fighting my own battles, my lord."

"Are you indeed?"

She became suddenly aware that he still held her wrist in a hard grasp, and she wrenched it away. "You are a hateful villain. If I had a pistol, I would not hesitate to shoot you myself!"

He regarded her with interest. "Really, ma'am? Well, you're in luck, for I just happen to have one to hand. And loaded, too," he added as an afterthought. He stepped to his desk and produced a handsome silver-mounted pistol from the top drawer. He cheerfully held it out to her on his open palm. She stared at the pistol and then up at his laughing, mocking face;

then, sensing that frustrated tears were only moments away, she moved to the door and, flinging it open, swept from the room, the echoes of his malicious laughter following her down the hall.

Stanton abandoned his plans to go to the club and instead returned to the fire and flung himself down in an armchair. The situation was going from bad to worse. He had succeeded in breaking his engagement, but making an enemy of Elizabeth Sherwood had not been part of his plan. He realized that he should have sent her away immediately, and under no circumstances should he have discussed his engagement with her. But somehow she seemed to sense that his behavior toward Charlotte had been a feint. He knew that she lacked the experience to be a worthy opponent, but he couldn't resist the temptation to outrage her. Now he regretted it, for he admired her spirit and her loyalty to her family and would have preferred her not to think ill of him.

Elizabeth returned to Mount Street in a vile mood, with righteous indignation at Lord Stanton's improper behavior warring with self-recrimination for her own crass stupidity in putting herself in his power. She wanted nothing more than to seek the privacy of her bedchamber and soothe her wounded pride by imagining any other ending to their interview than the one that had actually taken place. If only she had had the courage to take the pistol and put a bullet through him! That would have taken the smirk from his face!

Chapter 11

THE SHERWOOD FAMILY had varied reactions to Charlotte's announcement that she and Lord Stanton had decided that they should not suit after all. Elizabeth was puzzled when Richard showed little inclination to question Charlotte closer on the subject, but she was at the same time relieved, for the fewer questions Richard asked, the less likely it was that he would discover Lord Stanton's behavior toward Charlotte and Elizabeth's own improper interference in her sister's affairs.

Several days later, the Sherwoods received an invitation from Lord and Lady Kemp to join their party at Vauxhall Gardens on the following Friday evening. Lord and Lady Sherwood and Charlotte were already engaged to attend the theater with Harriet, who had been back in town only a few days and was impatient to join her husband on the Continent. Elizabeth had not committed herself to the play that evening and expressed a wish to visit Vauxhall.

"I am promised to Charles Warmington on Friday," Richard said, "but we haven't made definite plans. Shall we escort you, Lizzie?"

"Yes, please," she replied. "I shall write at once to Lady Kemp and accept for the three of us. That is, if you are sure Mr. Warmington will wish to go?"

Personally, Richard thought that Charles would rather go to the play, or indeed anywhere where he might expect to find Charlotte. But as it was impossible to say this, he only replied, "I'm sure he'll be delighted."

On Friday evening, Charlotte and her parents left the house first, and when Elizabeth descended, she found that Mr. Warmington had arrived and was with her brother in the salon. She entered the room to find him engrossed in an animated recounting of the curricle race that had taken place that morning between Lord Granbrooke and Viscount Stanton. He paused to greet her and then at her insistence continued his narrative.

Elizabeth had forgotten that the race was to be run that day, although in contemplating it before the event, she had thought that nothing would be more pleasant than for the two contestants to entangle their racing carriages and somehow manage to break each other's necks, for two such odious, abominable men deserved no better end. But to her disappointment, there seemed to have been no such satisfactory conclusion to the race. Lord Stanton's pair had won by a good margin.

"It isn't that Granbrooke didn't have good cattle," Charles was saying. "They were fine-looking beasts—showy, but plenty of substance. The man's an excellent whip, too, but Julian has always had the edge on him. This is the fifth time they've raced, and the fifth time Granbrooke has been beaten.

I personally think that it's Julian's method of conditioning his grays that gives him the advantage. Always knows how to bring them along just right for a big race."

Their carriage was announced and they rose to leave, but Elizabeth was sure that she had not heard the last of the race. No doubt it would be one of the major topics of conversation among the gentlemen that evening.

They arrived at the gardens in good time and soon found the box that Lord Kemp's party had taken for the evening. Mrs. Ellis and Miss Ellis were both present, and Lady Kemp was grateful to Miss Elizabeth for bringing two gentlemen as escorts, thereby somewhat evening their numbers. Dancing had already begun in the pavilion, and Mr. Warmington soon asked Miss Ellis to take the floor. Not many minutes had passed before Lord Kemp asked Richard if he had heard about the race between Granbrooke and Stanton, and with the men well launched on this subject, the women settled into a comfortable coze.

Richard later danced with Mrs. Ellis, and Elizabeth stood up with Mr. Warmington before they all partook of a delicious supper. Just as they were finishing, Elizabeth's enjoyment of the evening came to an abrupt end as Viscount Stanton and Sir Hugh Broughton came strolling past the box, stopped to exchange a few words, and were invited by Lady Kemp to join her party.

When the viscount greeted Elizabeth, she reluctantly placed her hand in his and then flushed indignantly as he held it overlong. A few moments later one of Miss Ellis's London cousins came to collect her for a stroll in the gardens, and after she had gone Sir Hugh suggested that the rest of the party go for a walk as well.

Lady Kemp demurred. "No, no. You young people go ahead. His lordship and I are much too sedentary for such exercise."

Richard made a point of taking Elizabeth's arm and strolled off with her down one of the lantern-lighted walkways through the gardens. Mrs. Ellis, in high spirits, found herself with no less than three escorts and laughingly took the arms of two of them as they followed along the same path. She insisted that the viscount give them a personal account of his race that morning, and she asked so charmingly that he could not resist her. His story-telling style was amusing, and since both his cousin Charles and his friend Sir Hugh had failed to get him to enlarge much upon the race, they hung upon his words quite as much as Mrs. Ellis did.

Some distance ahead, Richard was taxing his sister on the manner in which she had greeted the viscount. "Don't be rude to Stanton because of this situation with Charlotte, Lizzie," he said. "She's well out of any connection with him."

"That is what he said," she responded without thinking.

He looked at her sharply. "You spoke with him about this? You should not have done so. It is none of your concern."

They were walking quickly and had outdistanced the rest of their party. As they came round a bend and continued down a long stretch of deserted pathway, Elizabeth realized that the conversation was taking a dangerous turn. She had not intended to mention her meeting with Lord Stanton, and if she didn't change the subject quickly, more likely than not Richard would have the whole story from her. There was no mistaking the disapproval in his voice, and on top of her humiliating treatment at Lord Stanton's hands, she didn't think she could bear a lecture from Richard.

Even as she tried to think of an answer that would direct them to a safer topic, there was a rustle in the shrubbery to their right as two burly men leaped from the bushes and hurled themselves at Richard. Elizabeth opened her mouth to scream but was suddenly grabbed from behind as her mouth and most of her face were covered by a large foul-smelling glove. Large man that he was, Captain Sherwood nevertheless had his hands full with two heavy opponents, so he never saw the fourth man who approached from behind and dealt him a stunning blow to the head. Elizabeth did not see her brother fall, for she was already being dragged off through the shrubbery, held fast in an iron grip.

When the rest of the party rounded the corner a few moments later, they were shocked by the sight of Captain Sherwood struggling to his knees on the path before them. Of Miss Elizabeth there was no sign. Mrs. Ellis uttered an exclamation as Stanton broke into a run. He reached Richard in seconds and knelt beside him.

"Richard, what happened? Where is your sister?"

Richard tried to speak and then closed his eyes as he fought to overcome a shuddering wave of nausea. As the rest of the party came up the viscount said, "There was no shot, so he must have been struck down." He ran his hand carefully over the back of Richard's head, and it came away covered with blood. Taking a large handkerchief from his pocket, he placed it over the wound.

"Should we help him up, Lord Stanton?" Mrs. Ellis asked, reaching to hold the cloth in place.

"No, ma'am. We'll leave him as he is for the present and allow him to overcome the dizziness. Richard, you've got a nasty bump, but you *mustn't* pass out. Did you recognize any of them?"

"Julian . . ." Richard finally managed. "Lizzie . . ."

"Yes," Stanton encouraged. "Someone has taken Elizabeth. But who? Did you recognize them?"

"No," Richard answered more clearly. "There were three . . . no . . . four, but it had to be Granbrooke."

"Granbrooke?" the viscount asked in astonishment. "Surely not!"

"Indeed, my lord," Mrs. Ellis confirmed. "Elizabeth refused his offer of marriage several weeks ago, and at the Sherwood ball he so forgot himself that Captain Sherwood asked him to leave the house."

Sir Hugh now joined in the conversation. "His losing that race to you this morning probably put him over the edge, Julian. He's rolled up; probably decided this was the only way."

As Stanton rose to his feet, Richard grasped his wrist. "It had to be Granbrooke. He needs a rich wife . . . and Julian . . . he'll give her no choice."

"I know," Stanton replied gravely. "I'll find them, Richard. Trust me."

Richard only nodded, but the effort made his head throb.

Stanton turned his attention to his friends. "Charles, you must get him to a doctor as quickly as possible. And Hugh, if you could stay with Mrs. Ellis and make our excuses to the Kemps. Tell them that Miss Elizabeth was taken ill and Richard and Charles have taken her home. Dispose of me any way you please." He turned and was gone into the night.

Stanton was crossing the river to Westminster in a matter of minutes but then swore impatiently as he had to wait more than five minutes for his coach to be called up. As the carriage stopped before him and the footman jumped down, Stanton handed him some coins. "Take a hackney home immediately, Tim. Have the strongest coach team harnessed to the light traveling-chaise. Take the chaise immediately to St. James Square and await me there." As Tim turned and jogged off to the hackney stand, Stanton ordered his coachman to Lord Granbrooke's residence in St. James Square, but even as he drove, he knew he would not find Granbrooke at home. The question was: Where *would* he find him?

Within five minutes of the viscount's departure, Captain Sherwood was assisted to his feet, leaning heavily on Charles and Sir Hugh. Mrs. Ellis accompanied them to a scull and across the river, and there she and Sir Hugh saw Richard safely off to the doctor in Charles's care. They then recrossed to the gardens and strolled back to the boxes. Mrs. Ellis marveled at the ease with which Sir Hugh delivered his fabricated excuses.

"I am sorry to say, Lady Kemp, that our party has been greatly depleted. Miss Elizabeth became suddenly unwell, and Captain Sherwood and Mr. Warmington thought it best to convey her home."

"Ah, the poor child," Lady Kemp sympathized. "It was probably those shrimp. I, myself, never eat seafood away from home, for you never know when it might not be quite fresh. But what of Lord Stanton, Sir Hugh? Have we lost him as well?"

"Alas, I fear so, my lady. We came upon his brother Henry, and he was dragged off to recount the story of his race yet once again."

"Poor Lord Stanton," her ladyship replied. "I think that before the night is over he may regret that he ever ran that race."

"Indeed, ma'am," Sir Hugh replied, "I am beginning to think that he regrets it already."

Mrs. Ellis regarded Sir Hugh critically but couldn't decide whether he had intended his words to have a double meaning. During the remainder of the evening she tried to assume a normal mien, but it was difficult, and she could only be thankful that neither Lord nor Lady Kemp was particularly perceptive.

Once, while they were dancing, Sir Hugh taxed her with her demeanor. "Come, Mrs. Ellis, smile! To look at you, people will think that it pains you to dance with me."

"I am sorry, Sir Hugh. Indeed I am. It is just that I consider both Captain Sherwood and his sister my friends, and I am worried and feel useless dancing here. I would rather be anywhere else, doing something to help."

"We are helping by keeping up an appearance of normalcy. Julian was right, you know. If we had all left suddenly, it would have presented a very strange appearance and would perhaps have given rise to speculation. As it is, I don't think anyone will be the wiser. As far as Miss Elizabeth is concerned, if anything can be done, Julian will do it. And as for Richard, he has taken many knocks harder than that one. He has a hard head—he will be fine, depend upon it."

At Granbrooke's house in St. James Square, Stanton was informed that his lordship was not at home, which was nothing more than he expected. When he offered to leave his card, the footman told him that his lordship had gone out of town. Not wishing to arouse suspicion, Stanton said no more but retired to his coach and instructed his man to drive round to the mews. Here he alighted and casually walked into the stables. There were several grooms working there, and Stanton was relieved to recognize one of them. He walked directly to the man, who paused in his work to say, "Good evening, m'lord."

"Good evening. . . . Riddle, isn't it?"

"Indeed it is, m'lord," the man said, flattered that his lordship should remember him.

"Well, Riddle, I came by to see the bays. After I raced them this morning, I couldn't stop thinking what a fine pair they are, and I asked your master if I could come by and take another look at them. I have a similar bay pair, and I've been considering whether they might be made to go together as a team."

"Aye, I know your bays, m'lord, and mayhap you're right, 'twould be an impressive team." The man's eyes were sparkling at the thought, and Stanton knew that he was off guard.

They went together to the boxes to inspect the horses, and conversation progressed easily enough, for they were indeed a handsome pair of animals.

"Well, that's it, then," Stanton said decisively. "I must have them. Your master may name his price." Stanton was smiling openly at Riddle by this time, and the man felt favored to be sharing confidences with one of the most noted whips in the city. "Where is he now, Riddle? Do you know? He is usually at Watier's at this time of night, isn't he?" He turned to hurry away. "I'll make him an offer yet tonight."

"Wait, m'lord! I'm afraid you'll not find his lordship at the club, for he's gone out of town."

Stanton's face registered immediate disappointment, and he had to bite his tongue to keep from screaming—*where*? But he was immediately rewarded for his patience when Riddle said bracingly, "But I don't think he intends a long stay at Epsom, m'lord, and should return in a few days' time. I will tell him you called about the horses."

"Yes, please do, Riddle. And tell him to call on me. I will be impatiently waiting to hear from him." Stanton turned and moved without apparent haste back to his waiting coach. He proceeded to the end of the street, and then turning again into St. James Square, his town coach with two horses pulled up beside his traveling-chaise and four. As Stanton stepped down from the coach, he nodded for his coachman to come down as well. "Come along, Sweet, we're for Epsom, and I'll put my money on you to get me there as fast as any man can."

Sweet grinned as he jumped down from the box and quickly climbed up onto the chaise. "We've almost a full moon, my lord; that will help. And a fair road. Should be no problem to make good time."

"Let's be off, then. We'll make a change at Merton and stop at the King's Arms in Epsom for information."

Stanton ordered his town coach home, and without further ado, mounted into the chaise and set out. He was aware that he had lost valuable time in inspecting the horses in Granbrooke's stable, but it couldn't be helped. He must make the time up elsewhere. Epsom was no more than a twelve-mile journey and could be accomplished in one stage. Stanton was hoping that Granbrooke would take one team the entire distance. By changing horses himself at the halfway point, the viscount planned to finish the journey with a fresh team while Granbrooke continued with a tiring one.

The change at Merton was accomplished quickly, but more importantly, they learned that a chaise had passed through perhaps thirty minutes earlier, traveling south. To Stanton's relief, no change of horses had been made. From this point, with a fresh team, they should be able to gain on Granbrooke's coach.

Stanton found himself increasingly concerned with what

was happening in the coach ahead. If Granbrooke had employed ruffians to overpower Richard, he would not need their services once he had the girl safely away. It was most likely that he and Elizabeth were traveling alone, and the viscount found the thought disturbing. With a man of Granbrooke's temperament there was no predicting how he would behave. Having laid such careful plans to abduct the girl and keep her hidden for a few days, he could certainly be patient enough to delay his seduction until he found himself in a more comfortable place than a rocking, bouncing carriage.

If Granbrooke did make some attempt in the carriage, Stanton had no doubt that Elizabeth would make an effort to defend herself. She had a good right arm! He smiled at the memory of the day she had slapped him. She had plenty of courage, Richard's little sister! But slowly, as the miles passed, the viscount's smile faded, and an irrepressible rage began to take its place.

At the King's Arms the proprietor knew Lord Granbrooke well and gave them simple directions to his house, less than a mile away.

Chapter 12

STANTON WOULD HAVE suffered less anxiety had he known that Lord Granbrooke did indeed choose to curtail his advances until he and his "guest" reached the privacy of his secluded Epsom home. Having decided on this extreme course of action, it seemed to him the perfect place to take Elizabeth until she should agree to marry him. Few people knew of his house outside London, as he had kept it very close, retiring there on more than one occasion when his debts had made the town too hot for him.

"What is the meaning of this, my lord?" Elizabeth snapped,

as she fixed her captor with a cold, furious stare. "Where are you taking me?"

"Somewhere where we can be alone together without fear of interruption, my dear."

"You're a fool, sir, if you think Richard will not follow me!"

"I am sure he will try. But from what my hirelings tell me, he will be incapable of doing so for some time at least, and by then I fear he may experience some difficulty in finding us. It was considerate of the two of you to walk off alone like that. You made my job so much easier."

"What have you done to Richard?"

"Nothing more than a slight knock on the head, I assure you. You can't think that I should wish any permanent injury to my future brother-in-law."

The meaning of these words could not be misunderstood, and the image they produced sickened her. "I will never marry you, Lord Granbrooke. You cannot force me to do so."

"Can't I, my dear? I rather think you are wrong. You may be opposed to such an alliance tonight, but I think that in the morning you will have very different feelings in the matter."

"Why are you doing this to me?"

"Because you have a handsome marriage portion, Elizabeth, and I am in desperate need of it. If I could have been victorious over Stanton this morning, things might have been different. But the fellow has the devil's own luck, so you are my last hope. I never cared much for the idea of marriage, but I must say I can almost countenance it to a morsel as choice as you." He reached forward to fondle a curl that had escaped and hung loose by her face, and she shrank from him.

He laughed. It was not a pleasant sound. Elizabeth did not answer him, and when she made no response to the next several comments he addressed to her, he relapsed into silence and didn't speak for more than an hour until the Epsom house was reached and the coach rolled to a stop.

Elizabeth had by then had time to consider the seriousness of her situation. She was anxious for Richard and prayed that he was not badly injured. She knew that the rest of the party were close behind, and Richard would not have been long without help. Had any of that party rounded the bend in time to see her dragged away? The attack took place so quickly that she thought it unlikely. Perhaps one or more of the other gentlemen would try to come after her. But how could they, she reasoned, when they had no way of knowing who had taken her, or where? She decided she could not depend upon outside help and must discover a way to deal with Lord Granbrooke herself. There were no pistols in the coach holsters, and she wondered if he carried one upon his person.

Arriving at their destination, Granbrooke descended from the coach and waited for Elizabeth to alight. When she hesitated, he said imperatively, "You may walk into the house under your own power, ma'am, or if you prefer these men shall carry you."

One look at the stocky footmen at his side convinced her that they would not hesitate to obey him, so reluctantly she descended and entered the house. She knew she had no hope of prevailing against three men. She must bide her time until she had his lordship alone and then apply all her efforts to thwart him. She forced herself to remain calm. She must think. If there was a way to escape, she would find it.

Once inside, they ascended the stairway to a salon on the first floor. Elizabeth watched as Granbrooke closed the double doors behind them, locked them, and placed the key in his pocket. Her eyes swept the room quickly. There was only the one door, and the windows would all be too high from the ground to offer any possible escape. Food and wine had been set upon a sideboard, and a large fire crackled on the hearth. There was a small table and several chairs scattered about the room and a large sofa standing against one wall. Granbrooke went to pour himself some wine, and Elizabeth pretended to warm her hands at the fire. It had occurred to her that a poker might make a formidable weapon, but she saw to her dismay that there were no fireplace tools.

She turned suddenly to find his lordship directly behind her, and as she tried to move away he put his free arm around her and pulled her close, attempting to kiss her. She jerked away sharply, knocking the wineglass from his hand and spilling its contents over them both. He swore beneath his breath and, as she spun away, caught her right hand in his and crushed it ruthlessly. The pain stayed her momentarily, and as her eyes met his he said, "You would do much better to face the inevitable with dignity, my dear. I do not wish to hurt you, but if you fight me, I may be forced to do so."

With superhuman strength, Elizabeth pulled her hand free and tried to turn away, but he grabbed for her, catching her by the shoulders, and as she struggled wildly to free herself the shoulder of her gown came away in his hand. She tried to slap him, but he caught both arms, pinning them to her sides and forcing her relentlessly back upon the sofa. She felt his great weight descend on her, and as his face came close, she turned her head to avoid him, but his hand was in her hair, viciously twisting her head, forcing her face to meet his. He pressed his wet mouth to hers, crushing her lips cruelly against her teeth, and then she felt his hand at her breast and thought she must faint. She fought against a growing cloud of dizziness and continued feebly to struggle, even though she knew she was no match for him and in the end he would have his way.

Stanton's greatest concern upon arriving at Granbrooke's house was that he would be denied entrance at the front door. If it wasn't opened to him willingly, he doubted if he would be able to gain entry by force. He removed a pair of pistols from the interior of the carriage and, putting one of them into his pocket, handed the other to Sweet. The undergroom remained on the box, holding the team.

Stanton sounded the knocker and was immeasurably relieved when the door was opened almost immediately by a footman. "Viscount Stanton to see Lord Granbrooke," Stanton announced, stepping into the hall.

"Lord Granbrooke is not in residence, my lord," the man replied, and then took an involuntary step backward as the viscount produced his pistol and leveled it.

"Isn't he? Well, I hope you won't mind if I take a look for myself."

Sweet now entered the hall in his master's wake and closed the door behind them. Stanton glanced at the various doors around the hall and at the stairs ahead and demanded impatiently, "Where are they, man? Tell me now, if you value your life!" Sweet raised his own weapon threateningly, and the cowed footman nodded to the stairs.

"First door on the right, at the top."

Dropping the pistol into his pocket, Stanton took the stairs three at a time and then hesitated outside the double doors. He could hear no sound from within. He gently tried the handle and found it locked. Mentally preparing himself for what he might find, he took a step backward and then, raising his booted foot, planted a violent kick just below the handles. The wood splintered as the lock and the latch gave way and the doors flew wide.

Lord Granbrooke leaped from the sofa and turned furiously toward the door. When he saw who stood there, he was bereft of speech. Stanton's gaze alighted only briefly on Elizabeth, but even so took in her torn dress and her bruised, bleeding lips.

As Stanton continued to stand rigidly in the doorway, Granbrooke mastered his surprise and shouted, "You will explain yourself, sir! By what right do you force your way into my home? Your presence here is unwelcome!"

"To you, sir, no doubt it is, but perhaps the lady feels differently."

"What the lady and I choose to do is none of your affair, Stanton!"

"True enough, Granbrooke, if the lady accompanied you freely. Did you do so, Miss Elizabeth?"

"No, sir," she answered breathlessly. "His lordship brought me here against my will."

Stanton nodded in assent. "Just so, ma'am—as I thought."

"Get out of my house, Stanton," Granbrooke shouted wrathfully. "None of this is any concern of yours!"

"But I am making it my concern, my lord. I thought I had already made that clear." He advanced slowly on Granbrooke and stopped a few feet short of him. "You know, Granbrooke," he said thoughtfully, "during all the years of our acquaintance I have always fancied that there was a smell of the barnyard about you, but it is only tonight that I have discovered why that is." Granbrooke stiffened and unveiled hatred gleamed in his eyes, but the viscount continued calmly. "Your manners would offend a pigsty."

Granbrooke started forward, then stopped again, clearly needing every effort of will to restrain himself. "You will meet me for this, my lord," he growled, between clenched teeth.

"Certainly," the viscount answered amiably. "When and where you please. Sir Hugh Broughton will act for me. You may send your man to call upon him in the morning." Then, deliberately turning his back on Lord Granbrooke, Stanton took Elizabeth's cloak from where it lay on the floor and put it gently about her shoulders as she rose from the sofa. Without another look at Granbrooke, he escorted her from the room, down the stairs, and into his waiting carriage. The door closed behind them, the horses were set in motion, and the lights of the house faded into the distance.

If Elizabeth had been able to speak, she would have been unable to think of anything to say. Her first reaction to the viscount's violent eruption into the room had been gratitude that her fervent prayer had been answered and that she had been delivered from Lord Granbrooke's evil plan for her. This feeling was quickly replaced by acute embarrassment at being discovered in such a compromising situation, with Granbrooke lying on her, and with her dress torn and her person disheveled. But nothing could equal her shock when she realized that Stanton was purposely forcing a quarrel on Lord Granbrooke. The very man who less than three days ago had insulted her himself was now challenging Lord Granbrooke to a duel to defend her honor! How could she expect a man she despised to defend her? It was ludicrous! Unthinkable!

She started violently as Stanton laid his hand on hers, and as he quickly withdrew it, she looked up to meet his eyes in the dim light cast by the coach lantern. He was seated opposite her, with his back to the horses.

"Elizabeth," he said softly. "Please say something. You are frightening me."

I am frightening *you*, she thought. It should be Lord Granbrooke who frightens you. He is the one who will take a pistol and shoot at you in a few days' time. But she said nothing and only continued to stare at him. Then suddenly she remembered her brother and found her voice. "How is Richard?"

"He has a nasty lump on the head, but I think he'll be all right. The others were seeing to him as I left."

"Thank God," she whispered.

Impulsively he leaned forward to examine her more closely. "Elizabeth, I *was* in time, wasn't I? He didn't hurt you?" Even as she nodded and assured him that she was fine, he saw that she was shaking, and, pulling his evening mantle from his shoulders, he moved across to her side of the coach to put it round her. She instinctively shrank from him, and he suddenly remembered the last time they had been alone together and could understand her anxiety. In her mind, she had only been conveyed from the arms of one scoundrel into the hands of another.

In an attempt to reassure her, he said, "You have nothing to fear from me, Miss Elizabeth. I followed you at Richard's request, and I would not betray his trust. You are shivering. Please, put this on." She leaned forward off the squabs as he drew the mantle around her. He then pulled one of the carriage rugs over her legs, and although he remained seated at her side, he did not speak again until they reached Merton.

"We left my carriage team here," he explained, "and will stop to collect them. I think we should make some attempt to set you to rights, ma'am, for if I return you to your family as you are, I think they will be more concerned than necessary."

Elizabeth was struck by the sense of his words and raised a hand to her disheveled hair but, beyond nodding her agreement, made no other response.

Stanton left his coachman in charge of the change and escorted Elizabeth into the inn, where he demanded a private parlor. "We were involved in a carriage accident, and the lady has been slightly injured," he explained to the curious landlord. "We would like some brandy, and a cloth and some water, and a hairbrush if you have one."

The landlord soon produced the things they required and left them alone. Elizabeth seated herself at a small table, and Stanton pulled up a chair beside her. She watched him abstractedly as he dampened a cloth in water and turned to her.

"Look at me," he commanded, and she did so. "Your mouth is cut and bleeding," he said. "Let me see to it." He took her chin in his hand, gently dabbing the blood away. Elizabeth steadily regarded his eyes as he concentrated on his work, forcing herself to remain still, willing herself not to pull away from his touch or to flinch at the discomfort he was causing her. "There," he said as he finished, "now hold this cloth to the split and perhaps the bleeding will stop. Now for your hand." He picked up her right hand and she stared in astonishment, for several of the fingers were covered with dried blood.

She hadn't even noticed. She watched as he washed the blood away and realized that it was the hand that Lord Granbrooke had crushed so cruelly.

Stanton was tentatively turning the diamond ring on her third finger. "This is what caused the damage," he said. "The stone and the setting have both cut deeply into your fingers, here, and here. I am afraid it must come off. It may hurt a little." He pulled the ring over her knuckle, and although it did hurt, it was over in a moment. He dropped the ring into the pocket of his evening coat and soon finished cleaning the wound. "I think that shall do. Can you manage your hair by yourself? I'm sure I can't help you there."

He held out the brush, and she took it from him and moved to a small looking glass on the far wall. She saw that her mouth was indeed swollen and discolored. She pulled the pins from her hair, and it fell in dark glossy waves to her waist. The viscount, pouring brandy at the table, watched her silently as she ran the brush through the long strands section by section. When she had finished, she gathered it up and with several clever twists and turns of the wrist, piled it neatly on her head and began to secure it with pins. When she finished, she returned to the table, and he handed her a glass of brandy.

"I have no doubt this will burn your split lip abominably, but try to drink some just the same."

Stanton was uncomfortable with this silent and brooding Elizabeth. Always before he had known her to be ebullient, frank to a fault, full of infectious good humor, or, at the very least, outspoken anger. During the past hour, she had hardly spoken at all, and he was finding himself at a loss to know how to revive her spirits.

They soon returned to the coach and continued their journey. For some miles Elizabeth remained silent, and when she finally spoke, her tone was stilted and sounded rehearsed. "I would like to thank you, my lord, for coming to my assistance tonight. You were very kind to—"

"Nonsense," he interrupted rudely. "You do not consider me in the least kind. If you have forgotten the terms you used to describe me only a few days ago, believe me, I have not. Let me see . . . despicable, hateful, contemptible. . . . I'm sure I've missed a few."

"Can you blame me, sir?" she was stung into retorting. "Your behavior was deserving of no better description!"

"You cannot have considered, ma'am, that you would not have been subjected to my behavior if you had not insinuated yourself into my home and into my affairs."

There was a slight pause before Elizabeth continued. "Is that why you behaved so to me?" she asked quietly, "to punish me for interfering between you and Charlotte?"

"Perhaps."

Elizabeth was silenced. She was still at a loss to understand what insane motive had caused Lord Stanton to force a quarrel upon Lord Granbrooke, but some instinct warned her that she should not introduce the subject. Had she done so, she would have found the viscount unwilling to discuss it.

It was close on two o'clock in the morning when Lord Stanton's carriage drew up outside the Sherwood residence in Mount Street. Williams alone of the servants had been taken into the family's confidence, and he waited patiently by the front door as the hours dragged by. Relief was clearly written on his face when he opened the door to admit his young mistress and Lord Stanton.

"The family is waiting in the small sitting room, my lord."

"Thank you. We'll go right up to them."

Charlotte had retired to bed soon after returning from the theater that evening, so was unaware of Elizabeth's abduction. Therefore, only Elizabeth's parents and her brother sat impatiently and impotently in the sitting room, praying for some word from either Elizabeth or Lord Stanton. They rose as one when the door opened, and there was a collective sigh of relief when they saw Elizabeth standing there. Richard was closest, and he received his sister against his chest gratefully, wrapping one arm tightly around her and extending the other to the viscount.

Their eyes met over Elizabeth's head, and Richard's look spoke volumes, but he said only, "I knew I could count on you, Julian. I can't thank you enough."

Stanton turned to Lady Sherwood as she held out her hands to him. "Indeed, my lord, we owe you a debt of gratitude we can never repay."

"Seeing Miss Elizabeth home safely is payment enough, Lady Sherwood." As she surveyed her daughter with a worried

97

frown, he took her aside and said quietly, "She has had a good scare, ma'am, and a little rough handling, but otherwise no harm has come to her. She would be better for a good night's rest."

Soon afterward, Lady Sherwood took her daughter off to bed, and Lord Sherwood also retired, gruffly informing his son that concussion could benefit from bed rest.

"Concussion, is it?" Stanton asked when the door had closed behind his lordship.

"So the doctor says. My parents have been plaguing me for two hours past to go on to bed, but I couldn't rest until I had some word of Lizzie."

"He took her to a house he keeps in Epsom," Stanton supplied. "I had the information from a talkative groom at his London stables. I took my traveling-chaise and four horses, changed to a fresh team at Merton, and made up some of the time I had lost."

"Is Lizzie really all right?"

"She assures me that she is. When I broke in on them, he hadn't gotten past the kissing, if you could call it that, and mauling stage. My God, Richard, the man is an animal! It was all I could do to keep from strangling him on the spot."

"Oh, no, my friend," Richard returned. "That pleasure shall be all mine. If Granbrooke thinks to get away with this, he'll learn his mistake before he's much older!"

"Well, I'm afraid your revenge must wait upon mine, for he is promised to meet me at the earliest convenience."

"What?" Richard thundered. "Julian, you didn't call him out?"

"Well, no, not exactly, but I did say that his manners reeked of the barnyard."

"Oh, Julian, that was not well done of you! You should have left this matter to me."

"That I should not have. You've a concussion, man! You're in no condition to be fighting a duel! I had already decided to bring the fellow to book while I was chasing him, but even if I hadn't, one look at your sister would have decided the matter instantly. Her dress was torn, her mouth bleeding, and the look of horror in her eyes I will not soon forget. It was more than any man could bear. Besides, I think I shall thoroughly enjoy putting a bullet through Granbrooke's ignoble person."

"You can't mean to kill him?"

"No. Unfortunately, that would create too much embarrassment for all of us, and I wouldn't like to be forced to flee the country. But I must tell you that I fear Granbrooke may plan to leave very soon himself. He lost a thousand pounds to me yesterday, and I'm sure that he cannot pay it. Now that he has failed with your sister, he will probably be hounded out of the country. I daresay he wouldn't hesitate to shoot to kill either one of us."

"If what you say is true, then you are placing yourself in considerable danger, Julian, for Granbrooke is accounted no mean shot."

"Very true, Richard, but you will perhaps recall that I am accounted an excellent shot, and if I fire first and place my ball in Granbrooke's shooting arm, I think that his aim will not be so good."

"Perhaps. But are you sure you can do it?"

The viscount smiled at him. "I wouldn't wager against it, my friend. I wouldn't wager against it."

Chapter 13

THE FOLLOWING MORNING, when Sir Hugh Broughton entered the gates of Hyde Park, he found the viscount awaiting him at their normal rendezvous. "I wasn't sure I would find you here this morning, Julian. What happened last night?"

The viscount briefly sketched the previous evening's events for his friend, as he had done for Richard, but leaving out such personal items as the condition in which he had found Miss Elizabeth. He said only that she had been unhurt and safely returned to her family.

"Mrs. Ellis and I found little enjoyment in the evening after you left," Sir Hugh said. "She was particularly concerned for Miss Elizabeth's safety, and I had the devil's own time trying to cheer her up. Unlike me, she has no intimate knowledge of your resourcefulness, Julian, and therefore couldn't place as much confidence upon the success of your mission as I could. Shall we call on her when we finish our ride and set her mind at ease concerning the Sherwoods?"

"I shall call on her, if you like," the viscount answered, "but I should like you to stay home this morning, Hugh, if you would. I am expecting Lord Granbrooke's friend to call upon you."

Sir Hugh turned to him in surprise. "The devil you are!"

"Indeed, I am, and please spare me any lecture. I have already had one from Richard, thank you. Granbrooke is a blackguard, and clearly must be dealt with, and as Richard is in no condition to settle the matter himself, I am the logical person. Besides, the impulse to insult Granbrooke last night was irresistible, I promise you."

"Very well," his friend answered resignedly. "I will stay home to await his second."

"And, Hugh," the viscount added, "make it soon, tomorrow morning, if possible."

Mrs. Ellis spent a restless night, her mind in a flurry of concern in almost equal parts for Captain Sherwood and his sister. Her anxiety brought her at an early hour to the Sherwood residence. When she inquired for Elizabeth, she was informed that Miss Elizabeth was ill and would not be receiving visitors. Sarah then asked to see Lady Sherwood and was informed that her ladyship was still breakfasting. Sarah was about to leave her card and go away when Captain Sherwood appeared through a door at the back of the hall.

"Good morning, Mrs. Ellis."

"Good morning, Captain. I have called to see your mother."

"She is just finishing her breakfast and will be with us directly," he replied smoothly. "Shall we await her in the salon?" He offered his arm to escort her upstairs.

No sooner were they inside the room than she turned to confront him. "Surely you should be in your bed, Captain, after the blow you sustained last night?"

He smiled at the concern in her eyes. "I'm well enough, ma'am, believe me."

She looked unconvinced but continued quickly. "And Elizabeth?"

"Safe and sound, thanks to Stanton."

"Thank God," she said with relief, sinking onto a sofa. "Sir Hugh said that it would be so, but I could not be easy. I have been sick with anxiety all the night, worrying about you both."

"Both?" he asked quizzically.

"Certainly, both," she affirmed.

"You had no need to concern yourself for me, ma'am."

"Oh, really?" she said scornfully, rising once again to her feet. "You were unconscious when we put you into the coach, sir, and it was your blood on my hands!" She held out her hands in a gesture to reinforce her statement.

Richard grimaced apologetically and, stepping forward, took both her hands in his. "I'm sorry," he said. "It must have been dreadful for you."

"Dreadful for *me!*" she exclaimed. "Don't be ridiculous, Captain! You are the one who was injured, and I cannot believe that you escaped as easily as you pretend from that encounter."

"I have some slight concussion, Mrs. Ellis, nothing more," he insisted.

"If you have concussion, you should be in bed," she said acidly.

"Perhaps. But I have a great dislike of pampering myself."

"You are foolish beyond permission, sir."

"I daresay I am."

"And stubborn and willful."

"So I have been told," he agreed.

"And you will not get round me by being so agreeable, sir," she declared.

"Won't I?" He smiled charmingly at her then, and she could not resist the appeal in his eyes.

She smiled back at him despite herself and said quietly, "Well, perhaps this time." Their eyes held for a long moment, and then he dropped her hands as the door opened behind them and Lady Sherwood entered the room.

"Here is my mother now. I must go. Will you tell Jimmy, ma'am, that I cannot take him out today, but that I shall call for him tomorrow at the usual time?"

"I'm so sorry, Captain Sherwood," she said sweetly.

"Jimmy will be unable to accompany you for several days, *at least*. He is not feeling quite the thing, you see, and knows better than to *foolishly overtax his strength*."

"I did not imagine you capable of such underhanded tactics, ma'am."

"Didn't you, Captain? Ah, well, I daresay it's not the first time you underestimated an opponent," she said archly as she held out her hand to him.

He took it briefly in his own but only said, "Your round, ma'am, but we shall meet again." When he had gone, Mrs. Ellis sat down with Lady Sherwood. For the next half hour they discussed Elizabeth and the best way to help her forget the unpleasant experiences of the previous evening.

Elizabeth slept until midday but woke feeling unrested and ill at ease. Her sleep had been troubled by dreams, most of them unpleasant. She moved to her dressing table and sat down despondently, gazing in the mirror at her swollen and discolored lips. Now she understood why young girls were continuously warned about men and the passions that ruled them. But certainly no warning any girl could receive would prepare her for the situation Elizabeth had found herself in last night.

She sighed. Things were happening too quickly in her life. Just two years ago, she had lived quietly in the country, never imagining that such violence would ever enter her world. Her father and brothers represented her total experience of men. They were passionate, yes, and intense; but they were also compassionate, and principled, and, above all—loving. She had been warned that there were evil men in the world, and she believed this to be true. But anything she had imagined or read about such men could not prepare her for the shock of Lord Stanton's assault on her several days ago or the terror she had experienced during Lord Granbrooke's demonstration of unbridled, lustful passion.

Even as Elizabeth considered both men in the same light, she found herself comparing their behavior, or rather, the differences in their behavior and her own reactions. Lord Granbrooke wanted to possess her, and, in attempting that possession, he had not hesitated to physically abuse her. If Lord Stanton was to be believed, he meant only to punish her for meddling. And yet, even though his attack was also physical, he did not hurt her, nor frighten her, but only succeeded in arousing her fury.

For a moment she allowed herself to remember his kiss— the softness, the intimacy, her total inability to think or move because her entire being had been caught up in the touch of his lips on hers. In that moment of memory, Elizabeth sensed that Lord Stanton, given the opportunity, would not have used her as Lord Granbrooke had, and therein lay the difference between them. Lord Stanton, Richard's friend, had acted for Richard on the previous evening, and had, in fact, conducted himself much as she supposed Richard would have. Lord Stanton's only intention had been to find her; his only motive, to protect her. He had treated her with consideration, kindness, and concern. And what had she done? She had been sullen and uncommunicative, distrustful and ungrateful, and when she finally did force herself to thank him, she expressed herself so clumsily that any fool could see that she wasn't sincere.

What must he think of her? He had rendered her supreme service and had even challenged a man to a duel for her sake, and she had left it to others to thank him. Her behavior could be described as nothing less than rudely discourteous and ill-bred, and she couldn't think how she would bring herself to meet him again.

She slept again in the afternoon and by evening felt well enough to join the family for dinner. Afterward she sat with Richard over a game of cards and found an opportunity to ask him about the duel. "Is Lord Stanton still determined to meet Lord Granbrooke, Richard?"

"It is not something for you to be thinking about, Lizzie."

"Well, I can't help thinking about it, and I will worry less if I know what is happening."

"They will be meeting at dawn tomorrow."

"I wish he knew that I appreciate everything he has done for me," she said miserably.

"He knows, Lizzie."

"No, he doesn't. I know it sounds terrible, and I am ashamed to admit it, but I never thanked him for helping me."

Richard was startled. "Why not?"

"It's hard to explain. We haven't been on the best of terms."

"Yes, I noticed that last night when Hugh and Julian first

came up to our box at Vauxhall. In fact, we were discussing that very thing when we were set upon."

"Yes, we were, but I didn't wish to discuss it then, and even less do I wish to discuss it now." She rose agitatedly from the card table. "If you don't mind, Richard, I think I should like to go and read for a while." He nodded his dismissal, and Elizabeth excused herself to her parents and left the room.

In Park Lane, Viscount Stanton dined that evening with his brother Henry and Sir Hugh Broughton. After dinner, Stanton declined an invitation to accompany the other two men to Watier's, saying that he was promised to Richard Sherwood for a game of billiards.

Stanton lingered over his wine when the others had left and at one point glanced up to see his valet standing just inside the dining room door waiting to be noticed. "Yes, what is it, Peplow?"

"Excuse me, my lord, but I found this ring in the coat you wore last night and was wondering what you would have me do with it. It appears to be a fine stone but seems a bit loose in the setting." He walked to the table and placed the ring into Stanton's outstretched hand.

"Thank you, Peplow. I will see that it is returned to its owner."

Stanton stared at the ring for some time and then slowly turned it in his fingers. Surely her hands couldn't be so small? And yet he had drawn the ring from her finger himself. There were no traces of the blood that had been there the night before; no doubt his meticulous Peplow had cleaned it thoroughly.

He wondered how Miss Elizabeth was recovering from her adventure of the previous evening. From the moment he came up with Richard on the pathway until the moment he kicked in the door of Granbrooke's salon, he was driven by one thought, and one thought only—to find Richard's sister, and to find her quickly. It was only when he had her safely in the coach that he took time to think that she might not consider herself safe with him. Her silence and withdrawal showed him plainly enough that she had neither forgotten nor forgiven his previous behavior, and she was not prepared to accept him in the role of knight errant. He could see she was badly frightened, and he wanted nothing more than to take her in his arms and soothe away her fears, as he was sure Richard would have done. But he was not Richard, and she did not trust him. It was a sobering thought.

Stanton rose from the table, Elizabeth's ring in his hand. He decided he would see to having the stone tightened. Before he quit the house to keep his appointment with Richard Sherwood, he left the ring with his secretary, along with his instructions concerning it.

Elizabeth sat in her father's book room, trying to read but constantly finding herself at the bottom of a page remembering nothing. She decided that the sonnets of Shakespeare, which she usually enjoyed, were too intense for her mood. Perhaps a novel could more easily hold her attention. She was about to replace the sonnets upon the shelf when the door opened behind her and a quiet voice said, "Richard said I should find you here reading, but I didn't know if I should believe him. Never tell me you're a bluestocking, ma'am."

Elizabeth turned quickly and observed Lord Stanton enter the room, close the door, and slowly cross toward her. She took in the elegance of his well-cut, blue cloth coat, his tight-fitting, buff-colored pantaloons, and his gleaming Hessians, but not one word would form itself in her brain, and so she spoke none but stood still, regarding him.

"I daresay you're wondering why I'm here," he continued. "I was engaged to Richard this evening for billiards. He just told me that earlier you had expressed a desire to speak with me. Do you still wish to do so?"

Elizabeth had dreaded this meeting, but she had not thought to face it so soon, and she was not prepared for the extreme embarrassment, the chagrin, and the shame as she remembered her behavior toward him when last they met. She shook her head in the negative, and he recognized it not only as an answer to his last question, but as a rejection of his very presence in the room. Silently Elizabeth laid down her book and started quickly for the door. When he realized she intended to leave him without a word, he took a step toward her as she passed him, and caught her hand, and held it.

"Elizabeth, please . . . wait. If you have nothing to say, then

I would beg of you to listen, at least, for I have something I would say to you."

She looked down at her hand where he held it but made no attempt to draw it away as he continued.

"I would like to apologize for my behavior when you came to my house. You've been having some unusually bad luck with men lately, and for that I am partially to blame. What I am trying to say is, don't judge all your acquaintance by Granbrooke and myself. Believe me, we are the exception rather than the rule."

"Don't compare yourself to him, my lord," she said vehemently. "You are not at all alike."

"We are alike in that we both grossly offended you," he insisted.

"But you meant me no harm, Lord Stanton," she returned.

"No," he agreed. "But that alone does not excuse me. My behavior led you to mistrust me, and that mistrust rendered my service last night next to useless."

She had been staring at their hands all this time, but as he spoke these last words, her eyes came up to meet his as she exclaimed, "Your service next to useless? I was never so terrified in my life as I was last night! That horrible man— kissing me—touching me!" She shivered at the memory. "I was ready to die when you came through that door! I was so frightened at the time that I can barely remember what I was thinking. In the back of my mind, I knew that I disliked you, but I was numb—incredulous that someone had come in time to help me. But I have had time to consider the matter since, time to realize that I treated you disgracefully, my lord."

He stood quietly looking down at her and watched as tears gathered in her eyes. With each word her voice lost more control. "You came after me when you had no obligation to do so. You are determined to meet Lord Granbrooke because of the way he treated me. You tried to comfort me in the coach, and I treated you wretchedly . . . and I never even thanked you . . . and I am so ashamed!" Her voice broke on a sob, and his hand tightened on hers and pulled her to him. She came willingly and buried her face in his shoulder as he held her close.

How long he held her he couldn't guess, but if anyone had told him that he would be comfortable holding a weeping female in his arms, he would have been aghast at the very idea.

It was a new experience for him, and he found it strangely exhilarating. He had known many women and without exception they had made demands upon him, and whether they were demands on his time, his wealth, or his person, they were all similar in the method of payment—he met all demands based on some feeling of responsibility, inclination, or desire. But here was Elizabeth feeling guilty and miserable, asking for no more than comfort, and he willing to give it, not for his own sake, but for hers.

Elizabeth had not shed a single tear during the entire course of her abduction and rescue, nor in the hours since her safe return home. But now, more than twenty hours of pent-up emotion would not be denied, and she found herself weeping bitterly in the arms of, strangely enough, Lord Stanton. It seemed natural for her to be there. As his arms went around her, she was reminded of the first time he had held her so, and although the situation was different, the touch of his hands was the same and seemed almost familiar. She couldn't understand why she should feel so secure in his arms, but she didn't question it. She recognized his embrace for what it was—an offer of comfort, and an acceptance of her unorthodox apology.

After a time, Elizabeth's tears subsided, and as she lifted her head, the viscount handed her a large handkerchief. She wiped her eyes and unceremoniously blew her nose, a childlike gesture that made him smile tenderly at her.

"Why did you try to make me think you were a terrible person?" she asked with brutal frankness.

"Because I didn't want you to encourage a reconciliation between your sister and myself," he answered with equal honesty.

"You never really wanted to marry Charlotte, did you?"

"No, not really." The girl is as intuitive as her brother, he thought.

"Then why did you offer for her?"

"Because of a dislike of being continuously plagued by my godmother to marry, and because of some misguided sense of what is due to my family." Because of a drunken wager. Because I was promised an eighty thousand pound inheritance. Impossible to say these things, of course, but she seemed to accept his first two reasons as explanation enough.

"Did Richard ask you to stand away from Charlotte?"

"No. He simply told me that the question of Charlotte's happiness should be a matter for my conscience."

"So he knows then why the engagement was ended."

"I'm sure he suspects."

"Then that explains why he didn't seem surprised when Charlotte said she no longer wished for the connection. Wouldn't it have been easier for everyone involved if you had simply told Charlotte that you wished to be freed from your obligation to her?"

"I considered that possibility," he said, "but I couldn't think of any explanation to give her that would not be offensive, and I wanted to leave her pride intact."

Elizabeth could see the wisdom of this. He could hardly say: I offered for you because my godmother wanted me to, and now I have changed my mind because I realize I don't really wish to be married to you.

"Well, I must say that your method worked admirably, my lord," Elizabeth said now. "Charlotte said you frightened her, and that was enough to make her cry off, although I couldn't understand it myself. Your behavior did not frighten me in the least. It only made me angry."

"Did Charlotte tell you what passed between us?"

"No," she answered quickly. "And I don't wish to know. It is not my concern."

"Do you intend to tell Charlotte what you have learned of my part in this?"

"No, I don't think I shall. I think her experience with you has been beneficial, for it has made her think that she should not marry where she cannot first feel some affection."

"And that's good?"

"Of course it's good. Despite what she says, I don't think she would be happy without love in her marriage."

"Personally, I feel that love would be catastrophic in marriage—at least in my marriage."

She looked at him strangely. "Then I am glad you will not be marrying Charlotte, my lord."

"Yes, and so am I," he agreed amiably, and then added conspiratorially, "but we shall never let her know it. Tell me, Miss Elizabeth, are we ready to put all the misunderstandings of the past few weeks behind us and begin our relationship anew? I think we could be friends if we tried." He took her chin in his hand, turning her face up to his. He was rewarded by a warm smile.

"I should be pleased to think that you considered me your friend, my lord."

"Good. Then come with me, and you will observe the game as I soundly beat your brother at billiards. And then, when we decide that his concussion has had enough abuse for one day, you can lend me your support as I send him off to bed."

He turned and offered his arm to escort her from the room. When they reached the door, she paused. "My lord," she said, "there is one thing more."

He saw that the worried frown was back on her face as he asked, "Yes, what is it?"

"Tomorrow morning. Promise you will be careful."

"I promise."

They went on to the billiards room, where they found Richard awaiting them. No further mention was made of the duel during the remainder of the evening, and of the three of them, the one who was about to fight it thought of it the least. Elizabeth could not keep it from her mind, and that Richard was thinking of it as well was evident when Stanton finally suggested that they call it a night. Richard made no objection to retiring early and said that he expected Stanton to do the same, since he could not help but benefit from being clearheaded and well rested when the dawn arrived.

Elizabeth tossed and turned for hours and then finally drifted off some time before dawn. She was shocked when she awoke to see her maid opening the curtains to bright morning sun. Her clock showed half past ten! The duel had taken place hours ago! Why hadn't Richard come to waken her? As the light from the windows fell across the table at her bedside, she saw a note lying beside her morning chocolate. It was Richard's hand. She plucked it quickly from the tray and tore it open.

Lizzie,
There has been no meeting, as Granbrooke failed to appear at the appointed time and place. It seems the man's effrontery is equaled only by his cowardice. Julian is mad as fire. I'll be home for luncheon, and we will talk then.

R.

Thank God was all she could think. It didn't matter to her that Lord Granbrooke was guilty of an unforgivable breach of honor. She cared only that no one had been hurt or killed because of her.

This unexpected turn of events acted as such balm to Elizabeth's spirit that she appeared at the breakfast table in the best of humors, entertained her parents and sister with a flow of lively conversation, and dragged Charlotte off shortly afterward on a shopping expedition. She left her parents with little doubt that their sensible Lizzie had taken control of her feelings once again and had already put her experience with Lord Granbrooke behind her.

"There is no one like Lizzie when it comes to bouncing back after rough weather," her father said proudly.

"Yes," Lady Sherwood agreed. "I think we were justified in allowing her that private conversation with Lord Stanton last evening. Richard was convinced that it would help her, and I believe he was right, for she seemed more herself after she had spoken with his lordship. And this morning, I must admit that I see little amiss with her."

"Our Lizzie is a fighter, my dear," her husband replied. "She's not one to let anything keep her down for long."

Chapter 14

THE FOLLOWING MORNING Harriet called in Mount Street to share the news of her imminent departure for Belgium. "Jonathan has made arrangements for me to join him," she said joyfully. "I sail in four days' time."

"We shall certainly miss you, my dear," Lady Sherwood said, "but you may be home again sooner than you think, for Jon has promised to try for a short furlough in the new year."

"I am sure he will do his best to get leave," Harriet said. "I

110

know he misses you all a great deal, even though he likes the army."

Harriet soon departed London to join her husband, and the remainder of the Sherwood family continued to enjoy the Season. Charlotte had expected to experience some awkwardness in meeting Lord Stanton following their broken engagement, but she found that it was not to be so. His manner toward her was easy and relaxed, and the obvious friendship that existed between his lordship and both Richard and Elizabeth had no little influence in reestablishing Charlotte's comfort in Stanton's presence. They never spoke of the previous relationship between them, and Charlotte never regretted ending it.

After his failure to appear on the morning of the duel, nothing further was heard of Lord Granbrooke. There were rumors about town concerning his sudden disappearance, and the consensus seemed to be that he had fled the country to avoid his creditors. Only a handful of people knew that he had also fled to avoid a meeting with Stanton.

Lady Sherwood was planning another entertainment to take place in late October. She presented her husband with a guest list of nearly forty persons and proposed an evening of dancing and a buffet supper. His lordship gave his wholehearted approval to the plan, asked if he could keep the guest list for a short time (to see if there was anyone he should like to add to it), and later that evening spoke privately with Richard.

"Your mother has planned a party. Here is the guest list. What do you think?"

"It appears to include most of our closest friends in town, and a few of the girls' friends, and a number of their male admirers as well. I would say that it includes most of those persons who call here regularly."

"Do you think our information seeker may be on it?" his lordship asked.

"Well, we are agreed, are we not, that if such a person desires to be invited here, he must cultivate the acquaintance of one of the family at least. Yes, I would say there is a good chance of his being on this list."

"Think carefully, Richard. Who has been calling? Who joins you when you ride with the girls in the park? Who dances with them frequently? Who pays the most court? If you think of anyone fitting that description who is not already on the list, then put him on. If we could encourage our meddler to enter my book room in search of information on that evening, we could cut our list of suspects considerably. And if we are clever, perhaps we can catch him as well. I have considered taking one of the footmen into our confidence, someone who could sit by the keyhole of the salon across the hall from the book room and keep watch while we do what's proper by our guests. As long as we are very visible in the drawing room, our traitor will feel himself safe in coming downstairs."

"It sounds like a good idea. Whom did you have in mind?"

"I thought James would do nicely. He has some military experience; he's young, strong, and, above all—we can trust him implicitly."

Richard nodded. "Let's do it then. I'll get this list back to Mother as complete as I can make it, and we can speak with James tomorrow."

"We shall continue to keep this to ourselves, Richard. The less your mother and sisters know, the safer they will be."

On the night of the Sherwood party, Elizabeth wore a new gown, just delivered that day from the dressmaker. It was of white satin, with a delicate pattern of leaves and flowers finely embroidered in pale lime green silk. The skirt opened at the front to reveal an underslip of matching green, and the low scooped neckline and short puffed sleeves set off her shoulders to perfection. She fastened a fine string of matched pearls around her neck, pulled on her long gloves, and her ensemble was complete.

Elizabeth had stopped wondering what had become of her diamond ring, which had been a gift from her father. She could vaguely remember the viscount taking it from her hand the evening of her abduction, but since he never mentioned it, she assumed it lost or left behind that night at the inn where they had stopped. It was such a trifling thing when compared to the great service he had rendered her that she was never able to bring herself to mention it to him. She gave herself one final look in the glass and then went down the hall to Charlotte's room to collect her and take her along to dinner.

Later that evening, Lord Stanton and Henry Ferris were

among the first guests to arrive. Elizabeth greeted them as they entered the room, and Mr. Ferris insisted that she save a waltz for him. As he was by far her favorite dancing partner, she readily agreed.

"By the way, Miss Elizabeth," Mr. Ferris said. "I saw you in the park this afternoon with your sister and my cousin Warmington. Couldn't take my eyes off that bay mare he was riding! What is she? Welsh?"

"Yes, she is," Elizabeth confirmed, "and he is very proud of her. He says he was lucky that both you and your brother were out of town last week when she came up for sale, otherwise he would never have gotten her for the price he paid."

"Damn Charles, Julian. He is always doing this to me! Remember that brown gelding that he beat me out of last year while we were home for Public Days? Where is he? I must have a word with him." Muttering a hasty farewell, Henry went off to find his cousin, leaving Elizabeth alone with the viscount.

"You and your brother are not very alike, my lord," she said.

"So you have said before, Miss Elizabeth. But in this one area actually, we do have a lot in common. We both have an excellent eye for a good horse, and neither of us often finds himself in possession of a bad one. Will you allow me to say that you look charmingly tonight, ma'am. That color becomes you."

"Thank you, sir. Let me tell you that I consider it a great victory to have my mother agree to so much green in this dress. She considers too much color unbecoming in a 'girl of my age,' particularly in an evening gown."

"I have something that belongs to you, Miss Elizabeth. I would have returned it sooner, but I had it sent to the jeweler to have the stone tightened. It was returned while I was out of town, and I have brought it tonight." He held out her ring and she looked at it with a happy smile.

"I thought it lost that night," she said. "I didn't expect to see it again."

"Would you like to put it on?"

"Yes, please. It fits tightly. I must take off my glove." This she promptly did and then held out her hand to him.

He took it in his and surveyed the fingers critically. The cut had healed perfectly, leaving no scar. He slipped on the ring and held up her hand for her inspection. "It looks as good as new," he said.

"What? The hand, or the ring?"

"Both."

The musicians were striking up for the first country dance, and the viscount asked Elizabeth to join him. "I cannot aspire to Henry's proficiency, but I think I can manage to avoid treading upon your toes." She went off happily on his arm and for the next hour never found herself without a partner.

The dance was a waltz, Elizabeth's partner the incomparable Mr. Ferris, and as the orchestra reached the last bars of the piece, he swung her round with a flourish and brought her up breathlessly at the edge of the floor. She was smiling and radiant and thanked him prettily.

As she stood catching her breath, she allowed her gaze to roam over the room. Lord Stanton had danced the same waltz with Charlotte, and Elizabeth saw them now, standing only a few yards away, engaged in earnest conversation. She was pleased to see that they were comfortable together. She unfurled her fan and was raising it to her flushed face when her gaze was arrested by a man standing in the shadow of the draperies in a bay window not far from where they stood. She laid her hand impulsively on Mr. Ferris's arm and said in an urgent undertone, "Mr. Ferris. Look! 'Tis Lord Granbrooke!" He followed her gaze but was unable to understand her tone, for to him Granbrooke was only a debtor gone to ground to avoid his creditors.

To Elizabeth, however, he was much more, and she sensed instinctively that he had an evil purpose. As she watched him, he stood motionless, staring unwaveringly at Lord Stanton. She wondered fleetingly how he came to be there and then realized that a man of his athleticism would have little difficulty climbing one of the rose trellises that extended from the garden below to the balcony outside the window where he stood. As she hesitated, wondering what to do, she saw Lord Granbrooke bring his hand from behind the drapery and was stunned to see that he held a pistol. Not for an instant did she doubt his intention.

Even as Granbrooke raised his arm, Elizabeth threw herself

across the space that separated her from Lord Stanton, crying his name. Hearing his name shouted, Stanton turned his eyes from Charlotte to encounter Elizabeth's face close at hand. He had time only to register the terror in her eyes when a deafening report sounded in the room, a stab of fire tore his chest, and he slipped almost immediately into darkness and oblivion.

The room was an immediate scene of chaos. Several women were screaming. The three gentlemen closest to Lord Granbrooke leaped upon him, searched his person for further weapons, and dragged him from the room. Charlotte stood for an instant frozen with shock, staring down where both Lizzie and Lord Stanton lay in a heap at her feet. Then she dropped to her knees beside them, feeling helpless yet wanting desperately to help. Richard was there, tearing the cravat from around his neck and folding it into a thick pad. He laid it over a fast-spreading stain on Elizabeth's shoulder, and when he said, "Charlotte, hold this!" she didn't think, she only obeyed him.

Henry Ferris was reaching inside his brother's coat, where an already blood-soaked waistcoat and shirt gave evidence that Julian had been seriously injured. Sir Hugh Broughton was endeavoring to clear the room. Lord Sherwood knelt, and as he surveyed the scene, his words were more a statement than a question: "The one ball has injured them both?"

"Yes, sir," Richard answered. "It has passed through Lizzie's shoulder and taken Stanton in the chest." Turning to Mr. Ferris, he said, "Henry, get us a surgeon quickly. Two if you can manage it. We will see to Julian. Go on!" Mr. Ferris rose and left the room immediately, and within a very short space of time, both Elizabeth and Lord Stanton were carried abovestairs to await the ministrations of the surgeon.

The remainder of the guests were encouraged to go down to supper, but they did so reluctantly, their enjoyment of the evening at an end.

When the first surgeon arrived, Richard directed him to his own room, where Lord Stanton had been taken. "My sister has a shoulder wound, Doctor, but we have managed to stop the bleeding. The ball is lodged in his lordship. . . . The wound is directly over the heart." The doctor frowned and shook his head forebodingly but went away with Sir Hugh to the viscount's room.

When the second doctor arrived, he was led immediately to Elizabeth. He dismissed everyone from the room, with the exception of Mrs. Ellis, who had offered to assist him. Richard and Lord Sherwood found themselves banished to the corridor, where Richard took his father aside. "I wonder that shot didn't bring James to the drawing room."

"His instructions were to sit tight and guard that room, but we should let him know what's been happening here."

"I'll go," Richard offered. He went quickly downstairs and, pausing outside the book room door, glanced about to be sure no one was in sight and then entered the salon directly opposite. He was surprised to find the room empty. He stepped back into the hallway and cautiously turned the handle of the book room door. He opened it slowly and then nearly fell over James's body as he stepped inside. A quick sweeping glance showed him that they were alone, and he closed the door before turning his attention to the footman. He rolled the young man over on his back, and almost immediately James groaned and began to regain consciousness. As far as Richard could tell, he had received no more than a sharp blow to the head. How long he had lain there unconscious there could be no way of knowing.

"James! James! What happened?"

James struggled with the effort of memory. "I heard a shot fired somewhere in the house," he replied, "but decided to stay put as I was told. Some time after that, a gentleman came down the hall and made himself free of m'lord's book room. Couldn't see anything but his back through that hole, but it was a man, definitely, and dressed in evening clothes. Well, I give him a few minutes to get his fingers well into m'lord's papers, and then I carefully opened the door to surprise him like. But when I looked in, there weren't no one in the room, and when I stepped in to see if perhaps he had left through a window, I must have been struck from behind, for I saw no one, and remember naught else."

Richard shook his head with understanding. "Our friend was evidently expecting to be followed or observed. He was very clever. He simply waited behind the door in the event anyone attempted to come after him. Then, once he had laid you low, he could peruse my father's papers at his leisure. He knows now that we suspect him; he will not be so careless again."

"I was a fool to fall into such a trap, sir, and it's that foolish I feel."

"Don't concern yourself. He found nothing in those files that will profit him."

"But what was the shot I heard, Captain! I wondered but dared not budge."

"The shot was fired by Lord Granbrooke, James," Richard answered grimly. "Tonight he attempted to murder Lord Stanton."

Chapter 15

VISCOUNT STANTON OPENED his eyes to a strange room and a strange bed. For a moment he couldn't think where he was or why. He felt tired and listless, and his chest ached as if there were a huge rock sitting upon it. He brought his hand up to see if this were indeed so, and this slight motion brought his valet, Peplow, to the bedside. Stanton looked at him questioningly—at least his face was familiar. Peplow glanced anxiously at his master and then quickly left the room saying, "I will fetch the doctor, my lord."

Evidently this worthy was not far to seek, for in a very few moments he had returned with the valet and approached the bedside. "Please, my lord, you must endeavor to lie still. You have suffered a bullet wound. . . ." Memory came flooding back. Elizabeth calling his name and the report of a gun.

"Who shot me?"

"I am given to understand that it was Lord Granbrooke who fired the pistol, my lord."

"What?" he shouted, and then regretted the way he had wrenched his body as a sickening pain spread over him.

"Please, my lord, you must lie still. The ball was lodged in the wall of the heart muscle itself. There has been considerable damage. I cannot be responsible for the consequences if you refuse to take care."

Stanton's face registered his disbelief as he gingerly brought his hand up to feel where the heaviest bandages lay on his chest. "Are you serious, man? If what you say is true, I should be dead!"

"I said the ball lodged in the *wall* of the heart, my lord. It did not enter the heart itself, and I was able to extract it without doing any further damage."

"I appreciate your effort, Doctor, but I don't understand how a ball could strike me in such a place and fail to enter the heart. Was it deflected?"

"No, my lord. By the time the ball reached you, it was nearly spent."

"Nearly spent? You are making no sense, sir!"

"Lord Stanton," the doctor said with finality, "I can tell you no more than that. My advice to you is to rest and allow your body to heal. You have a strong constitution, but you cannot afford to aggravate such a serious wound."

As the doctor walked away, Stanton frowned after him and then spoke to his valet. "What time is it, Peplow?"

"Two o'clock in the afternoon, my lord."

"Two o'clock! I've been out for nearly twelve hours? Is this the Sherwood house?"

"Yes, my lord."

"So I thought. Find Captain Sherwood, and tell him that I would speak with him immediately."

This was soon done, and within a few minutes Richard entered the room, greatly relieved to see his friend returned to consciousness. "Julian, you can't know how good it is to have you with us today! For I must tell you—when I saw where you had taken that ball last night, I thought you'd surely had your notice to quit."

"That crazy sawbones is trying to tell me that the ball didn't do more damage because it was spent."

"He's right. I had begun to suspect as much myself when several minutes had passed and you were still with us, for I knew that if the ball had entered the heart you would have been dead within seconds after the shot was fired."

"You are being no clearer than he was, Richard," Stanton said in exasperation.

"He was only trying to protect you from anxiety, but I can see that it won't serve. The ball was spent because it struck Elizabeth first. It passed through her shoulder and then hit you, but didn't have enough momentum to cause a fatal wound."

The viscount stared for a moment in disbelief, and then asked quietly, "How is she?"

"She's in considerable pain, and the doctor expects there will be some high fever." Stanton moved restlessly, and Richard added, "He also predicts the same for you if you don't behave."

"She must have seen him there," Stanton said thoughtfully, "and she was trying to warn me."

"Yes. I think she was."

"Richard, you must believe I would give anything not to have had this happen to her."

"You would have given your life, my friend. There is no doubt that Granbrooke meant to kill you and would have done so if Lizzie hadn't stepped in the way."

"Your sister is mad, Richard! Why should she endanger herself to protect me?"

"How can you ask that, Julian? You know that she feels under an incredible obligation to you for rescuing her from Granbrooke. When she saw him last night, she had to know that he was after you because of her. She was only repaying the debt when she tried to warn you."

"But, my God, Richard, she could have been killed doing such a foolish thing!"

"Yes, she could have. And you could have been, too. But you weren't, and with any luck you'll both come through this with flying colors. You should know by now that Lizzie thinks with her heart. Believe me, if given the choice again, she would much sooner accept the wound she now has than the picture of herself standing safely out of harm's way, watching you die. If I were you, I should be thanking God right now for the brave, quick-thinking foolishness of my little sister."

The doctor returned soon afterward and insisted that the captain leave so that the viscount could rest. Stanton did eventually sleep again but not before another thought had come unbidden into his mind and would not be dismissed. Perhaps

Elizabeth's motive was only to warn him, and she had accidentally gotten in the way. But what if it hadn't been an accident? What if she had purposely placed herself in what she knew to be the direct line of fire? What if she had intentionally used her body to protect his? He could think of only one reason why she should wish to do so, and that thought would haunt his dreams and disturb his waking moments for many weeks to come.

He passed the better part of that day, and the next night and day as well, sleeping. He knew the doctor was keeping him sedated, and he didn't much care, but on the fourth evening he declined any offer of laudanum.

"You will not sleep without it, my lord," the doctor objected.

"I shall sleep well enough. The worst of the pain is past, and I would prefer to have my wits about me. I can deal with some discomfort, I assure you."

The doctor went away but confided later to Captain Sherwood that Lord Stanton would in a few days' time prove an impossible patient. "He already speaks of removing to his own home, insisting that he is a burden on your household."

"I will speak with him," Richard promised.

As the doctor had predicted, Elizabeth had a bout with fever lasting a night and a day. Then on the second night it had suddenly receded. After spending many hours in exhausting delirium, she had woken to recognize her mother and sister, and then almost immediately drifted off into a deep, restful sleep.

During the next several days, Elizabeth's condition continued to improve and Stanton greeted this news with profound relief. He demanded to be assisted to sit up in bed while he talked with Richard, and although Richard complied with this request, he found an opening to discuss the viscount's behavior. "The doctor says that you are becoming a difficult patient."

"Well, I hope you don't intend to lecture me. I believe it was you who not so long ago chose to ignore your doctor's instructions concerning a certain concussion."

"The situations are hardly the same, Julian. You mustn't think of removing to your own house. Your valet has taken full responsibility for you. He has left very little to the hands of others, believe me. When the doctor gives his permission,

I will convey you home myself. Meanwhile, I shall endeavor to keep you suitably occupied. In proof of that statement, I will tell you that Mrs. Ellis is belowstairs at this very moment and has offered to give you a game of chess if you should desire it. But let me warn you—she is a formidable opponent."

"Help me into that infernal dressing gown, then, and send the lady up," the viscount said. "I am in the mood for a good challenge!"

Mrs. Ellis played chess with Lord Stanton until nearly ten o'clock, and as Richard had promised, she was an excellent player. She left him then, offering him a game of piquet on the following day.

With Peplow's help Stanton was soon ready for bed, but he slept fitfully, and he dreamed. Once again he heard Elizabeth call his name, heard the report of the gun, saw the terror in her eyes . . . and suddenly he woke, her eyes still burningly visible in waking. That was what had been eluding him these past days! That look in her eyes. It was terror—blind terror. It had startled him then, and it startled him now. It could have been terror of Lord Granbrooke, but somehow he felt that it wasn't. Somehow he felt that that look of terror had been for him—fear for his safety.

Suddenly he had an overpowering desire to see Elizabeth. He carefully pulled himself up in bed and, moving slowly to the edge, lowered his feet to the floor. He saw no slippers but couldn't be bothered. Slipping his arms into his dressing gown, he tied the sash at his waist and then rose to his feet. He felt no dizziness and only a little pain as he made his way cautiously to the door and through it. He knew that Elizabeth's room was only a few doors away. Two small tables had been placed in the hall for the use of servants carrying trays to and from the rooms. There was one outside his door, and another, three doors down, told him which room was Elizabeth's. He hesitated only a moment and then turned the handle. There was a young maid seated near the bed, and she rose as he entered. She was surprised to see him there but said nothing when he motioned for her to leave. She closed the door behind herself and took a chair in the hall. When the gentleman left, she would take up her post again.

Elizabeth was sleeping soundly, and he had no intention of waking her. He moved stiffly across the room and stood silently by the bed. She looked tired. Her face was very pale, with just the slightest tinge of color in her cheeks. She was tiny, he thought, in the big bed, her dark hair spreading over the pillow.

"Why that strange look of terror in your eyes, little Elizabeth?" he asked aloud. "Was it fear for me? And if it was, then you deliberately took a bullet intended for me. You place a higher value on my life than you do on your own." Even as he spoke these words, their implication acted upon him like a physical blow. "You cannot, must not, love me, Elizabeth. You would find no joy in loving me, for there can never be any future for us." He leaned over the bed then and kissed her gently on the forehead. She didn't stir. He had no way of knowing how long he stayed there, but his feet were cold and his chest aching when he finally let himself out of the room and accepted the young maid's offer of her arm back to his own room and into bed. It was a long time before he slept again.

It was nearly two weeks before Lord Stanton was permitted to remove to his own home, and four days later he made a call in Mount Street to ask after Elizabeth. During the days that followed, he called each day to inquire after her health, and on one occasion, when Richard asked if he would like to come up to her room to see for himself how well she was mending, he declined the invitation, saying he would rather not intrude. Richard did not press him. The situation was an unusual one, to say the least, and there would no doubt be some awkwardness when Elizabeth and Stanton met again.

It was soon decided that Elizabeth should be moved to Sherwood Manor, where the relative quiet of the country and the decidedly fresher air would speed her recovery. Mrs. Ellis offered to cut short her own stay in London by two weeks in order to accompany Elizabeth on the journey and to keep her company once they arrived in Surrey.

"I can come over as often as you like," she said. "Perhaps your brother could take us driving. And then, when you feel stronger, we can go for long walks."

It was Richard, in fact, who had suggested that Elizabeth come to the country with him. He had been intending to return there the day after the party, but the shooting had made it impossible for him to leave as planned.

Miss Virginia Ellis had her father's permission to extend her own stay in London under the chaperonage of Lady Kemp, and Elizabeth was secretly relieved that it was to be so, for as much as she liked Sarah, she couldn't bring herself to enjoy the company of Virginia, who simpered, she thought, and giggled a great deal.

The journey south was accomplished with relative ease, Sarah keeping Elizabeth company in the chaise while Richard took Jimmy up with him as before. Elizabeth had her shoulder well supported with pillows, and the coachman had been instructed to take particular care when they neared Dorking and the rougher roads beyond.

Jimmy was destined to enjoy this trip more than any he had ever taken, for he had persuaded Richard to allow his team to gallop for a time, something they were seldom permitted in London. The boy's enthusiasm was so great that Richard had to smile, and it occurred to him that he was missing a great deal in not having children of his own. Until he had met Jimmy, children had not often come in his way. Being the eldest, his mother had teased him good-naturedly about settling down and supplying her with grandchildren. Well, the pressure was off him now, he thought, for surely Lizzie or Charlotte would marry before long, and with Jon already wed, no doubt Lady Sherwood would have a grandchild or two in the near future.

Their first days in the country passed pleasantly. The weather was cool but remained clear. Sarah came each morning to Sherwood Manor and stayed throughout the day. She and Elizabeth would talk, sew, read, or try to increase their skill at piquet. They were fast becoming close friends. Jimmy spent each morning with his tutor but came every afternoon to the Manor. He accompanied Captain Sherwood on visits to the village or the tenants and even sat in on several meetings between the captain and his agent. Sometimes he employed himself running errands for his mother and more than once he offered to entertain Miss Elizabeth.

Late in the afternoon on the third day after their arrival, Sarah left Elizabeth to take a nap, and coming downstairs she found Jimmy and the captain in the hall, just returned from the village.

Richard handed her a small parcel. "Here is the blue silk

you needed, ma'am." Then he added impulsively, "Why not come out for a walk with me, Mrs. Ellis? You have been with Lizzie almost continuously since we arrived. I am sure the exercise will benefit you."

"I doubt if Elizabeth will sleep longer than an hour, Captain," she objected.

"Go with Captain Sherwood, Mama," Jimmy encouraged. "I will stay to keep Miss Elizabeth company when she wakes. I can read to her, or give her a game of piquet if she prefers."

Sarah smiled proudly at her son, thinking how mature he was, and how generous. "Very well," she said, "I will go for a walk. I must admit it sounds tempting." She went upstairs to change her light shoes for serviceable half boots and to collect a warm pelisse. She had brought these things with her only today and planned to leave them at Sherwood Manor against the day Elizabeth decided she would like to venture out of the house herself. Sarah soon joined the captain in the hall and they strolled out together to enjoy the crisp November day.

They walked for some time in silence, westward along the floor of the valley in which the Manor was situated. Tree-covered ridges rose on both left and right, and although there were a number of pines, there were several deciduous varieties as well, and the leaves they had recently shed carpeted the ground. The rustling of the leaves and the occasional call of a bird were the only sounds to disturb the silence.

"Captain Sherwood," Sarah began, "I have a great deal for which to thank you."

"I was just about to say the same thing to you, ma'am! You have been a trooper these past weeks—helping me to entertain Lord Stanton, with no thought for the inconvenience to yourself, and giving your assistance to Elizabeth, first as a nurse, and now as a companion."

"I was more than happy to do it, Captain, and I have enjoyed the time I spent with them both. The gratitude I feel toward you concerns my son. It has been a little more than two months since the day you brought Jimmy home in the rain, and from that day to this I have seen a steady change in him. I had thought myself to be doing a good job in rearing him, but I have been brought to see that I was doing far less than I should have been."

He started to object, but she forestalled him. "Please, Captain, allow me to finish. Jimmy was always a considerate, thoughtful child, but I have never known him as animated as he has been since meeting you. He takes so much more interest in life, and in the people about him. He has been growing up in many ways that I never realized, and he seems to me years older since knowing you. I have seen his self-esteem grow considerably. He is more courteous than before and seems to be so naturally, and not through any conscious effort. He shoulders responsibility capably and readily and is willing to take on even more than I feel his age requires. I know that all this is due to your influence, and I am truly grateful."

"You give me too much credit, Mrs. Ellis," Richard objected, "and yourself not nearly enough. Jimmy is a fine boy, but his friendly good humor, his notion of what is fair or unjust, his honesty, his sense of responsibility, his pride in his family and his country, these are all things that he was taught long ago—taught by you. If you have noticed a change in him, then it is only a matter of his personality flowering under what I hope is a good influence."

"You may call it a flowering if you like, Captain, but it has happened because you have taken a special interest in my son."

"I have grown very fond of Jimmy," Richard admitted, "and yet I felt in the beginning that you did not welcome my interest in him."

"That is true," she admitted. "I have been jealous of letting anyone influence him. I have particularly dreaded Sir Winston taking an interest in him."

"Why?"

"Because Sir Winston is not a man after which I would like to have my son model himself."

"And I am?"

"Yes. Most definitely," she said frankly. "You are not like any man I have ever known. Please don't misunderstand me when I say this, Captain, but I find your personality more like that of a woman than a man."

He stopped, startled, and stared down at her. "If you were a man, ma'am, I think I would be forced to call you out for that!"

She smiled. "I asked you not to misunderstand, and I do not

mean it as an insult, sir, but as a compliment. You are gentle, tender—you do not threaten a woman with your manner."

"But certainly these can be male traits, ma'am?"

"Perhaps, but I have never seen them in any male of my acquaintance."

"Then I think you have been singularly unfortunate in your male acquaintance, Mrs. Ellis."

"Maybe so, and I suppose by some standards I have not known many men. I had cousins when I was young, but I didn't know them well. I was certainly well acquainted with my father, however, and my husband, James, and, of course, Sir Winston. They were, and are, all quite different from you, sir, I assure you. Many men in society are polite to women, and their manners are polished to just that end. Your manner with women is something you have not practiced, I think, but something that is part of your nature. I don't mean to imply that there is anything feminine about you, Captain. Quite the opposite, in fact. I find you commanding . . . athletic . . ." They had come to a stile, and he offered her his hand to come over. As she came to the ground, he retained her hand in a hard clasp. "And you are strong," she said, looking pointedly at his fingers where they held hers. Keeping his hold, he drew her closer, and she brought her free hand up to lay it flat against his chest. "And you are very attractive," she finished, as she brought her eyes up to meet his.

"You don't know how relieved I am to hear you say so, ma'am," he murmured. His next intent was clear. Mastering her will, Sarah pulled her hand away and quickly turned to continue walking. Richard frowned but fell instantly into step beside her. After a few moments, he said, "Let me understand you, ma'am. You find me attractive, but you do not welcome my attentions. Have I that correctly?"

"I wasn't saying these things to encourage a demonstration, Captain Sherwood. I was simply trying to make a point."

"I see."

She stopped once again to look at him. "Please, let us not spoil our friendship. I value it highly, and I would wish for it to continue."

Richard was puzzled and hurt by her behavior, but he couldn't resist the appeal in her voice. He held out his hand, palm up, and she hesitantly placed her own in it. His strong fingers closed around hers and then lifted her hand to his lips. "Friends, then, Mrs. Ellis—if you insist. But if you wish me to believe that you enjoy your time with my sister, then you must believe that I enjoy the time I spend with your son. Let there be an end to any feeling of obligation between us, for friends do not question a gift or the motive in giving."

Chapter 16

IN EARLY DECEMBER, Lord and Lady Sherwood and Charlotte arrived in Surrey, intending to remain in the country for some months. During the weeks preceding their arrival, Sarah continued to call daily at Sherwood Manor, but Richard made no attempt to advance their relationship beyond the limits of friendship she had prescribed. This he did partly because he knew it was what she desired and partly because it would be improper for him to take advantage of her presence in his house. There were numerous instances during those weeks when they found themselves alone together, sometimes for a few minutes, other times for several hours, but he allowed no repetition of his behavior on the day of their first walk.

More than once, Sarah had puzzled over her own behavior that day. She had told him she was not trying to encourage his advances, and yet, if she were entirely honest with herself, she had to admit that she did encourage him. She had begun her description of him simply to explain herself. But as she realized the effect her words were having on him, and when he held her hand in that possessive manner, she added her last comment deliberately, wondering what kind of reaction it might bring. Then, when he had responded, she pulled away, suddenly realizing that the very last thing she wanted was an emotional involvement with Captain Sherwood. Having suffered five years of domination by her husband, and another five since his death under the thumb of her father-in-law, she was not eager to give any man power over her. She knew better than anyone that she must continue to bend to Sir Winston's will while he lived, but what little freedom of choice and will her widowhood gave her, she was determined to keep to herself—completely to herself.

Less than a week after Lord and Lady Sherwood's return, Lord Stanton and his cousin, Charles Warmington, arrived for a week of shooting. Having been invited by Richard, Stanton considered that although he did not wish to encourage any tender feelings in Elizabeth, he could offer no plausible reason for refusing the invitation. And, if he was honest, he had to admit to a strong desire to see Elizabeth again. He had not seen her since the night he had stood in her room, watching her sleep, more than six weeks ago. He had never thanked her for saving his life, and although he suspected that she had done it purposely and not accidentally, to admit as much would be to admit that he guessed how she felt about him. He shuddered as he realized the kind of uncomfortable situation that would create! He couldn't imagine what he could possibly say to her when they met, so he tried not to think about it but just to let it happen.

He and Charles arrived early in the afternoon, but there was no opportunity for private conversation with Elizabeth until after dinner that evening. When the gentlemen joined the ladies in the parlor, she was sitting alone near the fire reading, and when he came to sit beside her, she put her book aside.

"I meant what I said earlier," he said. "It is good to see you looking so well."

"You had a serious wound, too, my lord, and you also look fit."

"I've had all these weeks to think of an adequate way to thank you for what you did, Miss Elizabeth, but it hasn't served. There is no way to properly thank someone for saving your life."

"There is no need to thank me, my lord. If I rendered you a service, you may consider it repayment of a debt I owed you. For if my being wounded delivered you from death, you may be sure that I feel your action for me, on an earlier occasion, delivered me from a fate that I considered worse than death."

"Richard said that you would probably view the situation in

this light, but still, it was an insane thing to do. Courage is a good thing, but it can be carried too far."

"I don't know that courage had much to do with it," she said. "I wanted to warn you, and I didn't stop to think about anything else. I daresay I didn't expect Lord Granbrooke to fire unless he had a clear shot."

Richard soon joined them, and the conversation turned to other subjects. Stanton had to admit to himself that seeing Elizabeth again had brought him no closer to understanding her actions. Her conversation seemed to indicate that gratitude had been her only motive, and yet he sensed that there was more to it than that. Either Elizabeth intended to be very careful to hide her feelings from him, or (and this was a totally new thought to him) she didn't realize herself why she had protected him. If she was in love with him and didn't know it herself, he had no intention of doing anything to enlighten her.

The intricacies of the situation were beginning to make his head ache, and he decided that the best course would be to put it all out of his mind and try to enjoy a good week of shooting. He and Elizabeth traveled in the same social circle, and he was destined to meet her. He would neither encourage her nor avoid her, and let the chips fall where they would.

The following evening the Ellises were invited to dine at Sherwood Manor. The presence of Sir Winston, Sarah, and Virginia swelled the number of the dinner party to ten and gave Lady Sherwood the satisfaction of having her numbers equal. Lord Sherwood viewed the gruff Sir Winston with tolerance, and if Lady Sherwood didn't quite cherish Miss Ellis, she had nothing but praise for Mrs. Ellis, who had proved herself indispensable in the days and weeks following Elizabeth's injury.

After dinner, Elizabeth played and sang for them, and she even coaxed Charles into joining her for a few songs of the sea that her father had taught her and that Charles also knew. Richard slipped away after a time and went to the library, where he was surprised to find Sarah.

"I thought you went to fetch a shawl for my mother?" he asked.

"Yes, I did," she said, indicating the shawl over her arm. "I just stopped here to pick up a book that I was reading several weeks ago and that I wanted to discuss with your father. It was some kind of a log from one of his ships. Here it is." She pulled the volume from the shelf and turned to find Richard close behind her. She raised her eyes to his. Taking the book from her hands, he laid it on the edge of the desk and then disposed of the shawl in the same manner. He pulled her into his arms, and she came rigidly. Clearly feeling her reluctance, he bent his head anyway and covered her mouth with his own.

Sarah braced herself for the bruising, possessive kiss that had been her husband's sole technique, and then was startled by the touch of Richard's lips. Soft, so soft, and yielding, yet strangely compelling. If this was a kiss—surely she had never been kissed before! The shock and the newness kept her from responding, and even as he released her, she felt a rising desire to do so, but the moment was lost, and they stood apart. She stood staring at him for a few moments in silence. This time there could be no mistaking his confusion and the pain of rejection in his eyes. She deliberately picked up the shawl and the book from where he had laid them and walked silently from the room.

From that evening, Sarah noticed a distinct change in Richard's attitude toward her. When they met, he was polite and civil as always, but gone was the light of humor in his eyes. He seemed restrained, controlled, unnatural. During the remainder of Lord Stanton and Mr. Warmington's visit, she saw little of him. He was occupied with entertaining his friends, and she was busy with some new thoughts of her own, for Sir Winston had shared with her his plans for moving the family to Jamaica in the spring.

The idea was not a new one, for Sir Winston had for many years had business concerns there and had considered a move. Now it seemed his enterprises were flourishing and would benefit even more from his personal supervision. Sarah wasn't sure how she should greet this news. Her first reaction was that she should not like to leave England permanently. She had never yearned for travel, and a primitive island thousands of miles away held little attraction for her. But she was practical enough to realize that if Sir Winston wanted her to go, she would have little to say in the matter.

Several days after the departure of his friends, Richard arrived unexpectedly one morning at Ellis End and asked to speak with Sarah. She made her way to the salon nervously and tried not to show the anxiety she felt as she held out her hand in greeting. He took it as briefly as possible, she thought.

"There is something I wish to discuss with you, Mrs. Ellis. It concerns Jimmy."

"Yes, certainly, Captain."

"I was wondering if you would object to my taking the boy out shooting with me. He has several times asked if he could come along. There are some fine birds to be had, but I know that some people have strong feelings about guns and that others are opposed to killing of any kind."

"I am not opposed to taking game birds for food, Captain Sherwood."

"Jimmy would be along only to observe, of course. He is a bit young to take a gun out himself. I promise you he will come to no harm."

"I have never been concerned for Jimmy's safety when he is with you, Captain. Surely you must know that."

"Perhaps he would like to come out tomorrow, then."

"You may ask him yourself before you leave, but I think we both know what his answer will be. And thank you for asking me before you said anything to him."

"I would never approach Jimmy without consulting you first, ma'am. It would be most improper for me to encourage him in any activity that ran counter to your wishes. I will see him then, before I leave. Good day, Mrs. Ellis."

Sarah could have wept at the cold formality of his words. The warmth and closeness they had shared just a few days ago seemed to belong to another lifetime. As he turned to leave, she took an impulsive step toward him. "Captain Sherwood . . . must there be such tension between us?"

He turned to look at her, noting the uneasy frown and the sadness in her eyes.

"I know that what happened the other evening has changed things for us," she said, "and I am so sorry—"

"No. Don't apologize, ma'am," he interrupted. "There is no blame attached to you in this. The problem is mine, and I shall deal with it . . . if I can." He turned and left on the words, and she stood pondering the last part of his sentence.

"And if you can't deal with it, Captain," she said to the empty air, "then I shall have lost a dear friend."

Richard *was* trying to deal with his feelings for Sarah Ellis, but he was finding it a difficult task. The lady wanted him simply as a friend, and he knew that such a relationship would never be enough for him. He had been attracted to her from the moment of their first meeting, even when he had thought her a married woman. Their acquaintance had not progressed far at all before his interest in her had far exceeded that of mere friendship.

He was intrigued by her behavior at the stile and thoroughly confounded by her reaction in the library, for although she said she wanted only friendship from him, surely he saw the promise of more than that for them. Apparently he saw something that wasn't there, or perhaps he was seeing only what he wished to see. At any rate, the lady made it clear that she wanted none of him. Easy enough to say it. Much harder to accept it.

Never before in his life had Richard known such a one-sided affection. Always when he had given love, it had been returned. It was a pain, he decided, worse than any other he had experienced, for it carried with it an overwhelming sadness and hopelessness that permeated the fiber of each thought and every action. It was a pain that dulled the bright side of the spectrum in everything he did, taking the joy from laughter, the glitter from the stars, the glory from the sunset.

The final days of December passed, and Richard found himself eagerly awaiting the diversion that would be created by the arrival of Jonathan and Harriet for the New Year. He didn't avoid meeting Sarah, for it made little difference whether he saw her or not; she was constantly on his mind, within his sight or out of it. Throughout the month of December he had taken Jimmy out shooting with him or driving when the weather permitted, and his relationship with the boy thrived. But with the mother he could find no solid ground for creating a comfortable bond between them, and their friendship floundered.

One afternoon just four days after Christmas, while Richard was sitting in the parlor reading the newspaper, and Elizabeth and Charlotte were chatting idly nearby, Charlotte said something that turned his thoughts in a new direction.

"Do you remember Jessica Roth?" Charlotte asked Elizabeth. "Lord Burridge showed a decided interest in her, but you can be sure it wasn't marriage that he had in mind!"

" 'It wasn't marriage that he had in mind.' " Richard repeated the words in his head and found himself wondering if Mrs. Ellis had questioned *his* intentions. He had never considered offering her anything less than marriage, but he had never made his intentions clear to her. Could she think that he was interested in her only as his mistress? Surely a widowed woman could be forgiven for having such a thought, for it was not that unusual after all. And if she did think so, was that why she had repulsed him? Would she perhaps show him a different front if she understood that it was marriage he was offering?

By the same time next day, Richard had decided that he must speak with Mrs. Ellis and make his intentions absolutely plain, even at the possible cost of the additional wound to his pride should she continue to reject him. So when he found her sitting in the parlor with Elizabeth, he did not hesitate to ask if she would care to step to the library for a few moments, as he had something of a private nature to discuss with her and they were less likely to be disturbed there. She went with him willingly, thinking he wished to discuss Jimmy, so it was with some surprise that she listened as he began to speak.

"Mrs. Ellis, it has occurred to me quite recently, yesterday, in fact, that you may have thought, perhaps still do think, that my interest in you is something less than honorable. If that has been the case, then I beg of you to banish the thought, for nothing could be further from the truth. I have had only one intention where you are concerned. I want you as my wife, nothing less, and I—"

"No, please," she interrupted. "Please don't say any more. I cannot!"

"Why?"

"I do not wish to marry again, Captain."

"You don't wish to marry? Or you don't wish to marry me?"

"I don't wish to marry anyone." She walked to the windows and stood looking out, her back to him. "I will not marry again."

"I know you haven't given me any encouragement," he continued, "and yet—I can't explain it—I have sometimes felt that you are not indifferent to me. . . . I love you, Sarah, with all my heart, and I think that you care for me."

She turned to face him then, and as he stepped closer and took her by the shoulders, she brought her hands up to his chest. She was shaking her head no, but her eyes were trapped by his and she could not pull them away. She knew he was about to kiss her again, and all she could think was: Would it be that same tender touch? ... It was the same, and she felt herself responding as if she were another person. Her mouth softened and moved on his. She began to tremble violently, and strong arms pulled her close. She felt as if his kiss were consuming her, and she was spinning, falling, forgetting all she thought she had ever known about love. Surely the winter sun must be shining into the room, beating on her head, heating her through, for she felt on fire. The kiss went on and on, sensual, intimate, and then, again with a strange abstraction, she realized Richard would misunderstand, and she pulled away. She was amazed to find herself capable of speech.

"Please, Captain, you must stop. This is not seemly!"

"Say you will marry me, and we need not concern ourselves with the proprieties."

"I have already told you that I cannot marry you."

"Cannot? Or will not?"

"Both."

"How can you say that to me now, after what has just passed between us?"

"A kiss has passed between us, Captain, nothing more. You place too much significance upon it."

"No. I don't think I do," he said thoughtfully as he reached for her once more. She avoided him and made her way to the door, but he was there before her and blocked her exit. She hesitated, lifting her eyes to his, and they held steadily for some moments, his questioning and speculative, hers defiant.

"You have made your request, and you have had your answer, Captain Sherwood," she said formally. "I beg you to let there be an end to this subject between us."

He moved out of her way then, and she was distressed to see that her hand shook as she reached for the door handle, but she soon had it open and was gone.

Lady Sherwood had her wish, and the entire Sherwood family spent the beginning of the new year together, a time made even more special this year by the addition of a new daughter.

Everyone was in spirits except for Richard, who Elizabeth thought looked rather more melancholy than festive. The whole family was aware of his regard for Mrs. Ellis, and they could see that the relationship was not prospering, but they did not plague him with their concerns. Richard preferred to keep his affairs private, and they respected that, knowing that if he desired advice from any of them, he would seek it. Elizabeth was the only one Richard ever permitted to trespass on forbidden ground, and she did so now, as they sat alone in the parlor after dinner.

"Your private conversation with Sarah the other day—it didn't prosper?" she asked.

"No. I'm afraid not. I asked her to marry me, Lizzie, and she has refused."

"You love her a great deal, don't you?" He didn't answer her, and she didn't seem to expect him to as she continued, "It must be terrible for you. I love her, too, but not, of course, in the way you do. I find it hard to believe she doesn't love you, for to me you are quite the easiest person to love."

He smiled and, putting an arm about her shoulders, drew her close to him on the sofa. "I don't think she is indifferent to me, Lizzie, but she insists she won't have me just the same. Says she won't marry again."

"Maybe she just can't like the idea of marriage, like Lord Stanton. You know—the vows of faithfulness to one person, the lifelong commitment, the responsibility. He finds all those things foreign to his nature. Perhaps she feels the same."

"Oh, come now, Lizzie, you know that those are only words when love is involved. Love doesn't fear faithfulness, or responsibility, or commitment. Look at Mama and Papa if you need proof of that."

"I agree with you," she said, "but there are many who don't. Perhaps you should ask her why she doesn't wish to be married again."

"No, Lizzie, I can't force myself on her further. I've already pushed her so far that there is only the thread of a relationship between us. And I will honestly admit that I have had enough rejection in the past two months to last me a lifetime. I have been thinking about Charles Warmington's invitation to Leicestershire. Do you still wish to go?"

"Yes, of course, but you said you couldn't leave until the end of January."

"Well, I've changed my mind. We'll not stay a moment longer than Jon does. When he and Harriet return to Belgium, we'll be off to the hunt. Stanton and his brothers will be there, and perhaps Sir Hugh. It will be an excellent house party. I will write to the countess today and let her know when to expect us, and I will make arrangements to send the horses ahead in plenty of time."

When the time came for Harriet and Jonathan to leave, it was not a sad occasion, for this was a family well accustomed to the farewells and long separations imposed by life in the military. Every time Lord Sherwood had sailed they had missed him dreadfully, and each time he returned home he was somewhat older but the same loving, caring father they remembered. And so it had been with Richard in the army, and now with Jonathan. The leave-taking was lighthearted and tearless. Harriet promised to write, as indeed she had done faithfully since her marriage, and they all looked forward to the next furlough and the next reunion.

Two days after Jonathan's departure, Richard and his sisters journeyed to Leicestershire, and Lady Sherwood stood on the front steps of the Manor, watching their coach disappear down the drive and pondering the strange parting words of her younger daughter. Elizabeth had kissed her mother good-bye and then startled her by whispering close to her ear, "If you see Sarah while we are away, Mama, try to discover why she doesn't wish to marry again, for Richard's happiness may depend upon it."

No matter how Lady Sherwood tried to interpret this remark, each time she came to the same conclusion. Richard had apparently asked Mrs. Ellis to be his wife and had been rejected, and Elizabeth seemed determined to take a hand in the affair and to involve her mother as well.

Chapter 17

VISCOUNT STANTON'S MAJOR seat was a large rambling Tudor mansion in Hampshire, but as he and his brothers had no other family, they habitually spent Christmas and the hunting season in Leicestershire with the Earl and Countess of Haigh. The countess and Stanton's father were brother and sister, and although Lady Haigh had never held a high opinion of her brother during his lifetime, she was fond of all three of her nephews and always made them welcome in her home. She had three sons and two daughters of her own and seemed most content when her house was overflowing with young people.

The Sherwoods arrived in the early afternoon, and Elizabeth found herself confronted by a roomful of people, half of whom she did not know. She had previously met Charles Warmington's parents, the earl and countess, and greeted them first, thanking them for their kind invitation. Next Charles introduced her to his sisters, Lady Mary and Lady Sophia; then to his eldest brother, Lord Flint, and his wife; and his second brother, the Honorable Stephen Warmington, and his wife. Elizabeth, of course, knew Sir Hugh Broughton, Lord Stanton, and Henry Ferris, but Charles made her known to Giles Ferris, Stanton's youngest brother. Finally she greeted Mrs. Polk, a widowed cousin of the earl, and Miss Templeton, daughter of Lord Templeton, a near neighbor.

Elizabeth thought that between them, she and Charlotte should be able to remember everyone, and all in all it seemed a pleasant group. They sat down eighteen to dinner that evening, and the talk was all of hunting, for they planned a meeting the next day, weather permitting.

Elizabeth was seated at dinner between the Honorable Stephen Warmington and Mr. Giles Ferris. She found Charles's brother to be a warm and intelligent gentleman, but it was Mr.

Ferris who intrigued her. She remembered that Mr. Henry Ferris had told her that his youngest brother was twenty, just one year older than she. It did not take her long to decide that Giles was by far the handsomest, and perhaps the most engaging, of the three brothers. Later in the evening, after the gentlemen had left their port to join the ladies in the salon, Elizabeth found herself again near Giles Ferris.

"What do you think of this style of tying a cravat, Miss Elizabeth?" he asked hopefully. "It is all the crack at Queens."

Before she could think of an appropriate answer, she heard the viscount's voice close behind her. "I would rather call it a massacre than a style," he said dampingly.

"Oh, Julian, the devil fly away with you!" Giles objected. "You know I will never aspire to your splendor." His eyes lingered jealously on the splendid effect created by his brother's neckcloth, and he said wickedly, "You have had so many more years to practice than I, and then, of course, you have the incomparable Peplow."

"Peplow should receive no credit for my accomplishments. What you see is the work of my hands alone," Stanton returned.

"So you have always said," Giles countered, "but you will never allow anyone in the room while you are tying your neckcloth, so you cannot prove that the skill is only yours."

"I can understand that his lordship should wish to be alone at such a time, Mr. Ferris," Elizabeth said. "My brother Richard insists that a more delicate operation does not exist, and it is imperative that there be nothing to break the concentration, and although he *has* allowed me in the room, he will *never* allow me to speak until he is quite satisfied with his effort."

"Spoken like a sensible woman," the viscount approved. "But I'll tell you what, Giles. Rather than have you continue to disgrace the family with your appearance, I will break my hard and fast rule. Come to me in the morning, and I will permit you to observe a master at work." He raised a finger as Giles would have spoken. "But . . . you must abide by the same rule that governs Miss Elizabeth. You must watch and listen only and not speak. If you are an apt pupil, you may return to Oxford with a style all your own."

There was no question but that Giles was flattered by this offer, and Elizabeth thought that despite his bantering tone,

Giles Ferris viewed his eldest brother with considerable respect.

Stanton soon left them, and they spoke of other things. Elizabeth had dreaded the thought that someone would mention the shooting incident of last October and was relieved when several days passed and no one introduced the subject. She knew it had caused a considerable stir in London. The story told was that Lord Granbrooke, angry with Stanton after losing the race and half crazy with worry over his debts, including his debt to Stanton, had tried to kill the viscount, and Miss Sherwood had accidentally stepped into the way. The exact nature of the wounds was never disclosed, so it was not general knowledge that Stanton was alive only because of the providential placement of Miss Sherwood between himself and the bullet. Such a story would have been sensationalized beyond all bearing, and so the facts were closely guarded. Elizabeth was certain that the silence of this house party on the matter stemmed from a wish not to remind her, or Lord Stanton, for that matter, of a time that was painful for them both.

The first day's hunting was excellent, the weather clear and bright, and the exercise exhilarating. As they rode home, Elizabeth found herself beside Henry Ferris.

"Lady Flint tells me that you and your brothers have been here since before Christmas, Mr. Ferris," she said.

"Yes, we have. We have been spending Christmas at Haigh Court for, oh, it must be seven years now since our father's death. I fear the winter would be long and dreary if we spent it alone at Stanton Castle."

"But surely your mother—"

"Our mother no longer lives in England, Miss Elizabeth. She returned to France soon after our father died. She is French, you know, and she was never happy here."

"Yes, Richard said she was French, but I didn't know that she had left the country. Surely that was hard for you?"

"Not really. I was nineteen and Julian twenty-one at the time. We were old enough to accept her decision. If anyone really suffered, it was Giles, for he was only thirteen."

"Certainly very young to lose both parents at once," Elizabeth sympathized.

"My mother wanted to take Giles with her to France, Miss Elizabeth. You mustn't think that she wished to desert him."

"Then why did she?"

The question was out before she could consider that he might view it as an impertinence, but he raised no objection and answered without hesitation. "Because Julian refused to allow her to take the boy with her, and she had no say in the matter, for by my father's will Julian was our guardian until we came of age."

If Elizabeth thought twenty-one a young guardian to nineteen and thirteen, she didn't say as much, but asked instead, "How did your brother manage his military service abroad and his guardianship at home at the same time?"

"That's where the countess helped us the most," Henry replied. "I daresay Giles feels this is more his home than is Stanton Castle, for he spent his vacations here while Julian and I were in the army. I served only two years with the regiment and then took a position in the Foreign Office, so Giles was able to come to me when he wasn't at school. I'm sure that if Julian hadn't had our aunt to rely upon in those early years, he would never himself have joined. As it is, I think things have worked out for the best, for Giles has become the most civilized of the three of us. He never gets into trouble at school, or, at least, very little," he amended.

"And you and Lord Stanton did?"

"Lord, yes! But don't tell Julian I admitted it!"

Two evenings later, Lord and Lady Haigh held a hunt ball, which for a country affair was very grand, with more than eighty persons in attendance. Elizabeth, who always loved to dance, and who especially enjoyed a party where she had the opportunity to take the floor with the light-footed Mr. Ferris, had a delightful time. She danced the quadrille with Sir Hugh Broughton, a country dance with Henry Ferris, and was pleased when Lord Stanton requested her hand for the waltz. Charles Warmington and Charlotte stood up for the same dance, and Stanton remarked conversationally, "My cousin Charles and your sister make a charming couple."

"Yes. I have often thought so," Elizabeth agreed. "I think he shows a decided preference for her company, and I know she thinks highly of him."

"It is not perhaps a connection you should encourage, however, Miss Elizabeth."

"Why not?" she asked, surprised by his remark.

"It would be rather an uneven match, ma'am, don't you think?"

"It surprises me that you should say such a thing of your own cousin, my lord, for certainly his birth and breeding are unexceptionable."

"I do not dispute his birth, Miss Elizabeth, which is actually better than my own, but there is the matter of fortune to consider. Charles is a younger son, and his injury some years ago curtailed any career he may have had in the army. He has a small property in Kent, but aside from that he will have little to offer a wife."

"But you are forgetting that Charlotte has a fortune of her own, my lord!"

"I am not forgetting it, Miss Elizabeth, but I think your sister's fortune will do more to hinder such a match than promote it."

Elizabeth frowned, but as the dance was ending she had no opportunity to pursue the conversation. Stanton did not ask her to dance again, and she found that perplexing, for it had not been uncommon for them to dance two, and occasionally three, times during the course of an evening.

From the moment Lord Stanton had discovered that Elizabeth was to be a member of the hunting party that season, he had determined to limit the time he spent with her, not enough to arouse any suspicion but enough to reduce the risk of any further intimacy between them. He had underestimated Elizabeth's sensitivity. Fewer than four days had passed since her arrival in Leicestershire, and already she sensed the change.

She watched him now as he danced with Miss Templeton and gritted her teeth as the girl's shrill laughter rose above the strains of the music. Miss Templeton was the only member of the house party whom Elizabeth had taken in almost immediate dislike. She was a pixyish blonde with angelic features and a tiny, perfect figure, but Elizabeth thought her giddy and considered her boldness and continuous flirting unseemly.

Elizabeth watched as the viscount flirted, in his turn, with Miss Templeton and was puzzled at the change in his behavior. In the past, they had such an easy, friendly comradeship, but now he seemed to be holding her at arm's length. He seldom sought her out, never seemed to have flattering things to say about her appearance, and rarely asked her to dance. She knew he had no romantic interest in her and that he had no desire to marry, and she didn't think he would be concerned about what others thought of their friendship. She was aware that the shooting incident had changed things between them, but she was at a loss to understand why and was hurt by his rejection.

So blithely unaware was she of her growing attraction for him that she allowed herself on the following day to fall into an embarrassing, uncomfortable scene. Elizabeth, Miss Templeton, Charles Warmington, and Lord Stanton made up a riding party early in the afternoon of the day following the ball. There was no meeting planned for that day, and most of the ladies preferred to remain at the house, recovering from the rigors of the previous evening. The four had ridden far, and when they came to a small brook, Miss Templeton expressed a desire for a drink.

"We have no cup, Miss Templeton," Lord Stanton said, "but if you would not object to my hands, ma'am, I will endeavor to make them into a cup for you."

"I am sure water could never taste sweeter than from your hands, my lord," she replied.

Since this was just one in a string of similar comments that she had been uttering for the past hour, Elizabeth rolled her eyes in disgust and, catching Mr. Warmington's eye, nearly laughed aloud at the barely suppressed grimace on his face.

Meanwhile, the viscount dismounted and took hold of Miss Templeton's horse as she began to dismount. Somehow she seemed to tangle her feet in her skirts, and she half slid and half fell from her horse. As she staggered against him, the viscount clasped her to his chest to keep her from falling. Stanton was smiling, Miss Templeton was laughing, and to Elizabeth's eye the viscount held her much longer than was necessary.

As Elizabeth realized that Charles was waiting for her to dismount, she said suddenly, "No, thank you, Mr. Warmington. I don't think I will stop after all. I shall meet you all back at the house." Wheeling her horse, she cantered away. The viscount spun around at Elizabeth's uncharacteristic tone, and Charles called after her, but she paid no heed.

"See to Miss Templeton's drink, Charles, if you would," Stanton said to his cousin. "I'll go after her." He caught his horse's bridle as he spoke and set off after Elizabeth, already a goodly distance away and covering ground rapidly.

Elizabeth rode recklessly, blinded by tears and shaking with a rage she could not understand. She was rapidly approaching a pasture hedge, started to pull her horse up to turn off from it, and then at the last instant decided to take it anyway. Her horse was confused and uncollected. He took the jump off stride, caught his hind legs as he went over, and stumbled on the uneven ground as he landed. Elizabeth was pitched forward over his head, landing unceremoniously in a pile of rocks and wind-blown winter leaves. Her horse scrambled to his feet and trotted a few paces away. She regarded him critically. No harm to you, old fellow, she thought with some relief, as she began to brush leaves and twigs from her dark red riding habit.

Moments later she heard the sound of hoofbeats approaching on the hard ground and looked up angrily as Stanton pulled his horse up beside her and dismounted. "What kind of mad stunt was that?" he asked wrathfully, hoping his anger would hide the concern he felt. "Are you all right?" He knelt beside her and took hold of her arm, but she shook him off resentfully.

"Save your assistance for Miss Templeton, my lord. I assure you she has more need of it than I!"

He saw instantly that her tears were emotional and not physical and that she had no thought for the nasty fall she had just taken. He seated himself on a large rock no more than two feet from where she had landed, thinking that she was fortunate to have missed it. "Would you like to tell me what all this is about?" He spoke in a calm, matter-of-fact voice that seemed to have the desired effect, for when she answered she was less angry and more civil.

"I'm sorry. I just couldn't remain another instant in that girl's company. If I had stayed, I would have said something unforgivable to her. And *you*, my lord," she said accusingly, "*you* encourage her, hugging her as you did!"

"I was not *hugging* her," he objected. "I simply tried to keep her from falling."

Elizabeth struck a pose and batted her eyelashes as she gave a creditable impersonation of Miss Templeton. " 'I am sure water could never taste sweeter than from your hands, my lord.' Ugh! How can you listen to such rubbish? It's disgusting. And don't laugh at me! I'm not trying to entertain you!"

He had found her performance delightful, but he suppressed his laughter as he answered. "I see that you have strong feelings about Miss Templeton, but was it worth making a scene?"

"I didn't mean to make a scene," she said, "but I can't bear the way she throws herself at you."

Stanton thought Elizabeth had reacted from simple jealousy, but she didn't seem to realize it, and he prayed she wouldn't. "Tell me, Elizabeth," he said carefully, "even if Miss Templeton continues to 'throw herself at me,' as you so colorfully put it, do you think it likely to profit her?"

"I couldn't say. Only you know the answer to that question."

"Miss Templeton is an extremely silly, entertaining chit, who happens to be a first-rate horsewoman, and that is as far as my interest in her goes or ever will go. She is no threat to our friendship, believe me." He had come to his feet, and now he smiled warmly at her and held out his hand. "If you're sure you're not hurt, I think we should be getting back."

Elizabeth found it curious, as she had on other occasions, that he used her Christian name so easily when they were alone together. It didn't seem at all inappropriate to her, but rather more a manifestation of the closeness they sometimes shared. He dried her eyes, helped her brush the leaves from her skirts, and then caught her horse. He helped her to mount, and they rode back to the house in relative silence, good-will having been reestablished between them.

The viscount's mind was in turmoil. Surely this uncharacteristic outburst from Elizabeth supported his theory that her feelings for him far exceeded those permitted by friendship. And while it warmed his heart to have this further proof of her affection, he chided himself for being pleased by her jealousy. He could not afford to encourage her, and yet, when she put her small hand in his, it had taken every ounce of willpower not to take her into his arms. How would she react if he kissed her now? He was hopeful that she would not slap him again. But would she welcome his embrace? Would she return it? This situation must not be permitted to continue, he thought, mentally shaking himself. I cannot be continuously in her company without causing more outbreaks of a similar nature, and sooner or later I'm bound to give myself away. He decided during that ride back to Haigh Court that he must leave Leicestershire as soon as he could reasonably do so and thereafter take care to avoid meeting Miss Elizabeth Sherwood.

Miss Templeton, deeply mortified when the viscount had turned his back on her and ridden off after Miss Elizabeth, had, for whatever reason, chosen not to mention Elizabeth's strange behavior. But that evening after dinner, she recommenced her fatuous attempts to attract the viscount, giving him so little peace from her constant inane prattle that by the time the tea tray was brought in he had had more than he could bear and dragged Richard and Giles off for a game of billiards. When he finally retired for the evening, he and Sir Hugh went upstairs together and settled in the viscount's bedchamber with an excellent bottle of cognac.

"How would you feel about loping off to London, Hugh?"

"I thought you intended to stay till the end of the month?"

"I did, but things here are getting damnably uncomfortable." He related to Sir Hugh the incident with Miss Templeton at the brook and Elizabeth's reaction to it.

"Sounds like jealousy to me. Has she made any effort to attach you?"

"No. There is no way I can be certain how she feels."

"You know, Julian, I think you are more than half in love with the girl yourself!" Sir Hugh accused.

"Much more than half," Stanton admitted.

Sir Hugh's eyes widened in surprise. "Well, now there is something I never thought I would live to hear! You admitting that you were in love with *any* woman!"

"You may believe me when I say I wish I weren't. It's a cursed position to be in. I very nearly gave myself away today. She frightened me half to death when she took that fall! She's so headstrong, Hugh—endangering herself in such a heedless manner!"

"Seems to me most of the danger she's been in lately is directly connected with you—the attempt by Granbrooke and now this incident with Miss Templeton," Sir Hugh pointed out.

"Exactly, and that is why I feel I must remove myself from her vicinity. Every time I'm with her or even near her, I am taking a great risk. Stay on if you like, but I think I shall leave for town, or perhaps Stanton Castle, by the end of the week."

"There is another solution to this problem that you are overlooking, Julian, and it is far simpler than running away. You could ask her to marry you."

"No. That is the one thing I am determined not to do."

"Why not? What have you to lose?"

"For myself, not so much perhaps—but for her, if she accepted me, a great deal. I wouldn't wager a groat on a happy ending to any marriage with me, and I will not gamble with her happiness. It means too much to me."

"I would never have picked you as the man to fall in love with an unsophisticated innocent like Miss Elizabeth," Sir Hugh mused.

"Nor would I," Stanton agreed. "And yet, my friend, it appears that I have, and I can't tell you why. I won't deny that it shook me a great deal when she took that bullet for me. It's a humbling experience to realize that someone is willing to offer their life for yours. I had similar experiences in the war, but aside from Henry, or perhaps you, no soldier would risk his life for mine out of affection but rather duty, which is a very different thing. Elizabeth acted out of pure selfless instinct, and a motive of that nature is hard to comprehend. But even though that night made me question *her* feelings, I think *I* was attracted long before that—the night Granbrooke took her from Vauxhall, or perhaps even earlier." When I kissed her in my library, he thought. "I can't explain my feelings for her—they defy description."

"You needn't explain, Julian. I know what you mean. I've been there myself."

"Harriet Putnam?" the viscount asked. Sir Hugh nodded, and Stanton continued speaking as he refilled his friend's glass. "Did she ever know you cared for her?"

"No. She had no thought for anyone but Jonathan Sherwood. I think she was in love with him even before she came to London, for they were neighbors in Sussex."

"So, my dear Hugh, we are quite a pair, are we not? Here you are with the woman you love married to another man, and here I am, destined no doubt for the same fate, for I cannot think that Elizabeth will remain unmarried for long."

"I don't suppose that there is anything I could say that would make you reconsider your decision, Julian?"

"Absolutely nothing, my friend, so let us pour some more

of this excellent brandy and toast the numerous benefits of bachelorhood."

Chapter 18

LORD STANTON WAS wakened the following morning by the tittering sounds of Miss Templeton, her shrill voice echoing in the corridor outside his room. As her voice and that of her companion faded down the hall, he sat up in an attempt to shake off the drowsiness caused by too much brandy the previous night.

How could Elizabeth imagine for one instant that I could be attracted to that silly chatterbox? he asked himself. Just listening to that voice could drive one mad in a fortnight. As he swung his legs out of bed and rang for his valet, he wondered briefly if Elizabeth would be sore this morning after her tumble yesterday. Then he frowned, realizing that his waking thoughts were of Elizabeth Sherwood, and he had just sworn the previous evening to put her from his mind.

Determined to master his obsession with her and stick by his resolve to avoid her, he descended to the breakfast parlor sometime later, took a seat beside the earl's cousin, Mrs. Polk, and set about to please her. She was an attractive woman in her late twenties, who had been widowed for nearly two years. She had met the viscount socially on many occasions, but never had she known him to be so congenial. She responded to his conversation enthusiastically and by the time they rose from the table had agreed to ride with him later in the day.

For her part, Elizabeth felt extremely foolish about her behavior at the brook on the previous day. What concern was it of hers if Miss Templeton wished to flirt with Viscount Stanton and he with her? She wasn't his keeper, and it wasn't her place to be either offended or incensed by his behavior. She was willing to admit that having his friendship meant a great deal to her and she had felt threatened by Miss Templeton, for it seemed to Elizabeth that the viscount preferred Miss Templeton's company to her own. She recognized that such jealousy was childish, and she resolved to overcome it.

Elizabeth kept herself busy for the next several days. She hunted every morning a party went out. She spent her afternoons chatting with the other young ladies, or playing piquet with Giles Ferris, or learning billiards from Richard. She noticed that Lord Stanton was spending less time in the company of Miss Templeton and seemed to be seeking out Mrs. Polk. Elizabeth admired the older woman. She was quiet and circumspect, a restful companion when compared with Miss Templeton. Elizabeth's admiration for the widow Polk was not destined to last.

One evening Elizabeth was enjoying a game of piquet with Giles Ferris while at a table nearby, Lord and Lady Flint, Viscount Stanton, and Mrs. Polk made up a table of whist. Elizabeth glanced occasionally at the other table, noticing that the foursome seemed in high spirits. She and Giles played until it was quite late, but even so, Elizabeth found it hard to sleep after she had retired for the night. Each time she closed her eyes she would see either the viscount's amiable face or Mrs. Polk's smiling, pleasant countenance in her mind's eye.

She tossed and turned for nearly an hour and finally sat up and relit her candles. Elizabeth did not often suffer from insomnia, but when she did, she knew that the best way to tire her eyes was to read. She reached for the book at her bedside and then remembered she had left it behind in the library, where she had been reading earlier in the day. Pulling on her dressing gown and slippers, she left the room. The house was dark and quiet, the last of the guests having passed her door sometime earlier. By the light of her single candle she made her way to the ground floor. The door to the library was slightly ajar, the fire still burning high, its light flickering off the walls and furnishings. She padded silently to the door, pushed it open on well-oiled hinges, and then stood frozen on the threshold. Before the fire, locked in a passionate embrace, were Lord Stanton and Mrs. Polk. As the light from Elizabeth's candle fell upon them, they broke apart and turned to face her.

Elizabeth blushed and stammered, "Ex . . . Excuse me, my lord, ma'am." She sketched a curtsy and, turning quickly, fled down the hall and up the stairs. Slamming the door of her room, she leaned breathlessly upon it, shaking like a leaf, tears standing in her eyes. She closed her eyes, and the painful scene she had just witnessed came clearly to view. The viscount's handsome head bent over Mrs. Polk, her face turned up to his, their lips melting together with passion, his hands at the small of her back, holding her tightly against him.

Suddenly Elizabeth remembered that day in his library. He had held her as close, his mouth on hers, and she imagined herself responding as Mrs. Polk had. Slowly she bent her knees and slid down the door until she crouched against it. "Why can't he want me like that?" she whispered to herself. "Why not me?" She sat huddled against the door until she was cold and stiff and then forced herself to go back to bed. She had found no satisfactory answer to her question, but one thing she did know. She wanted more than anything to put herself in Mrs. Polk's place, for what she felt for Lord Stanton was something much, much stronger than friendship.

Elizabeth slept poorly and made an excuse not to join the hunt the next morning. She kept to her room until early afternoon and then sought out Charlotte to see if she should like to walk to the village.

"I promised to tour the succession houses with Lady Sophia and Lady Mary," Charlotte answered. "Why don't you come with us?"

"No. Maybe another time. I would rather walk. I'll take my maid."

Charlotte looked doubtful. "Is something wrong, Lizzie? You don't look well."

Elizabeth shook her head. "It's nothing. I didn't sleep well last night, that's all. I need some exercise."

"Very well then, enjoy yourself, but don't be gone too long. Some of the gentlemen were saying at luncheon that it could snow before evening."

"I won't be long. I'll see you at dinner."

Elizabeth soon left the house with her maid and had walked nearly fifteen minutes before she became aware that her companion was sniffling almost continuously into a handkerchief. She stopped walking suddenly and stared at the girl. She had been so wrapped up in her own thoughts that she hadn't taken time to consider Molly.

"Molly, you have a cold."

"Yes, miss," the maid answered in surprise. "I have had it for the past week, as you know."

"Yes, I do know. How could I be so thoughtless? I should never have asked you to come with me. It is much too cold. Why, you could catch your death!"

"No, Miss Elizabeth. I shall be fine. 'Tis not so cold, and I can manage."

"I don't want you to manage. I want you home, and that is where you are going—instantly. And since I won't need you until it is time to dress for dinner, you may go to your room and rest until I ring for you upon my return."

"You intend to continue your walk alone, miss?"

"Surely; why not? We have walked to the village before. We have never met anyone who was not a member of the house party. I could be naught but safe on Lord Haigh's land."

"I don't know, miss," Molly said doubtfully. "The captain wouldn't approve of my leaving you on your own."

Elizabeth would not hear her objections. "Go home, Molly. You will be warm and comfortable in no time, and I will have my walk. I will go to the village and back, no farther, I promise, and I will stay to the private road."

When Molly was gone, Elizabeth was glad of the solitude. There was a post road that ran through the village and passed the gate house and the main drive into Haigh Court, but Elizabeth was following a cart track that ran from behind the stables along a winding route through the home wood and eventually to the village. She walked at a brisk pace, her mind working just as quickly.

What she had seen last night was not a bad dream, but the pain of heart she had felt during the long hours of darkness had vanished with the light of day. Now she chided herself for a fool. How could she ever have convinced herself that she admired the viscount as a friend when in reality she had been attracted to him as a man almost from the very beginning of their acquaintance. She thought back again to the day he had kissed her in his library. She had been shocked by his behavior, but she had also been strangely attracted by it. Although she had vehemently denied it at the time, he had been right when he accused her of enjoying his embrace. She *had* enjoyed it. More than that, it had thrilled her. Frightened of such overwhelming feelings and far beyond her experience with this worldly man, she had hidden her insecurities from him and from herself with an admirable show of anger. Then, on the night they had both apologized, and she had thanked him for rescuing her from Lord Granbrooke, and he had held her as she wept—that night, for the first time, she had seen his humanity and felt she could trust him. She could see now that from that moment her love had grown steadily, until his life had been threatened by Granbrooke, and she had moved instinctively to protect him, never counting the cost.

"You're a fool, Elizabeth Sherwood! He probably won't ever marry. And if he should, he would choose an experienced woman like Mrs. Polk, or at least an accomplished one like Charlotte, not an outspoken, impetuous schoolgirl like you!"

Eventually Elizabeth slowed her pace. Alone with her thoughts she had opportunity to dissect them, to look back over the events of the past several months. Most of what she remembered was not encouraging. When she reached the village, she made a few small purchases and was soon on her way home again. She had barely left the village behind when the snow began to fall in earnest.

When Lord Stanton drove his curricle up the drive in the late afternoon, he met Richard Sherwood coming out of the house. He handed the reins to his groom, stepped down from the carriage, and started up the broad stairway as Richard greeted him.

"Well met, Julian! I was just on my way to the stables. Will you loan me your carriage?"

"Gladly," Stanton responded, "but I would advise against going out in this weather. It's bound to be treacherous before long."

"I'm sure you're right, but Elizabeth walked to the village earlier and has not yet returned. I thought I would go out a little way to meet her."

"She hasn't gone alone, surely?"

"Yes, I'm afraid she did. She started out with her maid but then became concerned for the girl's cold and sent her back alone."

"That sounds like your sister," Stanton agreed.

"She's been gone quite a long time," Richard continued. "She's bound to turn up soon, but it's growing dark, and I won't be content until she is safely in for the night."

"Do you know which way she went?"

"Yes. Her maid said she took the old road through the home wood, the one that leads from the stables."

"Do you know it?" Stanton asked.

"No. I've never been that way."

"Let me go, then. I know it well."

"You don't mind?"

"Not at all. She can't be far. I'm sure we'll be back in no time."

Turning, Stanton mounted into his curricle again and dismissed his groom, curricles not being built to accommodate three persons comfortably. As he turned his carriage and headed toward the stables, he noted that the tracks he had made in the snow just a few minutes earlier were nearly covered, for the snow was falling heavily, obscuring the ground and making visibility impossible beyond several hundred feet.

When Elizabeth had covered nearly half the distance to Haigh Court she stopped and stood still in the road. The snow was falling faster now. There was no wind, so the large flakes fell straight down. It was deathly quiet, so quiet that if she listened carefully it was possible to hear the hiss of the snow itself as it struck through the bare branches above and settled on the woodland floor. Newly awakened to love, everything looked different to her somehow. The snow had quickly turned her world white, and she felt tiny and insignificant but at the same time very aware of the life that flowed within her. She moved to a large fallen log at the side of the road and sat down upon it, folding her hands in her lap. She sat motionless, imagining herself part of the landscape, allowing the snow to settle on her. Slowly her lap and arms turned white. She had been thinking of the viscount, so when she heard the jingle of harness and looked up to see him coming toward her, she decided she must be imagining him. She did not move but continued to sit as he brought his horses to a standstill beside her.

The steaming horses seemed very real, and his voice was clearly concerned. "Miss Elizabeth, are you all right?"

"Yes, my lord, thank you."

"Are you resting, then?"

"Not really, just sitting, enjoying the snow."

He glanced around at the wooded scene before them and had to admit that it was appealing. Hundreds of branches both large and small were outlined by the damp, clinging snow, creating intricate networks of dark and light.

"May I offer you a ride back to the house, ma'am?"

Suddenly she saw him again with Mrs. Polk in his arms, and she resented his intrusion on her solitary walk. There was a militant look in her eye as she responded, "I am content to walk, my lord."

"Perhaps, but your brother is not content that you should. The snowfall is heavy, and it will soon be dark. I met him as he was coming in search of you, and I offered to come in his stead."

"How *galant* of you, my lord."

"He is not familiar with this road. I am," he said shortly.

"I am also familiar with it, sir. I have walked it several times."

"Come, Miss Elizabeth, let us not spar. Your brother is concerned for you. You cannot wish to worry him."

She rose then, shaking the snow from her skirts. His horses backed as she approached the carriage, but he quickly steadied them and then held one hand down to assist her into the curricle. Elizabeth watched with silent admiration as the viscount accomplished the difficult but seemingly effortless feat of turning his carriage and pair in a very restricted space.

She waited until he had set his horses in motion toward the house and then spoke in a conventional tone. "I am sorry if my interruption last night spoiled your evening with Mrs. Polk, my lord."

"What?" he asked sharply.

"I said that I am sorry—"

"I heard what you said," he interrupted.

"Then why did you ask me to repeat myself?"

"Because I cannot believe that you said it! Who taught you your manners, Miss Elizabeth?"

She lifted her chin. "My mother, sir. But I am afraid in some areas she was not entirely successful."

"That, ma'am, is an understatement! In some areas she has failed totally! You begin conversations that are wholly inappropriate, you make comments that are, to use your own word, impertinent, and you have the most unsettling habit of intruding yourself into the private affairs of others!"

Elizabeth was well aware of her shortcomings, but somehow on his lips they seemed ten times more damning. A moment of silence followed his ringing speech, and then Elizabeth said quietly, "I know, my lord. That is why I wished to apologize."

Feeling he had been too harsh, he relented a little. "As far as last night is concerned, no apology is necessary. You spoiled nothing."

"Mrs. Polk does not share your opinion, Lord Stanton."

"She spoke to you about it?" he asked, his voice incredulous.

"I met her as I was leaving the house today. I believe she was angry with me."

"What did she say?"

"I would rather not repeat it, my lord."

"You started this conversation, Miss Elizabeth, and you shall finish it! Tell me what she said, word for word, as well as you remember it."

Elizabeth repeated the words for him, but she left out the biting sarcasm that had laced the older woman's bitter comment. "She said, 'Such a good idea for you to take a walk, Miss Sherwood. If it is a long and tiring one, perhaps you will not find it necessary to wander the house at night.' "

The viscount was silent. It wasn't difficult for him to interpret this comment or to add the inflection Elizabeth had omitted. Clearly he had raised some hopes in the widow's breast with his recent attentions. He had been mildly amused by his flirtation with her, but if the truth were told, the kiss in the library had been more her idea than his. He was not opposed to a liaison with her and had been enjoying her skilled kiss when Elizabeth interrupted them. Elizabeth's face, briefly though he had seen it, had driven all desire for Mrs. Polk from his mind. She stood there only a moment, her face illuminated by her candle, but it was all there—first the surprise, then the shock, the disappointment, and finally the resignation—all there for him to read as clearly as printed words upon a page. He had no intention of ever allowing Elizabeth Sherwood to play a major role in his life, but he admired her more than any woman he had ever known, and he valued her good opinion.

"Elizabeth, what you saw last night was nothing, it was less than nothing."

"Just another interesting interlude," she said flippantly, "a new woman each month." She shrugged her shoulders. "Variety adds spice, they say."

His eyes narrowed as he glanced briefly at her. "So it does. I believe I told you once that no woman can hold my attention for long."

"I didn't believe you."

"Perhaps you should." When she didn't answer, he continued solemnly. "Elizabeth, we have a strange friendship, you and I. We have shared a scrape with death, and that binds us in an unusual way. You saved my life, leaving me with a debt I can never repay. We may always be friends—I should like it if we could be—but we cannot use our friendship as an excuse to trespass in certain areas of each other's lives. We are very different people. You are traditional and romantic, and you believe that people are basically good. I, on the other hand, am . . ."

As he paused, searching for the proper word, Elizabeth supplied it. "Cynical."

He nodded in agreement. "All right, perhaps I am. It is true that I have little faith in my fellow man. I have no grand plans for the future. I live from day to day, and I worry about tomorrow, tomorrow. I welcome your friendship, but we cannot remain friends if you insist upon placing your values on me and then are disappointed when I fail to live up to them."

"But I don't do that!"

"I think you do. You were scandalized when Charlotte announced that I had frightened her into breaking the engagement. In your ordered, well-regulated life, engagements, like marriages, are made in heaven and not intended to be broken. You came to see me determined to set the world right again, and when I foiled your plans to do good, you were furious with me. Then when I kissed you, I spoiled your image of the ideal brother-in-law—wealthy, titled, the perfect gentleman—and you were angry at me for that, too. Deny it if you can."

"You're right," she admitted. "You did take a perfect situation and spoil it, and I did resent you for it. But I have learned a great deal in the past months. I am not so naive as I was.

But you are also right when you say it is not my place to judge you."

"Then you agree to accept me, just as I am?" he asked.

"Yes, I do." Then she smiled up at him, and when he responded in kind, she tucked her hand in his arm and leaned her shoulder against his as she thought, I love you just the way you are. I wouldn't change a thing.

The following day Lord Stanton received a letter from his steward at Stanton Castle, which he viewed as the hand of providence. It informed him that one of his race mares had foaled and included a description of the foal, but he led his aunt to believe that the letter had a far more serious import, and that its content required that he leave immediately for Stanton Castle to attend to urgent business. The entire party expressed their regret that he must leave so soon. Giles decided to accompany his brother and spend the few remaining days of his vacation in Hampshire; they made hasty arrangements to leave the following morning.

The Sherwoods remained at Haigh Court through the first week in February, and Elizabeth had numerous opportunities to observe her sister and Charles Warmington together. She no longer questioned Charlotte's attachment to Charles and one evening taxed her with it.

"I think you have finally found the man you decided to wait for—the one for whom you could feel some affection?"

"More than affection, Lizzie," Charlotte confided. "I am afraid that I have fallen in love with him."

"Why afraid?" Elizabeth asked. "I think it's wonderful!"

"Do you think he cares for me, Lizzie?"

"I'm sure he must. His attentions have been most marked."

"I have certainly felt that he liked me a little, but he has said nothing."

"Nor should he! It would be most improper for him to speak to you before he had received Papa's permission."

"Are you sure that's all it is?" Charlotte asked doubtfully.

"Of course. What other reason could he have? Wait until we are in London again in the spring. I will be willing to bet that he calls upon Papa the moment we arrive in town."

Charlotte seemed reassured by Elizabeth's words, but even as she spoke, Elizabeth was remembering the viscount's comments concerning a match between his cousin and Charlotte, and she determined to discuss the matter with Richard at the earliest opportunity. She found her opportunity two days later when Richard offered to drive her to the village where she had engaged herself to run some errands for Lady Haigh.

"Richard, have you ever noticed that your friend Charles seems to have an interest in Charlotte?"

"Lord, yes. I noticed it years ago."

"Years ago!"

"Yes. One of the first times he ever came to Sussex. I had that shoulder wound, and he had already been invalided out and came down to stay. Charlotte couldn't have been more than seventeen at the time, but he was instantly taken with her."

"Was it a serious interest, do you think?"

"I would say very serious."

"Then why did he never speak of it?"

"I daresay he intended to when she was older, but by the time Charlotte turned nineteen, Father had inherited and that changed things."

"His feelings for her changed because Papa inherited?"

"I don't think his feelings have changed at all, Lizzie, but when Father inherited, he settled a handsome fortune on Charlotte, and that, unfortunately, creates an obstacle for Charles."

"That's exactly what Lord Stanton said, but I don't see why it should change anything, except perhaps to make things better."

"I don't think Charles would offer for a woman whose fortune far exceeds his own," Richard explained.

"But, Richard, that's foolish. They are the same people they were before Papa inherited! If he loved her then, and he still loves her now, he should not allow the money to influence him!"

"You may see it that way, but I assure you that Charles does not. He permits himself to enjoy Charlotte's company, but I don't think he has any intention of offering for her. I feel for him in this, for Charlotte will eventually marry, and I think it will be difficult for him."

"Do you think that Charles is right to give up so easily?" Elizabeth asked with spirit. "He seems to accept his unhappy plight tamely. Would he not be wiser to fight for Charlotte if he wants her?"

"I cannot advise him to do so, Lizzie. I can't say what I would do under similar circumstances, but I do know that a man cannot compromise his principles for the gratification of desire. Some obstacles are too great to overcome, even with the greatest will in the world."

She knew he was thinking of his own involvement with Sarah, and she hoped that her mother was taking advantage of their absence to encourage Sarah to confide in her. Elizabeth forced her thoughts back to the question of Charlotte.

"And what if Charlotte should return Charles's regard, Richard? What then?"

"Then I suppose it would be Charlotte's place to encourage him to overcome his scruples. But I wouldn't place any dependence on her being able to do so, for he feels very strongly in this matter, and I doubt if he will ever declare himself, even if he thought she cared for him."

"Then I am afraid that you will continue to have an unhappy friend, Richard, and we will have an equally unhappy sister, because Charlotte told me just two days since that she is in love with Mr. Warmington."

Chapter 19

SOMETHING LESS THAN two weeks after she had seen her three children off to Leicestershire, Lady Sherwood found her first opportunity to act on Elizabeth's parting request. Lord Sherwood had offered to take Jimmy shooting in Richard's absence, and the enthusiastic hunters had just departed. The ladies sat alone in the parlor, occupied with their embroidery.

"That is a fine boy you have, Sarah," Lady Sherwood said. "You must be very proud of him."

"I am. He has been the only true joy in my life."

Lady Sherwood looked up from her work and regarded her companion critically. "Certainly your husband, Sarah?"

"I never loved my husband, Lady Sherwood. I know that must seem strange to you, for I can see that there is great tenderness between you and his lordship."

"It doesn't seem strange to me, my dear. Many marriages are not love matches. You were married very young, perhaps before you had time to meet a man you could care for."

"My marriage was arranged by my parents when I was seventeen. I was not consulted."

"And the man they chose for you—you disliked him?"

"It wasn't that I disliked him, for indeed, I barely knew him. We had met only a few times before we became engaged, and the engagement lasted only one month."

"Then you were wed, in fact, to a stranger," Lady Sherwood said. "I imagine that must have been difficult for you, especially at so young an age."

"It *was* difficult, for I was very innocent and had received no instruction concerning my duties as a wife. I wanted to be a good wife, and I wanted to please my husband." She paused for a moment while Lady Sherwood waited patiently. Finally Sarah continued in a harsh tone. "I must not bore you, ma'am, with the sad history of my marriage. All in all, it is not a pleasant story."

Lady Sherwood regarded Sarah sympathetically. It was easy to see how Richard could love this woman, but it was also easy to see that she was deeply troubled. "Nothing you could say would bore me, Sarah. Sometimes I think that if we have painful memories that we are accustomed to bearing alone, we can render them less painful if we share them with a sympathetic ear." Lady Sherwood paused for a moment, but when it became clear that Sarah had no intention of speaking, she continued mildly. "His lordship and I had a fifth child, another boy, born between Richard and Jonathan. When Richard was barely six and Jon not yet a year old, young Thomas was taken from us by the fever. My grief was so great that I could not bear to mention the child's name or see anything that reminded me of him. I refused to allow Richard to speak of his dead brother, which I know now was not the proper way to help him deal with his own grief, which was, in its way, as profound as my own. Jarvis was at sea at the time, but when he came home nearly six months later, he wasted no time in encouraging me to speak of my loss, of our loss, and in that way I began to come to terms with the pain. These days, I am able to think back fondly on the three years I had with my second son, and my memories of him are pleasant ones."

"There was nothing pleasant about my marriage to James Ellis," Sarah said bluntly.

"You have Jimmy," Lady Sherwood argued. "Certainly he is a pleasant product of your marriage, however unhappy."

"Yes, you're right." Sarah admitted. "And Jimmy was my one anchor to some kind of sanity during those years. But my marriage was not unhappy, Lady Sherwood—my marriage was a nightmare."

"In what way?" Lady Sherwood asked gently. "I am willing to listen if you would like to tell me about it."

"James, my husband," Sarah began, "was domineering and autocratic. Many of his attributes I have seen in Sir Winston, and I think Lady Ellis was quite as unhappy as I in her own marriage. James had very definite notions about what I should do, and how and when I should do it. I was not expected, or even permitted, to have an opinion of my own. He thought mending a menial task, so I was not permitted it even though I enjoy sewing. He did not consider it proper for women to be educated, so I was forbidden his books and his library. He felt that newspapers were printed for the exclusive use of men and were not for my eyes. He decided what I should wear, who my friends should be, how much exercise I should or shouldn't take while I was increasing, and what name my child should have. He considered that my sole responsibilities as his wife were to plan his entertainments, be the perfect hostess at his dinner table, and warm his bed."

Lady Sherwood listened to Sarah's story with growing incredulity, and the bitterness of the last words was not lost on her. She leaned forward sympathetically and laid a hand on Sarah's knee. "He didn't abuse you?" Her voice revealed her shock at the thought.

"I suppose that would depend on what you mean by the word *abuse*," Sarah answered. "He came to me on our wedding night and frightened me witless, for he offered me no reassurances or instruction and had no patience with my ignorance. For a full week I became nauseated at the thought of his touching me, and then, slowly, I began to accept what I could not change, as a blind man accepts the darkness. During the day, I could bear his behavior, for I learned to keep myself above it—I bent continually to his will, and I never fought back, so he never knew how much I despised him. But at night ... at night he had everything his own way, for then he would strip from me every shred of dignity. I felt that I had no more worth than a piece of clothing, to be used and then cast aside. I had decided that I would rather be dead than married forever to this man when I discovered I was to have a child.

"After Jimmy was born, things were better, for James didn't concern himself with the nursery, and I finally found one portion of my life that he did not control. He undoubtedly considered the rearing of children an unmasculine activity, and beneath him. He was just beginning to take an interest in Jimmy when he was killed. I had so dreaded his influence over my son, for I could not bear the thought that Jimmy would grow up like his father. Now I have Sir Winston to contend with, and although he has not yet tried to take control, I fear the day when he may decide that Jimmy could benefit from a man's influence in his affairs. I know he would not hesitate to order my son's life as he does mine. I also know that I would be powerless to prevent him from doing precisely as he wishes. He never seeks my opinion, and if I do happen to voice it, he invariably overrides me, and his will consistently prevails."

"Have you considered, Sarah, that if you were to marry again, you could remove both yourself and your son from the power of Sir Winston?"

"Yes, and place us once again in the power of a husband!" Sarah replied scathingly. "I have sworn I will never give a man that kind of control over me again."

"But certainly, if you were to choose the man yourself and not have him chosen for you ... ?"

"I would not trust myself to make such a choice, Lady Sherwood. I have known many charming men during the past five years, and some of them seemed the type to make fine husbands. But I think there are many men who leave their charm outside the bedroom door! I would be a fool to take such a chance. Sir Winston has a great deal of control over my life, but my body is my own, and I intend for it to remain so."

"I understand the way you feel, my dear, but you may be missing a great deal of happiness in your life by pursuing such a course."

"Perhaps I am," Sarah agreed. "But I assure you, ma'am, that I would much rather do without the happiness than take a chance on the misery again."

Lady Sherwood had discovered what Elizabeth wished to know, but she had a sinking feeling that this information would do little to aid Richard's suit. Sarah carried deep scars, and the years of trauma that had put them there would not be easily forgotten. She was a woman of strong convictions, and having once known the feel of a stranglehold on her spirit, Lady Sherwood thought it unlikely that she would turn from her decision to keep herself free in the future.

Her heart went out to Richard, for she knew he was not one to commit himself lightly, and he would find the rejection hard to accept. The sad thing was that she felt certain her son would be the perfect man for Sarah. She also believed that Sarah held Richard in affection, for no woman who viewed the majority of men with mistrust would allow her son to spend time with a man whom she did not hold in considerable esteem.

Richard and his sisters arrived in Surrey on the tenth of February after a long, cold journey, for the winter was one of the hardest in anyone's memory, with heavy snowfalls and bitter winds. They were travel-weary but spoke with enthusiasm of their stay in Leicestershire.

Two days later, Richard was driving his curricle home from the village when he met Sarah at the end of the drive to Sherwood Manor. He knew she was walking home, for she often did so, claiming that she enjoyed the exercise when the weather permitted. Richard pulled up his pair beside her. It was the first time they had met since his return home.

"Good day, Mrs. Ellis. You have been to the Manor?"

"Yes, Captain. I spent the morning with your mother and sisters. Did you enjoy the hunting?"

"Very much. We had some excellent meetings, and the company was congenial, but it is good to be home. May I offer you a ride to Ellis End?"

"I like to walk."

"I know you do, but I would enjoy the pleasure of your company." When she hesitated, he added, "I will not make things uncomfortable for you, I promise."

He had transferred the reins to his left hand and was reaching his right hand down to her, and in that moment she made her decision. She stepped up to the carriage, put her hand in his, and felt herself pulled easily up to sit beside him.

As he set his horses in motion she said, "I have never been driven by you, Captain. Jimmy says you are an excellent whip."

"Jimmy is biased. The next time we are in London I will have Lord Stanton take him up. One exhibition of Julian's skill will be enough to lower my meager talents in Jimmy's eyes."

He spoke in a light, bantering tone, but she answered in more serious accents. "You're wrong, Captain, for nothing could do that. I am almost certain that you have risen even above the Duke of Wellington in Jimmy's esteem."

He glanced at her quickly, suspecting her of mockery, but her face was grave. "I missed him while I was gone."

"He missed you, too, and is eager to see you. But I told him he must not present himself upon your threshold only moments after you had crossed it yourself."

They continued a light conversation until they were nearly arrived at the house, and then Richard said abruptly, "Mrs. Ellis, I have promised that I would not make this drive uncomfortable for you, and indeed, I do not wish to do so, but there is something I feel I must say. I have no wish to plague you with my attentions, for you have made it plain that you do not welcome them. But I wish you to know that my feelings are unchanged, and my offer stands. I promise that I will not mention this matter again if you will give me your assurance that you would inform me should there be any change in your sentiments."

I will never change my mind, she thought, but she said, "You have my promise, Captain. If you will give me your hand down, you need not see me in, for I know you will not care to leave your horses. Good-bye, Captain. Thank you for seeing me home."

Alighting from the carriage, Sarah entered the house and immediately summoned Jimmy. She had hoped that during his absence, Captain Sherwood would come to terms with her refusal and learn to accept it. After his words today, it was clear that he had no intention of doing anything of the kind. It was left to her, then, to bring to an end any hope for a future for them, so that he, at least, could forget her and get on with his life.

She thought once again of Sir Winston's intention to move the family to Jamaica. She had considered asking Sir Winston if she could stay on with Jimmy at Ellis End, promising to engage a companion if he balked at the idea of her living alone. But now, suddenly, Sarah began to think that Jamaica might be the answer to her problem, and as Jimmy entered the room in response to her summons she greeted him almost enthusiastically.

"Jimmy, I'm sure you've heard your grandfather speaking of his plans to move to Jamaica. What would you think of our going with him?"

"You mean to visit him there, Mama?"

"No, Jimmy. I mean to live there with him, permanently."

"Leave Ellis End! Leave England permanently?"

"Well, you would, of course, come back one day, my love, for this house will be yours when your grandfather is gone. But we must all hope that will be many years from now."

"Do you want to go, Mama?"

"Yes, I think I should like to go."

"But what about our friends?" he asked. "Won't you miss them?"

"Yes, of course we shall miss our friends, but there are times in our life when we must make changes, and sometimes that means leaving old friends behind. We will make new friends in our new home."

"And what of Captain Sherwood, Mama? Won't you miss him?"

"Yes, Jimmy, I shall miss him. Perhaps he would write to you." Obviously the boy found this suggestion unpalatable, for he stared stonily at her, saying nothing, and finally she continued, "Will it be so hard for you to leave him, then?"

"Yes, Mama, it will," he said with feeling, "for he has been more than a friend to me. He seems more like a father really.

And it isn't that he spoils me, either, although he has been awfully generous. He can be quite strict and demanding of perfection, yet at the same time he always makes allowances for my shortcomings and never fails to encourage me."

"In your driving, you mean?"

"In that, and in everything, for we talk of many other things besides horses, Mama."

She looked at him in surprise, for she hadn't thought to wonder what they discussed during the many hours they spent together. "What do you talk about?" she asked curiously.

"Oh, he's told me about the time he spent in the army, and we have discussed politics. He has taught me a great deal about farming and estate management. And we've talked about people, and the relationships between people, and the value of things like integrity and honor." Sarah stared at her son in amazement as he continued. "And he's answered some questions I had about girls."

"Jimmy!"

"Well, why shouldn't I have questions?" he asked defensively. "I'm not a baby anymore, Mama. And you must know there are things a fellow would just as lief not ask his mother."

"I told you long ago, Jimmy, that I would willingly answer any question you had."

"I know you did, Mama, but you must see that it is ever so much easier to ask such things of a man than of a woman."

She had to admit the truth of this, but her head was spinning with all he had told her—estate management, integrity, politics! She had never imagined. "I had no idea you had grown so fond of the captain, Jimmy. I can see that it will be harder than I thought for you to leave him."

"I am not fond of him, Mama. I love him. And somehow, I thought you did, too."

Soon after their return to Surrey, Elizabeth asked her mother what she had been able to learn from Sarah. Lady Sherwood told her daughter that she had discovered nothing that she felt could help Richard's cause, and she strictly forbade Elizabeth to involve herself further in the matter. Lady Sherwood could see little justification in revealing Sarah's confidences to her first born, and she had absolutely no intention of sharing such revelations with her youngest and most innocent child. But one morning nearly two weeks after their return, Charlotte came home from the village with two pieces of news, both of which the family found interesting, and one of which profoundly affected Richard and made Lady Sherwood reconsider her decision to keep Sarah's confidence.

Charlotte erupted into the parlor where Richard, Elizabeth, and Lady Sherwood had gathered before luncheon. "We have had a letter from Harriet, and it's the most wonderful news! She is increasing! You shall have your wish at last, Mama. You will be a grandmother by September!"

Clearly this was news to be exclaimed over, but since it was a subject soon exhausted, Charlotte recollected her other news and directed her question to her brother. "Did you know, Richard, that the Ellis family is planning a move to Jamaica? The vicar told me that the house is to let and has been on the market for nearly a week."

Lady Sherwood watched as her son turned noticeably pale, but he answered Charlotte's question easily. "No. I hadn't heard of it. I'm surprised that Jimmy said nothing. I was with him only yesterday."

"Evidently, they plan to leave quite soon. Sarah had mentioned that Sir Winston has property there, but I never imagined they would wish to live there. We will miss Sarah dreadfully, won't we, Lizzie? She has become much like one of the family."

Lord Sherwood joined them at that moment, and Charlotte turned the conversation back to her first item of news. Both Elizabeth and Lady Sherwood noticed Richard quietly leave the room, but when Elizabeth rose to follow him, Lady Sherwood took her arm and spoke quietly.

"Let me go to him, Lizzie. I think that perhaps it is time I tried to help—if I can." She caught up with her son in the front hall and asked if he would spare a moment for her.

"Could it wait until later, Mother?"

"It is about Sarah that I must speak with you, Richard, and no, I don't think that it can wait."

For a moment as he regarded her, she felt he was about to ask her, politely of course, not to interfere. But after a slight pause he said, "Very well, Mother. Shall we go into the library?"

Richard handed his mother to a sofa near the hearth and bent to add a few logs to the fire.

"Richard," Lady Sherwood began, "you know that I do not like to meddle in your private affairs, but it is not an easy thing for a mother to see her children unhappy. This is a subject that perhaps a mother should not speak of with her son, but if not I, then I cannot imagine who would speak. I think I know the kind of man my son is. I think I know that you value other people's feelings and their worth. I think I know that you would love and respect your wife, and do your best to make her happy and content. But if it is Sarah that you have set your heart upon, then there is something that you must know before you continue to pursue her."

"I suppose Lizzie told you that I asked Sarah to marry me?"

"Not in so many words, but she hinted as much."

"Then I suppose she also hinted that Sarah refused me and offers me no hope."

"I know why Sarah refuses to hear your suit, Richard. She was unhappy in her first marriage and fears a similar experience should she marry again."

"I guessed as much," he said, "but I don't know what makes her think she would be unhappy with me. I know she cares for me."

"Sarah fears placing herself in a subservient and defenseless position, and she also fears the physical relationship of marriage."

"But, Mother, that's not possible! She was married for five years! She has a child!"

"Listen to me, my son. She was married five years to a man who did not cherish her, a man who allowed her no freedom either in thought or deed, a man who came to her bed with no word of love for her, a man who used her, and hurt her, and never brought her any pleasure. I think I need not tell you that this was not a marriage in which any woman could be happy. Sarah must never involve herself in a marriage that will not offer her the kind of freedom and contentment that your father and I have found. If you persist in wanting her, and if you succeed in having her agree to become your wife, then you must be willing to be patient. She must have time to feel your love for her, time to trust you, time to believe that selfish passion is not your motive in seeking her bed." Richard had turned away to gaze into the fire but, seeing the tenseness of his broad shoulders, Lady Sherwood could sense his disgust for a man he had never known and who was long dead. "There is something else, Richard," she continued, "that you must consider. There is the possibility that the scars her first husband left cannot be erased and that they will cast a shadow over your own happiness. Yet I have reason to hope that it may not be so, for although I have seen some part of her pain and know that the wounds are deep, I have also seen her love for her son, which knows no bounds. If she is capable of such love for her child, can we not assume that such a love for you could be possible as well?"

"We must hope it will be so, Mother, for I will not give up seeking her hand."

"Even though you know she has a prejudice against your sex?"

"Especially now that I do know it." He turned and took her hands in his. "Thank you, Mother. You can't know how much you have helped me. There is no worse feeling than to be unaware of your enemy's position or his strength. I have been fighting this battle with my hands tied. But now that I have some idea of what I'm up against, I have more confidence that I can gain a victory in the end. I promise you I intend to put up one hell of a fight."

Lady Sherwood smiled. "I thought that was what you would say, and I am glad we had this talk. I would have all my children happy in life."

Richard bent his fair head and planted a kiss on her cheek. "And so we will be, if we continue to accept wise counsel."

Two days later, when Sir Winston drove Virginia over to visit with Charlotte, and Sir Winston himself disappeared into the library with Lord Sherwood, Richard had Sultry saddled immediately and rode to Ellis End, knowing that he would find Sarah alone.

A footman showed him into the salon, and when Sarah joined him a few moments later, he barely waited until the door was closed before he said, "Is it true that you plan to move to Jamaica?"

"Yes. Sir Winston has growing business concerns there. He

plans to build a house, and he wants me to take charge of it for him."

"Let his daughter keep his house," Richard said bluntly. "Sarah, don't run away from me!"

"You promised that you would not bring this subject up again, sir," she objected.

"That was before you decided to go halfway round the world to avoid me. My God, Sarah! Do you think that putting an ocean between us will make me care for you less?"

"Perhaps not, but it will be easier—"

"Easier for whom? For you? For Jimmy? Sarah, don't do this to us. You know that I love you, for I have told you so, and I have tried to show you in every way I know. You have tried to make me believe that you don't return my affection, but you haven't succeeded. You gave yourself away that day you kissed me, and I don't think you would feel the need to run away like this unless you cared for me. Do you have the courage to admit how you feel, or would you rather deny that you love me?" He took her by the shoulders and turned her roughly to face him. She looked up at him and as their eyes met he said, "Go on, Mrs. Ellis, deny that you love me, and try to make it convincing."

His hands gripped her painfully, but she was only dimly aware of it, for he was waiting for her answer and she could not will herself to speak against her heart. She felt tears stinging her eyes and said suddenly, almost angrily, "Oh, very well, I love you," and then repeated in a whisper, "I love you."

"Will you marry me?"

"No."

"Sarah, not every man is like your first husband!" Her eyes flew to his face, and he read the question in them. "Yes, my mother told me that James Ellis was cruel to you, but I had guessed as much myself. If you truly think that I would be the same type of husband, acquit me, for my tastes don't run to sadistic abuse." He let go her shoulders and took her hands in his, his voice softening as he added, "We can be happy together, Sarah, I know we can, but you must trust me. Give me a chance to prove that life can be special for us. Please, say you will marry me."

She jerked her hands away and turned from him. "How

many ways must I say no before you will understand? I have been married before. I do not wish to be married again."

"You have been married. You have never been loved. I am offering both love and marriage, neither without the other."

"I want neither from you, can't you understand that?" she shouted at him. "I must be free! I will not endanger my freedom for any man, regardless of my feelings."

He had never heard her speak with such passion, and he stared at her incredulously. "What did that man do to you?" He spoke it more as a thought than as a question needing an answer; but even as he heard himself utter the words, he decided that perhaps it needed answering, so he repeated it. "What *did* he do to you, Sarah? Tell me!"

"Didn't your mother tell you?"

"She said he allowed you no personal freedom, that he didn't love you or even treat you kindly, that he wanted you for self-gratification and nothing more."

"Is that not specific enough for you?" she asked bitterly.

"And you refuse to marry again because you fear a revival of that kind of treatment?" He felt a subtle rage building as the implications of her rejection materialized. "And you are refusing to marry me because you think that I . . . you think that *I* could behave in such a manner? Good God," he said, his words disbelieving, "I have been deluding myself from the beginning. If you could believe such things of me, then you know *nothing* of me. To know that you would even consider me *capable* of such behavior is a thought more humiliating than a hundred rejections, and there can be no hope for us—no hope at all." As he finished speaking he turned and walked toward the door. He had thought it impossible for her to hurt him any more, and yet she had managed to do so. He was a fool to have given her the opportunity. When he reached the door, he stopped with his hand on the latch and spoke again, making no attempt to hide the anger and bitterness in his voice. "If I don't see you again before you sail—*Bon voyage*."

Even as he turned the handle, Sarah cast herself across the room to him. "Richard!" she cried. "Please, please, don't go! Not like this." He turned to face her as she spoke his name, and now he found her anxiously grasping both his hands, unable to meet his eyes, mumbling a disjointed apology as her tears fell freely. "I'm sorry . . . please forgive me . . . you mustn't think . . . I didn't, I don't think you could be cruel . . . at least, perhaps once I did, but I don't now, not since I've come to know you. Oh, I'm not saying any of this properly! I love you, and I would like nothing better than to be with you always, *but I am afraid!*"

Richard pulled his hands from her grasp and, gathering her into his arms, held her close until she was calmer. And then, still without speaking, he tipped her face up to his and kissed the tears from her cheeks and then kissed her trembling lips until her senses swam and she was limp and nearly swooning in his arms.

"Trust me enough to say you will marry me, Sarah Ellis, and when you have promised to be my wife, then I will tell you the kind of marriage we shall have."

"I will marry you, Richard, I promise," she whispered.

"Good. And now I will make you a promise." He led her to a sofa and sat with her in the circle of his arm. "Never, from this moment forward, will you have cause to be frightened either of me or of any part of our life together. I think we will get on far better than you imagine, but if you have any fears or concerns, you need only voice them, and we shall deal with them, between us. You may have all the same freedom within our marriage that you now have, perhaps more, for you need not answer to Sir Winston for anything save his interest in his grandson. As far as Jimmy is concerned, I have no intention of ever bypassing your wishes. He is your son, and in all the months I have known you, I have never seen your judgment on matters concerning him to be anything but sound and sensible. I foresee no problems between us over him. And *please*, my love, you must *never* see me as any kind of a physical threat to you. I would not willingly harm a single hair of your head, and I swear to you, on my honor, that I will never force you to do anything you do not wish. It will require nothing more than the simple word *no* to deter me from any course. Do you understand, Sarah?"

"Yes, I understand."

"If you will give me the right to take responsibility for your welfare and for Jimmy's, and if you will give me the right only to call you wife—then all the rest can wait—for however long it takes."

They remained seated together on the sofa, heedless both of

time and convention. It was there that Sir Winston found them almost thirty minutes later, and it was he who was first to receive the news of their engagement.

Chapter 20

THE FOLLOWING MORNING at breakfast, Richard apprised his family of his engagement, and there were mingled expressions of surprise and delight. His mother and sisters were full of questions like when, where, and how, but Richard laughingly fended them off, saying that he and Sarah hadn't discussed it but no doubt the wedding would be quite soon.

Lord Sherwood congratulated his son warmly and some time later left the breakfast parlor to go to his study, but he returned a few moments later with the London papers in his hand. "Bonaparte has escaped from Elba," he said simply.

No one had an adequate response to this news. They had all thought that with Napoleon's defeat by the Allies the previous spring and his abdication and retirement to Elba, Europe had seen the last of him. During the days that followed, even as Richard and Sarah made plans for their wedding, it was learned that Bonaparte had landed in the south of France and was marching on Paris.

Lord Sherwood soon returned to London, promising that he would come down for the wedding even if it should be for only a day. Lady Sherwood reluctantly separated from her husband, remaining behind in Surrey to supervise the preparations for the marriage of her eldest child, the date having been set for the twenty-fifth of March.

On the morning following Lord Sherwood's departure, Richard received by special messenger a confidential letter from his father. He was alone in the library when it arrived, and he opened it with curiosity, but the expectant look on his face faded to a deep frown as his eyes traveled down the page.

Richard,

I arrived in town today to find the house and the servants in an uproar. It seems that last night someone managed to break into my book room from the outside. The place is a complete shambles. The intruder was not content with emptying all the desk drawers and files. Almost all the books were pulled from the shelves and scattered everywhere. God only knows what he thought he would find, but he left no possible hiding place unexplored. The carpets were taken up, pictures torn from the walls, sofa cushions slashed. Some documents are missing, of course. I will not be sure which ones until I have time to sort through the rubble. The most amazing thing is that none of the servants heard anything and were unaware of any problem until they opened the room this morning.

I feel I owe it to you to mention, in the strictest confidence, of course, that at a closed meeting at the War Office this afternoon, the name of your friend Charles Warmington was raised. It seems that he was in his cups several evenings ago at White's. That in itself is unusual for your friend, I think, but he was heard to say several less than respectful things about the army—his (your) regiment in particular. Most of them dealt with what he considered his unfair medical discharge. He insisted his present disability is not sufficient reason to bar him from his chosen profession. I need not tell you that in these troubled times such remarks do not always fall upon sympathetic ears. Mr. Warmington's comments do him no credit when there are several senior ministers suspecting spies under every rock.

Please understand that I make no accusation with my next words, but as memory serves me, Warmington was present at both functions where our spy made his intrusions, and the night of the shooting I cannot recall seeing him for some time after the shot was fired. He was not helping with either of the wounds initially, nor was he among those men who carried Elizabeth and Lord Stanton upstairs.

You must realize that under any other circumstances I would keep this information to myself, but as you were privy to the intrusions into my papers, and as Warmington is not only your best friend but soon to be your groomsman as well, I felt myself obliged to write. You may tell your

*mother and sisters about the break-in, as there will be no
hiding it from them. The room will need to be redone, of
course, and the servants will talk. I am letting it be called
a robbery.*

Yours, etc.
Your Father

Richard read the letter through again and then rose and
walked to the fire. He tried to picture Charles selling information to the French, Charles rifling through his father's desk,
Charles striking James down while his cousin lay seriously
wounded and perhaps dying abovestairs.

Even as he bent to lay the parchment on the flames, he reconsidered. Crossing to his desk, he drew a fresh piece of paper forward. He wrote a short letter to his father, refusing to
believe any ill of his friend, for disappointment over a lost career was a world away from treason. Then as he folded the letter he decided not to send it. He rang for Jepson instead and
ordered the chaise. He departed for London within the hour
and sat in conversation with his father by late afternoon.

Later that evening, Richard called at the Earl of Haigh's
town residence and found Charles at home. He was alone in
the library when Richard was admitted, and he smiled with
pleasure when he saw his friend.

"Richard! I didn't know you were in London. Did you have
my letter?"

"Yes, and I thank you for agreeing to stand up with me."

"Always pleased to lend my support to a friend. Can't say
I was too surprised when you wrote me of your engagement.
It's been easy enough to see these past months where your interest has been. Allow me to offer my congratulations in person. You and Mrs. Ellis are well matched. I hope you will be
very happy together."

"Thank you, Charles."

"But you haven't said what brings you to town. Is it this
news of Boney?"

"In part, yes. Charles—there is a matter I must discuss with
you. It's . . . awkward."

Charles sobered instantly at his friend's serious tone. "What
is it?"

"I received a letter this morning from my father, and it is

that letter that has brought me to town. The letter concerns you, Charles."

"Me? In what way?"

"I would like you to read it for yourself, but before you do, there is something I must explain. There have been several instances since last fall when my father's book room has been invaded by some unknown person. Once during our ball last September, again on the night Lizzie and Julian were shot, and most recently just two nights ago. Each time, delicate documents were taken."

"Military documents?"

"Yes."

"I fail to understand how this concerns me."

"Read the letter, Charles." Richard handed it over and Charles took it, moving to stand in the light of a candelabra on the mantel.

He began reading with interest, but as he continued down the page his face grew stern and then angry. When he finished, he looked across at Richard, and his eyes were both cold and bitter.

"Clearly Lord Sherwood believes me to be the spy he seeks."

"He thinks no such thing! In that letter he simply put some facts and possibilities before me and desired my opinion. Are they facts, Charles? Were you drunk and did you say those things?"

"Yes, I was drunk, and yes, I am sure I said those things your father credits me with and a great deal more besides. Does it therefore follow that I am a damned traitor?"

"No. And so I have just told my father. But the scene he describes is hard to imagine."

"The things I said were innocent enough, but I suppose they could sound less than loyal to a dedicated flag-waver. But part of it is true. I am bitter about the army turning me off."

"And it's partly because of Charlotte, isn't it?"

"If I had stayed in, I may have had a majority by now. As it is—"

"Your feelings for Charlotte haven't changed, then?"

"No. She's the only woman I have ever had any serious interest in. I suspect it was Rayburn's prattling the other night that got me started drinking so heavily. He was sitting at the next table, discussing your sister's many fine qualities and his intention to try to fix his interest with her in the coming Season. I tipped the bottle too often and took my frustrations out on the army. I never dreamt it would come to this." He slapped the letter as he spoke. "It won't happen again, Richard, you can assure your father of that."

"You have given up on Charlotte, then?"

"Your sister is not for me. There is too great a gulf between us. Nor can I think that Lord Sherwood would welcome me as a son-in-law after this." Once again he indicated the letter he held, and Richard twitched it from him and tossed it onto the fire.

"This is rubbish, and we both know it, and you wrong my father if you think he would judge a man based on suspicion alone. That letter was not meant to accuse, but to inform me of what was being said of you."

"Do you think your father meant you to show it to me?"

"I think he knew I would if I thought you innocent."

As the month of March wore on, everyone in the Sherwood household found themselves fully occupied, for in addition to preparing for the wedding, there were arrangements to be made for their removal to town for the Season soon afterward. Richard and Sarah would stay behind and begin their married life in the solitude of the country, but Lady Sherwood and her daughters were to leave for town soon after the wedding. In early March they made a short excursion to their favorite dressmaker in London to order new gowns. These arrived only five days before the wedding itself, and Mason, Lady Sherwood's dresser, had them unpacked immediately to be sure that no last-minute alterations were necessary.

Sarah arrived in Elizabeth's room that afternoon to find her stepping into a beautiful confection of white gauze over satin, and she exclaimed in delight as she saw the dress. "Elizabeth! How lovely! You will quite cast me in the shade!"

Elizabeth smiled at her soon-to-be sister but said only, "It is pretty, isn't it? But you know very well, Sarah, that your dress is nothing short of exquisite. What Richard will say when he sees you in it I can't imagine."

Sarah smiled as she considered the thought herself. From the moment she had agreed to marry Richard, she had been inextricably swept along on the tide of his family's enthusiasm. Although the thought of marrying again filled her with trepidation, and she was more than once assailed by doubts, she was determined to be Richard's wife and joined wholeheartedly in the wedding preparations.

Jimmy had been overwhelmingly relieved to learn that he was not to leave the captain behind but was to gain him as a stepfather instead. Sir Winston did not seem to consider it surprising that Sarah should wish to marry again. If he had misgivings or objections to Sarah's plans, he did not voice them but merely said that his daughter-in-law was her own mistress and must please herself. A tenant had been found for Ellis End, and he and Virginia were set to sail on the first of April. Sir Winston graciously accepted Richard's offer to oversee his property during his extended absence from England.

Charlotte's abigail stuck her head in at the door to ask if Miss Mason would step along to Miss Charlotte's room to assure herself that her dress would do. "Go on, Mason," Elizabeth said, "Mrs. Ellis will help me out of my gown—if you see nothing amiss?"

"No, nothing, miss. It looks perfect to me." She bustled off, and Sarah helped Elizabeth out of the gown again.

"I would love to have a gown slightly off the shoulders as yours is, Sarah," Elizabeth said, "but even if I were old enough for such a daring cut, I shan't ever be able to wear it now." She plopped herself down in front of the dressing table mirror and pulled her chemise from her right shoulder, exposing the puckered scar left by Lord Granbrooke's bullet.

Sarah watched her sympathetically. Even though Elizabeth was not in the least vain, it could not be easy for a young girl to accept such a disfiguring scar.

"It has been five months now," Elizabeth continued, "I think it has finished with fading away. What do you think, Sarah?"

"I think that it will fade a bit more, Lizzie. You have such lovely shoulders; does it fret you a great deal, having that scar?" There was so much concern in Sarah's voice that Elizabeth met her eyes in the mirror in surprise.

"No, Sarah, truly," she assured her. "I seldom think of it. It was a small price to pay to protect him. I would have died willingly." She was still watching Sarah in the mirror and saw the startled, arrested look in her eyes.

Sarah stepped around in front of Elizabeth, meeting her gaze directly, and her next words were as much a statement as a question. "You are in love with him, aren't you?"

Elizabeth could see no reason to deny it as she answered in her typical truthful and straightforward manner. "Yes, I do love him, though I try not to think of it."

"But Lizzie, surely—"

"Sarah," Elizabeth interrupted, "it can't signify. No doubt there are countless girls in love with him, for he is very eligible, you know."

"Countless girls who would risk their life for his? No. That I cannot believe!"

"Well, perhaps you're right, but it can make no difference, for he thinks of me only as a friend, and as his friend's little sister. He has no interest in me beyond that."

"Oh, Lizzie, are you sure?"

"Yes. I'm quite sure. He doesn't believe in love, you know, not the kind Mama and Papa share, and the kind you feel for Richard and he for you. He has told me that he has no desire to marry and is content that the title should pass on someday through Henry or Giles."

"The right woman might change his mind," Sarah insisted.

"Perhaps. But it won't be me. He likes me, I know, and he's been unfailingly kind, but he has shown no romantic interest in me, Sarah." When Sarah still looked doubtful, she added, "If he were to become passionate toward me, Sarah, I'm sure I would notice."

At that, Sarah burst out laughing. "Yes, Lizzie, I'm sure you would!"

Elizabeth leaned forward to take Sarah's hand and clasp it warmly. "You have made Richard so happy. I am pleased and proud that I shall have you for my sister."

As the days passed, the unrest in the country grew. There was now little doubt in anyone's mind that they would soon be at war again, and this time it seemed as if the Duke of Wellington and Bonaparte would meet at last on the same field of conflict. Napoleon had entered Paris on the twentieth of March to find that King Louis had fled the city and moved with his court to Ghent. The British Army had begun to muster in Belgium, and a letter from Jonathan made it clear that the army near Brussels expected action in the not-too-distant future, for he spoke of sending Harriet home if and when it became unsafe. Brussels, he wrote, was very gay, despite the French threat. Wellington was delayed at the Congress of Vienna, but they expected him in Brussels shortly, to take command of the Allied Forces.

Lord Sherwood was actively involved in commandeering ships wherever possible and arranging for transport of troops, horses, artillery, munitions, and supplies to Ostend. He was busy but wrote as often as possible with what news he could give. With little idea of how soon Napoleon would strike, it was imperative that Wellington have the troops and supplies he demanded as quickly as possible.

Just two days before the wedding, Richard and Sarah sat together in the library at Sherwood Manor. Elizabeth was reading on the other side of the room. For the past few days, Sarah had been aware of a growing restlessness in Richard, and she now decided to say what was on her mind. "You're concerned about the coming conflict, aren't you?"

"Yes, I am. An Allied army, thrown together in great haste, will not be an easy force to command."

"But certainly if anyone can do so, it will be the Duke?"

"I am sure he will be equal to the task. It's just bad luck that our best infantry, almost all the Peninsular veterans, are in America. I don't see how they can hope to be back in time."

"But your father wrote that he felt the cavalry would be under orders soon. Surely once they are in Belgium we can be easier?" He didn't answer, and after a moment she asked, "Do you wish you were going with them? With your old regiment?"

"Yes . . . no . . . I don't know. I feel so useless here. I know many untried troops will be sent over. I could make myself useful."

"Richard, if you feel it is your duty to rejoin, then you must do so. I wouldn't like to think that any consideration for me would keep you from doing what you feel is right. You mustn't think of me. . . ."

"Of course I must think of you," he objected. "What would you have me do? Marry in two days, and take ship for Belgium in three?"

"Yes, if you feel you must!"

"If you keep this up," he said, "you will have me believing that you wish to be rid of me."

"I wish for you to have the same freedom in our marriage that you have promised me."

"None of us will ever know any real freedom so long as Bonaparte threatens Europe. He must be stopped once and for all if there is to be any lasting peace."

"So will you go?"

"Not for the present. I will await developments and make a decision later. Come here, my love." His troubled frown lifted, and he smiled as he drew her into his arms. Sarah glanced anxiously at Elizabeth, but Elizabeth, deep in her book, or pretending to be, didn't even look up.

The twenty-fifth of March dawned cloudy and cool but with only a hint of rain in the air. Most of the wedding guests who were to stay at Sherwood Manor or Ellis End had arrived on the previous day. Lord Sherwood arrived late on the evening of the twenty-fourth, as he had promised, but could stay less than twenty-four hours. The wedding day itself was a cheerful, happy occasion, but at the back of everyone's mind was the gathering threat across the Channel.

Two months had passed since the hunting in Leicestershire, two months during which Elizabeth had examined and dealt with her feelings for Lord Stanton. But when he arrived on the afternoon preceding the wedding, she knew instantly that it had not been time enough. A large number of wedding guests were gathered in the parlor when the viscount and his cousin Charles were announced, and Elizabeth could only be grateful for the distraction that such a large group offered. She had thought herself prepared to meet him, but no sooner had she set eyes upon him than she found her pulse racing. How could she have gone all those months without realizing how she felt? She determined to greet him as normally as possible and then take care to avoid him for the duration of his visit. Certainly that should be easy enough with a houseful of guests and with the large number of persons invited to the wedding on the following day.

When the viscount finally came around the room to where she stood, she had gathered her senses enough to greet him calmly. She then greeted Charles and introduced them both to her mother's sister, Mrs. Wyeton-Smith, and then they passed on and she was able to breathe easier. She left the room soon afterward, making a quick stop at the dining room to be sure that she would be seated nowhere near the viscount at dinner. Somehow she managed to get through the evening, although she found her eyes often straying toward him when she knew he wasn't looking. How handsome he was, she thought . . . how dear . . . how foolish she had been to allow herself to love him.

The wedding ceremony was nearly unbearable for Elizabeth. She listened to Richard and Sarah exchange their vows with tears running unheeded down her face. Her mother handed her a handkerchief, but she didn't see why anyone should care. Everyone cried at weddings. It was expected. Everything was working out so perfectly for her brother and her friend. They loved each other, and they were getting married. Surely that was a simple enough thing to do. Not for the man you have chosen to love, Elizabeth Sherwood, she told herself. You have fallen in love with a man who has no use for marriage, so even if you could encourage him to care for you, it would lead nowhere.

Elizabeth had come to believe that Lord Stanton was a man who carefully guarded his heart, failing to believe that love could ever occupy any meaningful place in his life. In this weakness of his, she recognized her greatest strength. She understood love and knew its worth, but she also knew that her love alone would never be enough.

So she listened to Richard and Sarah pledge their love and faithfulness and found herself jealous of their opportunity to do so. She returned her mother's handkerchief and dug in her reticule for one of her own. She withdrew a large man's handkerchief that had been in her possession since Stanton had lent it to her in the book room the night after her escape from Granbrooke. She had never wanted to give it back, not really knowing why, and now it was all she had that belonged to him. She smoothed the fine lawn under her hands, studying the delicate monogram skillfully embroidered across one corner, JWF, and wondering, not for the first time, for what name the W stood. In less than a week, they would be removing to London for the Season, and she would meet Lord Stanton often. She couldn't decide if she should view this prospect with pleasure or regret.

Elizabeth managed to avoid any private conversation with the viscount throughout the day of the wedding, and she excused herself early in the evening, determined to make no appearance the following morning until she was sure he had departed for London. Richard and Sarah took leave of their guests shortly after nine o'clock and retired to their private apartments in the east wing.

Richard kissed his wife good night at her door and went on to his own bedchamber, where his valet awaited him. He was soon ready for bed, but he did not retire. He sat instead before the fire, staring into the glowing embers. There had been so many hopelessly depressing weeks in the past few months when he had been convinced that Sarah would never be his. Now, knowing that she was finally his wife, he was overwhelmed by almost equal portions of elation and relief, and he promised himself that he would never allow her to regret marrying him. He rose suddenly and, walking to the communicating door to his wife's room, passed through it without knocking.

Sarah sat before her dressing table in her nightgown and wrapper while her maid brushed out her hair. She turned her head as she heard her husband enter and then dismissed her maid. "You need not come in the morning until I ring for you, Betty. Good night." The woman left, closing the door softly, and as Richard crossed the room to his wife, she rose to her feet and turned to face him.

"I think I have wanted to see your hair down like this from the very first day we met. It's . . . indescribable." He swept the thick auburn hair from her shoulders and let his eyes travel down the gown she wore. "You are just as lovely in that, my dear, as you were in your wedding gown." He took her hands in his and brought them both to his lips. "My wife . . . I don't think I will ever tire of calling you that . . . my lovely, breathtaking wife." His voice was infinitely tender, his eyes smiling, and Sarah stared mutely up at him as he continued. "This is our wedding night, Sarah, and I do not wish to spend it alone. Can you understand that? Do you mind if I stay?"

She didn't know how to answer him, so she said nothing but went willingly into his embrace and raised her face for his kiss. They clung to each other as long minutes passed, and finally Richard put her from him and, taking her hands once again, said simply, "Come to bed." As he turned to lead her away, she hesitated, and he smiled indulgently. "You are too suspicious, my love. Just come to bed. It has been a long and tiring day, and we could both use some sleep."

She accompanied him to the edge of the bed, where he helped her out of her wrapper. As she got into bed he took off his own dressing gown, revealing his nightshirt beneath, snuffed the bedside candle, and climbed in beside her. He pulled his wife close, and she found the warmth and hardness of his body strangely comforting and restful. They lay together so, nearly motionless, for a long while. Neither spoke. After some time had passed, Sarah fancied that her husband's breathing had become more even and a bit deeper, and just as she decided he had fallen asleep, he said very quietly, "I wish that you were seventeen again, Sarah, and that this were your first wedding night. I would I had the opportunity to make your life over again, to erase the pain and the disillusionment. Dear God, if I could do that, I would ask nothing more from life." She felt his arm tighten convulsively about her, and she turned her face into his shoulder and felt his lips warm on her cheek, and so they lay until they fell asleep.

Sarah woke as the pearly light of the new day streamed through a crack in the draperies and was momentarily startled to find her husband sleeping beside her. James had never stayed the whole night in her bed but had, without exception, come to her early, taken his pleasure of her, and then left her sometime afterward for the comfort and privacy of his own room. She moved slowly so as not to disturb Richard and, raising herself on one elbow, stared down at his face. He lay on his back, his breathing quiet and even, a fine pale stubble clearly visible on his chin. Not since the birth of her child had she looked upon another human being with such love in her heart. She reached out and laid her hand softly on his chest, for she needed and wanted to touch him. Often during her first marriage she had wondered what she had done to deserve such a narrow-minded, tyrannical husband. Now, as she looked at Richard, she couldn't help wondering what she had done to deserve having this gentle, loving man in her life.

Richard opened his eyes and, instantly aware of her beside

him, turned his head to look at her, bringing his hand up to cover hers where it lay on his nightshirt. His eyes registered immediate concern as he saw the tears in hers, and he said, "What? Tears, my love?"

She reached out to smooth the frown from his brow. "Tears of joy, my Richard, only tears of joy."

Chapter 21

LADY SHERWOOD AND her daughters joined his lordship at their London town house in the early days of April, and by the time three days had passed, most of their London acquaintance had come to call. Charles Warmington came on the second day and made no attempt to hide his pleasure at seeing them in town again. But after five days passed with no sign of Lord Stanton, Elizabeth became curious enough to ask Charles if perhaps his cousin was out of town.

"As a matter of fact he is," Charles answered. "He's gone down to Stanton Castle. Said he had some things he must settle with his steward before he leaves."

"Before he leaves . . . ?"

"Yes. For Belgium." He could not fail to see the surprise this comment brought, and he added quickly, "Didn't he tell you? He has rejoined as a volunteer and is under orders to sail in about ten days."

"He has rejoined the army!" Elizabeth exclaimed, and found it impossible to hide the consternation in her voice. "But why?"

"He has a hankering to meet Boney at last, I suppose. Quite a few fellows are doing it, you know. And heaven only knows we will need good men with all the best troops in America. He feels confident that one of his old commanders will pick him up as a staff officer, but if not, he says he will be content just to see some action."

"What of Sir Hugh? Will he go back?"

"He says not, but I know he wishes he could. Thing is, he promised his mother when he sold out that he would stay out of the army. His younger brother was killed in Spain, and Hugh's the last of the line."

"I think Richard has thought about rejoining," Elizabeth said slowly, meeting her mother's eyes steadily across the room.

"Has he said as much, Lizzie?" her mother asked.

"He said that he feels he could be more useful there than here at home. I hope that he will decide to stay. It is enough to worry for Jonathan."

"And now for Lord Stanton, too," Charlotte added.

"Yes," Elizabeth repeated stiffly. "And now for Lord Stanton, too."

"Do you expect your cousin back in town before he ships out, Mr. Warmington?" Lady Sherwood asked.

"Yes, ma'am. He should be back tomorrow or the next day at the latest."

Lord Stanton did, in fact, arrive in town the following day and the day after made a morning call on the Sherwoods. Elizabeth had purposely kept to her room, hoping that he would call. When she heard that he was sitting with her mother and Charlotte, she hurried down to speak with the butler.

"Williams, when Lord Stanton has finished visiting with my mother, would you show him to the book room before he leaves the house?" The butler frowned at the impropriety of her request, but she was prepared for him. "I must have a few minutes to speak privately with his lordship, Williams. You know that I have been permitted to do so in the past." As he still seemed unconvinced, she used her final weapon. "Williams, his lordship has rejoined the army and leaves in a week for Belgium. I must speak with him, and you must help me!"

Williams finally relented. What harm could a few minutes do? His lordship was a fine gentleman and a good friend to the captain. Certainly he could be trusted to hold the line with Miss Elizabeth.

Viscount Stanton was disappointed when he didn't find Elizabeth with her mother in the salon, but he said nothing beyond politely inquiring after her. He and Sir Hugh had called together, and as they were leaving, Williams handed Sir Hugh his hat and gloves but did not offer Lord Stanton his.

"Miss Elizabeth desires a few words with you, my lord, and asked if you would step to his lordship's book room."

Stanton raised an eyebrow at this information and turned to Sir Hugh. "I'll meet you later at White's."

Sir Hugh nodded and left the house, and Stanton went with Williams to the book room where he found Elizabeth alone and clearly agitated. He crossed the room to her and took both hands she held out to him, although he noticed she was unwilling to meet his eyes. "I was hoping to see you today, Miss Elizabeth, although I had not expected a private interview."

"Your cousin said that you are leaving in a week, and I wanted to see you again, just in case—"

"In case I didn't come back? Haven't you heard of the Ferris family luck, Miss Elizabeth? You should believe in it more than most, for you have been part of it." He continued to hold her hands, and she continued to stare down at them until finally he said gently, "Frightened for me again, Elizabeth?"

Her eyes flew to his face then, and she brought her hands up against his chest in a protective, possessive gesture. "Yes, my lord, frightened. Frightened for all of you."

And then, without knowing how it happened, she was in his arms, and he was kissing her with all the insane abandon he had sworn he would never permit himself. During the past two months he had managed to convince himself that he had very nearly gotten her out of his system. And then one look, one touch, was enough to destroy everything. He had no strength, no will of his own when she was with him. What was it about this girl that made him feel as if all the light had gone out of the day if she wasn't there? Her mouth was soft and sweet, more passionate than he thought possible in one so young and inexperienced, and he knew that if the world would end that instant, he would have no thought for it so long as he held this tender girl in his arms.

"Marry me, Elizabeth," he said suddenly, and the words came as a shock to his own ears. "Marry me now, before I leave!"

"Marry you! But you don't wish to be married!"

"Can't I change my mind?"

"Of course you can change your mind. But why? Why now?"

"Because I want you, Elizabeth," he said simply. "Be my wife. I'll settle a handsome fortune on you, then if I don't come back when all this is over, Henry will have the title, but you will be a very wealthy woman."

She laid her fingers over his lips. "Do not say such things, my lord. I would not marry for wealth and position."

"Then marry me because you want me as much as I want you." His arms encircled her possessively, and he drew her body tightly against his own. "And don't say it isn't so, for I would not believe you."

Elizabeth's heart was racing, and her body tingled from the close contact with him, but she forced herself to think clearly—speak sanely. "I cannot deny that I am attracted to you, my lord, but passion is an untrustworthy emotion, I think."

"Ah, yes! Elizabeth—the incurable romantic!" he answered scornfully. "You would hear words of love, then, from the man you would wed?"

"I think I would not marry without love, my lord," she said quietly. *If he loves me, I have given him the perfect opportunity to say so,* she thought, and then felt crushing disappointment at his next words, which seemed to come to her ears measured and tense.

"I have my answer, then," he said, as he released her and turned away, "for you will hear no words of love from me."

His words hurt her almost beyond bearing, but she would not allow him to have the last word, and she forced herself to answer him distinctly. "I think you will come to thank me for refusing your offer, my lord, when you take time to consider that you may have tired of me before the week was out and then found yourself with an unwanted bride on your hands. Good day, my lord . . . and may God protect you." She left the room quickly, and a few moments later as she walked along the corridor upstairs, she heard the street door close behind him.

He had said he wanted her. He had offered marriage. Fool! Why couldn't she be content with that? Clearly she wanted all or nothing. Well then, she told herself, you will have nothing, because you are not willing to settle for what he has to offer.

If Elizabeth had entertained the slightest doubt about her exact feelings for Lord Stanton, his kiss had dispelled it. She had previously known security and contentment in his arms, but with his kiss came an unmistakable sense of belonging. The touch of his lips, the wondrous sensations, the new excitement, these were things too complex for her to attempt to define. But the belonging—that was easy for her—for Elizabeth had always known instinctively what was right for her, and with this man, in his arms, was her place in this world, of that she was absolutely certain. And if he would not take her to him, then she would be cast adrift. The thought filled her with a pervading sadness, but beneath her despair hope glimmered, for Elizabeth was a fighter, in the best tradition of her military family. It would never occur to her to give up the battle so long as there was a single spark of hope. For if he admitted to wanting her, wasn't that a step on the way to loving her? And if he came to love her, then perhaps he could be brought to change his opinions about love in marriage. She would pray that it would be so, for she could see no solution otherwise.

Her rejection by Lord Stanton weighed heavily on Elizabeth's spirits, but she was not the only woman wearing a long face in that spring of 1815. Husbands, sweethearts, sons, and brothers were daily leaving London, leaving England, to join Wellington's army in Belgium. Elizabeth did not see Lord Stanton again before he sailed, for she had taken care to avoid any function where she thought there would be the slightest chance of meeting him, and he did not call again.

The Duke of Wellington arrived in Brussels on the fifth of April, and everyone breathed easier knowing that he was with the army at last. By the end of April, the British cavalry was landing at Ostend in great numbers, and Jonathan, convinced there would be a major battle in the near future, decided to send Harriet home. He arranged for her passage to Harwich and wrote asking Richard to meet her there and convey her to London, where she would take up residence with her in-laws.

Harriet arrived in mid-May and, although pleased to see her family again, was clearly regretful at having to separate from her husband. There were hundreds of British in Brussels, she said, and a social season much like any she had known in London. "I didn't want to leave. Very few English have. Most of them feel quite secure since the Duke arrived. But Jonathan insisted that he couldn't rest easy or keep his mind on his work while he knew I was without family in an unfortified city."

"And he was quite right, my dear," Lady Sherwood said. "The hardest part for women is the waiting, but there is little else we can do. And you have not only yourself to consider now, but the child as well."

Richard stayed overnight in London and left for Surrey at first light. He had been gone a week, for Harriet's packet had been delayed in sailing, and he had been detained four days awaiting it. He arrived at Sherwood Manor before noon and found his wife alone in the parlor. She turned quickly as he greeted her, and ran into his arms. "Oh, Richard, I have missed you dreadfully. Our first separation!"

He raised her face with his hand to kiss her tenderly. She saw that his eyes were serious, and when he spoke, his tone was grave. "I fear it will not be our last separation, my love."

She didn't pretend to misunderstand him, and indeed would not have been surprised to have had a note from him telling her that he was taking the first available ship for Belgium. "You have decided to go, then?"

"Yes. I must. Harwich was a madhouse, and I can only assume the other ports are as bad. Father told me the quartermaster general still needs experienced men on his staff. I will try for an appointment there."

"When will you leave?"

"In the morning."

Sarah and Richard spent the remainder of the day together. They ate dinner informally at six o'clock, inviting Jimmy to join them. He was clearly concerned when Richard announced his plans to rejoin the army, but he said only, "You will be careful, sir?"

Richard promised that he would be, and after spending the early part of the evening with them, Jimmy said his farewells, promising in a very grown-up way to look after his mother during the captain's absence. Soon after Jimmy retired, Richard took his wife's arm and escorted her upstairs. He had brought the brandy decanter from the library, and he nodded at it significantly. "Come to my room when you are ready for bed, and we will drink to a speedy end to Napoleon Bonaparte."

Henchly had finished packing earlier in the evening, and Richard's room was neat and undisturbed. He was soon ready for bed and dismissed his valet. "I will ring for you early, Henchly, for I wish to be in London before noon."

"Very good, sir. All of our things have been carried down to the hall. It remains only to load them into the chaise in the morning."

"Thank you, Henchly. Good night."

When Sarah came to join him, Richard poured their brandy, and for some time they sat silently near the fire, both occupied with their own thoughts, until finally Sarah said, "What are you thinking?"

"I am thinking how much I love you, and how lucky I am." He turned to look at her and surprised a frown on her brow. "I didn't mean for that to make you scowl, my love. What, may I ask, are you thinking?"

"I have been thinking much the same thing, only I regret that I have not been a better wife."

"What foolishness! No man could have a more wonderful or loving wife than I! Believe me, I am perfectly content."

"I know you have never complained," she said, "and I know you never will. But it is not unreasonable for a man to expect his wife to *be* his wife in every way."

"Sarah," he said, possessing himself of her hands and holding them together between his. "We have had this discussion before. You cannot allow feelings of guilt to influence you in this matter. The physical relationship . . . the *best* physical relationship in marriage must grow from mutual love, and mutual need. I will not have you forcing yourself out of some misplaced feeling of duty or guilt."

"But, Richard, all these times we've been close, and when we're together at night, surely you must wish for more. Don't you find it difficult?"

"Yes," he admitted. "I do wish for more. And, *yes*, sometimes it is very difficult, but not nearly as hard as the months I slept alone thinking I had no chance with you. Compared with those dreary days, these weeks since our marriage have been heaven on earth for me. *Please*, for my sake, stop teasing yourself. We are just beginning our life together. We can take all the time we need to adjust to one another. We need not worry if things aren't perfect after less than two months of marriage."

"But we may not have the rest of our lives, Richard; perhaps we will have . . . no more than tonight."

"Sarah—"

"No, please," she interrupted him. "I have spoken with your mother about this. She told me what it was like for her all those years with your father at sea. She said she knew that each time she said good-bye to him, she might never see him again. Then, when you joined the army and the war in Portugal, she said it was the same feeling again, only the pain held a different place in her heart. Now she has her husband safely home, and it is Jonathan she prays for, and soon now, you again. I have known all these weeks that you felt you should go, and I have stopped myself a dozen times from begging you to stay because I was selfish enough to want to keep you safe. Well, I have come to terms with that, and I realize that you must do what is right for you, and I will not try to influence you otherwise."

She stopped speaking to regain some control over her voice, and Richard gently brushed a tear from her cheek. "I had decided," she continued, "that when the time came for you to leave, I would use your mother as my model, for she is so self-possessed, so brave, and so remarkably strong. It was only today that I realized your mother has something I don't have. She knows everything about your father there is to know. She has given all of herself to him, and has accepted, as her right, all he has to offer. In the early years, she would have had only her memories had she lost him then, but as time passed she had you and Jon, and the girls, *his* children. Please God, we shall have all the years ahead you speak of, but if it is not to be so, then I would not have you leave me now without knowing all I can of you, for I do not think I could bear a life without you, never having known what it was like to be loved, truly and completely loved, by you. Do you understand what I'm trying to say?"

He did not answer her but sat for a long time, staring at her in silence. Finally he stood and held out his hand for hers. She laid her own in it, and he led her to the bed and blew out the candles on the table there. Then, as so often in the past, he helped her out of her dressing gown, and this time her nightgown as well. When he had removed his own things, he joined her in the bed. The first touch of their bodies was electrifying. Sarah came eagerly into his embrace and found herself being kissed with a strange intensity. The room, the world, the past, the future—everything began to fade as she yielded to the passion of his mouth on hers, and soon there was no place in her thoughts for anything but Richard's lips, Richard's hands—and Richard's body.

Sarah awoke before the dawn, aware of a warm glow of contentment. As she moved and came fully awake, she felt her husband's body beside her, and her memory of the previous night flooded back, rich with the joy of their lovemaking. Never had she imagined that such a feeling of completeness existed in the world. She knew now what the Church meant when it spoke of the oneness of marriage. Richard stirred in his sleep, and she rolled against him, unable to resist touching him, allowing her fingertips to slip over the smooth, hard muscles of his chest, stretching to kiss his neck, and then his lips. Then, suddenly, Richard was awake, kissing her, caressing her, wanting her all over again, setting her body on fire with his touch, and fanning her desire with his own.

Finally, reluctantly, as the sun crept ever higher in the sky, they forced themselves to separate. They shared an intimate breakfast. The chaise was brought round, and while several servants saw the baggage bestowed, Richard drew Sarah into the parlor and pulled her possessively into his arms.

"I don't have any words for last night," he said.

She shook her head. "We don't need any. It was perfect for both of us. That's all we need to know."

He kissed her then, and when he straightened again, he said, "Sarah, I shall do my best to come back to you, but if—"

She quickly raised her fingers to stay the words. "Don't say it."

He gently took her hand away and held it tightly in his. "I listened to you last night, and now I want you to hear me out, for there is something I must say, something I have thought about a great deal since I decided I must go with the army. If I don't come back, I want you to swear to me that you will always remember what we had."

"Oh, dearest Richard," she exclaimed, "I could never forget!"

"No. That's not what I mean. I want to know that you will not stop living if you lose me." He saw a tear overflow and reached for a handkerchief and gave it to her. "This is not a time for tears, Sarah. I fought you for months because you insisted upon seeing all men as you had seen your first husband. You must learn to judge each man for himself, and himself alone. Don't let your memories of me keep you from giving yourself again someday. I am not, after all, the only man who could love you, or even the only man you could ever love." He could see that she was about to protest, but he lifted a finger to silence her. "I have every intention of coming home to you, but if the fates should decree otherwise, then you must swear to me that you will place a limit on your grief, and that you will form new relationships, with good judgment and without fear. Swear it to me, Sarah."

"I swear."

"Good. Now give me your prettiest smile, and a kiss passionate enough to last me the whole campaign."

Chapter 22

RICHARD REJOINED THE army in London, and in a very short space of time was under orders. He arrived in Brussels in the closing days of May and was successful in receiving an appointment on the quartermaster general's staff. He was kept busy, but found time to spend with both Jonathan and Lord Stanton, both of whom were billeted near Brussels. Richard and Jonathan both wrote to their wives, but their letters conveyed little real intelligence. Brussels continued its social whirl, with balls and parties nearly every night. The Allied armies continued to reorganize, and the tension seemed to mount each day in anticipation of the battle that was to come.

Neither Charlotte nor Elizabeth was enjoying the Season, even though they were both much sought after by any number of men, both eligible and ineligible. Elizabeth had not wanted to come to town because she had dreaded meeting Lord Stanton, and now that he was gone, she found little in the Season's amusements to interest her. Charlotte had come to town with the liveliest expectation that Lizzie's prophecy would come true and Charles Warmington would speak to Lord Sherwood at the earliest opportunity. But Charles had not spoken, and since it was now early June and they expected to remove to the country in a few days, she had come to the conclusion that Lizzie was mistaken, and that she herself had misinterpreted Charles's attentions. She had done everything she knew, short of speaking to him directly, to encourage him, but she had not succeeded in bringing him to the point.

"Well, Lizzie," she said one evening as they sat together before retiring, "it seems that we were both mistaken in Charles, for we are to leave at the end of the week and he has said nothing."

"You don't think that perhaps he has spoken to Papa and been rejected?" Elizabeth asked. "He is a younger son, after all, and if Papa thought it an unequal match. . . ."

Clearly this thought had not occurred to Charlotte, and she grasped at it now. "Do you truly think it may be so? I hadn't thought that Papa would interfere, but if he has, then it would explain a great deal. I shall speak with Papa about it immediately, Lizzie. He is still in the book room, is he not?" She rose and abruptly left the room, neither awaiting nor seeming to expect an answer.

Lord Sherwood glanced up as his eldest daughter entered the room, and smiled when she asked if she was disturbing him. "Not at all, child. Did you wish to speak with me?"

"Yes, Papa. I was wondering if Charles Warmington had spoken to you . . . about me?"

"Were you expecting him to, my dear?"

"Well, yes. I thought he might speak . . . rather, I had hoped he might. Lizzie thought that perhaps you would not grant Mr. Warmington permission to address me. Is that so, Papa?"

"No, Charlotte. I have not denied Mr. Warmington, for he has not been to see me. But you must know, Charlotte, that just because a man shows a liking for a woman, it doesn't necessarily follow that he is considering marriage with her."

"I know, Papa, but I have felt that there was more than

mere liking between us. If he comes to you, then, you will not reject him for his lack of fortune?"

"I cannot deny that I would like to see a brilliant match for you, Charlotte," her father replied, "but I will always be disposed to look kindly upon any man of your choosing."

Charlotte smiled and stood on tiptoe to kiss her father's cheek. "Thank you, Papa, but it does not now seem as if Mr. Warmington will speak, for we are to leave town soon and then will not see him for some months, I think."

She spoke sadly, and Lord Sherwood was sorry to think that she had formed an attachment for a man who did not return her regard. It was puzzling, for he thought himself that Warmington showed a partiality for Charlotte, and he had been immeasurably relieved when Richard had assured him that Warmington was not the spy they sought. If Charlotte had come to him sooner in this matter, he could have discussed it with Richard, for Warmington was a close friend, and perhaps Richard was privy to some information that might be helpful. However, Charlotte had not come, and for the time being Richard was out of reach, and no doubt had more weighty problems to deal with than Charlotte's romantic hopes. Time enough to think of Charlotte's future after they had dealt with the threat of Bonaparte.

At the end of the first week in June, the Sherwood ladies removed to the country, leaving Lord Sherwood behind in London. Both Harriet and Elizabeth were depressed by the constant talk of impending war, and Lady Sherwood felt they could all benefit by leaving the gossip and rumors of town behind. She was also concerned that Sarah had been so long alone, for Richard had been gone nearly three weeks.

During the third week in June, news began to trickle into London of the French advance across the frontier and a major encounter with the Prussians at Ligny and the Dutch-Belgians at Quatre-Bras on the sixteenth of June. Some hours later, Lord Sherwood received the information that the 1st Guards had been engaged late in the day at Quatre-Bras. He considered sending off a quick note with this news but then decided against it. There was no reason to alarm them at home until he had more information. But when, some days later, he did have confirmed information, he found it was something he could not bring himself to write, and so instead he sent a message to Charles Warmington, asking him to call.

"You have some news, my lord?"

"I have news, Mr. Warmington, that must be conveyed immediately to Surrey, and since I cannot myself leave London, I was hoping you would act as my deputy." Lord Sherwood's voice was unsteady as he continued. "It is not such news as I would wish to write. The Guards were engaged on the sixteenth, and Jonathan is included on this casualty list." He handed a paper to Charles, but Charles took it without looking at it as his lordship continued. "It will not be an easy errand, Mr. Warmington, but you are a friend of the family. My wife . . . the girls . . . Harriet . . . I would rather not send a stranger." He paused briefly and then added, "There is no news of Richard or your cousin Stanton. As I understand it, no cavalry was engaged at Quatre-Bras, and although we held the ground, our losses were heavy. The Prussians were soundly beaten at Ligny and have fallen back before Bonaparte."

Charles tried to express his regret to Lord Sherwood, but his words of sympathy sounded empty even to his own ears. Sensing that his lordship would rather be alone, Charles promised to leave for Surrey immediately and quietly left the room. He went home to change into riding clothes, ordered his horse brought round, and within half an hour was on his way. When he arrived at Sherwood Manor in the late afternoon, he found that Charlotte and Sarah had driven to the village and that Harriet was resting. Lady Sherwood and Elizabeth were alone in the parlor when he was shown in.

Both ladies rose instantly to their feet as Charles was announced, and Lady Sherwood stepped forward, but his name as she spoke it was more question than greeting. "Mr. Warmington?"

"How do you do, ma'am. I have come with a message from Lord Sherwood."

His countenance and his tone could leave her in little doubt of the nature of his news, but she asked automatically, "You are bearing ill tidings, I think, sir?"

"Yes, ma'am . . . the worst," he said quietly.

"Richard?"

He stepped forward to take her hands in his own. "No, ma'am—Jonathan."

She nodded mutely and allowed him to lead her to a sofa. She sat down slowly, closing her eyes and folding her hands in her lap.

Charles transferred his gaze to Elizabeth and found her staring at him in stunned silence. Then after several minutes had passed she went to her mother and laid a hand on her shoulder. "Mama, we must tell Harriet."

Lady Sherwood roused herself from her abstraction and raised her eyes to Charles. "You will stay to dinner, of course, Mr. Warmington, and if you need not return to London immediately, then you must stay the night as well." She pulled the bell-rope as she spoke, and when the butler appeared at the door, she said, "Jepson will show you upstairs, Mr. Warmington. I am sure you would like to freshen up after your long ride."

They all left the room together, and as they ascended the stairs, Elizabeth turned to Charles and asked quietly, "My father has had no word of Richard or your cousin?"

"No, none."

Elizabeth nodded, and when they parted at the top of the stairway, Charles gazed after the women as they moved away down the hall, marveling at the courage they displayed in the face of such a devastating loss. He couldn't know that they were each trying to be strong for the other, but at Harriet's door, Elizabeth's courage failed, and she grasped her mother's arm painfully. "Mama," she said, her eyes filling with tears, "I don't think I can face Harriet. How can you be so calm?"

"We must be brave, Elizabeth. We have no other choice. We all knew we could expect this kind of news, and we must accept it."

"Why must we accept it?" Elizabeth cried. "It's not fair! Jonathan was barely twenty-three, with his whole life before him, his child soon to be born! And it's only the first battle, Mama! Are we to accept it if Richard is next, and then Lord Stanton?"

Lady Sherwood took her daughter by the shoulders and shook her. "Elizabeth, calm yourself! Jonathan is dead. Nothing we can say or do will change that. He was fighting to protect his family and his country, and he knew the risks inherent in the profession as well as any man. War is the greatest evil on earth, and it leaves no one untouched. I carried your brother within me, and I brought him into this world, and no one could love him more than I, but he served his country proudly, and it is with pride that we will remember him, for that is what he would have wished." She paused for a few moments and then continued gently, "I will speak to Harriet alone. Why don't you go outside. Perhaps take a walk in the garden. Do not deny your tears, Lizzie, for we are not forbidden to mourn, but do not allow yourself to become bitter, for such an emotion is unworthy of you." She kissed her daughter gently on the cheek and then turned to enter Harriet's room as Elizabeth hurried down the hall and then down some service stairs and out a side door into the garden.

Harriet did not take the news well, and Lady Sherwood sent a message that they would not be down to dinner. Sarah, Charlotte, Elizabeth, and Charles sat down to one of the cook's best efforts, but it was a desultory meal. None of them had any appetite, nor could they think of anything to say, but since they were all equally disinclined for conversation, no one seemed to mind the silence.

They adjourned to the parlor together, Charles declining any offer of port. Sarah asked Charles to tell them what he knew of the action on the sixteenth, and though he knew little more than what Lord Sherwood had told him, he shared this information with them. Elizabeth interjected an occasional question, but Charlotte sat listening in stony silence, until suddenly she leaped to her feet and ran from the room. Sarah rose to follow her but Charles stayed her.

"Please, Mrs. Sherwood, let me go."

Charles didn't see Charlotte on the stairs, but he heard a door close down the hall and realized she must have gone to the library. He followed her there and entered quietly, closing the door behind him. As she turned to face him, he saw she held a slender volume in her hand that she had apparently just taken from the shelf.

"Jon gave me this book of poetry on my last birthday," she said. "There were only thirteen months between us, you know, and as children we were loyal comrades. I can remember when we were very young—we got into terrible scrapes and nearly drove our nurse to distraction. I can't believe that he's gone."

Charles crossed the room to stand before her. "Why did you run from the room just now?"

"I couldn't bear to listen anymore. I was looking at Sarah, thinking how horrible it must be for her with Richard over there, and as worried as I am for him, I suddenly realized how lucky I am that you hadn't gone, and I felt guilty. . . ." She stopped speaking abruptly as she realized what she had said, and she looked up to see an arrested expression on his face.

He brought up one finger to wipe a single tear from her cheek and then cradled her chin in his hand, gazing intently and steadily into her eyes. And then, very slowly, he bent his head and gently touched her lips with his own. Charlotte's response was instantaneous, and as she raised her arms about his neck, he took her waist and drew her to him. For some moments they remained so, caught up in the waves of emotion pouring over them, and then suddenly Charles put her from him, and she stared in surprise to see him shaking his head vehemently.

"No, Charlotte, this will never do. I'm sorry. I didn't mean to . . . I must go. It is highly improper for us to be here alone. Will you come back to the parlor?"

She gazed at him in some confusion but only said, "No, thank you. I would rather stay here."

"Very well, then," he replied stiffly. "I shall bid you good night." He turned and was gone on the words, and when Charlotte finally quit the library, she did not return to the others, but instead went upstairs to the privacy of her own room.

Charles left Sherwood Manor the following morning, promising to return should he have any further news. But it was Lord Sherwood himself who arrived two days later with the news of Napoleon's complete defeat by the Allied Forces just south of the village of Waterloo on the eighteenth of June. The British and Prussian armies had not been able to join forces, he said, and the British and some Allied troops had fought valiantly all day to hold the position until the Prussians could come up in support. The battle had raged for more than eight hours, but by nightfall the French Army was in full retreat. The Allied Forces had been victorious, but the price had been dear, the losses on both sides staggering. He had no information on the casualties of that battle and was sure it would be several days at least before they had any reliable word. He returned to London the following morning, and several days later the casualty lists began to come in. There was no mention of either Lord Stanton or Captain Sherwood.

The interminable days of waiting continued, and then finally news arrived in an unexpected way. One evening, just at dusk, a chaise turned in at the gates of Sherwood Manor, and a few moments later the women were drawn into the hall by the sounds of an arrival. Sarah was shocked to see her husband being more or less carried into the house supported between Charles Warmington and Henchly. His left leg was swathed in bandages above the knee, and he appeared unable to rest any weight upon it. His face was pale, but he smiled at Sarah's worried frown as he bent his head to kiss her briefly.

Charles hastened to reassure her. "He looks much worse than he is, Mrs. Sherwood. The jolting of the coach these last few miles was too much for him, I'm afraid. I tried to convince him to stay in London for a few days, but you know what he is. Said he would come home to you straightaway and wouldn't listen to any sage advice."

"Yes, Mr. Warmington, I know what he is. To travel at all in such a state is unthinkable." She tried to keep her voice lightly critical, hoping that her tone would in some part hide the overwhelming relief she felt in knowing that Richard was alive.

"He will be better here at home than elsewhere, ma'am," Henchly added. "The number of wounded in Brussels is appalling, and there is no way to care for them all properly. Those wounded who felt they could travel were encouraged to do so."

Richard insisted that he could hop up the stairs, but there was a general outcry and Charles refused to be bullied. With the help of two footmen, they lifted the captain and carried him up to his bedchamber. Once there, he desired to be placed upon a couch and insisted that if he should be given a glass of brandy, he would do nicely.

With his arms finally freed, Richard took his wife into them and kissed her properly, heedless of all eyes upon them. Then he accepted in turn the embraces of his mother, his sisters, and his sister-in-law. As Harriet bent to kiss his cheek, he took her hand. "Sit a moment, Harriet. I have a message for you from Jon." Silence fell in the room as Harriet sat facing him, and for a moment it seemed to the two of them that they were alone. "I saw Jon the day before Quatre-Bras. He was in high spirits—excited that we were to see some action, but he did get serious for a few moments and he said, 'If I don't make it through this, tell Harriet that I love her. And tell her to name our *son* after me.' "

Harriet smiled crookedly through her tears and said, "I will, Richard. I will."

A short time later, Lady Sherwood took Harriet away, and Charlotte, made decidedly uneasy by Mr. Warmington's presence in the room, went with them. Elizabeth, no longer able to control her anxiety, blurted out, "Do you know anything of Lord Stanton, Richard? We have heard nothing."

"I'm afraid I know very little, Lizzie, for I left Brussels early on the morning of the nineteenth. Julian was attached to General Grant's brigade. When the Prussians fell back from Ligny on Havre, we were forced to fall back to Waterloo to maintain communications. All the cavalry was kept to guard the retreat, and the 7th Hussars were heavily engaged at Genappe on the seventeenth. I know he came through that, for someone told me they saw him the next morning, but I have heard nothing since. We took a tremendous beating on the eighteenth, and our losses were heavy. By the time the Prussians were able to join us, many of our units were fighting as a last line of defense, with no reserves whatsoever. But they stood their ground to the last, against some of the heaviest artillery fire I have ever seen, and massive attacks of both cavalry and infantry. When the French mounted their final general advance sometime after seven, the Prussians had arrived in some force on our left, and we were able to turn the French from the field. Their army was fairly routed, and the Prussians took up the pursuit as they retreated. Most of our fellows dropped right where they were for the night, too exhausted to take a step in any direction.

"I arrived in Brussels during the night and was sent out with some of the first wounded who were able to travel. The town was already overflowing with wounded from Quatre-Bras. I can't imagine how they are dealing with the masses of wounded from Waterloo."

Richard noticed that Elizabeth had become alarmingly pale, so he hastened to add, "If Julian hasn't been on the casualty lists so far, Lizzie, that's a good sign, for bad news travels fastest."

Henchly had been hurrying about the room preparing the captain's bed, and at this lull in the conversation he made so bold as to say that he thought the captain would be better between sheets. Sarah agreed, so Charles bore Elizabeth off, promising to stay long enough in the morning to take his leave of them.

"Why don't you leave me to Henchly, Sarah," Richard said. "He can scrape some of this dirt from me and get me into bed."

"I would much rather stay and help."

"And I would much rather you stayed, my love, but I think it would shock Henchly profoundly if you did." He smiled as he spoke, and she relented and went away.

When she returned some time later, she found him washed and shaved, in a clean nightshirt, and snugly tucked up in bed. "Are you hungry?"

"Yes, and I have already sent Henchly to fetch me something from the kitchen."

Sarah sat gently on the edge of the bed and laid her hand on the coverlet over his leg. "What is the nature of your wound, and how did you come by it?"

"It was a musket ball, lodged deeply in the thigh. It bled freely at first, but I managed to tie a cloth above it and that helped some. I did well enough until my horse was hit. I don't remember much, but he must have come down on the same leg, for it's badly bruised, and I remember someone saying that I had to be pulled from under him. By the time I regained consciousness, I had been carried to Waterloo, and the ball had been dug out and the leg dressed. I was lying under the prettiest elm you can imagine. I don't remember ever finding a tree so attractive, but after six hours on the battlefield, the relative quiet behind the lines seemed like heaven.

"Henchly helped me to sit up against the tree, and we stayed there until after dark. There were quite a few wounded waiting to be conveyed to Brussels, and we managed to stay informed of how the battle was progressing by shouting to an occasional officer or troop that passed by, or from information from the wounded who were continuously streaming back from the front. By the early hours of the morning we had received positive confirmation in Brussels that the French were in full retreat and in such disarray that the Duke thought it unlikely that they would be able to make another stand before the Allies hounded them into Paris.

"Lizzie looks terrible. Is it Jon?" he asked.

"Partly Jon, and partly her concern for you and for Lord Stanton. She is in love with him, Richard."

"Oh, no," he said on a sigh. "I have been afraid of that, but I kept hoping that it would not be so."

"I think it is the waiting that is hardest. At least if she knew one way or the other, she could begin to deal with it."

"It is amazing to me that anyone could come unscathed through that battle. Never have I seen such violent conflict or such staggering losses. It was a sight I shall not soon forget. And then Jon. . . ." A shadow crossed his face, and he reached out a hand to his wife. "Come here, Sarah."

She leaned closer, and he pulled her against his side. As she laid her head on his chest, he slowly lowered his chin into her hair, closing his eyes and allowing his body to relax. He savored the warmth and softness of her body in his arms and the familiar and comforting scent of her hair, and they sat so, in companionable silence, until Henchly arrived with the captain's dinner.

The following morning Charles entered Richard's room in the company of the village doctor. The doctor examined Richard's leg and said that he saw nothing amiss and was convinced it would heal splendidly if the captain kept all weight off it for a full two weeks at least. He was amazed at the extent of the bruising and remarked that the captain was fortunate that his horse had not broken the leg when he fell on it.

The doctor was soon gone, and Charles reached out to take Richard's hand. "Well, I'm off, then. I'll stop at Mount Street to tell Lord Sherwood that I saw you home in one piece."

"Thank you, Charles, for all your help. And please, tell my father also to let us know immediately if he has any news of Julian. We are all concerned for him."

It was another three days before they had any word of Stanton, and then the news didn't come from Lord Sherwood, but from Charles, who had met in London a wounded Hussar from the 7th who had seen Julian on the nineteenth of June.

. . . He said that aside from a few flesh wounds and a rather nasty saber cut on his right forearm, Julian was well on the morning of the nineteenth. He had come in to have the cut stitched but insisted upon returning to the brigade and moving on with them to Paris. I don't think we need concern ourselves for him. Please convey my compliments to your family. I will write again if I receive further news.

Yours, etc.,
Charles

Richard read this aloud to Sarah, and when he finished, she reached to take it from him. "May I take this to Lizzie?"

"Yes, please do. I think she went riding with Jimmy this morning."

By the time Sarah made her way to the stables, Elizabeth and Jimmy were returning from their ride. Dismounting, Elizabeth turned to see Sarah hurrying toward her with a letter in her hand, and she turned suddenly pale.

"It's good news, Lizzie," Sarah called to her. "Lord Stanton is well and still with the army, following Napoleon back into France."

Elizabeth, who had wept unreservedly for Jonathan on the day they learned of his death, had not allowed herself to give in to such weakness since; but after the intervening days of anxiety and the sleepless nights, she could not deny her overwhelming relief. She threw herself into Sarah's arms, weeping like a child. Sarah cradled her in her arms until the sobbing subsided, and then as Elizabeth raised her head, Sarah brushed a few loose strands of hair from her face. Elizabeth was dabbing her eyes with a large man's handkerchief.

"Where did you get that?" Sarah asked.

"It's Lord Stanton's," Elizabeth explained. "He lent it to me a long time ago, and I never returned it. I keep it with me most of the time. I know it's foolish, but I like having it."

"No, Lizzie, it's not foolish, but I think you have kept these feelings to yourself long enough. When you see Lord Stanton again, you should tell him how you feel. If he knew you loved him, it might change things between you." Elizabeth shook her head, but Sarah said quickly, "Don't say no. You can never be sure of anything where love is concerned. Look at your brother and myself. Richard didn't allow his pride to stand in the way of telling me he loved me, and it's a good thing he didn't, for otherwise we would never have found the happiness we now share. If you tell him how you feel and he still rejects you, you can feel no worse than you do now, don't you see? You are the one who is always saying that honesty is important above all things. Well then, practice what you preach! Tell him the truth, and see what he will do with it."

Chapter 23

BONAPARTE'S BRIEF REIGN had come to an abrupt end. He was banished to the bleak island of St. Helena, and Louis XVIII was once again placed upon the French throne by the Congress of Vienna. During the summer, great numbers of men were demobilized, and Charles wrote to Richard that Julian had come home at last, tanned and healthy, and in excellent spirits.

Lord Sherwood finally came to the country for a well-deserved rest, but he was less than pleased with the conditions he found at Sherwood Manor. Richard was up and about the affairs of the estate, and it was plain to see there was nothing amiss with his marriage, but Charlotte and Elizabeth were both looking poorly, and he could not help exclaiming to his wife when they were alone.

"The girls are looking burnt to the socket. What ails them?"

"I have tried speaking with Elizabeth," his wife said, "but she will not confide in me, and Richard says that I should not press her. Charlotte admitted that she has formed a *tendre* for Charles Warmington. She said she had spoken to you."

"Yes, she did. She seemed surprised that the young man had not approached me, for she felt he returned her regard. I had decided to speak with Richard, and I will do so immediately. He is in a better position than most to know where Mr. Warmington stands in the matter."

Lord Sherwood spoke to Richard at length that very evening, and although he did not share the substance of their conversation with his wife, he told her that Richard felt the situation between Mr. Warmington and Charlotte did not look promising.

But two days later, all thought of Charles Warmington was put out of their heads by the precipitate arrival of Sir Hugh Broughton just as the family was gathering in the drawing room before dinner. He was shown in immediately, greeted everyone politely, but seemed disappointed as his eyes swept the room. "Julian is not here, then?"

"No," Richard replied, puzzled. "Did you expect him to be?"

"I suppose not really, although I had hoped he might stop here. I shall push on to Stanton Castle immediately and hope to find him there. We have had the most unsettling news in London this morning. It seems that Henry Ferris is a spy for the French—has been for years." Sir Hugh was speaking to Richard and could not fail to see the look that passed between Richard and his father at his words. Sir Hugh turned to Lord Sherwood and asked brusquely, "Did you know, my lord?"

"No, Sir Hugh," his lordship replied. "Richard and I knew that there was a traitor among our acquaintance, but we didn't know who, until now. The night of our ball in Mount Street some delicate papers were tampered with in my book room, and on the night that Lord Stanton and Elizabeth were shot, we made an attempt to capture the man, but he overpowered the footman who had been set to watch for him. Most recently, he broke into the house in London and ransacked the entire room."

"I can't believe it," Richard said in a dazed voice. "Not Henry. We fought together. He put me on his own horse when I was wounded in Portugal. It's just not possible."

"I would have been the first to agree with you," Sir Hugh said, "but I am afraid it is true, nevertheless. They discovered some papers in Paris that showed Henry's activities without question. Right up until Waterloo, he was sending the French whatever information he could about our troop strength and movements. When they confronted him yesterday at the Foreign Office, he made no attempt to deny anything but astonished everyone by leveling the nearest minister and casting himself through a second-story window. Before anyone could respond, he had disappeared into the side streets, and nothing has been seen or heard of him since. The story was all over town this morning, and I was with Julian when we first heard it. He would not believe the rumors but went immediately to the Foreign Office and demanded to be told the facts as they knew them. When they were finished, he never said a word but only walked out to the coach. When I tried to follow him, he said that he wished to be alone and that he must go home to Giles.

"That was the last time I saw him. I spent the better part of the day trying to run him down in London. All I know is that he did go home, but Giles had already heard the rumors and left the house. Whether Julian ever found him I don't know. His servants were being awfully close, even with me, but I could see for myself that Julian's curricle and team were gone, so I concluded that he had left town, but I can't imagine where he has gone."

"I doubt that he has gone to Stanton Castle, Hugh," Richard said, "and I see little reason for you to seek him there. You know Julian. If he wants to be alone, you can be sure he will go nowhere he would expect to be found. Stay to dinner, stay the night, and go back to London in the morning. When he has come to terms with this, he will go back there, I have no doubt of that."

"I'm sure you must be right," Sir Hugh answered. "The thing is that I never should have let him out of my sight. I have racked my brain trying to think where he may have gone, but I can come up with nothing. I can't rid myself of the idea that he has gone after Henry, and I shudder to think what may happen if he catches up with him."

Giles Ferris heard the rumors about his brother Henry almost simultaneously with Stanton. Unlike Stanton, he had no thought of having the allegations confirmed. By the time Stanton had parted from Sir Hugh and arrived home, he found that Giles had ordered the post chaise and left the house nearly an hour earlier. Stanton instantly ordered his curricle and team. He did not doubt for an instant where Giles had gone, for he had had the same thought himself. The only safe place for

Henry was France, the quickest way to get there—across the Channel.

What the Ferris brothers knew, and no one else, was that Stanton owned a piece of property on a stretch of lonely coastline in Kent. It was no more than a modest manor house on the edge of the marsh, presently let to a tenant. Julian and Henry had spent several summers there as boys, and once, when Giles was seventeen, Julian had taken him there and shown him where he and Henry had played at being pirates and smugglers. It sickened him now to think that Henry had probably found the place convenient for meeting his confederates from across the Channel.

Stanton changed teams often and made good time into Kent. He abandoned his carriage at Tenterden and hired a horse for the last twelve miles of his journey. He had no intention of stopping at the manor house and gave it a wide berth. It was growing dark as he directed his horse out of a stretch of timber and onto the broad expanse of the marsh. He followed a narrow sheep track that wound erratically over the ground. In all these years, he thought, the path had not changed. It had neither widened nor narrowed and seemed not to have moved an inch from its original meandering trail.

It had by this time grown quite dark, and sensing that he was close to the shepherd's cot he sought, Stanton dismounted and tied his horse to a thorn bush a little way off the path. It wasn't a very substantial tethering place, but the animal was tired, and the viscount judged that he would not attempt to break free. He had walked only a few paces when he heard a sound to his right and, peering through the twilight, saw a horse tethered nearby—probably Giles's, or perhaps Henry's. A few more minutes brought him to the tiny hut. Although it had been carefully shuttered inland, there were several cracks with light showing toward the southeast. Stanton approached soundlessly and made his way round to peer through one of the chinks in the wall. His brothers were both inside, apparently alone. He heard Giles's voice raised in righteous wrath.

"None of what you are saying makes any sense to me. You can't feed me any rubbish about loyalty to the Empire! Julian was engaged at Waterloo, wounded there! He could just as easily have been killed, and you would have been instrumental in your own brother's death! My God, Henry, so many of our friends died there! Your friends!"

"I have no friends in this country." Henry's voice was passionate; he spoke with finality. Giles took a menacing step forward, and Stanton saw for the first time that Henry held a pistol, leveled almost nonchalantly at his young brother.

Hoping his arrival wouldn't startle Henry into unwary action, Stanton called out, "Henry, it's Julian. I'm coming in." He lifted the latch and bent his head to enter the dimly lit interior.

Obviously viewing Stanton as a more tangible threat than a mere schoolboy, Henry pivoted, aiming his weapon at his elder brother.

"I thought this place forgotten," he snapped. "I did not expect to have my entire family descend upon me!"

"I shouldn't think that anyone beyond we three knows of its existence," Stanton replied. "But I must ask you either to use that pistol, Henry, or put it down. You are wondering if I am myself armed, and the answer is yes. But there is no provocation that could induce me to fire upon my own brother, so you may rest assured that I will not make the attempt."

Seconds passed, and then, slowly, Henry lowered his pistol and laid it on the table before him. He watched his own motions carefully, staring at the piece as he put it down, and then suddenly looked up to meet the viscount's eyes defiantly. "Well, I am waiting to hear your tirade of disgust and incredulity, Stanton. I have already endured one from this whelp. I am sure you will be more eloquent than he."

"I have not come for that, Henry. You know what you have done, and I know full well that your activities were not accidentally entered into or taken lightly. I am sure that you are fully committed to your cause in every way that a man can be."

Giles started to speak, but an uplifted hand from Stanton silenced him immediately as he continued.

"I know how much you hated my father, and I also know how deeply you loved Mother. To a large degree, we share those feelings. I disliked Father intensely and decided early on that he was a perfect model of the man I would never wish to be. As for Mother, I loved her, yes, but not with the dedication you felt. It was not an unbreakable tie for me. I want you to know that I understand your position; we are, after all, half French. You had a choice to make, and you made it. But even though I understand your sympathies, Henry, I cannot forgive your activities on these shores. You have forsworn an oath of allegiance to the king. You are a traitor to this country and to your family here, and I will not protect your life at the risk of my own or Giles's. I plan to call on the district magistrate at dawn with the intelligence that I own property here, property with which you are familiar, and that you could be using as a place of concealment. If you have friends over the water, I hope that they plan to collect you tonight, for after tomorrow morning I have only one brother."

He turned to look at Giles as he spoke these last words and could see that the boy was trying hard to control his emotions, but his eyes were glistening, and one tear had already coursed a track down his cheek unheeded.

"But . . . we are brothers," Giles stammered, "and we love one another. Does that not count for anything?" He was vainly seeking answers—solutions that would fall short of tearing them apart forever. The cold reality was that after tonight they would never see Henry again, and he did not want to face it. He looked from Henry to Julian, but he could not speak.

"Love between brothers counts for a great deal, Giles," Stanton said, "but there comes a time in each man's life when he must follow the dictates of his conscience, and sometimes in order to do that, he must sever old bonds. Henry has severed his bonds with us, and if the truth be told, he did so many years ago."

They stood for a few moments in tense silence, and finally the viscount spoke again. "Is that your horse a little way down the path, Giles?" His brother nodded mutely, and Stanton continued. "Go to him, and wait for me there. I will be along shortly." Giles stood his ground anxiously until Stanton took his shoulder and turned him toward the door. "Go now, Giles. We will be fine, and I will come soon, I promise."

As Giles left and Stanton turned back, Henry came from behind the table and took a step forward, leaving less than two feet between them. "Julian . . . if you could think of the good times, when we were young, and we didn't have much except each other . . ."

"I won't forget them, Henry. Our father did us a great disservice when he brought our mother to England. He cast the dice for us even then." He held out his hand and was not surprised to see it shaking. Henry took it in his own, but as if by mutual consent they felt it not to be enough, they embraced each other suddenly, and then, just as suddenly, stood apart. "Good-bye, Henry. If you see Mother, give her my love, and tell her that she need lack for nothing so long as I live." For the first time in his life, Stanton experienced the sensation of hot tears rising to his eyes, and he turned away quickly, passed through the door, and found himself struggling for breath in the cool night air.

He soon came up with Giles, and they walked together to where Stanton's horse waited. As he mounted, Giles finally found his voice. "Julian ... I feel ... I can't describe it."

"Sick—and empty," Stanton supplied. "But there is no help for it, Giles. We must learn to live with it and hope that in time it will fade."

"Do you truly intend to lay information in the morning?"

"Yes. I won't say that I suspect Henry of being here, but only that I own property in the area. You needn't worry for Henry. There are at least a hundred places where he can hide until they come for him, and he knows them all. We haunted this marsh for three long summers. We left no stone unturned." He stopped speaking suddenly, and Giles knew he was remembering those carefree summers, and he, too, relapsed into silence. They rode on side by side without speaking for many miles.

After several weeks passed with nothing being heard of Henry Ferris, most people assumed that somehow he had escaped to France. If he was willing to change his name and settle quietly in some remote village, it was unlikely that anything would be heard of him again.

Lord Sherwood returned from a short visit to London with the information that both the Prince Regent and the Duke of Wellington had personally communicated with Lord Stanton regarding his brother's activities. "They both felt that he should hear from them directly, so he would understand that there was never any question of his loyalty. The Prince said something to the effect that the Ferrises had been loyal subjects of the Crown for over two hundred years, and there was no reason to doubt them now simply because there had been one rotten apple in the barrel."

"I think it showed great sensitivity for His Royal Highness to speak to Lord Stanton," Lady Sherwood said. "It must be reassuring for him to know that his allegiance is not in question."

"Yes," added Elizabeth, "but I'm not sure that I understand. Was Henry Ferris an agent for the French, or a traitor to Britain?"

"He was a British subject, Lizzie," Richard answered, "and as such owed his allegiance to the king. But there is little doubt now that his sympathies have always been with the French, and therefore to some degree you are right—he was a French agent and no doubt highly valued by them."

"Still, it must have been a great shock for Lord Stanton to discover that his brother was a French sympathizer," Charlotte added, "for I think that he and Henry were fond of each other."

"Yes," Richard agreed, "they were very close."

The following evening after dinner, while Harriet and Charlotte went for a walk in the garden, Elizabeth found an opportunity to bring up the subject of Charlotte's floundering affair with Charles Warmington. "Papa, is there nothing we can do to encourage Mr. Warmington to ask for Charlotte? She is so miserable."

"She is looking poorly," Lord Sherwood agreed, "but there is nothing we can do, Lizzie."

"But couldn't you talk to him, Papa? Explain that the money isn't important when weighed against Charlotte's happiness?"

Lord Sherwood looked across at Richard. "I have talked to him, Lizzie," Richard said. "I got nowhere. He is determined that Charlotte can do better for herself. He will not make an offer."

"Did you tell him that Charlotte loves him?"

"No. I didn't think I had the right, since I was speaking without Charlotte's knowledge. But I think he knows how she feels."

"Is he really so poor, Richard?"

"No, actually. His house in Kent is very well—much like the one we grew up in. And with Charlotte's fortune, I am sure they would be very comfortable there. But we can't force him to offer for her, Lizzie."

"He can't really love her," Elizabeth said with conviction, "or he would not allow such foolish scruples to stand in his way. If there was just some way we could get around this stubbornness of his," she mused, more to herself than to her family. "Perhaps we could devise a way to have him compromise Charlotte. Then he would be forced to offer for her."

"Really, Elizabeth!" her mother objected. "I must beg you not to voice such improper thoughts. Whatever will you say next!"

Elizabeth was silenced, but Richard was much struck by her casually uttered words and he met his father's eyes speculatively. Shortly thereafter, Lord Sherwood and his son went off together to the library, and his lordship left a message with the footman in the hall that he wished Miss Charlotte to join them as soon as she returned.

When Charlotte came into the house nearly an hour later, she was directed to the library, where she found her father alone.

"You wished to see me, Papa?"

"Yes, Charlotte. Do you remember, some weeks ago, speaking to me about Mr. Warmington?"

"Yes, Papa."

"You said you thought that Mr. Warmington might speak to me concerning you. Why did you think that, child?"

"I thought he might be interested in asking for my hand, Papa."

"But why?"

"I suppose because we enjoyed each other's company. He seemed to seek me out, and I thought, as did Lizzie, that he showed a decided partiality for me. I suppose also that I hoped he cared for me."

"Because you care for him?"

"Yes, Papa."

"So it was all conjecture on your part? Did he never say or do anything to make you certain that he cared?"

"Why are you asking me this, Papa?"

"I am merely trying to obtain a clear view of the situation, Charlotte. *Did* he say or do anything?"

Charlotte did not answer immediately but instead stared

down at her hands, and Lord Sherwood felt a faint glimmer of hope as he asked again, "Well, Charlotte?"

"At the time I spoke to you, Papa, no, he had done nothing. But since that time, something has happened that made me more certain that he cares."

"And what was that?"

"When you sent him down with the news of Jonathan, I was upset . . . and I blurted out how I felt about him . . . and he kissed me." She raised her eyes to her father's, and he saw that they were full of tears. "For a moment I thought he would admit that he cared for me, but he didn't. He just said that it was wrong, and apologized, and left. I was confused, Papa, and I didn't know what to think. All I know is that I love him."

"Where did all this take place, Charlotte?"

"Here. In the library. I had come to find the book that Jon had given me for my birthday, and Charles followed me."

Lord Sherwood rose from his desk and walked over to embrace his daughter. "Take heart, Charlotte. I intend to see Mr. Warmington and have a talk with him. If there is anything that can be done to advance your cause with him, you may believe that I shall do it. But you must promise to stop moping. No young lady ever won a man's heart with a worried frown and dark circles under her eyes. Have some faith in your father, who loves you more than anything, and who will do all in his power to see you happy."

Charlotte soon left him, and Lord Sherwood returned to his desk very pleased with himself. Lizzie's remark, Richard's suggestion, and his inquisition had yielded the weapons he needed to proceed. He sat for some moments in contemplation, and then, choosing a quill, pulled a piece of writing paper forward and began a letter to the Honorable Charles Warmington.

Lord Sherwood received an immediate answer to his letter. Mr. Warmington replied that he would be happy to visit Sherwood Manor and hoped that Thursday next would be a convenient day for his arrival. Charles arrived late in the afternoon and was not surprised to find himself the only house guest.

After dinner that evening, the ladies retired to the parlor, and as a footman set the port upon the table, Richard rose and excused himself, and Charles had the distinct feeling that he was about to discover Lord Sherwood's purpose in summoning him into Surrey.

"You will have port, I believe, Mr. Warmington?" his lordship was saying.

"Yes, thank you, sir," Charles answered automatically, and then noticed that Lord Sherwood signaled for the footman to leave the decanter and motioned him from the room.

"You will no doubt have guessed that I have something of import to discuss with you, Mr. Warmington?" his lordship asked.

"Yes, my lord."

"It concerns Charlotte."

Charles had also suspected this, but he said nothing and waited for Lord Sherwood to continue.

"Charlotte confided something to me several days ago that has caused me considerable disquiet, but I have determined to make no judgment in the matter until you have had ample opportunity to defend your position."

A frown creased Charles's brow, but he continued to regard Lord Sherwood steadily as the older man continued.

"Charlotte has told me that during your visit here in late June, you shared a conversation with her in the library."

"Yes, sir. I did. She was grief-stricken over Jonathan, as we all were. It was not a pleasant evening for us."

"Charlotte has admitted to me, Mr. Warmington, that you and she were quite alone in the library, and that you did more than talk." He paused meaningfully and waited for Charles to respond.

"What exactly are you saying, Lord Sherwood?"

"I am saying, sir, that I asked you to come to my home because I thought you a man to be trusted. My wife, daughters, and daughter-in-law were all residing here without the protection of any male relative. I had expected that you would deliver my message in good faith. I did not expect that you would take advantage of the situation to make advances to Charlotte."

Lord Sherwood watched as Charles's jaw hardened into a firm line, and he answered stiffly, "Is that what Charlotte said? That I made advances?"

"She said, Mr. Warmington, that you kissed her, and I hope

you do not expect me to doubt her word, for Charlotte would not lie to me."

"No, sir, I would not expect you to doubt her. I did kiss her. I don't deny it."

"Then, may I ask you, sir, what you meant by it and what your intentions are toward my daughter?"

"I meant nothing by it, my lord, and I have no intentions toward your daughter. I apologized to Charlotte, and I will apologize to you if necessary."

Lord Sherwood rose suddenly from the table with all the appearance of a man overcome by righteous indignation. "You force your attentions upon a young, unmarried girl in her own home, when you know she has no protection by; you take advantage of her grief and then have the audacity to sit there and tell me that it meant nothing and that your intentions are dishonorable! You are insulting, sir!"

Charles rose to his feet as Lord Sherwood finished speaking and spoke in a steady, carefully controlled voice. "I do not mean to be insulting, my lord, but I do not know what you would have me say."

"I would like to hear the truth from you, young man. Why did you feel yourself constrained to kiss my daughter?"

"I kissed her because I find her very desirable."

"And . . . ?"

"And because I am in love with her."

"May I ask if Charlotte returned your embrace, Mr. Warmington?"

"Yes, sir, she did."

"In my day, young man, when a gentleman loved and desired a young, unattached woman and went so far as to kiss her and receive her kiss in return, there was one more requirement that went along with the desire and the kissing."

"An offer of marriage," Charles said flatly.

"Yes, sir. An offer of marriage!"

"And you are demanding one from me?"

"I expect one from you, Mr. Warmington, if you consider yourself a gentleman!"

There was a pause before Charles spoke again. "Charlotte would be throwing herself away on me, my lord."

"The day the daughter of a simple sea captain throws herself away on the son of an earl is the day hell will freeze over, my boy. You and Charlotte have both admitted that you love each other, and you have taken the first step toward a physical commitment. There is no honorable way to turn back now. . . . I am waiting."

The two men stood staring at each other across the width of the dining room table, and finally Charles spoke. "I would like your permission, Lord Sherwood, to pay my addresses to Charlotte."

"You have my permission, Mr. Warmington, and you may do so without delay." Lord Sherwood moved to the door of the parlor and, throwing it open, strode in. Charlotte was sitting with Harriet near the empty fireplace, and he spoke to her directly. "Charlotte, will you step back into the dining room for a few moments? Mr. Warmington would like to speak with you."

All five women stared at his lordship in silence, and Charlotte rose mechanically and walked past her father into the dining room. He pulled the doors to behind him, leaving her alone with Charles. She stopped just inside the doors, and Charles stood beside the table, fifteen feet away.

"Charlotte," he began, "your father has given his permission . . ." And then when he saw the joy in her eyes, he could only say "I love you." He was walking toward her then, and she met him more than halfway as he folded her in a hug that took her breath away and left her in no doubt whatsoever of his intentions.

Chapter 24

TWO DAYS LATER, the engagement of Miss Charlotte Sherwood and the Honorable Charles Warmington appeared in the columns of the *Post*, and two days after that, Lord Sherwood and Captain Sherwood were still chuckling over the way they had used Charles's overly fine sense of the proprieties to turn his own hand.

Charles realized, of course, that he had been manipulated, but having once admitted his love for Charlotte, he could not wish any of it undone, and he confessed ruefully to Richard that he should have given in to his friend's initial arguments. "I should have known that if the entire Sherwood clan united against me, I would have no chance. You are a ruthless, disreputable lot, and it is clear to me now that you will go to any length to win."

Lord Sherwood agreed to a wedding date in late December, allowing for six months strict mourning for Jonathan, and insisted that the ceremony be private and simple. Charles spent much of the remainder of August in Surrey, but early September found Lord and Lady Sherwood, Charles, and Charlotte back in London with plans to remain. Lady Sherwood, of course, would come down for Harriet's lying-in. Elizabeth vaguely planned to spend some part of the Little Season in London, but for the present she chose to remain in Surrey and work around Harriet's schedule, whatever that might turn out to be.

One sunny afternoon just four days after she had seen her parents and sister off to town, Elizabeth was alone in the hall arranging some late summer flowers that she had gathered. When a knock sounded on the door behind her, she turned to see Viscount Stanton admitted to the house. There was a shattering crash, and she stared down in amazement at her feet. Her flowers were scattered in every direction, the lovely blue glass vase broken into several dozen pieces. She looked up again as she exclaimed, "My Lord Stanton! This is a surprise. We did not expect you."

"Apparently not," he said, smiling. "I am sorry if I startled you. I hope it wasn't a valuable piece?"

She gazed at him uncomprehendingly for a moment and then recalled the broken vase. "No ... no, not at all. How foolish of me." She stooped immediately to collect the flowers and then unthinkingly swept her hand over the marble floor, gathering the broken slivers of glass.

Stanton bent quickly, grasping her wrist in concern. "No, ma'am, you must not. You will surely cut yourself. Leave it for the servants."

She stared for a moment at his hand on her wrist and then, looking up into his eyes, suddenly realized she was acting a complete fool. It had been such a shock to see him standing there. It was nearly five months since she had last seen him—the longest five months of her life.

She rose unsteadily and, recalling her manners, invited him into the parlor. "Richard and Sarah are visiting with the tenants at Ellis End, and Harriet is resting, so I fear I am the only one to entertain you. Will you have some wine?"

A footman responded to her pull on the bell. He was sent for refreshments and soon returned. While he was in the room, serving the viscount, Elizabeth's mind was racing. The last time she and Lord Stanton had been together he had proposed to her, and in the months since then she had passed through a wide array of emotions: her realization that she would never be complete without him; her terrible concern when he and her brothers had gone with the army; the shattering news of Jonathan's death, followed by days and nights of tortured waiting for some word of Richard and Stanton, praying constantly for their safety, fearing them dead; Richard's safe return home, and news that the viscount was alive; and finally, the discovery of Henry Ferris's treason. She knew it must have been devastating for Stanton, and she wondered how he was coping with it. She wanted to say something now, but no words would come, and as the footman left the room, she heard herself ask, "What brings you to Sherwood Manor, my lord?"

"You . . . and Richard, and Jonathan's wife. I wanted to tell you all how sorry I am about Jonathan. I wanted to come sooner . . . but I couldn't. I called on your parents yesterday and found Charles there. I have rarely seen two people happier than he and your sister seem to be. I am pleased that things worked out the way they did, for Charles is the perfect man for Charlotte, and he will make her happy, as she deserves to be."

"And she will make him happy as well, my lord."

"Yes. I am sure she will. How is Jonathan's wife handling his loss?"

"As well as can be expected. None of us will ever stop missing him, but we are learning to accept that he is gone. He was buried on the battlefield, you know, as were thousands of others, but Papa has put up a memorial stone, and we pretend that he is here with us. Harriet has been very brave, and in about two weeks her baby is due. I think it will be a great comfort for her to have Jon's child."

At that moment Richard and Sarah returned home, and the tête-à-tête between Elizabeth and Lord Stanton came to an end as greetings were exchanged. The viscount took Sarah's hand briefly in his and then grasped Richard's warmly.

"Charles said you had a nasty leg wound, but I see no evidence of it now."

"No, none at all," Richard responded. "Not even a limp. It healed beautifully. How did you come? In your curricle? Will you stay?"

"Yes. I drove myself. And, yes, if you will have me, I would like to stay, overnight at least. I was hoping to have your permission to ride with Elizabeth this afternoon, and I was also hoping that you could lend me a horse."

Elizabeth looked startled at the suggestion, and Richard gazed at her inquiringly. "Well, Lizzie?"

"Yes, of course, my lord. . . . I should be happy to ride with you if you wish it."

"Then have John saddle Sultry for Lord Stanton, Lizzie, for I shan't need her today."

Elizabeth nodded to her brother and turned to the viscount. "I will go and change and shall be down directly." She hurried to her room to don her riding habit. She wasn't sure she was doing the wise thing, but the opportunity to be alone with him was too tempting to be denied.

Elizabeth had told no one about the offer of marriage she received shortly before Stanton left for Belgium. She had very few secrets from either Sarah or Richard, but that offer was one of them. Lord Stanton desired her physically and had admitted as much. He had made his proposal based upon that desire. It had been painful for her to receive such an offer from a man she loved with her whole heart, and that pain was too intimate, too humiliating to share with anyone.

When Elizabeth returned to the parlor and Lord Stanton rose to join her, she caught Sarah's eye across the room and suddenly remembered Sarah's words on the day they had learned that Stanton was safe. "When you see Lord Stanton again, you should tell him how you feel." Elizabeth wasn't sure that Sarah was right—wasn't sure she could make such an admission even if she wished to.

"Which way will you ride?" Richard asked.

"Over the Downs, I think," Stanton answered. "I am in a solitary mood."

Elizabeth turned to him in surprise. "Are you sure, then, that you want company, sir?"

"Yes, indeed," he promptly replied. "For either I shall include you in my mood or you shall shake me from it. In either case, I desire your company." He turned to Richard. "You won't worry if we are gone for some time?"

"No. I won't worry."

As Elizabeth and Stanton left the house and walked across to the stables, Richard moved to the window and watched them go. "He will refuse to take a groom along, and he will keep her out for hours," he said thoughtfully to his wife. "He's troubled. Anyone can see that."

"Troubled over what?"

"Over his feelings for Lizzie."

"Romantic feelings? Do you think he has any?" Sarah asked.

"I think he is attracted to her, yes."

"You have never said so before. What makes you think it?"

"You never knew this, Sarah, but on the night Julian rescued Lizzie from Granbrooke, he challenged Granbrooke to a duel. I had every intention of taking the same step myself, despite the promise I had made to Lizzie on the night of the ball. The man had gone too far—something had to be done about him. I was surprised by Julian's challenge, because it was not his place to defend my sister's honor, and I have never known him to provoke a fight. In fact, I have heard him speak out strongly against dueling. But I accepted his explanation that the provocation had been great, and I also believed that he was acting in my interest, thinking that the blow I received would make me a poor candidate for such deadly sport. I accompanied Julian and Hugh to the dueling ground on the appointed morning, but Granbrooke never appeared. Julian was furious, angrier than I have ever seen him, and his unusual behavior made me begin to question his involvement with Lizzie. His anger seemed disproportionate for a breach of honor, cowardly though it was. I had the impression that he was looking forward to shooting Granbrooke, and his anger stemmed from the lost opportunity. My suspicions were strengthened shortly after Lizzie and Julian were shot."

"Why then?"

"Lizzie's maid told me that Julian came to Lizzie's room in the middle of the night and stayed at the bedside for more than two hours watching her sleep."

"Perhaps it was a vigil," Sarah suggested. "She was very ill, and she had saved his life."

"It could have been that, of course, but I don't believe so, for she had already passed the crisis and was resting peacefully when he made his visit. He stayed with her for two hours at a time when he was still very ill himself and in considerable pain. Something drew him there at that time of night, and I don't think it was anxiety or even gratitude. I think it was something closer to curiosity. He was asking himself, as he had asked me earlier, why she had done it. Perhaps by being there, close to her, he thought he would find the answer.

"There was one more incident," he continued. "When we were in Leicestershire, the relationship between those two seemed strained to me. There was one day when Lizzie had walked to the village alone, and when it started to snow and she hadn't returned, Julian went to fetch her. They arrived home safely, but I could tell instantly that something had taken place between them, for you know how attuned I am to Lizzie. I don't think they had argued or even disagreed, but the air seemed charged between them. That day I began to suspect that Lizzie cared for him. He left suddenly soon after that, on the slimmest pretext. My conviction grew steadily from that day—a conviction that there was strong attraction on both sides."

"Why has he come today? Do you think he intends to make an offer?"

"I can't say. I know he has little use for marriage. I was astonished when he offered for Charlotte—it seemed out of character somehow. He seems to lack the confidence of a man ready to make a declaration. My guess is that he wishes to spend time with her to more carefully weigh his feelings and perhaps try to discover hers."

"I advised her to tell him of her love," Sarah said.

"Really?" he asked in surprise.

"I cannot see who is served by her keeping it to herself," Sarah answered defensively.

"Such a confession by her could destroy their friendship if he doesn't return her love."

"As it destroyed ours? You faced a situation similar to Elizabeth's, yet you did not withhold your feelings from me."

"No. I admitted my love for you, and I destroyed our friendship in the same moment. There were many times when I regretted my impulsiveness, Sarah, and wished to have my friend back again. I gambled on a chance to win all—and when I lost, I was left with nothing—no lover, no friend, and very little hope."

"But don't you see, Richard, Lizzie is just like you. She doesn't want Lord Stanton as her friend, she wants more, as you did. And for my part, I hope she goes after it, and I wish her luck. Lord Stanton will be giving your father ample ammunition to force a declaration from him," Sarah suggested. "Riding unchaperoned for hours over deserted commons is a great deal more compromising than a brief kiss in the library."

Richard turned to his wife and took her into his arms, smiling down at her. "The tactics that my father employed on Charles would never serve with Julian. He is not the man to allow himself to be tricked, coerced, or threatened into any action. If ever he offers for Lizzie, it will be of his own volition, his own choice, freely made."

The horses were soon saddled, and Stanton himself put Elizabeth up. He moved to Sultry's side, and as he gathered the reins and prepared to mount, the mare turned her head round and gently nudged him. He smiled at her and reached to stroke her muzzle. "What's this? Disapproval?"

"Curiosity, I should think," Elizabeth said. "No one ever rides her but Richard. I am sure she is wondering who you are." Elizabeth was surprised when Stanton told the groom they would not need him, but she said nothing, and they rode off in silence, neither of them speaking until the road had diminished to a cart track and the horses had begun to pick their way up the steep ridge of the Downs.

It was a cool, sunny day with only a light breeze, a beautiful day for riding. They rode side by side, their legs occasionally touching, and finally the silence became too much for

Elizabeth, and she spoke suddenly. "My lord, there is something I wish to say to you, but I cannot think how to begin."

"Something concerning Henry?"

"Yes," she said gratefully, for now that he had spoken his brother's name, it seemed somehow easier to continue. "I was concerned—we all were—when Sir Hugh told us about your brother. We were so shocked; Richard was incredulous; and we realized how hard it must have been for you. I wish you had come to us then. Perhaps we might have helped."

He smiled at her tenderly. "Perhaps so, but I think it was best that Giles and I dealt with it ourselves. Strangely enough, I didn't have that much difficulty accepting Henry's French ties. What I found so hard to overcome was my own blindness and insensitivity where he was concerned. Here was a man, my own brother, whom I thought I knew better than any other person on this earth, and I found that I didn't know him well enough to understand those things that were most important in his life. When we were young, we were very close. My father was a wastrel. He made my mother's life miserable, and the less we saw of him, the happier we were. Giles was much younger, but Henry and I were inseparable as boys—and even as young men. We knew each other so well that I sometimes felt we were thinking with the same mind. But now as I look back, I can see that things changed for us when my father died and my mother returned to France. We grew apart, even though I told myself that we were as close as ever. We had become men, and we each chose the life that was right for us. Henry chose the side of our mother's blood. We have both lost brothers, Elizabeth. I wish that I could have lost mine honorably, as you did."

"But surely you must know that no one attaches any blame to you for Henry's activities," Elizabeth said. "Papa told us that both the Prince Regent and the Duke spoke to you personally. Surely that reassured you!"

"Believe me, Elizabeth, having them speak so only made matters worse."

"But why? If they said that your loyalty was not in question—"

"Elizabeth, you don't understand! I let Henry get away! When everyone was looking for him, I guessed where he had gone, as did Giles. We found him, and I let him go. I didn't help him, but I didn't hinder his leaving the country."

"And you think that was wrong?"

"Wrong? It was treasonous!"

"But what could you have done instead? Shoot him?"

"Yes! That is exactly what the Prince or Wellington would have expected me to do!"

"But, Julian," she said, forgetting in her anxiety to use his title, and addressing him as she had thought of him all these months. "We are speaking of your *brother*! Certainly when such horrible decisions must be made, love must be the first rule to govern us."

"As it was when you purposely intercepted a bullet meant for me?"

"Yes," she answered without hesitation. "As it was then."

He pulled Sultry to a standstill, and she did the same as he continued, "Had you no thought for your own safety?"

"No. I thought only of protecting you and didn't count the cost to myself."

"There is a name for that kind of selfless giving, Elizabeth."

"Yes," she agreed. "Sarah says I must have loved you even then, although I didn't realize it at the time." She kicked her horse into a walk again, unable to bear his steady regard.

"Oh, Elizabeth," he said, and the words were almost a groan. "Everything is so simple for you. You can say you love or hate a person as easily as you discuss the weather. Everything for you is either right or wrong, black or white. To me the world seems always gray, and saying 'I love you' is harder for me than leading a cavalry charge against impossible odds."

"You loved your brother a great deal, didn't you?" she asked simply.

"Yes. I love both my brothers, although I daresay I have never said as much to either of them. And now, for Henry at least, it's too late."

"No. It's not too late. Surely he knows why you let him go. Only love between brothers could have seen you through the difficult moment that must have been."

"Giles said, 'We are brothers, and we love one another. Does that not count for anything?' And I thought to myself, It should. It should count for everything."

They rode on for several minutes in silence, and finally

Stanton continued, his voice low and unsteady. "Elizabeth, the last time we met, the day I asked you to marry me, I know it must have hurt you to think I didn't care for you, and although it can't change anything between us, I think that the truth can't be any more painful than the lies. I love you, Elizabeth, and I have for a very long time." He turned to look at her, but she seemed unwilling to return his regard and kept her eyes firmly fixed on the meandering path ahead as he continued. "I suspected your feelings for me after the shooting incident." A sad smile crossed his face. "I wasn't sure until today. I have tried to keep my feelings in check because I have nothing to offer that you could ever be content with. I tried to explain to you once before how different we are. That hasn't changed. We want different things from life. I cannot make the kind of commitment you want, because I know that in the end I would fail you and make you unhappy."

"I cannot believe that you really love me," Elizabeth said quietly in a dazed voice. "I have prayed that it would happen, but I never believed it would."

"Oh, you can believe it!" he said. He pulled both horses up suddenly, reaching to take her chin in his hand and forcing her to look at him. "I love you madly, passionately . . . I lie in bed at night and torture myself wondering what it would be like to hold you . . . touch you. I would like nothing better than to keep you to myself and protect you from the world. But it would never work, Elizabeth! I know you so well! You would always stand by me. Constancy is part of your nature. But it is not part of mine, and wishing will not make it so. If I could be sure that I would always feel the same . . . but I cannot be sure, and I will not risk hurting you."

"But you are hurting me now!"

"Yes. I know, and I'm sorry. But you are young, and if you stay free of me, in time you will forget."

"I don't want to forget!" Elizabeth returned passionately. "You ask for too much, my lord. None of us is ever guaranteed happiness. Think of Jonathan and Harriet! But certainly we will never be happy if we never *try*! You may not win every battle, but you cannot make me believe that you ever led your men expecting to lose. You make plans to win—and sometimes you do!"

"Yes. And sometimes you lose," he replied dampingly. "And always the cost is dear."

"I would rather have whatever time you are willing to give me," she insisted, "than none at all. If it is marriage you fear so much, then take me as your mistress. Then, when you tire of me, as you seem so certain you will, there need be no bonds to tie us."

"This is no time for jest, Elizabeth."

"I am not jesting. I care not for my reputation. I don't think it likely that I will ever love any man but you, so why shouldn't I be with you while you want me? Then I will be able to say that at least once in my life I knew what it was to be loved."

"I will pretend you didn't say that, Elizabeth," he said wrathfully, "because I am convinced that you are too innocent to fully realize what you say. I wish never to hear you repeat such a sentiment again. You will never be my mistress, nor any man's. Do you understand?"

Elizabeth had expected him to be flattered by her offer, not angered, and she looked away in confusion, only nodding her head in answer to his question. Several minutes passed before she spoke again. "I think I understand the difference between the kinds of love we feel. My love for you seeks to remove the obstacles and find solutions. Your love for me views every stone in the path as a boulder, and you fear real problems and imagined ones as well. You lack faith in us," she said sadly, "and faith, like love, cannot be taught. It is something that must be experienced, and shared."

He gazed at her wonderingly. "How can you see so much so clearly at your age?"

"I have always understood love," she said. "I cannot remember a time in my life when I didn't feel completely loved and secure."

"I envy you that."

"You may say you envy me, but you don't want the same thing for yourself," she pointed out. "Otherwise you would not hesitate to take the love I am offering you—which is all, and everything, I have to give."

They rode on in silence for some time, each of them realizing that the conversation had come to its inevitable conclusion. There was no more to say. There was no solution, no future. Finally Elizabeth spoke again. "Would you tell me about your life when you were young, and about your relationship with Henry during those years?"

"Yes, if you like. And later, you can tell me what it was like to grow up in a seaport and what mischief you got into as a child."

She turned her head to smile at him and said saucily, "I was a perfect child."

He returned her smile. "Now, why do I doubt that?"

Lord Stanton and Elizabeth rode for more than four hours, and to Sarah, they seemed to return in much the same manner as they had departed—amiable but strained. It was impossible to tell what had passed between them but easy enough to see that they had not made any commitment to each other. If Elizabeth had found the courage to tell him she loved him, it clearly hadn't changed the gentleman's opinion about marriage, for there was no joy between these two, only resignation.

Dinner was a fairly pleasant meal if one didn't take into account the fact that Lord Stanton ate little, and Elizabeth ate nothing at all. Exercise generally improved her appetite, but apparently it had not been so today, for she simply pushed the food about on her plate, refusing to be tempted by any of it.

The post that day yielded a letter from Charlotte, and as Richard was best at deciphering her scrawl, he had agreed to read it after dinner. Taking the letter from a table in the parlor, he crossed to a chair near the fire and sat with his back to the blaze, allowing the light to fall over Charlotte's scribbled news. Elizabeth sank to the carpet near his knees, the soft folds of her pale blue muslin spreading about her on the floor. Charlotte's letters were always amusing, and Elizabeth looked up expectantly as Richard broke the seal and spread out the pages. Sarah knew that the Sherwood children had always gathered so about their mother's chair whenever there had been a letter from their father. Elizabeth's pose was perhaps too informal for company, but she was consistently uninhibited in the viscount's presence, treating him more like a member of the family than a guest.

Elizabeth presented a charming picture, Sarah thought, with the firelight shining softly upon her uplifted face. Sarah turned her gaze to Lord Stanton and saw that his eyes, too, were fixed on Elizabeth, but the look she saw on his face both startled and shocked her. Surely she saw great pain and longing in his eyes? He is as much in love with Lizzie as she is with him! she thought. Then why are they both so blue-deviled? And what is keeping them apart?

The remainder of the evening passed uneventfully, and after the tea tray had been removed, Sarah and Elizabeth rose to retire, Harriet having been encouraged to go much earlier. The viscount took Sarah's outstretched hand. "I will say good-bye now, Mrs. Sherwood, for I plan to leave very early in the morning. I must thank you for your hospitality toward an unannounced and uninvited guest."

"Nonsense, my lord. You know you are always welcome here. We are pleased to have our good friends call to see us."

Stanton turned to Elizabeth and took her cold hand in his warm one. "Will we have the pleasure of seeing you in town for any part of the Season, Miss Elizabeth?"

"I think not, my lord. I am determined to stay to help Harriet with the baby, and I find that London has little appeal for me. I much prefer the country."

Elizabeth was aware of her heart pounding painfully in her chest, but still the viscount held her hand as he spoke again. "Thank you for riding with me today. I enjoyed it a great deal." When she didn't answer, he said, "Good-bye, Elizabeth."

"Good-bye, my lord." His fingers tightened on her hand, and as she looked up to meet his eyes, he bent, and to her surprise, kissed her lightly on the cheek. It was a brotherly kind of caress, but it was so unexpected that it brought sudden tears to her eyes, and taking her hand from his, she turned and fled the room. Hurrying across the hall, she was already started up the stairs before Sarah could catch up with her.

"Lizzie, please wait." Elizabeth turned in obedience to the pressure of Sarah's hand on her arm, and Sarah was shocked to see tears pouring down the girl's face. "Lizzie, please, tell me what has happened."

"I can't, Sarah." Elizabeth sobbed. "Not now." She turned and fled up the stairway, while Sarah stared helplessly after her.

The following morning, Viscount Stanton left for London. For several days, Sarah could not bring herself to press

Elizabeth for an explanation of the ride she and his lordship had taken. But slowly, as the September days passed, Elizabeth began to confide in her, and little by little, Sarah came into possession of the facts. It was a weighty problem, for, like Elizabeth, she could see no clear way to overcome Lord Stanton's resolution.

Chapter 25

ON THE TWENTY-SECOND of September, Harriet Sherwood was delivered of a strong, seven-pound son. Her labor, although difficult, had been blessedly short, and both she and her son were prospering. Elizabeth and Sarah delighted in the new baby as much as did Harriet, and Richard made his wife blush one evening at dinner by saying that if she had such a liking for babies, he must see about giving her one of her own as soon as possible. Both Elizabeth and Lady Sherwood were present at the table, and Sarah was moved to expostulate, "My goodness, Richard, have you no delicacy?"

"What? Have I embarrassed you? But I assure you, my love, that Mama knows where babies come from, and so does Lizzie—I believe. *Do* you know where babies come from, Lizzie?"

"Yes, certainly I do, dear brother," Elizabeth answered promptly. "And I have not the slightest objection to another niece or nephew. I think it would be splendid!"

Sarah's eyes met Lady Sherwood's resignedly, but her ladyship only said, "It is as I have always said, Sarah. There is no way I will ever be able to moderate Elizabeth's behavior so long as her brother encourages her thus. But so it has always been," she said in mock dismay. "No one pays the least heed to me. They will all go their own way." She rose from the table, and Elizabeth immediately leaped to her feet.

"I am off to the nursery to help with Jonathan Edward," she said.

"Honestly, Lizzie," her mother objected, "the child is only three days old. He sleeps most of the time!"

"I know. But I like to watch him sleep. And I promised to read to Harriet. We are in the middle of a romantic novel. The villain is about to get his just deserts." As she left the room, Sarah turned to her mother-in-law.

"She seems somewhat improved these last several days," Sarah said, "but her mood underneath remains the same. Richard and I have discussed it, and if you have no objection, I would like to accompany you to town at the end of the week. I have taken a leaf from your book, ma'am. I think it is time one of us approached Lord Stanton, and I think it should be me. Matters can become no worse, and perhaps I will be able to help, because I think that better than anyone else, I can understand his pain."

On the last day of September, Lady Sherwood and Mrs. Sherwood arrived in London. Sarah immediately had a message carried to Lord Stanton's house in Park Lane, informing his lordship that she would appreciate the opportunity to speak with him at his earliest convenience. She went on to say that she would be at home that evening, and the following morning as well, should he find an opportunity to call.

This communication from Mrs. Sherwood was conveyed to the viscount while he was dressing for dinner, and it puzzled him. He hadn't known that she was in town and thought it strange that she should write to him requesting an interview. When he had finished dressing, he sent a footman round to Sir Hugh Broughton's rooms in Ryder Street, begging to be excused from his engagement for the evening. He then set off to pay a call on Mrs. Sherwood in Mount Street.

Lord Stanton was shown into the salon, where Lord and Lady Sherwood greeted him warmly. He then took Sarah's outstretched hand. "You wished to see me, ma'am?"

"Yes, my lord. I would like to thank you for calling so promptly."

"I believe my daughter-in-law wishes to speak with you privately, Stanton," Lord Sherwood said easily. "So, if you will excuse us, my wife and I will leave you."

Lady Sherwood rose as he spoke, and they quit the room

together. As the door closed behind them, Sarah said, "I am sure you must be wondering why I have asked you here, my lord. Please, won't you sit here by the fire? Will you have some brandy? Richard and I always enjoy it at this time of night."

"Yes. Thank you," he said, reaching automatically to take the glass she offered him. "Richard did not come up to town with you, Mrs. Sherwood?"

"No, my lord. He did not come, and I have not come to stay. I came only to see you, and I may leave again as early as tomorrow. . . . Lord Stanton, there is something I wish to tell you, and although it may seem strange to you at first, I beg that you will bear with me, for in the end it will all become clear to you, I believe."

He regarded her with polite interest as she continued. "Unlike you, my lord, I was not born to wealth and position. My parents were simple country gentry, my father the son of a village rector. I was an only child, and from the moment my parents decided that I would be handsome, they thought of little else besides selling me for a title. When I was barely seventeen, they discovered Sir Winston's son, my first husband, James. It was not the peerage my parents sought, but when Sir Winston died, I would be a lady at least, and they decided to settle for that. I was not consulted in the matter of my marriage. My husband, like my father, was . . . a worthless man, and Sir Winston is little better. I had no use for men, any men, until I met Richard Sherwood.

"From the very beginning I found myself drawn to him, for I saw something in him, and later, in his family, that I did not know existed. When I was with him, or with them, I felt as if I were standing outside a window in the cold, looking in on them, seeing their warmth and their love, and feeling as if they were part of another world—a world in which I would never belong. I wanted desperately to pass through that window, and yet, I was afraid that once inside, I would discover that it had all been a mirage, and I would find the same desolation and humiliation that I had known in my childhood and my marriage.

"Nevertheless, I was drawn against my will to Richard, each day needing him more, each day missing him more, each day wondering just a little more if perhaps life had something to offer that I had missed. And then, when my wanting him became a pain equal to the pain of my memories, I said I would marry him. I was terrified of giving myself to him. I felt as if I were standing on the edge of a deep pool, unable to swim, knowing that if I jumped in, I would surely drown. And yet, there was Richard, asking me to jump, telling me to trust him to keep me safe. And finally, I did decide to trust him, and I found the courage to go to him. Partly, I suppose, it was because of my son Jimmy, who loved this man with such intensity, and who encouraged, nay, begged me, to allow myself to love him, too. And partly it was my need, which had become an ache nearly impossible to bear. But most of all it was my response to Richard's need, which he had never hidden from me. I found it impossible to live with the pain my rejection was causing him.

"But now I come to the end of my story, my lord. I jumped into that pond, and the feeling was exactly as I had imagined. The water was cold and terrifying, and it closed over my head. But when I rose to the surface, I discovered I could swim! I needed help. I needed guidance and teaching—but I *could* swim. I saw the love in that family, and I took a chance that Richard would be able to show me the way to find it, and he has. I'm not saying that it will always be perfect. I know there will be troubles, but I'm not afraid to face them, because my love has kindled a strength in me that I never knew I possessed.

"The last time we were together, I saw the way you looked at Elizabeth. I saw the combination of pain and longing in your eyes and recognized it. I can't be certain how you feel about Elizabeth, but I think you love her a great deal. She has told me that she is in love with you, and that she has told you so—so there can be no misunderstanding on that score. I think perhaps you are afraid of your love, afraid that the feelings you have, the images you behold, will vanish if you reach out to take them. I, too, felt that way. The very day of my wedding I felt as if I was moving in a dream; that the fates were playing a cruel trick on me; that Richard was no different from any other man; that my love had made me blind; that I was seeing an illusion, an image of what I wanted my lover to be. Imagine my shock on my wedding night, when my husband came to me the same tender and gentle man I had married— not changed beyond recognition into the embodiment of my fears. My commitment had not endangered me, it had set me free."

Sarah paused, but Stanton did not speak. He was staring now into the fire. Finally she continued. "I think that we are not offered love so often in our lives, my lord, that we can allow ourselves the privilege of snapping our fingers at it. Elizabeth is young, but she knows her heart, and she has given it to you." He looked up at her then, but she continued without pause. "Hers is not a volatile nature, and her feelings will not easily be swayed. If you continue to reject her, she will continue to suffer. For now, she is devoting all her energies to Harriet and the new baby, and Harriet needs her support, so she feels somewhat fulfilled. But the days will come when Harriet needs her less and less. Jonathan's loss in time will fade, for Harriet has no hope and knows that he will never come back to her. The pain will lessen, the sorrow become easier to bear. Lizzie will not be so fortunate. For her, the hope, and therefore the pain, will live on, and she will never give up hope, my lord, so long as you are free.

"I truly think that in the end you must go to her. I think that, like me, you will find yourself drawn against your will. But I also think that because you are much stronger than I, you will fight your inclinations longer than I did, and you will both suffer unnecessarily as a result. Does this make sense to you, my lord? You say nothing, yet I feel I have come close to the truth."

"I feel as if you have crawled into my head, Mrs. Sherwood. It is a queer feeling, I can tell you. You have correctly interpreted the look you saw, and you see my fears far clearer than I see them myself. Elizabeth said that a complete love requires faith, and you are telling me that a proper commitment requires courage. But I do not think I possess your courage, ma'am."

"I did not find the courage within myself, Lord Stanton. I found it in Richard—and you must seek it in Elizabeth."

Sarah returned to Surrey the following day but had nothing concrete to report to her husband. Lord Stanton had listened politely to all she had said but had given her no indication that he would change his mind about involving himself in Elizabeth's life. "I think perhaps he will reconsider his decision," she said, "but I cannot be sure. I don't think there is anything more we can do except give him time to come to terms with his fear and hope that in the end he will decide that he needs Lizzie enough to come to her."

But as the autumn days of October passed, and then the weeks, any hope that Sarah had held of having altered the viscount's resolve faded. Elizabeth did not mope about the house. She had too much pride to wear her heart upon her sleeve, and her youth and natural liveliness helped her to deal with her rejection. But beneath the surface, all could see the change in her. The perennial optimism that had been her trademark was often absent. She took long walks and rides alone, refusing to take a groom with her and sometimes worrying her family by not returning for hours. When Richard remonstrated with her, he did not meet with the spirited argument of the old days but with a meek apology and a promise to be more considerate in future. She objected vehemently to any suggestion that she go up to town for part of the Season, and she was adamant in refusing any and all invitations to various house parties.

The month of October was drawing to a close, and Charlotte and Charles's wedding was now less than seven weeks away. One afternoon while Richard sat in the study, going over some accounts, he looked up as the door opened and the butler announced, "Lord Stanton, Captain Sherwood."

Richard rose and moved forward to greet his guest. "Julian! What brings you to us this time? Or can I guess?"

"I have come to see Elizabeth, but I wish to speak with you first. You know, of course, that your wife came to see me nearly a month ago in town." Richard nodded, and Stanton continued. "Do you share her hope, Richard, that Elizabeth and I should marry?"

"Yes, Julian, I do."

"Not so very long ago you made it quite plain that you did not desire me as a brother-in-law."

"At that time, we were discussing your position as husband to Charlotte. Elizabeth is not Charlotte."

Stanton smiled ruefully. "No. Elizabeth is not Charlotte. Then you would not object to my asking for Elizabeth?"

"You don't need my permission, Julian."

"No. I know I don't. But I know that Elizabeth is your favorite, and it is important for me to know that you approve."

"I approve wholeheartedly, my friend," Richard assured him. "I have known for months that Lizzie's happiness lies only with you."

"Where is she?"

"She and the baby's nurse usually take him for an outing at this time of day. You will probably find them in the gardens behind the house."

One of the footmen showed the viscount the direction Elizabeth and Nurse had taken, and he was not long in finding them. As he came round the end of a tall hedge, he saw them seated on a rustic stone bench, the baby on Elizabeth's lap.

Both women glanced up as they noticed someone approaching, and Elizabeth's heart thumped uncomfortably when she recognized who it was. She rose to her feet as Stanton came closer, still holding the child in her arms. He stopped about ten feet away, and they stood staring at each other, neither of them willing to speak.

Finally Nurse broke the silence. "Shall I take the babe back to the house for you, Miss Elizabeth? He will be hungry soon, I think."

Elizabeth dragged her eyes away from the viscount and forced herself to attend to Nurse. "Yes, of course you may have him." She handed the child to the older woman, tucking the shawl closely around his tiny face as he settled into Nurse's arms. Nurse walked quietly away, and Elizabeth turned back to Stanton.

Slowly he covered the space between them, and she held out her hand instinctively. It was her right hand, ungloved, and as he took it in his, her diamond ring caught the afternoon sun and brought a rush of memory. It seemed years ago that he had taken it from her injured hand the night Granbrooke abducted her from Vauxhall. And then he had returned it the night she saved his life. He continued to regard the ring steadily until Elizabeth startled him by saying, "I have not taken it off, not since the night you put it there."

His hand tightened painfully on hers, and he drew her roughly into his arms, bringing his lips down on hers in a kiss that was hot and hungry and demanding. And then, suddenly, he released her mouth and crushed her against him in an urgent embrace. His breath was quick and rasping, and she could feel his body tremble against hers. His fingers were gripping her so tightly that she knew she would be bruised by them, but she didn't care, and she clung to him, allowing the wonderful intimacy of the closeness of their bodies to wash over her. For so many months she had felt desolate and alone. She had yearned to have him hold her, dreamed of having him want her, and now, in his arms, she knew she had come home.

Long minutes passed as he held her close. Slowly his breathing evened, and finally he loosed his hold and put her a little from him. She looked up to meet his eyes shyly. "You have not come into the country for solitude this time, I think, my lord."

"Certainly not! I have come for companionship. Will you give it to me?"

"Gladly."

He took her face in his hands and allowed himself the pleasure of running his fingertips over the softness of cheek and chin. Then, very slowly, he bent his head and kissed her again. This kiss was as different from the last as midnight was from noon. It was infinitely soft and sensual—a brush, a touch, a whisper—a lingering, languishing caress, a kiss so intimate that Elizabeth was breathless and blushing when he finally held her away. He drew her to the stone bench and down onto it beside him, holding her hands firmly in his.

"I once made you an offer of marriage, Elizabeth, and I couched it in such terms as to make it totally unacceptable to you. I intend today to make you another, and I hope to do better this time. First I will tell you that I love you—more than I thought it possible to love any person or anything in this life. I told you once before that I wanted you, and that also is true, even more so now than it was then. But there are several other things that I want as well."

"What is it that you want, my lord?"

"I want you to be the first thing I see each day when I open my eyes and the last thing I see each night before I close them. I want you to teach me the secret of making love grow each day. I want the chance to prove to you that I am the kind of man who can love one woman truly and honestly all his life, and I want you to give me a reason to prove it to myself as well. And most of all . . . I would like to see you hold a child of mine in your arms."

"I want all those things, too," she whispered, her eyes suddenly filling with tears.

"Elizabeth, will you be my wife?"

"Yes."

"When?"

"Whenever you like."

"As soon as possible?"

"Yes. As soon as possible."

He took her once again in his arms and held her close, and for the second time in his life felt the threat of tears. But this time he made no attempt to stop them, for he no longer feared them. All the faith, all the love, all the courage that he needed in his life was in his arms at that moment—all that he would ever need to make himself complete.

At Daggers
Drawn

"We never meet together but we be at daggers drawing."
—John Palsgrave, *Acolastus*. Fo. 1. (1540)

Chapter 1

IN THE VILLAGE of Paxton in northern Hertfordshire, a cluster of somberly clad mourners stood in the churchyard near a newly dug grave. Their heads were bowed in prayer, their backs turned against a sharp northerly wind and a misty November rain. The Reverend Swinton had left his prayer book behind today in deference to the weather and now recited the burial service from memory.

When the rector had finished, the family of the late Baron John Hargrave turned away and filed through a narrow gate in the cemetery fence. Several of them spoke quietly to the rector and then, since there was no carriage waiting, moved off down the lane toward their home, nearly a mile distant.

Stephen Hargrave, now Lord Hargrave at the age of nineteen, silently offered his mother his arm as he raised a shabby umbrella to shield her from the weather. Close behind this pair followed the late baron's three other children—his younger son Miles, and his two daughters, Caroline and Patience.

The Hargraves' home lay north of the village and they were forced to walk into the wind, the rain steadily increasing as they progressed. They walked briskly, warmed by the exercise and anticipating a dry, if not particularly warm, home awaiting them. Arriving at Paxton Hall, they hurried inside and stood dripping onto the stone floor of the entry hall as they relieved one another of sodden cloaks.

Lady Hargrave was a fair, handsome woman in her early forties. Her children closely resembled her, all four being blue-eyed and fair. Patience had brilliant golden hair, while Caroline's was lighter, tending toward flaxen when exposed to the sun. The boys were blond, too, but of a darker shade. Both were tall and slender, each blessed with a pleasant countenance.

"Where can Wilcox be?" Stephen wondered, his arms full of wet clothing.

His question was answered immediately as an old man in an outmoded butler's uniform shuffled forward. "Here I am, Master Stephen—I should say, your lordship." He took the wet things young Lord Hargrave held. "His lordship's man of business is in the library, sir. He arrived while you were at the church and said he would be content to wait. I gave him some tea, my lady," he added.

"That was thoughtful of you, Wilcox. Did he say which of us he wished to see?"

"All of you, my lady, for he has brought the will."

"I see. Thank you, Wilcox. If you could see to tea now for the rest of us, that would be lovely."

As the butler departed, Lady Hargrave considered her children. Caroline, at twenty-three, and Stephen, as her late husband's heir, must hear the will. At sixteen, Miles should no doubt be present as well, but she hesitated over thirteen-year-old Patience.

Caroline took the decision from her mother's hands as she addressed her younger sister. "Lawyers are prosy and boring, Pay. How fortunate for you that you need not join us. Be a dear and run to my room to let Leo out. He has been locked in all afternoon." A bright smile lit Patience's face at the opportunity to play with Caroline's King Charles spaniel. No longer quite a puppy, he still loved to frolic, especially after a period of confinement.

As Patience hurried up the stairs, Caroline moved toward the library. "Must we hear the will? We know that Papa's passion for the gaming tables has left us little but our pride. Must we have the details read to us?"

"I would know the worst," Stephen said.

"In the letter I received yesterday," Lady Hargrave offered, "Mr. Birmingham said there is no debt."

"No debt, but little income either," Caroline added. At her mother's frown she said quickly, "It is not for myself that I care, Mama, but for Stephen. It isn't fair he should inherit this great house and all these acres with small hope of caring for them. The tenant farms yield less each year. Without adequate money to restore the estate it is only a matter of time before we will be forced to take desperate action. You cannot close your eyes to it any longer!"

"Caro is right, Mama," Stephen added. "You know yourself that without your income we would have gone hungry long ago. Yesterday I rode round to most of the tenants. The farms have been so neglected it will take years to set them right; I find it difficult to demand rent from people who are living in poverty and struggling to survive."

"We must join Mr. Birmingham," her ladyship said. "We have kept him waiting long enough."

The reading of the will was all they expected—the heavily mortgaged house and land descending to Stephen by law. There was a small jointure for Lady Hargrave; Caroline and Patience would each have four hundred a year. There were no other bequests—nothing left to servants.

Stephen, who had spoken several times during the early part of the reading, now grew silent. He had hoped his father had provided adequate dowries for his sisters, but as Mr. Birmingham drew to the final paragraphs of the document, he realized those hopes were in vain. He was both shocked and ashamed. He raised startled eyes to the solicitor as he realized he was being addressed.

"As you can see, my lord, there is no capital. I thought if perhaps you sold some of the land . . . Lord Devereux has always fancied the woodland west of the stream. I believe he would pay handsomely for it. The piece produces little income, so would not materially lessen—"

"No," Stephen said quietly. "Five generations of Hargraves have held this land intact. I will not be the one to give it up."

"Respectfully, sir, your father has left you little choice. According to my records, some of the servants' wages haven't been paid for more than two months. Those who stay do so out of loyalty or because they have nowhere else to go. There is not enough cash for the spring planting—"

"I know all this, sir, but I will not sell any land. There must be another way." Stephen shifted uncomfortably in his chair, abruptly changing the subject. "Have you finished with the reading, Mr. Birmingham?"

"Very nearly, my lord. There is one addendum to the will, added quite recently. It concerns guardianship."

"Guardianship?"

"Yes, my lord. When your father realized the severity of his illness, he named Phillip Percival Brooke as trustee and guardian to you, your brother, and younger sister."

"What of my income, Mr. Birmingham?" Caroline asked.

"Your income and that of Miss Patience will be held in trust until you each attain the age of twenty-five, Miss Hargrave. You would, of course, be free of the trust before that time should you marry, provided Lord Brooke approves the match."

"And if he disapproves?"

"In that event the trust would continue until your twenty-fifth birthday."

"Twenty-five! Surely that is excessive?" Caroline objected.

"You may feel so, Miss Hargrave, but it was, nonetheless, your late father's wish and is legally binding."

Caroline subsided as young Miles spoke for the first time. "Who is Lord Brooke?"

"I am not acquainted with the gentleman," the solicitor answered. "Perhaps Lady Hargrave could inform us?"

"I am afraid I do not know him either," Lady Hargrave responded. "In fact, I can't remember my husband ever mentioning anyone by the name of Brooke."

"How peculiar," Stephen remarked.

Miles, who practically lived in the library and knew each book residing there, removed a copy of the *Peerage* from the shelf.

"Brooke," he said. "There is no Phillip Brooke, but there is a Baron Percival Randolph Reginald Brooke, born 1739, married 1775 to Martha Westbury Rivington, third daughter of the Duke of Cumberland. Principal residence, Southwell House, Southwell, Nottinghamshire. There were two children—Helen Francine, born December 2, 1777, and Phillip Percival Randolf, born June 5, 1782. There is no more, but this is an old publication, older than I, surely."

"That doesn't tell us much," Caroline added. "Only that *our trustee* will be thirty-five next year. We can assume his father is dead since he is now Lord Brooke. Have you written to him, Mr. Birmingham, to apprise him of my father's death?"

"I have indeed done so, Miss Hargrave, and hope to hear from him by return post."

* * *

Phillip Brooke sat at a large mahogany desk in the well-appointed estate office of Southwell House. Seated at his right hand was his personal secretary, Matthew Keating; standing nearby was his estate agent, John Crawford.

Lord Brooke addressed his agent in a pleasant baritone. "That will be all, Crawford. I am leaving for Lincolnshire tomorrow as planned. I will keep you informed concerning the things we discussed."

"Very good, my lord."

When Crawford had gone, Lord Brooke turned his attention to his secretary. Youngest of six boys and a distant cousin by marriage, Matthew Keating had applied to Brooke for employment immediately after taking a degree at Cambridge. With no particular affinity for the church and even less for the army, he had convinced Lord Brooke that he could be a useful member of his household. Now, after seven years of depending upon Matthew's quiet efficiency, Brooke couldn't imagine how he had ever managed without him.

"If we are finished, Matthew, I think I shall have a bath before dinner," his lordship remarked.

"There was one thing more, sir. The letter I mentioned from Hertford, from Lord Hargrave's man of business." Matthew watched as his employer's handsome face settled into a frown.

"I told you to deal with it, Matthew. I am certain you will handle whatever it is admirably."

"I read the letter, my lord, as you asked, but it is a matter you must attend to personally. I have it here. It's brief." He placed the letter into Brooke's outstretched hand, then watched to see what sort of response it would bring.

Brooke leaned back in his chair, his dark hair catching the rays of the late afternoon sun streaming through the high windows. After reading only a few lines, he rose impatiently and began to pace the room, his booted feet drumming against the highly polished floorboards. His fine eyes darkened as his brows drew together in disbelief. That expression quickly gave way to one of consternation, and when the gray eyes were turned to his, Matthew thought he recognized anger in them as well.

"What foolishness is this?" Brooke demanded. "How can I be appointed trustee to the children of a man I haven't seen in nearly eight years?"

"How did you know Lord Hargrave, sir?"

"He was my commanding officer in Spain. I saved his life once. I went back for him when his horse went down. Had to go through a couple of fellows to get to him and then took him up with me as we retreated. What does this lawyer say?" he asked, referring to the letter in his hand, " '. . . his lordship has entrusted you with the guardianship of his children . . .' If I had wanted children, Matthew . . ." He broke off suddenly, then quoted from the letter again. " '. . . Lord Hargrave is just nineteen and Lady Hargrave would welcome your support.' If these children have a mother, what need have they of me?" Crumpling the paper into a ball, he tossed it onto the desk.

"No, really, my lord," Matthew objected, reaching for the ill-treated letter. "You cannot do that! It is a binding obligation, however much you may dislike it."

"It is not binding! Not morally, at least, for I feel no obligation to Hargrave, alive or dead. The obligation was on his side, Matthew! I saved *his* life, not he mine."

"I daresay he respected you a great deal, my lord. Enough to entrust you with the well-being of his family, which, after all, is a man's most prized possession. You should be honored, not vexed."

"Well, I am not honored. Damn, Matthew! I am expected at Belvoir tomorrow!"

Matthew maintained a prudent silence as his employer crossed to his desk and reseated himself. When he extended an imperative hand, Matthew placed the crumpled letter into it. Brooke spread the single sheet upon the desk, mechanically smoothing out the creases but not attempting to reread it. He sat for several moments in brooding silence, then sighed and raised his eyes to his waiting secretary.

"Very well, Matthew; you must write to this lawyer, what's his name—no, better yet, order my chaise-and-four for six o'clock tomorrow morning. I will be in Hertford before any letter could hope to be." He rose and came around the desk, the letter and Mr. Birmingham's direction in his hand. "Unpleasant duties are best not delayed, Matthew. Don't you agree?"

"Absolutely, sir."

"Please write to His Grace of Rutland for me, Matthew. Advise him that I shall be a few days late to his shooting party as I am called away by business."

The clerk seated in the front office of Birmingham, Birmingham, and Smithe, Hertford, glanced up with casual interest as the street door opened, then came instinctively to his feet as he recognized a member of the Quality. On the threshold stood a very tall gentleman in buckskins and top boots. A drab multicaped driving coat swung from broad shoulders as he covered the space between door and desk in two long strides.

"I am Lord Brooke. I have no appointment but should like to speak with Mr. Jasper Birmingham."

"If you would be pleased to wait one moment, my lord, I will tell Mr. Birmingham you are here."

The young man hurried up a flight of stairs while Brooke turned toward the window. His carriage waiting in the street outside was drawing no small amount of attention. Children gathered to gape at the four splendid bay horses and at the coachman and footmen attired in handsome blue and gray livery.

Brooke heard muffled voices from the floor above, then feet descending the stairs. A slight, middle-aged man with balding head and graying sidewhiskers extended a hand, which Brooke took briefly.

"Lord Brooke!" the man exclaimed. "How do you do? I am Jasper Birmingham. I did not expect you. I had planned to attend you in Nottinghamshire, at your convenience."

"So your letter said. As it happens, it was more convenient for me to come to you."

"I see," the lawyer returned. "Would you care to step upstairs to my office?"

He stepped aside to allow Brooke to precede him up the narrow stairway. When the door was closed and they were both seated, Brooke stated bluntly, "I think you should know, Mr. Birmingham, that this trusteeship comes as a complete surprise to me."

The solicitor nodded knowingly. "I thought that perhaps might be the case when the family said they were unacquainted with you. Did you know Lord Hargrave well?"

"I knew him, I suppose, as well as comrades in arms ever

know one another. I was attached to his command for nearly eighteen months. If he ever spoke of his family, I don't recall it."

"He did not write to you recently?"

"How recently?"

"Within the last week or so."

"No. Unless he wrote me in London. I have been in the country since mid-November."

"He intended to write you," Birmingham said. "He told me so. You see, the will in which he named you was a recent document, executed barely a week before his death."

"Did he give you any reason for choosing me as trustee?"

"He did not confide in me, sir. I cannot say what his motives might have been. I had assumed you would know why he appointed you."

Brooke shook his head. He did not speak for some moments, and Birmingham remained silent as well. His handsome visitor looked troubled. No doubt, given time, he would share what was on his mind.

"I must say, Mr. Birmingham, that I find this situation highly irregular. I was no friend of Lord Hargrave, but an acquaintance only. I have never met any member of his family. Surely some male relative would be a more appropriate trustee than I."

"Perhaps, my lord, but as I understand it, Lord Hargrave had few close relatives, and it seems that over the years he alienated most of them. Is it your desire to relinquish the trust, my lord, or perhaps assign it to another?"

"I had considered that, yes. But as I drove down, I decided that since I have come, it could do no harm for me to at least see what the estate entails."

Mr. Birmingham began by displaying a succession of maps showing the boundaries of the estate, the timberland, the tillable acreage, the availability of water, the number and location of tenant farms. Nearly an hour later, he placed before Lord Brooke a balance sheet revealing the sad state of the Hargrave finances.

Brooke inspected the paper in growing disbelief, then searched for another sheet, and for some time compared the two. Finally he spoke. "It is nearly impossible to credit these figures when compared to those of ten years ago. What could possibly explain such gross expenditure, such depletion of capital?"

"Gambling, my lord," Birmingham answered simply. "I knew Lord Hargrave most of his life. To my knowledge he never indulged in the pastime as a young man. But he once admitted to me that he acquired a liking for it while in the army. After he sold out, it became a ruling passion in his life."

"He isn't the first man to have fallen victim to the lure of the gaming tables."

"No, my lord. Nor the last. Yet in this case he was not the only victim. His family must continue to pay for his indiscretion."

"Were you in my place, Mr. Birmingham, how would you administer this estate?" Brooke asked.

"I would allow young Stephen—Lord Hargrave, that is—a free hand with the estate income. The situation is grave, but there should be enough for him to meet the mortgage payments and perhaps a bit left over to do the spring planting. He is a sensible young man, and I believe can be trusted entirely."

"Very well; so be it. I see here that Miss Patience is only thirteen. What of Miss Hargrave? She is to have four hundred a year. Should she have it?"

"That is for you to say, my lord."

"How do you believe she would employ it, were I to put it at her disposal?"

"I believe, sir, that she would use every penny to assist her brother in his difficulties."

"I see. Admirable perhaps, but inappropriate. Shall we give her say, fifty pounds per annum, for pin money and expenses?"

"I believe that would be adequate, Lord Brooke."

"Good. Enter it so, then. Is there anything else?"

"I need your signature on several documents, my lord. I believe most of our communication can be handled through the post."

"Very well," Brooke answered as he skimmed the pages the solicitor presented and scrawled his name across the bottom of each.

"If, after you have met the family, Lord Brooke, you should wish to alter any of these arrangements, you need only inform me. You are at a disadvantage working with only my advice."

"Nonsense. You are a great deal more familiar with the Hargrave affairs than I, and therefore infinitely more qualified to offer an opinion. But I regret that it will be impossible for me to meet the Hargraves at present. I am expected at Belvoir Castle; I cannot tarry in Hertford.

During the early part of March it rained in Paxton almost continuously for six days. When the rain finally ceased, Caroline was frantic to escape the house. She and Patience walked to the village to call at the rectory, where Isabella Swinton, the rector's daughter, invited them for tea. When Patience went off to play with the new kittens in the stable loft, the two older girls sat alone in the garden.

"Have you heard anything more from Lord Brooke?" Isabella asked.

"No. He corresponds with Mr. Birmingham. Stephen has heard nothing since the letter he received before Christmas—and that his lordship didn't write himself. It was signed by a secretary, Mr. Matthew Keating. Mama thinks it odd that Lord Brooke has never visited, but I can only be glad. It seems unnatural to have our affairs in the hands of a stranger."

"My father thinks it will benefit Stephen to have an older man to advise him," Isabella offered.

"I don't see how that may be. Stephen's problems cannot be solved without funds, and even Lord Brooke cannot find money where there is none." Caroline smoothed her rumpled black skirt, eyeing it with disfavor. "How I loathe black. Mama says in May we may go into half mourning, though I don't see how it can help matters much. I have less gray than black. We sorted through some things in the attic looking for fabric we might use and found some dresses we put away years ago, thinking them too shabby. They look almost new beside the things we are now wearing!"

"Stephen stopped for a few moments yesterday as he was passing through on his way to Hertford," Isabella said. "I suppose he had to sell your father's stallion?"

"I'm surprised we were able to keep him so long. He was one of our most valuable assets. Stephen plans some major renovations to the home farm with the money he got for Jupiter. He hopes that with a good harvest we can show a profit this year and perhaps improve some of the tenant farms next year."

"And the house?"

"The house must continue as it is. Any improvement would yield only comfort, and comfort is something we can ill afford. Patience and I are envisioning a wonderful garden this summer," she added. "If you come over tomorrow, we will show you our plan."

When the Hargrave sisters returned home, Patience went immediately to the house while Caroline paid a visit to the neglected stables. They seemed very quiet now that her father's spirited stallion had gone. She strolled down the long row of empty boxes, remembering better days when all the stalls had been filled with fine horses. Gradually, they had all been sold. Now there was just one draft team, one older gelding that Stephen rode, and Caroline's old riding mare Blossom, retired to pasture after many years of service. For a time the work team had been used to pull the carriage, but when the carriage had been badly damaged on a rough road, there had been no money for repairs and it had been sold. The draft horses were not in their stalls today, and Caroline remembered that Stephen had said he planned to pull stumps as soon as the rain ceased.

Caroline smiled as she thought of her determined brother. He was such a dedicated, honorable young man. What wonderful things he could have done with the Hall if only his father had left him something to work with. As it was, he struggled along with small sums, trying to make them do miracles. He staunchly refused his mother's money when she offered it, suggesting instead that it be used for basic necessities within the house. He had ordered an adequate supply of coal and wood laid in so they would not spend another winter shivering.

Stephen and Miles Hargrave had come down from school the previous year when their father had been unable to provide their tuition. The rector had offered to help them continue their studies and the extensive library at Paxton Hall provided most of the resources they needed. But Caroline knew that Stephen's first love was the land; since his father's death it was all he thought of.

Not so with Miles. Miles loved learning and she knew he

feared he might never have the opportunity to attend university. He worked steadfastly at Stephen's side, willingly joining in each project, but at every opportunity he would escape to his room or to the library to bury himself in his beloved books.

Being the oldest, Caroline was in the habit of watching over her brothers and sister. Of the three, she supposed she worried most about Patience. The boys would make it on their own somehow—they were talented and they were men. But what would become of Patience, she wondered, with only a small income and no prospect of ever leaving Paxton? Patience had a gentle soul, and she would be a beauty; but would these qualities ever be recognized? In their present circumstances, Caroline had her doubts.

Chapter 2

LORD BROOKE SPENT the hunting season in Leicestershire with friends, was in London for the opening of Parliament, and stayed through the Season. During the months that had passed since his meeting with Mr. Birmingham, Brooke seldom thought of the guardianship, until by chance he remembered that an acquaintance, Viscount Ashton, hailed from Hertfordshire. Brooke asked casually if Ashton had been acquainted with Hargrave.

"I knew him well. He was a neighbor."

"What do you know of his family?"

"Quite a lot. Why do you ask?"

"His will appointed me trustee, and guardian to his three younger children."

"What?" the viscount asked in disbelief.

"Yes. Mad, isn't it? I hadn't seen the man for nearly a decade, didn't know him well to begin with, and he drops his family on me as if they were a rare gift."

"Since you're asking, I take it you haven't called upon them yet?"

"No, I haven't, nor did I intend to, but seeing you put me in mind of them. Surely they can't need a guardian?"

"Two of them are quite young," the viscount returned. "But I would say what they need more than a guardian is a fortune."

"Yes. I have seen the accounts."

"Hargrave drove them to it. He gambled and spent money like a madman. Drank himself into an early grave."

"I knew he gambled; I didn't realize he drank."

"He wasn't a drunkard; I didn't mean to imply that he was. He died of an acute liver ailment. He continued to drink even though the doctors warned him what the consequences could be." Viscount Ashton shrugged his shoulders. "He seemed not to care."

"The man I knew was a good officer—a brave man," Brooke returned.

"People change," Ashton said. "In any event, the estate is heavily encumbered and falling to rack and ruin. But the family is still holding on. They are a dogged bunch."

"You almost make me curious to meet these wards of mine."

"Do. They are most intriguing, I promise you. And a more handsome group you will seldom find. Besides, you must pass very near on your way north, and you have nothing better to do. If I know Southwell, it is running as smoothly as a well-oiled machine, and you will find little to occupy you there. The turmoil at Paxton Hall may interest you."

Lord Brooke arrived at the Inn of the Three Swans, Hertford, on a warm, sunny June morning. Since his coach and servants had preceded him by several hours, one of his own grooms was waiting to take charge of his mare as he dismounted in the cobbled yard. Inside he found that his rooms had been bespoken and his luncheon ordered. After an acceptable meal of steaming partridge pie, sliced cold beef, fresh asparagus, and strong ale, he strolled to the stables to see his mare resaddled. Asking directions from the landlord, he set off toward the village of Paxton, intending to make an unannounced, casual call upon the family of the late Baron Hargrave.

The Hargraves, blissfully unaware such an untoward honor was about to be bestowed upon them, were busy about their various tasks. Lady Hargrave and Patience were weeding in the kitchen garden, where a vigorous crop of young vegetables gave promise of a bountiful harvest. Stephen and Miles had spent the morning helping Walter Miller lay a second layer of thatch on his roof.

Caroline walked to the village just before noon with a basket over her arm and a straw bonnet shielding her eyes from the midday sun. Her knock at the cottage door was answered by Mrs. Miller, whose young freckled face lit with a smile when she saw who stood there.

"I have brought lunch for my brothers, Iris," Caroline said, "and a few things for the baby as well. How long will it be?"

"Just six weeks more, Miss Caroline," Iris said, taking the package Caroline handed her and untying the string that bound it. Inside were two infant nightgowns of pale yellow muslin. "Oh, miss, how lovely! Thank you ever so much. And thank her ladyship, too, for this lovely cloth. I never thought to have my young one decked out in such finery."

Caroline smiled. "The fabric is from a frock my sister outgrew; I'm pleased it can be put to good use. I've never before sewn anything so small; it goes quickly when the seams are short."

The men stopped work at noon and in the rising heat of the afternoon the Hargraves walked three abreast down the lane from the village, trailing the old gelding Hercules behind.

"Bother!" Stephen exclaimed. "It will be hot today."

"Was it hard work thatching the roof?" Caroline asked.

"Very hard, which I am discovering is true of most farm work. Miller says it's too warm to do a proper job. A damp day is better, for then the straw will lie together more closely."

"It is generous of you to help him. I know he is worried about getting it done before the baby arrives."

"Even so, he is one of the few tenants who will accept our help. He said he has never known gentlemen to do such work."

"We're not much use as laborers," Miles added, "but it was

us or no one. Every other able-bodied man on the estate has more work than he can do and no end in sight."

"Which reminds me," Stephen continued, "I must get back to the home farm. There are still many stumps to pull in the long meadow."

Caroline turned on her brother in exasperation. "Surely it is too hot a day for such work, Stephen. For the men and the horses. I think the stumps should wait, and for one afternoon at least you should relax." Her affectionate gaze took in Stephen's tired eyes and sagging shoulders. His buckskin breeches were stained and patched, and his worn cambric shirt clung to his sweat-covered shoulders and back. "Let's take our lunch to the creek!" she suggested. "It will be cool and clean, the perfect place on such a day."

"I don't have time, Caro," Stephen objected.

"Yes, you do. You must eat, after all," she countered. "We owe ourselves a holiday. Please, Stephen, just this once?"

"Oh, very well," he relented, "but only for an hour or so. Then I must get back to the stumps."

"You two go," Miles said, excusing himself. "There is some reading I need to do."

"Don't you want lunch?" Caroline asked.

"I'll get something at the house . . . do you mind?"

Knowing that study was relaxation for Miles, neither his brother nor sister objected. As Miles left them, Stephen mounted Hercules and reached for his sister's hand. "No sense walking when we can ride in style."

Handing Stephen her basket, Caroline placed her foot in the stirrup he freed for her and allowed herself to be pulled up behind him. As she threw her leg over, her skirt spread over the horse's quarters and skimmed up her leg, exposing a shapely calf. "So improper!" Caroline gasped in mock dismay.

Stephen put Hercules into a canter as he replied, "How fortunate for you that we will see no one, for I am certain your reputation in the neighborhood would be quite ruined."

In a few minutes they arrived at the stream and the special place where they had often played as children. At this spot the banks were low and the water flowed gently, eddying about several large, flat rocks stranded midstream. Trees near the bank offered shade to a comfortable grassy space where one could read or nap.

When Stephen had helped Caroline down, she went immediately to the water's edge to wash her hands and face and take a long, cool drink. Within moments Stephen was there beside her, stripping off his shirt and losing no time in washing the straw dust and sweat from his arms and chest. His face and hair also received a liberal dousing while his sister rinsed his shirt and spread it over a gorse bush in the sun to dry. They sat together in the shade to eat their simple lunch, and afterward Stephen yawned and stretched out full length on the grass. When Caroline saw his eyes close, she wandered downstream, gathering wildflowers.

Lord Brooke rode for several miles over what he assumed was the Hargrave estate. Everything he saw fit Mr. Birmingham's description of a neglected property. The village of Paxton appeared shabby and unprosperous, most of its cottages in need of extensive repair. Even the village church wanted a fresh whitewashing. Tillable fields lay fallow at the height of the growing season. The flocks of sheep he encountered were small, the cattle of inferior quality. He passed through woods and pastures littered with windfall, dotted with rotting stiles, broken and sagging gates, crumbling and damaged walls and fences.

Cresting the top of a gentle ridge sprinkled with ancient beeches, Brooke looked down upon a stream meandering in the valley below, then reined in as he glimpsed a young woman in a gray gown walking along its bank, picking flowers. She wore no bonnet, and her hair of palest flaxen glowed like spun gold in the brilliant afternoon sun. Seeming to have gathered all the blooms she wanted, she turned to walk back the way she had come.

Then Brooke saw the young man lying under the trees with the horse tied nearby. He reined back, thinking he had stumbled upon a lovers' tryst and not wishing to intrude. But before he could turn to leave, the young woman claimed his attention once again as she sat to remove her shoes. He continued to watch undetected as she stripped off her stockings, exposing long shapely legs as she did so. Then, hiking up her skirts, she waded to one of the large rocks midstream and perched upon it, trailing her bare feet in the water as it swirled by.

At that moment Brooke's mare whinnied in greeting to the horse in the valley. As the gelding answered, the young man sat up and the young woman turned to scan the ridge. Brooke knew he was well served for prying and had no choice now but to ride down and make himself known. After all, he was the trespasser; these young people probably had a right to be there.

As the stranger set his horse down the slope, Stephen, conscious of his bare chest, crossed quickly to retrieve his shirt, fastening the last buttons as the mare splashed through the stream. At first sight of the rider on the ridge, Caroline pulled her bare feet beneath the edge of her skirt, yet she was held prisoner on the rock, for she could not possibly wade back to shore in the presence of this magnificent stranger.

Broad-shouldered and long-legged, he sat astride a raking bay mare that was the handsomest animal Caroline had ever seen. The gentleman's bottle-green riding coat clearly owed its fashionable cut to no provincial tailor. Flawless buckskin breeches hugged muscular legs, while a thin layer of dust did little to dull the high polish of his top boots. His hands were closely encased in supple leather gloves; a curly beaver sat firmly over shining black hair.

He brought the mare to a standstill before Stephen. "Excuse me for disturbing you," he apologized. "I did not wish to intrude. I am looking for Paxton Hall."

"The Hall is a mile farther east, sir, but perhaps I may serve you. I am Stephen Hargrave."

Brooke was not wholly surprised by this claim. As he rode down the hill, he had obtained a closer look at the couple, noted the resemblance between them, and suspected he had stumbled upon his wards.

"I am pleased to make your acquaintance, my lord," he said, as he swung off the mare and extended a hand in greeting. "I am Phillip Brooke."

Stephen took the hand offered but shook it only briefly, a soft flush warming his cheeks as he said mechanically, "How do you do, sir?"

Stephen's discomfiture was acute and stemmed from several sources. When he had first learned he was to have a guardian, he had suffered conflicting emotions, for though he wanted a free hand with his land, he knew he lacked the experience necessary to manage a large property. He had hoped his guardian would advise him when it came to making those decisions that would affect the safety and well-being of his family and his tenants. But when Lord Brooke had shown little interest in the trusteeship, Stephen had proceeded with only his solicitor to guide him. He had worked diligently and felt some pride in his progress.

Stephen knew he was meeting Brooke under the worst possible circumstances. He was uncomfortably conscious of his informal, shabby attire in the face of his guardian's elegance; he knew Brooke could not fail to see the sorry excuse for a horse that stood behind him, but more important, he was chagrined that his guardian should find him sleeping in the shade in the middle of a workday. All this flashed through his mind in an instant as Brooke answered, "I am quite well, thank you. What a lovely spot this is. You *both* seem to be enjoying yourselves."

Reminded thus gently of his lapse in manners, Stephen said quickly, "Excuse me, sir. Permit me to introduce my sister, Caroline."

Unable to curtsy or offer her hand, Caroline simply nodded while Lord Brooke bestowed upon her an elegant bow and a smile that warmed her far more than the sun beating upon her head. She had not wanted a trustee and had spent some time speculating upon what sort of man Lord Brooke might be; but even in her wildest flights of fancy she had never imagined anyone approaching this dashing London swell.

Having introduced his sister, Stephen once again fell silent, causing Brooke to wonder whether this couple lacked proper manners or whether his unexpected appearance had quite overpowered them. Deciding that the second supposition was probably closer to the truth, he refrained from delivering the set-down he might issue should he encounter such rudeness in others of his acquaintance, and said instead, "Perhaps we should repair to the house? I should like to be made known to Lady Hargrave."

"Yes, of course," Stephen responded. "Mother will be so surprised; she wasn't expecting . . ." He stopped in confusion, and it was now Lord Brooke's turn to be a trifle embarrassed.

"I should have written," he apologized lamely. "But as I

made a hasty decision, there was no time." He glanced about idly. "Have you another horse—for your sister?"

"No. We both . . . we have only the one," Stephen replied.

Caroline suddenly spoke for the first time, and Brooke was pleased by the richness of her voice. "You ride back with his lordship, Stephen. I much prefer to walk. It's such a lovely day."

As Stephen went to untie Hercules, Brooke found his amusement growing. Clearly, brother and sister had ridden here together, very improper behavior considering the horse carried only a man's saddle. Also evident was the young woman's embarrassing situation. How awkward she must feel being introduced while sitting on a rock in the midst of a stream. He knew she was eager to have them gone so she could return to the bank and retrieve her stockings and shoes. The situation strongly appealed to his sense of the ridiculous, and he couldn't resist carrying it a bit further.

"But, Miss Hargrave, we couldn't possibly ride off and leave you here alone. I have a better plan. Lord Hargrave shall ride ahead to apprise Lady Hargrave of my arrival, while I stay behind to walk with you. I have been riding since early morning and will enjoy a stroll in your company."

Remembering he had left his mother and sister that morning on their knees in the garden, Stephen viewed this suggestion in the light of a reprieve. Before Caroline could object he accepted Lord Brooke's offer. As he mounted Hercules and rode away, it was obvious he had not fully comprehended his sister's predicament.

She called out to him, but he only raised a hand in farewell as he answered, "I will see you at the Hall."

Phillip Brooke tied his mare to the tree branch where Hercules had been tethered, then strolled to the water's edge. He knew Miss Hargrave to be nearly four-and-twenty but thought she looked younger. Now at leisure to study her, he found her remarkably lovely, with large blue eyes complementing her unusual hair and delicate, classic features.

He was enjoying himself tremendously as he said, "You must come ashore now, Miss Hargrave. Lady Hargrave will be expecting us, and a walk of a mile will occupy some time, I think."

"I would much prefer if you went on alone, my lord. I wasn't ready to leave yet. As you said, it is so lovely here."

"But I need you to show me the way to the house," he replied, "and we could use this opportunity to become acquainted."

"If you have waited six months to become acquainted, my lord, certainly a few more hours cannot signify."

Caroline watched his black brows rise and could have bitten her tongue in frustration. She suspected he was teasing her, but she hadn't meant to retaliate. She doubted she would fare well in any confrontation with him.

"Will you cross over now, Miss Hargrave, or shall I come for you?"

This threat brought her frankness to the surface as she responded readily, "Surely you must know, sir, that I had to wade here. I cannot wade back so long as you stay."

"But as I have already observed you wade across, what matter if I see you return?" he asked sensibly.

A fierce blush rose to her cheeks as she recalled how soon the horses had whinnied after she had crossed the stream. It was quite likely he spoke the truth—he had observed her wading. Then her flush deepened as she remembered that only moments earlier she had removed her stockings, exposing her legs in an unseemly fashion. Had he seen that as well?

Anger replaced embarrassment as she rose to her feet on the large flat rock, forgetting the bare toes that peeped from beneath her hem. "I think you are no gentleman, sir, to spy upon people when they believe themselves to be private."

"I believe you are right, ma'am," he replied promptly, "and I apologize. I will make amends instantly by removing you from the embarrassing position in which you find yourself."

Caroline's mouth fell open as she watched him wade purposefully toward her through the shallow water with no regard whatsoever for his costly boots. Reaching the rock, he swept Caroline from her perch and turned with her in his arms toward the bank. "Your mouth is open, Miss Hargrave . . . so unladylike," he murmured.

She snapped it shut, amazed at the strength of the arms that held her so effortlessly, for she was no featherweight. It seemed only an instant before she stood on the grass. "I will wait near my horse, Miss Hargrave, with my back turned, while you resume your shoes and stockings." As he moved away, she did as she was told, keeping a wary eye on him the while, but he kept his word and never turned.

When she finished, she collected her flowers, basket, and bonnet. "This way, my lord, if you please." As she headed east, setting a quick pace, he walked at her side leading the mare, instantly regretting his impulsive behavior as his wet boots made walking uncomfortable.

After passing through the trees near the creek, they crossed a large meadow, then joined a deeply rutted wagon track that led them through thick, shadowy woods. She had not spoken again, and he suddenly taxed her with her silence.

"Have you no conversation, Miss Hargrave, or am I being punished for teasing you earlier?"

"I have no conversation that would interest a Londoner," she replied briefly.

"I am not in London now, Miss Hargrave, and when in Rome . . ."

When she failed to respond, he stated unequivocally, "I am being punished for teasing you earlier." He stopped walking a moment, but when she continued without him, he had to hurry to catch up. He carefully observed her haughty profile as he continued, "I apologized once; must I do so again?" Once more the silence stretched on until he said, "You seem most unforgiving, ma'am."

That stopped her. She turned to face him, eyes blazing, proud chin raised. "I would forgive you freely, sir, if I for one instant believed you to be sincere."

She was right. His apology had not been sincere, and she had neatly bested him. He retreated. "Why all this concern over a pair of limbs?" he demanded reasonably. "Look at this mare!" He stepped back regarding her. "You or I, your brother, even Lady Hargrave could say, 'Look at her fine legs, how straight they are, how shapely.' Yet if by chance, by accident, a man happens to see a woman's ankle, the world is shocked and horrified. Why should this imbalance exist, Miss Hargrave? Tell me."

"You are ridiculous, sir."

She began walking again, and he fell in beside her. The smile playing over her face told him he had coaxed her from her sulks, yet he determined to be careful how he dealt with

Miss Hargrave in future, for this young woman had a proud heart.

At the end of the wood they passed through a dilapidated gate. Directly before them, across a wide expanse of unscythed grass that had once been a lawn, stood Paxton Hall. Brooke had seen so much neglect on the estate by this time that its continuation on the Hall grounds did not surprise him. The gardens and park were overrun with undergrowth and weeds, while the graveled drive was rutted and poorly maintained. The house itself, however, pleased him. Large and finely crafted of mellow stone, it stood as it had for several hundred years, reminding each generation it was there to stay despite an occasional imprudent owner who might neglect or abuse it.

They were met on the drive by a young lad who, Caroline guessed, had been called in from stump pulling to see to Lord Brooke's mare. There was no servant in the hall to meet them, so Brooke laid his hat, gloves, and whip on a small table before following Caroline to a pair of double doors on the ground floor.

"This way, my lord, if you please," she said. "I am sure everyone will be gathered in the salon."

This was indeed the case. Stephen had changed into his best coat; Miles had been dragged from his books; Patience was all curiosity in her simple gray muslin. When Lady Hargrave extended her hand to the visitor, he bowed over it with infinite grace while Patience's eyes nearly popped from her head. Then, when he took Patience's hand in turn, she blushed painfully and could only stammer a greeting.

Chapter 3

WHEN LORD BROOKE requested a private interview with Lady Hargrave, Caroline looked sullen and Stephen anxious, but Miles and Patience were eager to escape. When she was alone with his lordship, Lady Hargrave repeated her welcome.

"We have been eager to meet you, Lord Brooke. We had never heard of you, you see, until the day the will was read."

"I knew your husband in the army, Lady Hargrave. He was my commanding officer in Spain."

"I must admit it came as a surprise to me to find that my late husband had appointed you trustee," she continued. "He had said nothing to me."

"Nor to me, ma'am. The first I heard of the arrangement was when your solicitor wrote following your husband's death."

Lady Hargrave's features reflected her surprise. "You cannot be serious, sir! Are you saying my husband laid this responsibility upon you without your knowledge or consent?"

"That is exactly what I am saying."

"How strange. And how very unlike him. I can see how you might view such an obligation as an imposition, Lord Brooke. If you should wish to excuse yourself from the commitment my husband made in your name, I will perfectly understand."

Even as Lady Hargrave offered Brooke an honorable escape from his obligation, he felt perversely inclined to fulfill it, considerably surprising himself by saying, "On the contrary, Lady Hargrave. I have several weeks free, and would not be opposed to offering some assistance to your son. I have considerable experience in estate management, and if you'll forgive my saying so, this property is not in good heart."

"You will not offend me, sir, by speaking the truth. But little can be done without capital, and I must tell you plainly— there is none."

"There are sometimes ways to work around a shortage of funds, Lady Hargrave. I will meet with Mr. Birmingham again. Perhaps we may discover a solution."

As he waited for her to respond, he sensed her uneasiness and realized his mistake. He should not have been so forthright with her, nor admitted his surprise at being named trustee. He should have simply taken control, leaving her with nothing to say.

"I can't help but think we would be imposing upon your goodwill, Lord Brooke," she said.

Casting about in his mind for a way to retrench, Brooke hit

upon a solution. "Perhaps I should tell you, Lady Hargrave, that your husband saved my life in Spain," he lied. "I owe him a great debt, and I feel myself in honor bound to respect the terms of his will. At least I can help your son bring some order to this property. It is, after all, your livelihood, and your children's futures depend upon it."

In that one sentence he neatly packaged Lady Hargrave's fears, and for one glowing moment she imagined how wonderful it would be to have a strong, experienced man to shoulder the burden of responsibility. Lord Brooke seemed intelligent and capable; her solicitor had reported that his properties were extensive and profitable. If Brooke had the time and the inclination, why shouldn't Stephen have the opportunity to learn from him?

"My husband's will was very clear, Lord Brooke, and I must believe he knew best. I am certain my son would be grateful for your counsel. Where are you staying?"

"At the Three Swans in Hertford."

"There is a comfortable inn at Welwyn," she suggested. "It's only four miles away."

"I had hoped, Lady Hargrave, that I might stay here. But if it would be inconvenient . . ."

"No, no, my lord, certainly not. I would not have you think us inhospitable; but we live simply. I fear it would not be what you are accustomed to."

He smiled at her then—that same broad smile that had warmed Caroline at the stream. "You forget, ma'am, I am an army man. I have lived on army rations and slept many a night upon stony ground with only my saddle for a pillow. There is no possibility I could be uncomfortable in your home."

She returned his smile graciously. "Then you are most welcome to stay, my lord. When may we expect you?"

"I will send my people along in the morning from Hertford, and I will return directly I have finished with Mr. Birmingham."

She wondered briefly how many "people" his lordship had with him, and how many horses, but then dismissed it from her mind. He was in charge; she would be content to leave everything to him.

Having taken leave of Lady Hargrave and his wards, Brooke accepted Caroline's offer to accompany him to the stables. She dared not ask what he and her mother had discussed, but he soon satisfied her curiosity.

"I shall return in a few days, Miss Hargrave, to stay for several weeks. I know I can depend upon your cooperation as well as that of your brothers, for there will be much to accomplish." Turning away, he mounted his mare, then glanced down as Caroline took the rein near the bit.

"My lord, before you go, I was wondering if you might tell me—did you come to the ridge before or after I had taken off my shoes and stockings?" Unable to look at him as she asked the question, Caroline did not see the wicked gleam that lit his eyes.

"I arrived afterward, Miss Hargrave," he lied for the second time in the past hour. Then, turning the mare, he cantered away. For one instant he wished he had told the truth, just for the pleasure of seeing that delightful blush creep into her cheeks again.

As the social Season wound to a close, Gerald Layton, Viscount Ashton, departed London to return to his ancestral home in Hertfordshire. He made his first courtesy call upon the Hargraves on the morning following Lord Brooke's visit.

Ashton had spoken nothing less than the truth when he had told Brooke he knew the Hargraves well. Their families had been friends for generations. When young Gerald had finished at Oxford, he came home to discover that his childhood playmate Caroline had grown into a beautiful young woman. Two years later when she was nineteen, he had asked her to be his wife and she had declined.

Although it may be expected that such a declaration and such an answer would be cause for discomfiture between the parties, this was not the case. Gerald and Caroline had remained friends. They danced together at local assemblies; they rode and picnicked in perfect harmony. During her father's numerous and lengthy absences, Gerald had been instrumental in teaching her brothers to drive, shoot, and hunt. Patience was his special favorite. He had acquired the habit of collecting some trifle for her whenever he was away from home.

As Ashton slowly walked his horse through a beech copse, the early morning light thinly slanting through the leafy branches overhead, he thought it strange that Phillip Brooke should be appointed trustee to the Hargraves. The Hargraves, for all the faults and follies of the lately departed baron, were a tightly knit, fiercely loyal and devoted family. Brooke, from all Ashton knew and understood, was the opposite. His only family, so far as anyone knew, was a married sister off in India somewhere. He lived alone and seldom entertained in town.

Well known for his hunting parties, however, Brooke was a popular country host, his seat at Southwell in Nottinghamshire often praised for its picturesque setting and unrivaled terrain. Ashton had been invited to several of these gatherings and knew Brooke to be a meticulous landlord. Gerald doubted Stephen could find a better adviser than Brooke, yet he wondered if Brooke intended to take an active part in the guardianship. When they had spoken, it had seemed as though he might; yet Brooke didn't strike Ashton as the sort of man who would worry himself unnecessarily over the plight of others.

Gerald spurred his horse to a canter. Now that he was so close, he found himself anxious to see Caroline again. As luck would have it, he came upon her when he was still half a mile from the Hall. Picking berries along the lane with her small spaniel frisking nearby, Caroline glanced up at the sound of approaching hoofbeats and smiled warmly in recognition. She hadn't seen Ashton for more than five months, yet he looked much the same as always: dark brown hair short-cropped and curling naturally over a wide, intelligent brow; brown eyes smiling and twinkling in greeting; gray riding coat and buckskin breeches, London-tailored to a lanky, well-conditioned body. Dismounting, he took her hands in his, his grip as familiar to her as that of her brothers.

"Gerry!" she exclaimed. "How good it is to see you! We have been expecting you anytime this past week. When did you arrive?"

"Last Thursday, but I have been devilish busy. This was my first chance to get away. How is the family?"

"We are all well, though in a bit of an uproar at present. Our trustee appeared yesterday, quite unannounced."

"When I saw you at Christmas," he countered, "you said your father had named a trustee, but you didn't say who it was. I imagined someone older—a contemporary of your father's perhaps. I was amazed to discover it was Phillip Brooke."

"Do you know him?"

"Yes, of course. He is always in London for the Season, and one sees him everywhere. He remembered I hailed from hereabout and asked if I knew your family. That's how I came to know he was the man your father appointed. So you have met him, then. What do you think of him? Does he plan to stay?"

She nodded. "He plans to stay several weeks to advise Stephen. And Stephen is curious to see what sort of advice will be forthcoming. Lord Brooke is fine as fivepence, and Patience was blinded by his elegance. Mama seems to think he is the answer to our problems at last, though I don't see how he can be. He cannot create money where there is none."

"You haven't said what *you* think of him, Caro."

"I don't know what to think of him, for I barely spoke to him. We met under rather awkward circumstances." Briefly she described the scene at the stream the previous day, though it embarrassed her to recall it.

The viscount grinned appreciatively, pleased by her blush. "Lucky devil! I wish it had been me instead of him. I've been hoping for a glimpse of those ankles for years. If you would ever take my proposal seriously—"

"What? Another proposal? You have been here only five minutes. You become more impatient each year."

They stood smiling warmly at each other, for this annual proposal had become almost a game between them. Every year since that first proposal he had repeated his offer, usually when he came home at the end of the London Season.

"I speak sooner each year for we are neither of us getting any younger, Caro. I will be twenty-nine this summer. Time and more that I was married. Just ask my mother."

"There must have been any number of women in London setting their caps at you, for you are quite a catch."

Suddenly serious, he asked, "If I am such a catch, why will you not have me?"

"You know why, Gerry," she answered. "Because I am not in love with you, nor you with me. We both deserve a *grande passion*, and I believe that you, at least, will someday find one. If you continue to ask me, I will continue to say no. Then one spring you will ride home smelling of April and May, and you will not ask. Then I will know you have found that special person. And it will happen, my friend. I know it, and so do you."

As he reached to collect her basket, she noticed the package tied behind his saddle. "For Patience? What have you brought this time?"

He smiled again. "It's a length of muslin."

When she looked doubtful he added, "My mother chose it, blue-gray for half mourning. I think Patience will like it."

"How could she not? As she grows older, I think I may become jealous of these gifts you lavish upon my little sister," she said teasingly.

"Shall I walk you home?" he asked. "Or perhaps another time would be more convenient, what with Brooke here and all."

"He is not here," Caroline responded. "He has gone to Hertford to confer with Mr. Birmingham. Do come to the house. Mama will want to hear all the latest gossip from town. Patience will be delighted to see you, and not only because you spoil her with gifts. And you really can't deny my brothers the opportunity to admire this fine fellow." She ran her hand down the face of the handsome gray gelding standing quietly beside them.

While the two walked back toward the Hall, Gerald carrying her basket and leading his horse, the subject of Phillip Brooke cropped up again.

"Did your father give any reason for naming Brooke trustee?" he asked.

"No. It all seems very strange. Whatever could have led Papa to believe I should need a trustee at my age?"

"Perhaps his intimate knowledge of your willful, headstrong ways."

She gasped. "Gerald Layton! What a rude, ill-bred thing to say!"

"But true," he persisted. "You cannot deny it. This trusteeship will be no easy task. I wish Brooke joy of it and consider myself fortunate not to have been named in his place."

"What? This from a man who has six—no—seven times proposed marriage?" He only smiled in response as she continued. "It is wonderful to have you at home. It will be a comfort knowing you are close by this summer if I need help or advice."

"But I won't be here, Caro," he responded. "That's one of the things I came to tell you. Hubert is to take his grand tour this summer, and his traveling companion broke his leg last week. I have been petitioned to go in his stead, and I agreed. We leave in two days."

"Oh, dear," she sighed, truly disappointed. "Things shall be very flat here without you, but your brother must have first claim on you. We will miss you dreadfully."

"I will miss you, too, but I seriously doubt if your summer will be boring. Brooke's presence should rescue you from that."

They had come in sight of the house sometime earlier. Now as they crossed from the unscythed lawn onto the drive, Patience burst from the door and ran to meet them.

In the stuffy upper office in the heart of the town of Hertford, Lord Brooke sat on a hard, uncomfortable chair, his stern, uncompromising visage fixed upon Mr. Birmingham. Jasper Birmingham was not an aristocrat, nor was he wealthy, nor did he enjoy any of the privileges of the haughty lord before him, but he knew his business, better he would swear than his lordship did, and he refused to be swayed by any argument.

Brooke spoke patiently, succinctly, as if addressing a simpleton. "Would you for one instant simply consider what I am proposing, sir?"

"I have considered it, my lord, and I assure you it is impossible to secure another mortgage. The estate is already heavily encumbered, while the debt increases each year due to accumulation of interest. You have seen the condition of the Hargrave estate, sir. Even if we were able to raise enough money to effect minor improvements, there is no guarantee of success. Any number of things could go awry. The countryside could suffer drought; the crops could fail or the flocks take sick and die."

Brooke rose impatiently and strode the three paces the small room permitted him. "Did you not once tell me that there was some acreage free from mortgage?"

"Yes, sir."

"Then it must be sold."

"I have already suggested this to Lord Hargrave, my lord.

He would not hear of it. You, of course, have the power to do what you think necessary, but I beg you to consider carefully before taking such action. His lordship is adamant. If you decide to sell, I fear you will make an enemy of him."

"What I hear you saying, sir, is that there is no solution to this dilemma," Brooke offered.

"None beyond leaving things as they are. If the family practices economy, if the weather holds fair and the harvest is good, they have a chance."

"*And* if none of the disasters you spoke of earlier befalls them—bad weather, failed crops, sickening animals . . . In fact, you hope for a miracle!" Brooke walked back to the desk where Mr. Birmingham was seated. "Surely the Hargraves are fortunate to have such a staunch supporter in their corner, Mr. Birmingham. Clearly, you are an ethical, dedicated professional. Yet I wonder if with all this professional integrity there is any real feeling for the Hargraves as people, or are they just an account to you, a file in your desk, a column in your ledger? Because, you see, I met them only yesterday, but already I care about them a great deal. I am determined to find a way to help them, despite your gloomy forecasts."

Mr. Birmingham scowled at Brooke's words, but controlled his temper and answered with aplomb. "No solicitor likes to think personal feelings influence his professional judgment, my lord. I endeavor to keep them from coloring my opinion or advice. But to say I have no concern for the Hargraves is the outside of enough! My firm has served the family for generations, and I, as much as you, would like to see young Stephen recover from the ravages of his father's indiscretions."

"Would you be willing to practice a deceit to help bring about that recovery?"

Mr. Birmingham sat straighter in his chair as though the very word *deceit* was offensive to him. "What are you suggesting, my lord?"

"We are dealing with a family possessed of great pride. We have already agreed they would reject out of hand any overt offer I might make to help them. Therefore, I wish to invest a sum of money in the Hargrave estate. Unsecured. Confidential. We shall tell the Hargraves only that we have managed to arrange another mortgage on the property. How well do they understand the state of affairs? Do you think they would believe such a tale? And, more important, would you be willing to lend yourself to the scheme?"

"Were I your solicitor, my lord, I would strongly caution you against such a risky proposition. You will in all likelihood lose your entire investment."

"I can easily stand the loss, else I would not offer it."

Beyond raising one brow, Mr. Birmingham made no response to this comment. He had come to appreciate Lord Brooke's forthright manner, even though he was far from comprehending his motives. His lordship's comment left no room for argument. Therefore, the lawyer proceeded to answer Lord Brooke's earlier questions.

"Lord Hargrave has a general understanding of his situation, but has not been permitted to see any actual figures, as we agreed at our first meeting. I may be able to convince him that another mortgage was possible, but I believe he would be highly suspicious. What sum did you have in mind? Too large an amount would not be credible."

"I am well aware of that. We shall have to be crafty, Mr. Birmingham. We will have a modest influx of funds, but we must also have a total revamping of organization on the estate. Not one penny will be wasted; I will see to that. We must use sufficient capital to effect improvements, but not so much as to arouse Hargrave's suspicion. We will be treading a thin line, but I think we can manage it."

"And if we are discovered, my lord?"

"If we are discovered, you shall be absolved, for you are acting under my orders. I, no doubt, will be considered a cad and deceiver. But I prefer even that, Mr. Birmingham, to the alternative of Paxton Hall passing out of Hargrave hands."

Chapter 4

AS LORD BROOKE rode northwest from Hertford toward Paxton in the lengthening shadows of the afternoon, he reflected upon the events of the past several days. He had determined to call upon the Hargraves partly out of curiosity and partly because of a nagging guilt planted within his conscience by his secretary. He'd had every intention of introducing himself, then righteously excusing himself from any personal involvement in what he considered an unjust and ill-conceived guardianship.

But he had not done so. He could pinpoint the exact moment he had changed his mind—in the midst of his conversation with Lady Hargrave—but he was at a loss to understand what had prompted his uncharacteristic response. He was not generally given to sudden starts or erratic behavior. He was methodical and cautious. He seldom made an important decision without careful planning.

Why, then, had he felt this sudden impulse to involve himself further with the Hargraves? It was true they were a charming family, yet that alone could not account for it.

After a period of reflection he decided it was not only the residents of Paxton Hall but the property itself that attracted him. All his own property, and it was extensive—Southwell in Nottinghamshire, Bleak Priory in Somerset, Kilshire Hall in Norfolk, a tidy hunting box in Leicestershire, a mansion in Mayfair—had come to him in perfect order from his father. He had certainly improved and extended his holdings, but it had simply been a question of deciding what to do and when to do it. He had never needed to concern himself with the cost or the means. The well-organized and properly funded Brooke properties ran well and smoothly without him. In fact, they had ceased to be a challenge.

Brooke had to admit the Hargrave estate interested him. It was good land in a charming situation, and the widespread neglect fired a challenge within him.

He tried to imagine how he might have fared had his estates come to him heavily encumbered, as they had to Stephen Hargrave. Hargrave was only nineteen. As Brooke remembered himself at nineteen, his face slowly contracted into harsh lines and his lips tightened. He jobbed at the bit, and the bay mare threw her head in displeasure. Loosing the rein and soothing the horse with his voice, Brooke resolutely put aside all consideration of Lord Hargrave's youth and his own, bending his thoughts instead to a piece of neglected property and his intention to heal it.

Lady Hargrave had warned Brooke what he could expect at Paxton Hall, but he was certain she had made every effort during his brief absence to prepare her home for his visit. When he trotted his mare to the front door, his own groom came running from the stables to lead her away. He was admitted by the butler, greeted by Lord Hargrave, then shown to a room where his valet awaited him. He had been allotted a large bedchamber, handsomely appointed, showing little of the shabbiness evident in the more heavily used rooms downstairs. He frowned at the dark squares of unfaded paper on the walls, suspecting that the paintings that had once hung there had been sacrificed by the Hall's former owner for a stake at the faro table.

After bathing and changing, he descended to join the Hargraves for dinner. If he could find no fault with his dinner companions, all of whom took part in a lively conversation and seemed genuinely pleased to have him there, it could not be said his opinion of the meal was as generous. Never, even at the humblest rural tavern, could he recall having been served such a wretchedly ill-prepared meal. The soup accompanying the first course was watery and tasteless, while the fish he selected from a dish offered him was riddled with tiny, treacherous bones. The second course included chicken so dry it needed large quantities of an oversalted sauce to render it palatable. The vegetables were cold. Halfway through the meal he decided his first official improvement at Paxton Hall would be the replacement of the cook.

When the dinner concluded and the ladies retired, leaving

the gentlemen to their port, Stephen was first to speak. "I have read the letter you brought from Mr. Birmingham, my lord. You are aware, I believe, of its contents?"

"I am."

"I will admit I am surprised he was able to secure another mortgage, for we have tried unsuccessfully to do so for several months."

"Mr. Birmingham is a worthy solicitor, my lord, but you will agree, I think, that his influence is not nearly so far-reaching as mine." Brooke selected a nut from the bowl before him and cracked it between strong fingers.

Stephen nodded, his suspicions confirmed. "Then I am correct in assuming, sir, that to obtain this mortgage you made some assurances on my behalf?"

"This estate is a valuable property, and your desire to set it right is admirable. I would not hesitate to say as much to anyone who asked such an opinion of me. I would be remiss in my role as trustee if I did not make those efforts within my power to aid you. But tell me this: How best may this capital be used?"

As Stephen prepared to answer, he caught sight of his brother's long-suffering face. "You needn't stay, Miles, if you had rather not."

"I did have some work to do," Miles admitted, then addressed Brooke. "I don't have much of a head for estate matters, my lord. I leave that to Stephen. But I am willing to do my part; you need only tell me what to do."

Brooke rose, offering his hand to Miles. "I couldn't ask for a more cooperative attitude. If everyone is of a similar mind, we shall no doubt rub along quite well."

After Miles had gone, several moments passed in silence until Brooke broached a new subject. "Lady Hargrave has graciously invited me to stay, but you have not said whether this arrangement pleases you."

Stephen's eyes met his guardian's briefly, then dropped to study his wineglass. He slowly rotated the stem between his fingers, watching the candlelight play off the dark red liquid. When he seemed disinclined to speak, Brooke continued.

"I would prefer you be frank with me. I will not take offense at plain speaking."

Stephen glanced up, considering his words carefully before

replying. "I have often wished for someone to advise me, my lord; yet I would not care to see this property handled in a way I consider unfit. For all his strengths, my father did not respect the land. As guardian and trustee you have absolute authority. I admit it worries me."

"Then allow me to relieve you immediately of that anxiety," Brooke returned. "I, like you, love the land. I cannot think we will disagree over agricultural matters. I do not wish to be a dictating guardian, but I think we may disagree over domestic arrangements. Some changes must be made in this household, and I fear you may consider them intrusive. I ask only that you endeavor to see my view. Try to remember I am nearly twice your age. My years and experience do lend me some wisdom."

Since he could think of no reply, Stephen remained silent, and Brooke spoke again. "I had a trustee when I was younger than you are. I was only sixteen when my father died. I inherited a huge estate; my uncle was my guardian. He gave me a generous allowance, informed me that it would be immediately cut off should I do anything to disgrace myself or my family, and then never mentioned my inheritance to me again until the day I reached my majority. On that day he turned everything over to me, and all I can say now is thank God I had trustworthy solicitors, bailiffs, and agents in charge. I knew absolutely nothing about the property I had inherited—at least, not in any business sense. I disagree with this practice and have no intention of being the kind of trustee my uncle was. Mr. Birmingham tells me you have great interest in the land, and I can see he is right. I would like for the two of us to be able to work together. For the next two years I have the final word, but that doesn't mean I am unwilling to hear your opinions, your suggestions. I am asking for them now. How do you think the capital Mr. Birmingham has acquired can best be put to use?"

This speech was calculated to put Stephen at his ease, and it succeeded. Stephen visibly relaxed, and his ready answer to Lord Brooke's question launched them into a detailed agricultural discussion, which they unwillingly interrupted to join the ladies in the salon. After only the briefest of visits there, they adjourned to the estate office to spend several hours on the same and related subjects. They soon dispensed with formal forms of address and became Stephen and Phillip. When they parted near midnight, they did so in good humor, a comfortable friendship initiated between them.

The following morning Stephen went in search of his mother and found her alone in the morning room.

"If you have a moment, Mother, I should like to speak with you about Lord Brooke."

Lady Hargrave had been busy hemming a handkerchief, but she put the work aside, giving her son her full attention. "Your discussion with him last evening—it went well?"

"Yes. Much better than I expected. He intends to let me work with him, to help him reach decisions, to offer my opinion. He thinks I've done well over the winter, considering how little I had to work with. He won't tell me how much money he was able to borrow. In fact, he seems careful to avoid the subject. What I don't understand is how he was able to secure an additional mortgage, for Mr. Birmingham seemed definite about there being no hope for one. I thought perhaps Lord Brooke had sold some of the land, but he assures me he hasn't and promises he will not, since I am so set against it. I can't help thinking he is directly responsible in some way for getting the money. What I don't understand is why he should do so."

"I think I can answer your question," his mother said. "He told me your father saved his life while they were serving together in the Peninsula. Perhaps he feels that by helping you he can repay his debt."

Stephen's eyes widened with interest. "Do you think that was why Father chose him? Because of the obligation?"

"I don't know," his mother answered, "and it serves little purpose to speculate. Your father appointed him trustee, for whatever reason, and there is no question that we need his help. I intend to cooperate with him fully; I hope you feel you can do the same. He wished to speak with both of us this morning concerning some housekeeping matters. Perhaps we should join him now."

Later that morning Caroline sat at a rosewood *secrétaire* in the library, writing a letter to Viscount Ashton. She wore a simple gray muslin gown, free of any ornamentation. Her hair had been neatly braided and coiled tightly on the crown of her head. She responded to a gentle scratching at the door and looked up to see the cook, Mrs. Ribbon, standing there.

"Excuse me, Miss Caroline. I was hoping you might spare me a moment."

"Yes, certainly. What is it?"

"Oh, miss, now that I'm here, I don't rightly know what to say. I don't wish it to seem as if I was goin' behind her ladyship's back, so to speak, but you and I have always been friends, or so I thought."

"Of course we are. What's wrong, Mrs. Ribbon?" Caroline asked. "Please tell me. Perhaps I can help."

"I dearly wish you could, miss, but I fear the worst for myself, for I've gotten the sack, you see."

"Gotten the sack?" Caroline repeated, clearly puzzled.

"I've been let go, miss. Her ladyship has dismissed me from my position," the cook added dramatically, in an effort to clarify the situation for her young mistress.

"Dismissed you! But why?"

"She explained that his lordship requested it, miss, and she felt she should oblige him."

"But this makes no sense. Why should my brother recommend your dismissal?"

"No, no, Miss Caroline, 'twas not Lord Hargrave that wished it so, but t'other."

"Lord Brooke?"

"Yes, indeed, miss. Her ladyship says he has sent for a replacement, and my services will not be needed after Tuesday next. She said I could stay on in the kitchen if I wished, or she would give me a reference if I decided to go. I cannot support my family on a kitchen maid's wages, miss! I told her ladyship I would try my luck elsewhere. Well, it's shocked I was, Miss Caroline, having been cook in this house more than sixteen years, and never a hint I was unsatisfactory."

Startled by the cook's impassioned speech and convinced some mistake had been made, Caroline bade Mrs. Ribbon return to her duties.

"I will speak to my mother immediately."

"She has gone to call at the rectory, Miss Caroline, as she does every Tuesday."

"Then I will speak to his lordship."

Knowing that Stephen had left earlier to continue the stump

pulling, Caroline went directly to the estate office, where she expected to find Lord Brooke.

The door of the room stood open and she trod noiselessly through, halting just inside, waiting to be noticed. Lord Brooke sat at a large desk, a ledger before him, a quill in his hand. He was dressed in riding clothes—a dark brown coat and flawless buckskins. His glossy top boots were tucked back under the chair as he leaned forward, intently studying a long column of figures. From her position to his left, Caroline was given an excellent opportunity to study his aristocratic profile. She had decided he was equally handsome from any angle when he turned to face her.

"Good morning, my lord," she said as he hastily rose to his feet and cast his quill aside, a pleasant smile upon his face.

"Good morning, Miss Hargrave. Did you wish to speak with me?"

"Yes, sir, I did."

"Will you take a seat?"

"No, thank you, I prefer to stand. I have just had the most puzzling conversation with Mrs. Ribbon, our cook. She tells me she has been dismissed. I know there must be some mistake."

His smile faded, and a wary expression took its place. "There is no mistake, Miss Hargrave. Your mother dismissed her this morning."

"On your recommendation?"

There was the slightest pause before he answered. "I fail to see what concern this is of yours, Miss Hargrave. The hiring and firing of domestics is not your responsibility."

"Mrs. Ribbon came to me," Caroline returned. "I promised her I would look into the matter, and I intend to do so. I would ask you again, my lord, was it your recommendation that our cook be dismissed?"

"Yes," he answered simply.

Caroline's jaw set in a hard line as her breast rose and fell quickly in agitation. "Stephen will not approve."

"He has already done so."

Further perplexed, but determined to have an answer, Caroline demanded, "What is your reason for wishing her gone?"

"I am not in the habit of explaining my reasons—"

"Well, you will explain them to me, my lord," she interrupted rudely, "for if Stephen will not defend the rights of our servants, I will, and I will not leave this room until you have answered me."

He gazed at her consideringly. By God, she was a rare beauty! Proud as a lioness and, it seemed, equally as fierce. He had feared this reaction from either Stephen or Lady Hargrave and had been pleased and relieved to find them both reasonable and amenable. He was not accustomed to women so outspoken as Miss Hargrave—women who did not know their place.

"What is your reason, my lord?" she repeated. "She deserves to know that, at least."

"I fear I find her abilities woefully inadequate," he replied coolly. "If you found last evening's meal palatable, I assure you I did not."

Caroline knew she had a bad temper, but since she had outgrown her childhood it had seldom been provoked. Whether it was Brooke's autocratic cockiness, his condescension, or his overbearing arrogance that now awakened it, she was never afterward able to decide. She hardly knew what she was saying as she spit bitter words at him.

"I have no doubt our simple meals fall pitifully short of the banquets you are accustomed to, my lord, but I believe my mother warned you that we do not live in the lap of luxury here as you do at—Southwell, is it? Do you know anything of cooking? Surely not. I daresay you have never set foot in a place so lowly as a kitchen. Allow me to give you instruction, for I understand the kitchen and its workings well. A cook is only as good as her ingredients, and those are only as good as the budget allows. The budget for fine food here at the Hall is nonexistent! You cannot make a savory soup without spices— *very* expensive, spices are—and you cannot make an old, tough laying hen tender no matter how long you cook it. And you cannot keep vegetables palatable, even though they came fresh that day from an excellent garden, if your dinner guest comes thirty minutes late to table!"

All this she spilled out at him in a flurry of words tumbled one over another. As she came to a breathless halt, she suddenly realized the enormity of her rudeness to a guest in her home, a near stranger, and her trustee as well. She covered her mouth with both hands, a gesture too late to be anything but pathetic. Then, as tears glistened in her eyes, she turned and ran from the room.

She left Lord Brooke standing rigid with shock, feeling much as he had when he had been thrown from his hunter the previous winter—his breath taken away, his body bruised, his pride humbled. He had so wanted to avoid ruffling feathers at Paxton Hall, but he had been in residence less than twenty-four hours and already had a crisis on his hands.

All this passed through his mind in a matter of seconds, and he knew he could not allow things to rest as they were. He thought it likely Miss Hargrave would refuse to come if he summoned her, so he wrote a note instead, instructing a footman to carry it to her room. It was concise:

Miss Hargrave,

Please do not view me as the enemy. It is the last thing I want. There is justice in what you say, even though your manner of saying it was somewhat abrasive. You may tell Mrs. Ribbon, or I will tell her myself if you prefer, that she will be given a full week before any final decision is made concerning her position. Supplies have already been ordered from Welwyn and Hertford and should arrive this afternoon. She will have the ingredients she needs to prepare a proper meal and shall have opportunity to prove her ability. Can you be content with that? We seem to have gotten off to a bad start, and I am sorry for it. I am sure we can do better in future.

PB

Unhappily aware of the inappropriateness of her outburst, Caroline was in no way soothed by this missive. Brooke's seeming capitulation and willingness to compromise only made her behavior seem that much more disgraceful.

Mrs. Ribbon, advised of her reprieve, was delighted and determined to put forth her best efforts to please his lordship. Her delight was short-lived. When the supplies of which his lordship spoke arrived at the kitchen entrance in the early afternoon, she set to work with a will. But as the afternoon progressed she grew increasingly apprehensive. Did his lordship care for mushrooms or would they displease him? Which cheese did he favor? Would he prefer beef or fowl? Realizing she had less than four hours to present an acceptable meal to Lord Brooke—who now loomed over her future as both judge and executioner—Mrs. Ribbon rushed off in search of Miss Caroline to beg her advice.

Caroline was not the only one who caused Lord Brooke anxiety on his first full day at the helm of Paxton Hall. When Stephen and Lady Hargrave had left him that morning after a fruitful discussion, he had expected to see his young ward at luncheon. But when Brooke appeared in the dining room, he learned that Stephen had departed an hour earlier to work at the home farm. Brooke had much to do in the office so he contented himself there; but when Stephen did not return by three o'clock, Brooke ordered his mare saddled, asked Lord Hargrave's direction, and set off to find him.

With his earlier interview with Caroline still fresh in his mind, Phillip was not pleased with the sight that greeted him at the home farm's long meadow. Four men were digging stumps in the heat of the early afternoon sun. One man encouraged a draft team pulling in harness while the other three swung axes, severing roots as they appeared. The success of their labor was evident in the many unearthed, gnarled root-masses lining the edge of the meadow. Some of these had been clustered together in threes and set afire, but they burned sluggishly.

The men were stripped to the waist, their bodies bronzed from long hours in the sun, their shoulders glistening with sweat, their muscles rippling with the swing of the ax. They were also dirty, for as sharp blades struck dirt-covered tentacles, soil flew in every direction, pelting them liberally. Three of the men appeared to be farm laborers; the fourth was Stephen Hargrave.

Phillip frowned and set his heel to the mare. Riding to where old Hercules was tethered, he untied the gelding without dismounting, then collected Stephen's shirt from where it lay on the saddle. He trotted both horses toward the men, and they stopped work the moment they saw him, glad for a moment to rest. As Stephen lowered the blade of his ax to the ground, he reached for the shirt Brooke held out to him.

"Did you want me, sir?"

"Yes, I did. I hope you don't mind."

"No, not at all. But allow me to introduce my companions. Joe and Willy Meger and Jack Clegg, all workers here on the home farm."

Brooke greeted the men politely while they nodded and mumbled hellos.

As Stephen finished with his shirt and mounted his gelding, Brooke addressed the workmen. "I'm sorry to take his lordship away, but I need him at the house. I'm sure you understand." They nodded knowingly, and he was certain they understood far better than young Stephen did.

As the horses walked off toward the Hall, Phillip tried for the proper mix of admonition and sympathy. "Isn't it an odd time of year to pull stumps, particularly with fields lying fallow?"

"We planted as much as we could—till we ran out of money for seed. This field can be used next year if we finish clearing it and plow it down yet this summer."

"Do you often work so with your field laborers?"

"Pulling stumps?"

"No, shoulder to shoulder, doing common labor."

"Only since my father's death. I found I could not sit idly when so much needed doing. I work mostly on the home farm, for few of the tenants will accept help from me. They consider such work beneath my station."

"I am in complete agreement with them," Phillip said baldly. "I do not intend to lecture you on your place in society, for you understand what it is. Neither will I enter into a discussion on the merits or demerits of the class system that structures our society, for whether you approve or disapprove of it makes not one whit of difference. Things are as they are and we benefit no one when we run counter to accepted practice. The people who reside upon this estate, nearly two hundred of them, rely upon you for leadership, not muscle. You have the education and hopefully the wisdom to make decisions that profoundly affect their lives. They are more comfortable when they know you are doing your job and not theirs."

Stephen said nothing, and after riding for several moments in silence, Phillip spoke again. "I would ask that in future you restrict your activities to advice, supervision, and administration. I promise you will not feel useless, nor will you lack for work. I already have a list on your desk that should keep you busy for weeks.

Stephen smiled crookedly, and his guardian asked, "Have I said something humorous? I had not intended to."

"No, sir. I know you are right, and I will obey your wishes. I smiled because I was remembering the day we first met by the stream. I was ashamed that you had found me dozing in the sun in the midst of a perfectly good workday. I daresay you thought nothing of it."

"Not a thing. But I cannot guarantee I shall feel likewise should I discover you in such idleness again. We have much to do, and winter will be upon us sooner than you think. There will be no time this summer for *siesta*."

Chapter 5

WHEN THE FAMILY gathered for dinner that evening, Lord Brooke was prompt and Caroline absent. She had sent her apologies, saying she had the headache and would not be joining them as she wished to retire early. Phillip thought it more likely she was not prepared to face him.

When Lady Hargrave made a delicate, guarded comment to Brooke before dinner concerning the foodstuffs he had ordered, he replied offhandedly that he intended to personally settle all tradesmen's bills directed to the kitchens.

"Consider it my contribution to the restoration of Paxton Hall, ma'am. Though I must confess, I have been sadly spoiled by my French chef, Claude. If I had to choose, I would rather give up the Newmarket Races than do without his turtle soup."

"How fortunate for you that you need never make the choice, my lord."

He returned her smile. "How fortunate, indeed."

"Yet I think you misled me the other day, sir, when you said you had been content with army rations."

"Why, so I was, Lady Hargrave, when they were all that was available. But given a choice, only the most indiscriminate mouse would choose rations over Claude."

As he offered his arm to lead her in to dinner, she thought it curious how easily he fit in at the Hall. Two days ago, she would never have permitted him to supply food for her family; yet today she found herself raising no objection, for he had settled in with a friendliness that inspired trust and a generosity not in the least condescending. She took her seat at the table thinking her husband had shown uncommon wisdom in naming Lord Brooke trustee.

The meal began with soup as had the one the previous evening, but the difference was notable. Far from being unpalatable, this offering was robust. The soup was removed with game fowl cooked to a turn. There was sliced, tender beef, hare in rich sauce, and a variety of delicious, fresh vegetable dishes. Delicate pastry was offered for dessert. Still a simple country dinner by most standards, Brooke found it excellent and the Hargraves were delighted.

The major topic at dinner that evening was footpads, for Miles had come home from his lessons at the rectory with news of a robbery that had taken place not five miles from Paxton.

"Old Mr. Cunningham's coach was stopped last night, and the brigands took his money and even his jewelry!"

"Did they fire their pistols in the air?" Patience asked, blue eyes widening. "And demand that he stand and deliver?"

"I am certain they did," Miles replied. "They always do, don't they, Stephen?"

"They are rumored to. I have no personal experience, of course. Perhaps his lordship could say."

"I have been stopped only once in my lifetime," Brooke responded, "but to my recollection they did most certainly order us to stand and deliver."

"Truly, sir?" Patience demanded.

"Yes, truly. But they don't always take jewelry, at least not *all* the jewelry. I have heard it said no gentleman of the High Toby ever takes the wedding ring from a lady."

"Oh," Patience sighed. "How romantic."

"Romantic!" Miles snorted. "What do you know of romance?"

"More than you, master scholar," Patience snapped back.

"Enough, children," Lady Hargrave cut in. "If you cannot converse politely at table then you may return to the schoolroom for your dinner." This threat effectively silenced them as she continued. "Isn't this the third time during the last several months that there has been a robbery in the vicinity? Can't the authorities do anything?"

Phillip answered her. "It is always difficult to apprehend thieves who are continuously moving to another location, never establishing any pattern to their crimes. The best defense when traveling is to be prepared, even though the chance is slim that you will ever be stopped. And there is no dishonor in giving up your trinkets; such thieves are generally content with valuables and seldom harm travelers." He didn't add that the highwayman who had stopped his coach had not lived to stop another.

The excellence of the dinner raised numerous comments from the delighted participants, and all regretted that Caroline was missing such a treat. Phillip's thoughts strayed more than once to her during the meal, for he had never liked to have the sun set upon a disagreement. He made short work of his port after dinner, asking Stephen and Miles to excuse him. Repairing to the library, he dispatched a footman to request that Miss Hargrave join him there. If the girl had stayed away from dinner because of their disagreement earlier in the day, she was making too much of it. He was not one to bear a grudge, and she had been right after all. The cook had acquitted herself admirably, proving that with proper ingredients at her disposal she was more than qualified to hold her position.

When the footman returned to say that Miss Hargrave was not in her room, Phillip asked to have her maid sent to him instead.

The young maid, Ginny, soon appeared, bobbing a curtsy in the doorway. "You wished to speak with me, sir?"

"Yes. Tell your mistress I would like a word with her," he said.

"Miss Caroline is not in her room, m'lord."

"I am sure you have been instructed to say so, but please, tell her it is important I speak with her."

"You may come and see for yourself, m'lord, if you disbelieve me. Miss Caroline is not in her room nor has she been, not since the afternoon."

"The afternoon?" he said. "But she excused herself from dinner and intended to retire early," he mumbled, more to himself than to the girl. Abruptly returning his attention to her, he asked, "When did you last see your mistress?"

"This afternoon, m'lord. Mrs. Ribbon came to speak with her, and they went off together. I have not seen Miss Caroline since."

"Mrs. Ribbon?" Now thoroughly confused, Phillip thanked the maid absentmindedly, then left the library for the door at the far end of the hall. No one it seemed, including her family, had seen Caroline for several hours. If she had gone with the cook, then perhaps the cook would know something of her whereabouts. A scullery maid stopped work to stare as Lord Brooke made his way through narrow passageways to the kitchen, but her look of astonishment could not equal his own when he passed through a door to find Caroline standing before a butcher block, a mess of kidneys before her and a bloody knife in her hand.

He could not keep himself from exclaiming, "What the devil are you doing here?"

She couldn't begin to guess if he was angry or amused and didn't stop to think. She merely answered his question plainly. "Preparing your breakfast, my lord. These will make an excellent pie."

If he had been hovering between emotions, these flippant words put paid to any generous instinct he harbored. In his most cutting, authoritarian voice, the one reserved for those unfortunate enough to have displeased him utterly, he said, "You will go to the library, Miss Hargrave, and await me there." He immediately turned to the cook, so did not see Caroline's eyes light with the fire of battle nor her nostrils dilate with the quick intake of breath.

She obeyed him, however, stopping only long enough to wash her hands and remove her apron. She may have disliked the voice of authority, but she recognized it well enough. Her father had stood for little nonsense in his home. He had ruled his family, she supposed, much as he had ruled his troops—

issuing unequivocal orders and expecting them to be obeyed instantly without comment or excuse.

Lord Brooke's command fell perfectly into this category, and she obeyed from force of habit, even experiencing some of the trepidation she felt when she knew she had displeased her father and wondered what form his punishment would take. That Brooke was displeased she was certain. How he intended to deal with her was unclear, but she had ample time to consider the possibilities while she waited more than twenty minutes for him to join her.

When he entered the library, she was seated in an armchair pretending to read. Always preferring to meet adversity head-on, she put her book aside and rose to face him as he crossed the room.

"Is it your ambition to be a cook, Miss Hargrave? If tonight was a representative sample of your work, I am willing to admit you would make an excellent one. If you are interested in the position, I can offer you fifty pounds per annum and found."

She regarded him steadily but, uncertain where his discourse was leading, said nothing.

He soon continued. "What was in your mind? Did you intend a perpetual headache? How long did you think you could protect Mrs. Ribbon? Oh, yes, she told me you prepared the meal. It wasn't that hard to guess, although I daresay it was the knife that made everything clear. I must be getting slow. Clearly I should have made the connection between your absence from dinner and the high quality of the meal, but somehow it didn't occur to me you would find your way to the kitchen. It should have, for I recall you informed me only this morning of your intimate knowledge of that domain."

At his mention of their meeting that morning, a flush tinged her cheeks, but she still refrained from speech.

"Have I stumbled into a madhouse here?" he pursued. "Has none of you any notion of the proper way to go on?"

He finally struck a responsive chord in her. "If you are so displeased with us, my lord, why don't you take your sensitive palate and your disapproval and leave us in peace. None of us asked to have you here!"

"You're out there. Your mother asked me to stay, and I have no intention of leaving until I have accomplished what I set out to do. If that means I must endure ill-bred lectures and witness outrageous behavior in a young woman old enough to know better, then so be it."

Knowing she had no defense, Caroline wanted only to be gone. "May I retire now, my lord?"

"You may leave after you have told me, without heat, why you felt constrained to cook the meal tonight."

Caroline knew she had little choice but to meet his terms. "You had poor Mrs. Ribbon in a frenzy, my lord. She is a simple farmer's wife and had no idea what she should prepare for you. You expect too much from her; she was frightened by the prospect of losing her position."

"Servants should be turned off if they are not satisfactory."

"No, sir! Not in this house. It has never been so. Our people do their best and always have, but they have no experience of the style of life to which you are accustomed."

"Why were you cooking for her?"

"She came to me for advice. She had all the ingredients before her and feared to continue. Some of the spices she had never seen before, and she had no knowledge of your likes and dislikes. She has six children and a disabled husband and she needs her job. She knew she must present a meal that would please you."

"So you offered to help?"

"Yes."

"When did you learn to cook?"

"Each time Mrs. Ribbon needed time off for her children, the job was mine. Actually, I enjoy cooking, though I never had such raw materials to work with as I had today. With good ingredients it is rather simple to make a fine meal. If you have no objection, I thought I might teach Mrs. Ribbon how to prepare several dishes. She is more than eager to learn. I am sure in no time she could be preparing meals to please you."

"I have every possible objection to such a scheme," he replied dampingly. "The kitchen is no place for you. Your mother and I will deal with the cook, and I insist you steer clear of the matter entirely." When he saw her proud chin come up a fraction and the stubbornness return to her eyes, he added, "I hope you intend to oblige me in this, Miss Hargrave."

His words held a definite question and she responded lightly, "Why should I have any reason to disoblige you, sir?"

"I can't imagine."

"May I retire now?"

"You may. Good night."

"Good night, Lord Brooke."

The following morning Caroline presented herself very early for breakfast, took one look at the kidney pie Stephen was eagerly consuming, and promptly lost her appetite. She helped herself to coffee and a piece of dry toast, then seated herself beside her brother.

"Where is our esteemed trustee this morning?" she asked.

Stephen looking questioningly at his sister's Spartan breakfast, for she was normally a hearty eater. "You don't like him much, do you?"

"No, not much. And I can't understand why you agreed to his dismissing Mrs. Ribbon."

"I don't think you're trying to see his side, Caro," he offered. "You must not view his changes as a personal attack."

"But they are an attack—certainly an attack upon our cook."

"Mrs. Ribbon is not the only one to have fallen under his lordship's displeasure. I had a dressing-down yesterday for working on the home farm. Patience is to have a governess though she's not at all certain she wants one. He's right about me, and I think if you consider, you must admit he is right about Mrs. Ribbon. She's never been a very good cook. Although, I must say, she acquitted herself well last evening."

Caroline stood up suddenly, tossing down her napkin and glaring at her brother. "I will not stay and listen to you defend him, Stephen. Clearly you think him a paragon."

"I am not defending him. I am only asking you to consider whether he may have been right."

"I care not one whit if he was right or wrong! What I object to is his manner. He walked in here a total stranger and took charge as if he were the king himself, with no thought for the customs of the past or the feelings of the people. He issues orders and expects everyone to jump. Well, you may jump to his commands, Stephen, but I will not! I am not a puppet who will submit to having my strings pulled by Lord Brooke!"

At that moment Brooke strolled into the room, a friendly smile on his lips. "Good morning, Stephen . . . Miss Hargrave. May I call you Caroline?"

As Stephen returned the greeting, Caroline sank back into her chair. She knew not how much of her comment had been overheard, but any amount would have been too much. She couldn't bring her tongue to form a civil answer to the question Brooke had posed, so she remained silent.

In an effort to cover her rudeness and allow her time to compose herself, Stephen heartily recommended the kidney pie to his guardian.

During the days that followed, Caroline did her best to avoid Brooke. When she heard one maid and one groom had been dismissed, she was not in the least surprised. When she found the butler's position had been taken over by one of the senior footmen, she sought her brother for an explanation.

"Wilcox has been pensioned off," Stephen informed her.

"I need not wonder whose idea that was," she replied scathingly.

"Wilcox was well past the work, Caro, and you know it. How many times have we found him asleep in the cloakroom? It is too big a job for a man his age."

Caroline's eyes narrowed as she regarded her brother. "You are beginning to sound a great deal like Lord Brooke, Stephen. Wilcox is too old, therefore he should be cast aside and replaced by someone more efficient."

"Not cast aside. Retired. And, yes, replaced. We cannot save the Hall if we allow sentiment to govern us."

Caroline felt her eyes clouding with tears of resentment and turned away quickly to hide her disappointment. When she did not speak for several moments, Stephen began again. "Phillip has sent to Southwell for his chef. He is hoping Mrs. Ribbon will learn all she can from Claude while he is with us. If she applies herself, it may be possible for her to resume her former position after he has gone. Will you speak with her?"

Caroline nodded, her back still turned.

"Phillip's personal secretary is coming to help organize the household," Stephen continued. "He will be bringing Claude and several other servants, as well as a few more horses. We will need a room prepared for Mr. Keating. Since he is a distant cousin of Phillip's, I think it would be appropriate for him to have a room in the west wing."

"I will see to it immediately, Stephen," Caroline responded dully. "Was there anything else?"

"I don't think so. I shall see you at dinner, then?"

"Yes, certainly."

She left the room without looking at him again. She could scarcely believe this was the brother she had laughed with just two weeks ago. He seemed determined to pattern his will after Lord Brooke's, and she could see no way to stop him.

Her mother would be no help, for she, too, was blind to his lordship's machinations. Relieved of some of her anxieties concerning the estate, Lady Hargrave had returned wholeheartedly to her favorite pastime—charity work. If she wasn't at the church, she was at the rectory or in the village, planning, organizing, and working with the rector's wife and the village women.

Miles existed in a world of study. Lord Brooke had told him he could return to Eton in the fall. Caroline would find no supporter in Miles.

Patience had never altered the opinion she had formed of Brooke upon first meeting him. Dazzled by his smile and striking good looks, she saw in him the hero of all her childhood fairy tales. In her eyes he could do no wrong; she had even convinced herself she would like her new governess.

Why couldn't her family see the man for what he really was? Caroline wondered—a hard, uncaring, insensitive, manipulative egotist.

A late afternoon ride on Hercules with Leo for company did little to improve Caroline's spirits. When she returned to the stables, she was greeted with a piece of news that sent her fuming to the house. Webber, formerly footman, now butler, opened the door.

"Where is Lord Brooke, Webber?" she asked.

"Dressing for dinner, I believe, miss. It lacks only thirty minutes till the hour."

She hurried upstairs without answering, changed her dress in record time, and was waiting in the hall when his lordship descended the staircase. After the first night when he had been unwittingly late, he had made an effort to be down early.

He was straightening a wristband as he came into view and

descended four or five steps before he saw her. He paused, not liking her attitude or the grim lines of her face. He wondered how long it would be before he had the pleasure of seeing joy, or mirth, or even a simple smile on her face.

As he reached the last stair and came on a level with her, he said, "Good evening, Caroline."

"Good evening," she replied simply. She found it impossible to address him by his given name, as he did her, yet she tried to avoid the formality of giving him his title. "I had determined not to interfere since it is obvious my opinion counts for little, but I find I must speak with you, sir."

"Very well. Shall we step into the library where we can be private?" He held the door for her, then closed it firmly behind them. "How have I displeased you now, Miss Hargrave?"

His reversion to more formal address made it easier somehow, and she continued clearly. "I was told at the stables that you have ordered the mare Blossom to be sold."

"Yes, I have. The stables, as well as the house and farms, must be run practically to be profitable. I was told the mare is no longer ridden—indeed, that she has no use at all."

"No, my lord. She has no use. But she was my first horse, and I had intended she should live out her life here."

"The mare requires care and feed. There is no place for useless animals on a foundering estate. I don't think there is room for sentiment here, and I don't see any reason to keep her."

"*You* don't think! *You* don't see!" Caroline flared at him. "Are you the only one entitled to an opinion, my lord? Are you the only one with a mind or a thought in it? Can you never see any view but your own? You may have control of the purse strings, but you do not own us. That horse is mine, not Stephen's, and you have no right to dispose of her. If you will not permit Stephen to feed her, then I will pay for her feed myself. And I will groom her myself, too, if you cannot spare one of the boys to do it."

"It is the height of folly to squander what little income you have on a useless animal," he persisted.

"It is within your power to stop my allowance, sir. Do so, and this argument is decided."

Several moments passed in silence as she stood rigidly before him, her hands clenched at her sides. He, on the other hand, stood very much at his ease, regarding her with interest. Finally he answered.

"I will have my secretary give you an account on quarter day, and you may pay for the mare's keep yourself. I hope you don't find the cost of sentiment too dear."

"No, never that, my lord." She swept into the hall as she heard the others descending to the drawing room, and he followed slowly behind.

Chapter 6

DAYBREAK THE FOLLOWING morning found Phillip cantering his mare along the field roads of the home farm. The crops were thriving. Recent days had offered long hours of sunshine, and the fields flourished under it. This morning, however, there was a misty rain falling; heavy fog lay in the valleys, and even the joyful woodland birds and squirrels were silent. Phillip collected the mare to a trot, her hooves sounding a dull, steady rhythm on the damp earth.

Not for the first time, Phillip was wondering what he could do to improve his relationship with Caroline Hargrave. She seemed determined to dislike him; he knew she purposely avoided him. When they met at meals, she took part in the conversation but seldom addressed him directly.

Phillip hadn't been told that Blossom was Caroline's mare. He sympathized with the girl, for he knew it could be painful to part with an old friend, yet he still believed that to keep the mare was unwise. Caroline had played her cards cleverly. There was no way he could have carried his point without being cast as a complete tyrant, a role he was most unwilling to assume.

Returning to the stables, Phillip surrendered his horse to a groom and found himself strolling down the row of loose boxes. He found Blossom at the end of the aisle quietly munching hay. She perked her ears and interrupted her breakfast at his approach, then dropped her head over the half door to say hello. Phillip smiled and ran his hand down her face. She was chestnut with a broad blaze and widely spaced, intelligent eyes.

"Your mistress has come to your defense, old girl. Did you know that? And a formidable defender she is! She put me to rout easily enough—so you stay. And for today at least, you need not go without currying, for I intend to do it myself."

And he did. He asked one of the stable lads to fetch him brushes and combs and spent an enjoyable half hour with Blossom.

Late that afternoon Caroline was quizzing Miles on his Greek verbs when the first of the entourage from Southwell arrived. She and her brother stood at the window watching as a group of horses and riders came up the drive and passed on to the stables. Two mounted grooms were leading two horses each. The horses being led were grays, similarly marked.

"That will be Phillip's curricle team," Miles said. "Stephen said he had sent for them. Spectacular, aren't they? Arabian, don't you think?"

"I really couldn't say," Caroline answered, feigning disinterest. Privately she thought them spectacular indeed, but she was seldom in a mood to approve of Lord Brooke, and that included approval of his horses.

A coach following close behind drove round to the service entrance, where it unloaded the incomparable Claude and several other domestics. The coach containing Mr. Keating arrived nearly an hour later. Pulled by a handsome bay team, it rolled to a stop directly before the wide stone steps leading up to the front doors.

"This will be Mr. Keating, Miles. I must go."

"Need I come, Caro?"

"No, I think not. You will meet him at dinner. Shall we do the verbs–again tomorrow, then?"

"Yes, if you like."

Caroline knew that Webber would show the visitor into the salon. She made her way there, shaking the creases from her skirt and stopping briefly at a mirror to be sure her hair was tidy. Coming from the west end of the house, her route brought her to the salon via the drawing room, which adjoined it. She opened the doors to find that Matthew Keating was a man in his late twenties. Beside him stood a boy of perhaps fifteen, tall and dark-haired.

Caroline gave her hand to Mr. Keating, noticing how his brown hair curled naturally. "You must be Mr. Keating. I am Caroline Hargrave. Welcome to Paxton Hall."

He nodded and took her hand, his hazel eyes smiling. "Thank you, Miss Hargrave. It is a pleasure to meet you." Even as he turned to make his companion known to Caroline, the doors to the main hall opened and Brooke entered.

Caroline was intrigued by his strange behavior. His eyes skimmed over her, rested a moment on Mr. Keating, then moved to the boy. Brooke's face hardened noticeably, and Caroline had the odd impression he was in pain. He stopped abruptly two steps inside the doors and stared rudely as the boy returned his regard. Seconds dragged by until Brooke seemed to shake himself free of whatever emotion was controlling him. He moved forward to greet the boy.

"Phillip! Needless to say I did not expect to see you here. You are very like the miniature Helen sent last year. You are well, I see."

"Quite well, sir, thank you," the boy replied.

For a split second Caroline thought he intended to ignore Brooke's outstretched hand, but then he extended his own, taking the older man's briefly.

Brooke smiled and shook Mr. Keating's hand warmly. "It will be good to have you here, Matthew. I have missed your efficiency." He turned to Caroline. "Miss Hargrave, it seems Matthew has brought another guest. May I present my son, also Phillip Brooke."

It was now time for Caroline's face to betray her surprise. "Your . . . your son . . . How . . . How do you do, Mr. Brooke."

She extended her hand, and he took it. "My pleasure, Miss Hargrave, but I'm known by my second name—William. It makes for less confusion." Young William was smiling pleasantly, but beyond his shoulder Caroline saw his father's smile fade and one eyebrow rise. If William felt his father's gaze upon him, he showed no sign of unease.

"I'm sure it must," she replied. "I can't imagine having two people in the same house with the same name."

"We don't have that particular problem," Brooke interjected. "Phil—William doesn't make his home at Southwell. He has just arrived from India. I did not even know he was in the country, hence my surprise at seeing him."

"India! How wonderful!" Caroline exclaimed. "I have always longed to travel but have never had the opportunity. Were you gone long?"

William hesitated, and before he could reply, Phillip interrupted. "I think we must delay this conversation to another time. It is fast approaching the dinner hour, and you will both wish to change. Caroline, if you could have a footman show William to the room you prepared for Matthew, I will take Matthew to mine. Will that do?"

"Yes, certainly. And I will see immediately to a room for you, Mr. Keating."

"Thank you, ma'am. You're very kind."

They all ascended the stairs together and parted company in the upstairs hall. Phillip closed his bedroom door firmly behind himself and his secretary.

"What is happening here, Matthew?"

"I don't know. He arrived at Southwell just a few hours before I was scheduled to depart. He says Lady Crowly wrote, but apparently his ship made a faster journey than the one carrying her letter. In any event, I had no way to warn you and no choice but to bring him along. All he will say is that your sister sent him to England. More than that he would not tell me."

"My heart nearly stopped when I saw him standing there," Phillip said. "I knew him instantly. Even without the miniature I think I must have known."

"There is a resemblance," Matthew said. "How old is he now?"

"He and his sister turned fourteen this past spring. They were five when I last saw them."

"It must be strange to have children you never see."

"It is. But at the time it seemed the only thing I could do, and I am still convinced it was for the best. I wonder why he has come."

* * *

William Brooke and Matthew Keating were introduced to the Hargraves when everyone gathered in the drawing room before dinner. Observing Lord Brooke and his son together, Caroline decided there was little likeness beyond coloring. Although he was dark-haired and gray-eyed like his father, William's features were otherwise dissimilar. While Phillip's face was composed of strong lines and bold planes, William's was softer, his chin and nose less pronounced, his eyes less piercing than his father's.

Mr. Keating she liked instantly. Without being precisely handsome, he was a fine-looking man. Nearly as tall as his employer, he dressed soberly but was precise to a pin, his coat and breeches expertly tailored to his slender form. Flawless manners accompanied a warm, outgoing disposition. So unlike his cousin, she thought.

The dinner itself began routinely, but Caroline's knowledge that young Mr. Brooke was newly arrived from India soon brought the focus of the conversation to him.

"Did you enjoy your visit to India, Mr. Brooke?"

"I was not visiting India, Miss Hargrave. I live there with my aunt and uncle and my twin sister. I am, in fact, visiting England."

Phillip spooned his soup silently. William had handled the question well. How would Caroline respond now? he wondered. But it was Patience who spoke, addressing herself to Phillip.

"We didn't know you were married, sir, nor that you had children. Has your daughter come to England?"

He smiled at her. "I'm not married, Patience. My wife is dead. And no, I don't believe Beth has come to England." He raised a questioning brow to William.

"I came alone," William confirmed, his eyes never leaving his father's. "It was my aunt's idea, not mine."

His words seemed to hold both challenge and resentment. Phillip signaled for a footman to pour more wine, then helped himself to quail with mushroom sauce.

Miles then asked about the passage—how long it had taken and whether William had been ill at sea. The conversation progressed to the striking difference in climate between India and England and throughout the main course dealt with innocuous subjects.

Phillip listened with interest. Caroline, Lady Hargrave, and Stephen were purposely avoiding any question that might bring too personal a response. Miles and Patience seemed unaware of the undercurrent at the table.

During the dessert, just as the older members of the family felt they had managed to cover some rough ground fairly well, Patience asked William a seemingly simple question. Its effect was to bring acute discomfort to nearly everyone present.

"Why is it that you and your sister don't live in England with your father?"

After a lengthy, embarrassing silence, William answered. "You must ask my father that question, Miss Patience. I really couldn't say." Turning to Lady Hargrave he continued. "It has been a long day, ma'am. With your permission, I should like to retire."

"Certainly, Mr. Brooke. We so enjoyed hearing about your home. You must tell us more very soon."

"I would be happy to. Good night, everyone."

There was a chorus of good nights as his eyes swept the table. Carefully avoiding his father's stony regard, he followed a footman from the room.

After dinner Phillip joined Matthew and Stephen in a single glass of port, then excused himself, leaving them to become acquainted. Knowing that a confrontation with William was inevitable, he saw no reason to delay it. He entered William's room to find him standing between the open draperies of his western-facing windows, watching the sun set in a pink and azure sky.

"Why have you come, William? It is obvious you would rather be elsewhere."

William answered without turning. "I told you at dinner. It was Aunt Helen's idea. She feels it's time I had a proper education. Five generations of Brookes have attended Oxford. I dare not break with tradition," he added bitterly.

Phillip regarded his son with proprietary interest. He was tall; Phillip supposed he would be as tall as himself someday, perhaps taller. He had noticed at dinner that William's eyes were gray, not brown as his mother's had been, yet they held the same shape hers had, the same expression. Despite his son's obvious belligerence, Phillip's tone softened. "I'm sorry I wasn't at Southwell to welcome you home."

William swung to face him, his father's conciliatory tone making no impression. "Home? Southwell isn't my home. I'd never seen it until two days ago!"

"It will be your home someday."

"No! I don't want it. And I don't want to be here. I wish to God I hadn't come!"

He turned his back again, and Phillip allowed several minutes to pass in silence before he replied matter-of-factly, "If you wish to return to India, you may do so. I will not stand in your way. But before you make a decision, I suggest you consider the matter carefully. If you truly desire an education, England is certainly the place to get it. If it is my presence that concerns you, that problem is easily solved. You can stay at Southwell. I won't be there this summer. I can hire a tutor and you can study at home until the fall term starts at Eton. When you're older, you may attend whichever university you prefer. A break with tradition would not disturb me."

"I should like to think about it," William replied noncommittally.

"Certainly, take all the time you need. For myself, I should be pleased if you stayed here at Paxton Hall. Circumstances have kept us apart all these years. I would welcome the opportunity to spend some time together."

"Circumstances! What circumstances?" William asked brutally. "You gave us away! You didn't have to give us to Aunt Helen and Uncle George."

"Yes, I did," Phillip said softly. "I had to. Someday, perhaps, I will tell you why. Someday when you are less hostile and more willing to listen. I will leave now. You said you were tired. I ride before breakfast each morning; you're welcome to join me if you like. Good night."

By the time William mumbled a belated "good night," his father had already gone.

William didn't join Phillip for an early ride the following morning, but neither did he make any immediate plans to leave Paxton. Upon hearing his father would not hold him in England against his will, his first thought was that he would return immediately to India. But contemplation of his aunt's disapproval should he do so made him reconsider. She had insisted he go; she would be gravely disappointed should he return.

After being only a few days among the Hargraves, William discovered he wished to remain. He thought Caroline the most beautiful woman he had ever seen; in Miles he found a willing study companion; he admired Stephen's dedication to his family and his ambitions for his estate; he soon discovered it was an easy task to avoid his father. During the first two days of his visit they met only at dinner, and with the others present it was never uncomfortable.

Several days after William's arrival a letter was forwarded from Southwell to Paxton Hall, addressed to Lord Brooke from his sister. He was alone in the library when Webber carried it to him. Lady Crowly began with greetings and general news, then came to the subject of William:

. . . By the time you receive this William will be well on his way to England. I thought everything through carefully before sending him, and am convinced it is the proper thing to do. As you know, he has, all these years, been reluctant to speak of you, though George and I have encouraged him in every way we know. He has refused to write as Beth does (I have enclosed her latest letter) and I do not believe he reads your letters to him, though he does take them away to his room.

During the past six months, however, I have noticed a change in him. It is that, as well as my belief that he needs a proper English education, which has determined me to send him to you. One day recently he asked me several personal questions about you and Victoria. Did you love her? How old were you when you married? How old was she when she died? Some were a great deal more personal. Several I felt it wasn't my place to answer. For some I had no answers. I am sure you must understand that after years of silence from him concerning you, we were amazed at his sudden interest. From the general direction and tone of his questions I concluded that he holds some very strange notions of both you and your motives for acting as you did all those years ago. His questions should be answered and you are the only one to answer them. I know he loves us both, as we love him, but you are his father. Since he must some-

day assume those responsibilities that are now yours, we feel it is time he comes to you. I hope you will agree; somehow I know you will.

With deepest affection,
Helen

Phillip read the enclosed letter from his daughter Beth then reread that part of his sister's letter concerning William. He wished now he hadn't offered to allow the boy to do as he pleased, for Helen seemed determined that William remain in England. Phillip sighed as he tucked the letters away in his pocket. He had always wondered whether the time would come. Now it seemed that after fourteen years he was to have an opportunity to try his hand at fatherhood.

Returning to the house after a walk to the village, Caroline encountered her mother in the front hall. Lady Hargrave was moving toward the estate office with several jewelry cases in her hands.

Caroline's face clouded as she asked suspiciously, "What are you doing, Mama?"

"I am taking these trinkets to Lord Brooke. It is foolish to keep them when the money they will bring could be put to good use."

"Sell your jewelry!" Caroline exclaimed. "Mama, you mustn't."

"I have quite decided to do it, Caroline. I have no wish to argue." By this time Lady Hargrave had reached the office door. As a footman opened it before her, Caroline hurried after, forgetting in her anxiety that to do so would bring her in contact with Brooke, a person she avoided whenever possible.

"I have brought the jewelry, my lord," Lady Hargrave said, as both Brooke and Mr. Keating rose to their feet.

Phillip glanced past her shoulder at Caroline's troubled face. "Are you certain you wish to part with them, ma'am? No second thoughts?"

"No, sir. None," her ladyship replied.

"Very well, then. I will sell them for you on my next visit to London."

Unable to contain herself longer, Caroline spoke. "Is it really necessary to sell my mother's jewelry, Lord Brooke?"

Her mother answered her, quite sternly. "His lordship and I have discussed this subject and agreed, Caroline. It is not your concern. I am late. Thank you again, Lord Brooke. Good day. Good day, Mr. Keating."

As her mother withdrew, Caroline stood irresolutely. She must say something. But how could she? How could she tell her mother, how could she tell his lordship the jewels were worthless? Her father had had them copied years ago, disposing of the gems to retire massive gambling debts. What Brooke held were imitation—paste.

Phillip watched her closely as a succession of strong emotions passed over her face. When he spoke, it was to his secretary. "Will you leave us a moment, Matthew?"

When he and Caroline were alone, Phillip asked, "Had you expected these to come to you someday? Is that what concerns you?"

"No. Certainly not."

"They have considerable value," he persisted.

Stung that he should think her willing to benefit at Stephen's expense, she answered clearly, "My mother may dispose of her own property as she sees fit. I think it's wonderfully generous of her. She's helping Stephen in the only way she can."

She had moved to the window and stood looking out. Phillip studied her in profile, deciding that harsh sunlight did little to detract from her beauty. He moved to her side, stopping only inches away. "Was there one particular piece you wanted then? Something of your mother's that you would like to pass on to a daughter someday perhaps. I see no harm in retaining one piece."

She turned to look at him, something in his voice making her forget her immediate problem. Their eyes held for several moments until he dropped his to open the top box. "Diamonds—no, I think not; emeralds—charming, but not quite . . ." He left off his perusal of the jewelry case and brought his free hand to her chin, turning her head slightly so that her eyes caught the light angling in the windows. "Sapphires, I think, would be perfect, though your eyes would outshine any gem—"

He stopped suddenly as she jerked her face from his hand

and turned away. He snapped the case shut. "There was nothing you wanted to hold back, then?"

Freed from the unsuspected warmth she had seen in his eyes, she remembered her catalog of grievances against him. "My father had excellent taste in precious gems, my lord. I think you will be surprised at the value of those."

Let him find out for himself how worthless they were, she thought. She evilly imagined the scene when the haughty Lord Brooke asked a reputable jeweler to buy imitation stones. Let *him* decide how to tell her mother. She would be hurt whoever told her. Why not let his lordship be the bearer of bad tidings?

Caroline moved from the room with an unwelcome sensation of tightness in her chest and the memory of undeniable magnetism in a pair of dark gray eyes.

Chapter 7

CAROLINE ALTERNATED THE stiff brush in her left hand with the soft one in her right, sweeping down and back across Blossom's satiny coat. Stephen stood nearby, idly slapping his riding crop against one boot, waiting while a groom saddled the gelding Phillip had supplied for his use.

"You don't think it unusual, then, for him to have a fourteen-year-old son?" Caroline was asking. "He couldn't have been much more than twenty or twenty-one when William was born!"

"There is no law to govern when a man marries, Caro. Some men marry quite young, and I see nothing wrong in it. I would consider it myself if the opportunity arose."

"What do you mean?"

Stephen shrugged. "Only that if there were someone I cared for in that way, someone I wished to wed, I would see no reason to delay."

Caroline considered the idea and decided she could easily

envision Stephen married. He had always seemed years older than he was.

"It's different with you," she said. "You're steady; you know what you want; you accept advice and make careful choices."

"And how can you say Phillip wasn't the same at my age?" he asked reasonably.

She shrugged her shoulders. "Here comes your horse. Where are you bound this morning?"

"Ware. To look at ewes—breeding stock." He took the reins from the groom and mounted smoothly. "With Mama and Patience in the village and Miles and William studying at the rectory, you will have a quiet morning to yourself." He grinned down at her from his restless, sidestepping horse. "You must admit that doesn't happen often. Don't expect me before the afternoon."

He threw her a brief salute and trotted away. She watched him for a few moments, then transferred her gaze to the groom who held Lord Brooke's bay mare in the drive outside the house. Brooke was leaving for London and would be gone for several days. It would be wonderful to be free of him even for a short time.

Within the house Phillip made last-minute preparations for his departure.

"If you took the curricle," Matthew said, "you could put these stones in the hiding place under the seat. There were those reports of highwaymen."

"I will ride as planned, Matthew. Put them in the pouches, and I'll carry them in my pockets. I have seldom known footpads to be active in the daylight on a post road." He folded some papers from the desk and tucked them into an inside pocket of his coat. Then, taking the pouches Matthew offered, he stowed them away as well, pulled on his gloves, and picked up his hat and whip.

He paused on the top step outside, admiring the freshness of the day, looking forward to a long, invigorating ride. His eyes swept the drive and stable yard and came to rest on the old chestnut mare and the girl who stood near her. Caroline was gazing at him as well. Their eyes held for several moments until she looked away to continue her work. He stood a moment longer, then descended the steps, mounted his mare, and set off for London.

Several days of rain and mist had given way to a clear morning. Bright sunlight filtered through the leafy branches overhead, throwing dappled patterns on the winding woodland road. Phillip soon rode clear of the Hargrave estate and joined the post road toward Welwyn. He judged London to be a shade more than thirty miles; he had no intention of hurrying.

Less than two miles from the Hall, the trees began to thin while the undergrowth increased. Ferns mingled with brambles, and thornbushes crowded one another to the edges of the road. Idly watching the road ahead, Phillip spied what appeared to be the glint of metal reflecting sunshine. His recent caution from Matthew, years of military service, and a strong instinct for self-preservation caused him to rein back without conscious thought.

At that very instant a deafening shot rent the stillness of the morning. Pulled back violently, the mare reared on her haunches, even as a bullet cut a furrow across her shoulder and buried itself in the leather of the saddle. She squealed in pain and bounded sideways into the heavy undergrowth, startling herself anew as the rough vegetation dragged under her belly and tangled round her legs. She reared again, this time rising up under the low horizontal branches of an ancient oak.

Phillip struggled to control the mare, knowing he was little match for any adversary while on a plunging horse. When she reared the second time, a heavy branch struck the back of his head and he lurched forward across her shoulders, toppling headfirst to the ground.

Riderless and trembling, the mare stood still at last, while her rider lay motionless on the ground before her. A movement across the road brought her head up as her ears flexed tightly forward, every muscle tense. She waited while a strange man made noisy progress through the thick bushes. When he stepped into the road, she snorted once, turned on her haunches, and bolted for home.

Caroline led Blossom down the lane to the pasture gate and had just turned her into the meadow when the bay mare came thundering down the drive toward the stables, reins slack on her neck, stirrups flying.

Caroline smiled. The mare had seemed very fresh as she waited for her rider earlier. She had been pawing the ground impatiently, tossing her head, turning in circles about the groom. Clearly she had been fresher than his lordship suspected and had managed to unseat him. Caroline privately admitted to some surprise. She'd had many opportunities to watch Brooke ride, and she grudgingly admitted he was a first-rate horseman. Yet even the best riders came off occasionally, she reasoned. She felt cheated that she hadn't seen it happen. Lord Brooke in the dust—a rare treat indeed!

As Caroline walked back along the lane, the mare reached the stable yard and stopped as a groom ran to take her rein. Brooke's head groom stepped from the building and was soon beckoning Caroline. She quickened her steps to join them, for even from some distance she could see blood on the mare's shoulder.

"What's happened to her?" she asked, bewildered.

"Can't be positive, miss, but it looks like a bullet wound to me."

"A bullet! But I thought—"

"With your permission, miss, I'll take this horse and go back along the Welwyn road. His lordship hasn't been gone long—"

"No. If he's hurt, a horse won't help," she reasoned. "We'll need a carriage. Harness a team, quickly."

The head groom needed only to look at his underling, and the boy dashed into the stables.

"Bring the carriage when it's ready, Smithton," Caroline said. "And inform Mr. Keating. I shall ride ahead. Give me a leg up, would you?"

Smithton stared at her openmouthed, not nearly so shocked that she should wish to ride a bloodied horse astride as that she should contemplate riding into possible danger.

"You mustn't, miss. You can't tell what may have happened. You could be endangering yourself. Let me go."

"Nonsense. If someone has fired at his lordship, they would not stay about to be caught. They will run far and fast. I must go. I have helped my mother when she tended the sick and injured. If Lord Brooke is hurt, I may be able to help him."

Since she seemed determined and her words made sense, Smithton cupped his hands to receive her foot, averting his eyes as her skirt skipped up her ankles. He hurried to the stables to help with the coach as Caroline cantered down the drive.

Caroline gained the high road and turned toward Welwyn, talking quietly to the mare. She could see the wound wasn't serious, for the bullet—if it had been a bullet—had merely removed the hair and enough skin to cause minor bleeding. The mare was moving soundly and seemed calm, her ears back, listening to all Caroline said to her. As the road narrowed and the trees thinned, the mare's nostrils flared and she slowed her gait noticeably. Caroline was certain the animal was remembering the place she had been frightened earlier. Collecting the horse to a trot and then a walk, Caroline took a firm grip on the reins, her eyes studying the forest ahead. She saw nothing, heard nothing unusual. Only the normal woodland sounds and sights greeted her. She walked the mare slowly forward until she stopped of her own accord and stood.

"Lord Brooke?" Caroline spoke his name rather quietly. When there was no answer, no sound of any kind, she called louder, "Lord Brooke?"

She realized then that her heart was hammering within her breast, for even though she had told Smithton no criminal would remain at the scene of the crime, she was not entirely convinced of it.

She urged the horse forward again, then saw Brooke lying just a few feet from the road's edge amid a mass of trampled vines and brambles. He was on his side, facing away. She dismounted and with shaking fingers tied the mare tightly to a small tree.

Phillip lay still enough to be dead, but Caroline's mind could not envision him so. Yet when she reached him and with great effort rolled him onto his back, his bloodied waistcoat told another story.

"Oh, dear God," she mumbled as her hands took his limp wrist, seeking a pulse. It was there . . . weak, but there, and now her hands fumbled with his waistcoat buttons, knowing that to stop the bleeding was of utmost importance. The buttons undone and the shirt and waistcoat thrust aside, she found there was no blood beneath. Her fingers roamed over his chest but found no wound.

"How can there be blood and no wound?" she wondered

aloud. Then, as the mare impatiently pawed the ground, Caroline thought she had the answer. "He must have brushed the mare's shoulder as he fell. But that doesn't explain why he is unconscious."

Then she noticed the stump of a recently cut tree near his head. Had he fallen on that? Gently she brushed the hair from his forehead. There was certainly a lump there, already turning blue. She ran her hand carefully over his head, searching for other injuries. Toward the back was a large contusion, swollen and bleeding. Knowing there was little she could do for him until help arrived, she sat anxiously at his side until she heard the coach rattling along the road.

Matthew jumped from the box before the horses had come to a complete stop. He ran to Caroline's side and knelt on the ground near her.

"Is he . . . ?"

"No. He's not dead, only unconscious." As Matthew's eyes took in the bloody waistcoat and bared chest, she explained. "There is no wound there; I searched carefully. I think the blood must be the mare's. His head is badly injured, though. We must get him back to the house as quickly as possible."

Matthew lifted Phillip by the shoulders while Smithton hurried to take his legs. They placed him gently inside the coach, with Caroline cushioning his injured head in her lap. Then Matthew and Smithton carefully turned the carriage in the narrow road.

"Take the mare, Smithton," Matthew said, "and ride for the doctor at once."

"Can you handle the horses, sir?"

"Yes, I can handle them. Go now—and go quickly."

Smithton galloped off toward Welwyn, while Matthew started slowly back toward the Hall. He held the horses to a walk, but even so the carriage jolted roughly over the uneven surface.

Phillip had made no sound when they lifted him, but as the coach turned onto the Hall drive, he suddenly opened his eyes, focusing carefully on Caroline.

"Did they take the jewelry?" he asked.

Caroline had forgotten he was carrying her mother's jewelry to London, but she was relieved that he was awake and that his words made sense.

"It is of no importance, Lord Brooke. You have been hurt—"

"Did they get the jewelry?" he persisted.

Since it seemed important to him, and as it was clearly a great effort for him to speak, she didn't argue. "Where was it?" she asked.

"In my coat pockets."

She reached to feel in the closest pocket and found it empty. She tried the others. "It seems they did take it, but it—"

"Don't tell anyone," he said, his hand finding her arm and gripping it strongly. "Tell no one it was taken. Promise me."

"It cannot signify—"

"Promise me, please!"

"Very well, I promise, but you are worrying yourself unnecessarily. The stones were worthless—" She broke off as his eyes closed and his fingers relaxed their grip. He had lost consciousness again.

The doctor came and went, and the residents at the Hall could only speculate as to what had occurred on the woodland road. Matthew Keating joined Caroline and her mother in the salon to inform them it was certainly a bullet that had injured the mare, as he had dug it from the saddle himself. "Clearly, whoever fired the shot had robbery in mind. We can only be thankful his aim was poor."

"Oh, dear!" Lady Hargrave exclaimed. "I had forgotten Lord Brooke carried my jewelry today. Never tell me it has been lost?"

Before Matthew could respond, Caroline answered. "No, Mama. The jewelry is quite safe. It was on the horse, and she came home when his lordship fell." Gazing directly at Matthew, her eyes dared him to challenge her.

"Thank God for that, at least," Lady Hargrave responded. "Not that the jewelry means anything when compared with his lordship's safety," she said earnestly. "What does the doctor think?"

"He says there is severe concussion, but he considers it a good sign that his lordship spoke to Miss Hargrave," Matthew supplied.

"He thinks the fact that Lord Brooke recognized me and spoke sensibly shows the damage hasn't been too severe," Caroline added. "But he says we must wait until his lordship regains consciousness to discover how he got the terrible lump on his head."

"Did the horse trample him or fall on him?" her ladyship asked. "Perhaps the brigands struck him with some sort of cudgel."

"There is no way we can know," Caroline replied. "I'm sure Lord Brooke will tell us everything when he is able. Has anyone sent for Miles and William?"

"No," Matthew answered. "I thought it best to hear first what the doctor had to say. They should be back soon. Their lesson at the rectory finished some time ago."

"I thought I would sit with Lord Brooke for a time now, Mama," Caroline offered. "I think you should send William up as soon as he comes home."

As Caroline turned to leave, Matthew addressed her again. "May I walk with you, Miss Hargrave?"

She nodded, knowing why he wanted to speak with her. They were partway up the stairs before he began. "I, myself, saw his lordship put the jewelry in his pockets—"

"I lied, Mr. Keating. A despicable thing to do, I agree, but your cousin requested it of me—made me promise, in fact."

"Promise what?"

"To say the jewelry was not lost. That's what he spoke of in the coach when he regained consciousness. He made me promise to tell no one the jewelry was taken. And now I have told you and broken my word already." She paused as she reached the door of Brooke's bedchamber.

"Why should he extract such a promise from you?" Matthew asked, clearly puzzled.

"I am the last person you should ask such a question of, Mr. Keating. I have never pretended to understand his motives. I freely admit they are beyond my powers of reasoning."

"I think you underestimate yourself, ma'am."

"No, indeed, sir. Nor do I underestimate Lord Brooke. I am certain he had what he considers a valid reason for his request, and I am equally certain that whatever his reason, I would disapprove, for we are poles apart, your cousin and I."

Arriving at the house some minutes later, and informed by Matthew of his father's injury, William went immediately upstairs. He found Caroline arranging summer flowers near the window, while his lordship's valet stored linen into the deep drawers of a walnut chest. His father lay in the center of a large four-poster, his face pale except for a livid bruise high on his forehead.

Caroline moved to meet William and brought him to the bedside, where they stood for several moments in silence.

"Mr. Keating said he was set upon by thieves," William said.

"Yes. We think so."

"How badly is he hurt?"

"We're not certain. There's another wound on the back of his head. Both are severe, and the doctor is uncertain how much internal injury there might be."

"Is there anything we can do?"

"No. Only watch him carefully and try to keep him comfortable."

"Could I help? Sit with him, I mean."

She smiled. "Yes, of course. There are many hours in a day, and the doctor particularly requested that someone stay with him at all times."

In an unexpected and uncharacteristic burst of confidence, William said, "All the years I wondered about him—wondered what he was like—I imagined many different things. I have always known he was wealthy, powerful, and influential, and my images always included those things. I never thought of him like this—helpless, or in any way vulnerable."

"I know what you mean," Caroline responded. "I have only known him a few weeks, but to me he is the embodiment of the power and influence you speak of. I suppose there is a lesson for us here, William. No matter how strong, how influential your father may seem, he is only human, and he has human weaknesses, as do we all."

I could give you a list of his character faults a mile long, she thought, and then for a moment pondered what her life would be like tomorrow if Lord Brooke died today. Surprisingly, she found the thought unwelcome and briefly wondered why she had thought it at all. She soon left William sitting with his father and went in search of Miles.

Initially, the nursing schedule for Lord Brooke was random, various members of the family offering to relieve one another when they had time. But when Phillip's unconsciousness persisted into the second day, they realized a more formal schedule was necessary. Stephen and his lordship's valet saw to Brooke's personal needs. The other hours were divided into shifts of various lengths. Most of the nighttime hours were taken by Caroline and her mother, while during the day Stephen, William, Miles, and even Patience took turns.

For the first two days there was no noticeable change in Phillip's condition. Then, on the morning of the third day, he developed a fever and by evening suffered from delirium. The doctor's decision to bleed him resulted in some relief from the delirium but no decrease in the fever.

When Caroline relieved Stephen at midnight, she found the patient tossing from side to side as Stephen attempted to change a cold compress on his forehead.

"He's very restless tonight, Caro, though the fever seems no worse. Shall I stay?"

"No. I can manage."

"He's been delirious again. He was talking about his father. And someone called Victoria. It makes me uncomfortable; it's almost like eavesdropping."

"Victoria was his wife. He mentioned her this morning, too, and I asked William if he knew who she was."

For the first half hour Phillip's restlessness continued as Caroline changed compress after compress, trying to bring him some relief. Finally he slept.

It was nearing two in the morning when he stirred again, throwing the sheet from his chest as he rolled. Caroline moved to the edge of the bed and tried to cover him, but he resisted her. Taking her cool cloth she bathed his face. Then she opened the top buttons of his nightshirt, hoping to make him more comfortable.

She bathed his neck and upper chest, noticing again, as she had in the woods when she searched for a wound, how different he was from her brothers. While Stephen and Miles were fair and smooth-chested, Brooke's chest was covered with a thick mat of tightly curling black hair. She knew Brooke had deprecated Stephen's labor on the home farm, yet she could see he was no stranger to physical activity himself. His body was in excellent condition, his muscles well defined. She allowed her fingers to trail gently through the springy hair, then blushed in the candlelight.

"I must be quite mad," she whispered to herself, realizing she was sitting in a man's bedroom, willfully touching his bare chest. She had begun to redo the buttons of his nightshirt when he startled her by bringing up a hand to clasp her wrist. She looked into his face to see his eyes wide, watching her.

Embarrassed beyond reason she stammered, "I . . . I was . . . I was just buttoning these . . ."

"Victoria?"

"No. It's Caroline."

"It isn't my fault," he stated defensively. "There was nothing I could do. I was powerless."

"Of course you were," she agreed, not certain what she was agreeing to, but relieved to know he had not discovered her touching him. Clearly his mind dwelt on other things.

His grip was cutting off the circulation to her hand. When she tried to pry his fingers loose, he tightened them.

"Please, Victoria, don't leave me. Stay with me."

"I won't leave," she promised. "But you're hurting me."

Amazingly, he understood, for his grip instantly loosened, though he did not release her. "You will stay?"

"Yes. I will."

"I love you; you know that."

Caroline swallowed with difficulty. It was an amazing thing to hear from a man, even though she knew the man was delirious.

He knew she hadn't answered. His grip tightened again. "You do believe I love you?" His tone demanded an answer.

"Yes, I believe you love me."

His eyes in the flickering candlelight shone with a love lost, but not forgotten. "And you love me, too?"

"Yes, I do," she answered, unhesitating this time.

Then, acting not at all like a sick man, he moved his other hand behind her neck and drew her face to his, meeting her lips with his own. Caroline was stunned. Her breathing ceased abruptly as every nerve tingled. His fevered mouth claimed hers with passion, and she offered no resistance but returned the kiss as well as her inexperience allowed. Even when he brought his hand between them, against her breast, she did not pull away but only gasped for the air she had been denying herself.

When his lips left hers, she felt suddenly bereft.

"You're gone," he said.

"No, I'm not. I'm right here," she answered, taking his hot hand in hers.

"You're dead."

She hesitated a moment before replying, "Victoria is dead, yes."

"It's my fault."

"I'm sure it's not anyone's fault."

"I'm sorry—I'm so sorry. How many times must I say I'm sorry before you will forgive me?" His eyes were moist, and Caroline pitied him.

"I do forgive you; I did long ago."

"No, you didn't. You never did, and you never will. And I don't blame you, for I cannot forgive myself."

He started to cry then, silently, tears sliding one after another down his cheek. Shocked and embarrassed, Caroline knew she was the last person who should be sharing this man's private grief, his tormenting memories. William, even Matthew, had more right than she. But there was nothing she could do, no way to erase the past hour, no choice but to offer what comfort she could. So she simply held him in her arms and prayed his delirium would soon pass.

Chapter 8

WHEN LADY HARGRAVE came to relieve Caroline at four o'clock, Lord Brooke was sleeping again. Caroline was exhausted, too tired to attempt any sorting of the conflicting emotions she felt. She stumbled wearily to her room and was asleep seconds after her head touched the pillow.

When she returned to Phillip's room shortly before noon, she found William sitting with him.

"How is he this morning?" she asked.

"Better," William replied. "The fever broke near dawn, and he has been sleeping peacefully since."

"That's good. He was very bad last night—restless, delirious."

"I would feel better if he would speak," William said earnestly, "or at least open his eyes."

Caroline regarded William tenderly. He was a fine young man, sensitive and caring. He had harbored a good deal of anger for his father when he first arrived at the Hall, but this veneer of bitterness had vanished quickly when Phillip was hurt. William did more than his share of sitting with the patient and kept up with his studies as well. Caroline was growing fond of him.

"He spoke to me last night," she said, "and opened his eyes. But he didn't know me. He thought I was Victoria."

"My mother?"

She nodded.

"My Aunt Helen says he loved her very much."

"I'm sure he did. He still feels her loss deeply. Did she die recently, William?" she asked gently.

"No. She died when we were born, my sister and I. We never knew her."

"I didn't know . . . I'm sorry."

William inclined his head toward his father. "He didn't want us, so he gave us to his sister and her husband—my Aunt Helen and Uncle George. They raised us."

Caroline heard the resentment building in his voice. "You think that was wrong of him."

"Don't you? If you had children, would you give them away?"

"It would be easy for me to say 'No, certainly not,' but sometimes there are extenuating circumstances. Your father was very young when you were born, not much older than Stephen. Perhaps he didn't feel capable. His sister is older than he, is she not? Has she other children?"

"She is five years older. She never had children of her own," William answered. "Don't misunderstand me, Miss Hargrave. I love my aunt and uncle. They have always been good to us. It's just that I never understood. When my uncle was posted to India, my sister and I were five and my father twenty-five. He didn't want us then, either."

"Perhaps you could ask him to explain."

"How can I do that? He is a stranger to me!"

"He is now. But he won't always be. Unless you continue to avoid him."

"Is it so obvious?" he asked.

She nodded. Especially obvious to someone who is doing the same thing, she thought. "He seemed genuinely pleased to see you. Why don't you give him a chance? You may find you can like him."

William smiled at her, thinking he would do anything to please her. "Very well. I'll stop avoiding him and see what comes of it—that is, if he recovers from this injury—if he is ever himself again." He was sober now, the concern back in his voice.

"He will be. I am sure the fever leaving is a good sign. Have you eaten?"

"Yes. A tray was sent up earlier."

"Well, I haven't and I'm starving. I'll come back later. Try not to worry."

As she moved down the hall, Caroline considered the unusual conversation she had just shared with William. Why had she attempted to defend Phillip's position to William? Or if she hadn't precisely defended him, she had at least suggested Phillip could have had some acceptable reason for deserting his children.

Why did she do so? she wondered. It would be more in keeping with her relationship with her trustee if she had joined William in disparaging his father's behavior. It startled her to realize that even though she disapproved of nearly all Phillip's actions and opinions, she did not believe him to be morally lax. She found it impossible to visualize Phillip, at any age, willfully shirking a moral obligation.

She came to the top of the stairs and descended slowly, remembering the passion of the kiss Phillip had given, in his mind, to Victoria. Considering how she loathed the man, why hadn't she been repulsed by it? Was she playing Victoria's part so completely that she responded as she felt Victoria would have? No. No reason to deceive yourself, Caroline Hargrave.

You enjoyed it as yourself, not as Victoria. And you returned it, too. And you allowed intimacies ... I must be insane, she decided. How could I actually enjoy kissing a man I despise?

"Miss Hargrave!"

At the bottom of the stairs Caroline turned to see William beaming at her from the banister above.

"He's awake! He's awake, and he recognizes me!"

She smiled—a smile of genuine pleasure. "That's wonderful, William. Really wonderful." And she meant it.

Phillip's first words upon waking were, "I'm thirsty." While his valet poured water and held the glass for him, William darted into the hall with his news.

Now returned to the bedside, William asked, "How do you feel?"

"My head aches."

"I'm not surprised. You have a monstrous big lump. And concussion. Do you remember what happened?"

"Yes. I saw a reflection in the wood and then someone fired at me. My horse shied."

"She was hit by the bullet."

"Ah. That explains why she exploded so violently. She brought me up under a tree, and I came off. I remember falling. Nothing after that."

"We think you hit your head again when you fell. There was a tree stump and another lump on your forehead. You've been unconscious for four days."

Phillip showed his surprise. "Really?"

William nodded. "We thought whoever set upon you perhaps struck you down."

"No. There would have been no need if I was rendered unconscious by the fall."

William bit his lip for a moment and then said with difficulty, "They could have killed you."

"If that had been their intention, they could easily have done so," Phillip agreed, "but such brigands seldom intend murder."

"But they fired at you!"

"They had to if they were on foot. It is nearly impossible to stop a mounted man otherwise. I doubt they intended a fatal wound. My reining back no doubt made them miss their mark."

William shuddered at the casual way his father discussed the possibility of being shot.

"How did you find me?" Phillip asked.

"The mare bolted for home and alerted us that something was wrong. Miss Hargrave thought at first that you had been thrown, but when she and Smithton saw the mare's injury, they suspected foul play. Miss Hargrave rode immediately to your aid; she says the mare showed her where you were."

"Caroline rode after me?"

Phillip's disapproval was manifest as William tried to explain. "She and Matthew were the only ones here, and Smithton says she insisted even though he tried to dissuade her."

No, Phillip thought, Smithton would be no match for Caroline once she had set her mind to something. So that was how he came to be in the carriage with her when he regained consciousness for that brief period. He remembered it clearly. He hoped she had kept her word about the jewelry.

Thinking his father looked drained by the conversation, William left him to rest. The most important questions had been answered. The others could wait.

Phillip's progress was steady; each day he improved. He no longer needed constant attention, and Caroline was first to curtail her time with him. From the moment he regained consciousness she avoided the sickroom until one day he called out to her as she was passing the open door. Rose pink rays from a dying sun settled across the pattern of the Aubusson carpet as the curtains billowed in a steady westerly breeze.

She entered at his invitation and moved immediately to the open casements. "Shall I close these for you? The wind is becoming quite cool."

"If you like, though I enjoy the fresh air."

"It is possible to have fresh air without opening eight windows as far as they will go." She closed the four to the left of the bed, then moved round to the right side to continue with the others. When she came to the last, she left it slightly ajar.

He watched her silently. Her modest wheat-colored gown covered her from neck to floor, yet he found it provocative.

"We need to talk," he said.

"Do we?"

"William tells me you sat long hours here while I was unconscious."

"We all did." She fussed with the curtain, making the folds lie straight.

"You haven't been here since I awoke."

"You don't need constant attention now."

"Is it only that? Or would you rather not be near me when I am awake—when I can speak to you?"

She turned to regard him, her hands clasped behind her back. "We have little to say to each other, sir."

"On the contrary. We have a great deal to discuss. I understand from Matthew that you respected my wishes concerning the jewelry."

Caroline pursed her lips. She'd had more than one opportunity to regret the promise. Not only had she been forced to lie, but she had realized too late that having the jewelry stolen was the best possible thing that could have happened. Her mother would never have to know the truth, and since it was worthless anyway, there had been no real loss.

"I have told my mother it is in Mr. Keating's keeping," she said. "I don't care much for lying, Lord Brooke."

"No, I am sure you don't. Nevertheless, I am grateful you did. It is due to my negligence alone that those gems were lost. I intend to see Lady Hargrave paid their full value."

"She would never take it, sir! She would not consider you at fault, and she would never allow you to make good their loss."

"I know. That is why I have no intention of telling her they were stolen. Matthew has a list of the pieces. I am certain Rundell and Bridge is familiar enough with them to give me a fair estimate of their worth. I will deliver the money to your mother as if it had come from them."

"And you will, of course, expect me to say nothing."

"And I will, of course, expect you to say nothing."

Caroline paced to the far wall and turned to face him. "Webs of lies have a way of tangling one's life, my lord. You ask a great deal of me."

"I know I do. And I also know there is no precedent for you to oblige me. Yet I am hoping you will." She didn't speak, her face set in stubborn, rebellious lines. "I was hoping you could take to heart one piece of advice you offered William."

"And what was that?"

"You asked if he might give me a chance. You suggested he could come to like me."

"Did he tell you I said that?"

"No. I heard you say it myself."

She stepped closer to the bed. "You heard—?"

"I was half awake when you were talking here together. I think the advice you gave him was sound, and I thank you for it. I only wish you would practice what you preach. I don't think you have ever given me a chance, not from the beginning, and I know you don't like me, so I can't see why you should defend me to my son."

"I wasn't defending you. I merely suggested he should try to find answers to the questions that concern him. Since you are the only one who has the answers, what could serve better than for him to come to you?"

He made no reply, but after a few seconds began on a new subject. "There was another thing I wished to discuss with you. It is your mother's wish that part of the money from the jewelry be used for you, to give you a London Season."

"What?"

"It was her primary reason for wanting to sell it. She has always regretted not bringing you out in the normal way. As you know, a Season is rather expensive, and the dibs were not in tune."

"Look at me, my lord! I will be four-and-twenty in a few months. I am no blushing debutante!"

"One need not be a debutante to visit the metropolis. I think you would enjoy yourself, for there is much to see and do, many interesting people to meet." After a slight pause he added, "Unattached gentlemen, for instance."

"I see. And what if I were to tell you, sir, that I have no interest in meeting gentlemen—unattached or otherwise?"

"I would have to say you are the only unmarried woman I know who feels so."

She drew herself up. "Oh, really! You are insufferable. If you truly believe every woman is pining for a man, then I pity you. Such presumption!"

"I presume nothing. It is a simple, practical matter. Most

women don't care to spend their lives dependent upon their father, or in your case, your brother. They would rather find some independence through marriage. Most also want children. Will you live with Stephen all your life? Things will not always remain as they are. When Stephen marries, his wife will become mistress of Paxton Hall. Will you be content here then?"

Earlier she had considered keeping silent about the jewelry if it could help Stephen; but if the jewelry money was to benefit her . . . She moved to a chair near the bed and seated herself. "This entire conversation is pointless, sir, if my mother's jewels were to be the funding for my Season."

"I have said I intend to make good their loss."

She shook her head. "There was no loss. The jewelry was worthless; my father had it copied years ago."

He studied her critically for several moments before he replied. "It won't work, Caroline. I know a bluff when I hear one."

"What do you mean?"

"Simply that I don't believe you."

"It's the truth," she returned hotly. "If you had tried to sell the stones, you would have discovered just how worthless they were."

His eyes narrowed, regarding her closely. "I don't know what game you're playing, but you can't win. I have already written to my second cousin, Lady Henrietta Winfield. She is a widow who resides year-round in Bath, but she has agreed to act as hostess for me. You and your mother will stay at my house in Curzon Street, and Henrietta will do her best to see that you are comfortable there. You are going to London, Caroline; it has been decided."

She rose from her chair. "You may think all is decided, sir, but you have not heard the last of this, believe me."

He watched her leave the room in silence, and when she was gone, he sighed. Another confrontation to look forward to; he wasn't sure he was up to it. He closed his eyes and was soon asleep.

Caroline retired to her room to change for dinner. Think what you like, make what plans you will, my lord, she thought. You will not get me to London short of carrying me there!

Yet two days later, when a coach filled with parcels arrived from town, she knew the battle was fairly joined and she was already at a disadvantage. Coming down the stairs in the early afternoon, she found several footmen stacking boxes and trunks in the hall under the direction of her mother and Mr. Keating.

"All of these go to Miss Caroline's room, Webber," Lady Hargrave said. "Please have them carried up immediately."

"Mama!" Caroline exclaimed. "What is all this?"

"Some things his lordship and I ordered from London, dear. I believe he told you about them."

Caroline could think of nothing to say but simply followed her mother upstairs as the packages were taken to her bedchamber. She sat in silence as her ladyship opened a large trunk and after digging through sheets of tissue extracted a soft gown of primrose muslin.

"Oh, Caro, how lovely. Come see. You will look splendid in this."

Caroline moved to her mother's side, unable to resist taking the beautiful fabric between her fingers. "This was made for me?"

"Yes, it was. I gave Lord Brooke your measurements, and he had them sent to a very fashionable modiste in London."

Caroline flushed. "You gave him my measurements! Mama, how could you?"

"Well, I had to, my dear," Lady Hargrave replied reasonably. "How else could they make gowns for you?"

"Gowns? There are more?"

"Yes, several, and some for me as well, for I will be accompanying you to town. We will need to order a great many more things when we arrive, but these are a beginning. As things were, we hadn't even anything appropriate for the journey."

Taking Caroline's hands, Lady Hargrave pulled her down to sit close on the sofa. "I can't tell you, Caro, how much it means to me to be able to do this for you at last. The year you turned eighteen and every year after, I tried desperately to find some way to bring you out. But there was never any money, and I didn't dare sell my jewelry while your father lived, even though I never wore it and didn't particularly admire it. But now that I have the opportunity I intend to use it. You are a bit older than other girls making their first visit to London, but you are so lovely I can't think you will lack for admirers."

Lady Hargrave's eyes were moist, and Caroline knew she was realizing a lifetime ambition for her daughter. Caroline had intended to tell her mother she wanted no part of a London Season. Yet, she reasoned, perhaps she should agree to it after all. She would certainly appreciate having new clothes. She would enjoy the theater and the parties and entertainments. Perhaps she would even enjoy the male admirers if, indeed, she had any.

The only drawback was that Brooke would be paying for everything. She knew it was most improper, yet she had told him the jewelry was worthless and he would not believe her. What more could she do?

"What about our mourning, Mama? Have you forgotten that?"

"Of course not. I shall stay in black gloves for the full year, but I see no reason for you to do so, and his lordship agrees. Your father will be gone from us nearly ten months before the Season begins, and it's only the Little Season, remember. I can't think anyone would disapprove."

Lady Hargrave returned to the trunk, this time lifting out a sky blue sprig muslin trimmed with white ribbons and pink rosebuds. "Try this on, Caroline. I think you should wear it to dinner. You have worn gloomy gray long enough."

Chapter 9

IF IT WERE true that clothes made the man, then Caroline thought it must be doubly true for women. Until she started wearing gay frocks again, she hadn't realized what a dampening effect her other clothes had had on her. Years of penny-pinching had reduced her wardrobe to the boring basics. Most of her gowns had been remade from older fashions, while the past months of mourning had nearly made her forget that wonderful colors existed.

She and her mother had unpacked ten new gowns from the London trunks, each more lovely than the last. There was a walking dress in dark green, a morning dress in sunshine yellow, a dashing evening gown of burgundy satin. They all fit perfectly. Nor had Patience been forgotten. There were several pretty, appropriate dresses for her as well.

Wearing the yellow morning dress with its short puffed sleeves and flounces at the hem, Caroline crossed the hall to the library, humming to herself. It was a dreary, rainy afternoon, but in the pretty gown her spirits soared. She entered the room with a smile on her face, wondering what William and Miles would think of her new dress. Her smile quickly faded when she found Lord Brooke to be the room's only occupant. He had been seated in a comfortable chair before the fire but came to his feet when he saw her.

"Please, don't stand," she said quickly. "I did not mean to disturb you. I didn't know you would be coming down today; are you sure you should have?"

"I feel fine, thank you." He resumed his seat while she settled onto a nearby chair.

"You look well," she returned, though privately she thought him pale. He was dressed with typical precision. A russet cutaway coat hugged his broad shoulders, and his snowy cravat was arranged in a splendid waterfall. During the two weeks he had spent in bed, he had seemed more approachable. Now, seeing him dressed and in command again, Caroline found herself wary. "I was looking for William and Miles."

"We need two more teams for the harvest and fall plowing. They went with Stephen to the horse auction in Luton."

"On such a day as this?"

"The auction will be held rain or shine. If attendance is poor, they may get the animals at a lower price. That would be a bit of luck. I doubt they will be home in time for dinner. That's a very becoming dress, by the way."

She smiled. "You are praising your own taste, sir, since you chose it."

"Not I. I merely submitted your measurements and a description of your coloring. The modiste chose the fabric and patterns according to your mother's instructions. If this is a fair sample of their work, then they have done well. You look lovely."

The simple compliment took her by surprise, and she turned away quickly to hide the blush she felt creeping into her cheeks. "Are you testing me to see what my reaction shall be when gentlemen stand in line to shower compliments upon me?"

He knew she found the idea ridiculous but answered quite seriously. "There will be a surfeit of compliments, my girl, and not only from the men, unless I miss my guess."

She puckered her brows, not understanding him. At that moment Webber appeared in the doorway, delicately clearing his throat.

"Yes, Webber, what is it?" his lordship asked.

"Walter Miller is at the door, my lord, asking for her ladyship. I told him she was indisposed with a bad cold, and he asked if he could speak with Miss Caroline."

"What is it, Webber? His wife?" Caroline asked.

"Yes, miss. A trifle early it seems. Walter has been to fetch the midwife, but she was not at home. Seems she's gone to Stevenage. Walter says as how her ladyship told him he could always call on her—"

"My mother can't possibly go out in this weather," Caroline replied, "but I can. Tell Mr. Miller to go home. I will be along as soon as possible."

"Very good, Miss Caroline." Webber turned back into the hall, and Caroline rose to follow him.

"Who is Walter Miller?"

Phillip's voice stopped her. She had forgotten to excuse herself, almost forgotten he was there. "One of our tenants. I must go, my lord."

"One moment," he said, crossing to her and detaining her with a hand on her arm.

"What is this about his wife and a midwife?"

"His wife is expecting, and as you heard, they cannot locate the midwife."

"Surely *you* don't intend to go?"

"Yes, I do. Why not?"

"I can give you a dozen reasons, but one will suffice; I forbid it."

"That's unfortunate, my lord," she answered stiffly, "for Iris Miller needs help, and I intend to help her."

"You don't seriously mean to attend a birthing?"

"I do. My mother has done so—more than once."

"Your mother is a married woman."

"My mother is a widow."

"Very well," he returned exasperatedly. "She *was* a married woman."

"I have no time to argue with you, Lord Brooke. I must go."

She wrenched her arm free and hurried away, while Brooke stood alone in the library, a thunderous expression clouding his handsome face.

Phillip paced the room for more than an hour. He nearly went twice to speak with Lady Hargrave, thinking he could enlist her aid to bring Caroline home. In the end he decided not to disturb her. Knowing her cold was severe, he feared telling her anything that might bring her from her bed on a chill, rainy day.

As the afternoon gave way to evening, Phillip warned Webber not to mention Caroline's exploit to her ladyship, left word for Stephen where he might be found, and ordered a closed carriage. He left the house wrapped in a heavy cloak to protect himself from the damp night air.

Having asked the midwife's direction from Webber, he drove directly to her village and inquired at the tavern for her cottage. She was still not home. He drove on to Stevenage and after several inquiries located her there. She readily agreed to accompany him, yet it was past nine o'clock when they arrived at the Miller cottage.

"Tell Miss Hargrave I am waiting," Phillip told the midwife. "There is no need for her to stay now that you have come."

"Surely, m'lord, I'll tell her."

The woman disappeared into the cottage. Phillip waited five minutes, but Caroline did not come. After another five he stepped from the carriage impatiently and began pacing the length of the carriage and team. Smithton sat upon the box, the reins held slackly in his hands, while the horses stood steaming after their exertion over the muddy country lanes. The rain had stopped. There was little sound save the occasional jingle of harness and the slow drip of water into the rain barrel.

After another fifteen minutes, Phillip knew Caroline would not be coming. He walked toward the front of the carriage. "Take them home, Smithton. There's no sense making them stand about in this weather."

"And you, my lord?"

"I'll be staying here."

"Very good, sir."

Phillip watched the coach move off, then searched for a place to be comfortable while he waited. The Miller cottage was a rectangle perhaps ten feet by fourteen. Directly outside was a fair-sized garden beyond which stood a hen house and a lean-to filled with hay. Hercules was tethered to the near wall. Phillip settled in the hay to wait, pulling his cloak tightly about him. He was less than twenty feet from the house and could hear low-pitched voices, though the words were unintelligible.

Near midnight, as Phillip had been nodding asleep, a scream tore across the yard, bringing him wide awake and to his feet. By the time the woman screamed again several seconds later, he had broken out in a cold sweat. How well he knew the agony of childbirth; how easily he recognized the scream. In an instant he was carried back fourteen years, and it was as if the time between had never existed. Once again he felt the helplessness, the sense of uselessness. It had been the most frightening night of his life; it had been the most costly as well.

The cries soon ceased, replaced by an uncertain silence. When the wailing cry of a babe vibrated through the night air, Phillip hurried across the yard and pounded with his fist on the frail cottage door.

"I'll go," he heard Caroline say. A moment later she stood in the open doorway, her face lit with a smile. "I thought it must be you," she said. "It's a boy, a big, strong boy!"

"And the mother?" he asked.

"Fine. She's fine. Come in and see for yourself. I know she would like to thank you for fetching the midwife." Caroline was still smiling, and he remembered thinking she should smile more often. He didn't accept her invitation to enter the cottage but only shook his head and turned away.

Caroline frowned after him and stepped back for her cloak. "I must go now, Iris. I will stop by tomorrow."

The clouds had cleared during the past hour, allowing a half moon to throw indistinct shadows across the garden. Caroline followed Phillip to the lean-to, where he had returned and re-seated himself. She sat beside him.

"I know you're angry with me," she began, "and I'm sorry. I didn't wish to disobey you, but you gave me no choice."

He didn't answer her. He had forgotten both his anger and his disapproval.

"I don't think you should be here, Phillip. This was your first day downstairs, and it has turned out to be much longer than you intended. I will blame myself if you suffer a relapse."

"I'm all right," he said, brushing her concern aside, so lost in his own thoughts he didn't even hear her call him Phillip, though it was the first time she had ever done so.

"How can any woman wish for children when she knows she must endure that?" he asked.

"Childbirth is painful," Caroline agreed, "but they say the pain is forgotten the moment the mother holds the child in her arms. It is certainly true with Iris. She is smiling from ear to ear."

"I heard her screaming."

"The last moments were difficult for her, and I think a boy as first-born is always harder."

He turned to regard her in the dim light. "Yet men make it clear they would prefer their wives to give them a son."

"Yes. I think most men like a son first."

"It is a fearful demand to make of one you love," he stated flatly.

"Perhaps. But it is the proudest gift a woman can give her husband. Iris was delighted when she discovered she was to have a child."

"She couldn't have known how it would be."

"Oh, yes. She has seen several children born. She knew."

"It's inconceivable that anyone should willingly entertain such pain, such risk."

"You're not a woman—you can't understand."

"You understand?"

"Yes, certainly. It's God plan. If I should ever marry, I would want children—very much." When he didn't answer for some minutes, she continued. "I think we should go home. I have Hercules."

"Let's walk," he suggested. "It can't be more than a mile."

"All right, if you really wish it. Let's take the footpath; the road will be muddy."

Phillip untied the gelding, offering Caroline his arm as if they were about to promenade in a ballroom. She took it, grateful for the support in the darkness.

They walked a goodly distance in silence. Phillip had set a snail's pace, and with every step the tension built within Caroline until she had to speak. Afterward she wondered where she had found the courage. Perhaps it had been the alternating thrill and anxiety of the evening she had spent witnessing the miracle of birth; perhaps it was the darkness, in its own way a protection against the real world and the real problems in it; perhaps it was Phillip's discomfiture, an aura too tangible to ignore.

"It is wrong for you to blame yourself for your wife's death," she said simply.

"I don't," he returned.

"Perhaps not consciously," she persisted.

"What exactly does that mean?"

"When you were unconscious, you had a fever, and for several hours you were delirious. You thought I was Victoria."

"Good God."

"You have no memory of it?"

"No."

"You thought I was she, and for a moment, pretending to be her, I felt very close to her somehow. You kissed me, thinking you were kissing her."

He stopped walking and turned to face her. She couldn't see the expression in his eyes, but his voice was troubled, apologetic. "I'm sorry, I—"

"You needn't apologize," she interrupted. "I didn't mind, and I wasn't offended. It was the most tender, the most loving kiss imaginable. You loved her a great deal; those feelings haven't died. If your memories are so fond, so strong, perhaps you should share them with William. He wants to know about his mother; I can tell from some of the things he's said. I think you should tell him about the day she died."

"No. I can't ever tell him. It is something I never want him to know."

"Why?"

He didn't answer her question, but simply started to tell his story. He wasted few words, speaking slowly in a straightforward, abbreviated fashion.

"Victoria and I knew each other from childhood. We were neighbors in the country; our parents were close friends. I kissed her for the first time when she was sixteen and I eighteen. From that day we assumed we would always be together. Our families and friends seemed to assume the same thing. No one was surprised when we announced our engagement when she was eighteen and I twenty.

"She became pregnant the second month after we married. Eight months later she delivered twins, a boy and a girl. All three struggled for life for several days. William was holding his own after forty-eight hours. Then Victoria died. Beth was sickly for weeks, months really, but somehow she slowly gained ground, and by six months my sister says she was actually robust."

He paused, and Caroline maintained a strict silence as they walked on through the dim moonlight.

"The morning Victoria died, when the doctor pulled the sheet over her face, I remembered vividly a day five years earlier, when I had seen the same thing done to my father. I suddenly remembered the portrait of him that hung in the library and how many times I had looked at it during those five years, hoping for guidance, thinking perhaps he would know how much I missed him, how much I needed him. Then I was overcome with remorse because I had never had a portrait done of Victoria and now it was too late. . . .

"Her mother found me there in the library, standing before my father's portrait. She spent God knows how long berating me for what I had done. She accused me of monoplizing her daughter from the cradle, blinding her to the attractions of other men, insisting on an early marriage, and then having her with child indecently soon. 'Your selfishness has killed my only child.' That's what she said to me. And she was right. I couldn't answer her, and I think my silence made her lose what little control she had left. She began a pitiful wailing, beating her fists on my chest as if in hurting me she could find some relief for her own pain." He smiled wryly. "I made no effort to stop her; I didn't have the will. She was a small woman, but even so the next day my chest was a mass of bruises. When she finally subsided, I left her there. I had no comfort to offer her, nor could I find any for myself for a long, long time."

He stopped talking as suddenly as he had started, and they walked in silence for several moments.

"Do you still mourn her?" Caroline asked.

"I'll never forget her. But mourn her? No. I don't think so. It was all so long ago it seems like part of another lifetime."

"Yet you thought of her tonight?"

"Yes. But I'm sure my feelings tonight, as well as the delirium, are tied to my seeing William again after all these years. Having him back in my life is bound to rekindle some memories. I'm sorry about the kiss, though—"

"I told you," she interrupted, "I wasn't offended."

"I'm not sorry I did it," he explained. "I'm sorry I can't remember it."

His voice held a light, teasing note, and she was grateful he couldn't see her blush. They walked in amiable silence across the drive to the Hall, stopping before the front doors.

"I'll take Hercules to the stables," he offered. "You go on to bed; you've had an eventful day."

She knew better than to argue, so she simply bade him good night, watched a moment as he led the horse away, then turned and entered the house.

Caroline slept late the following day and even when she woke showed no interest in rising. She had fallen asleep thinking of Phillip. Her waking thoughts, too, were of her enigmatic trustee.

She thought it odd that her relationship with him should swing as radically as the sweep of a pendulum. She seemed to be violently at odds with him one moment, then sharing the closest of intimacies the next.

Phillip had treated her as a rag-mannered, ill-bred schoolgirl after she had prepared his meal, then kissed her as a man in love when he thought her someone else. She had boldly disobeyed him in the matter of Iris Miller, but instead of the repercussions she had expected, he had shared confidences with her—confidences she suspected no one before her had ever heard.

While she admitted her feelings were softening toward him, she was clever enough to realize why. She strongly disliked the Phillip Brooke she first knew, the one William had described as wealthy, powerful, and influential. To those traits she could easily add authoritarian, pompous, and dictatorial.

During the last several weeks she had caught glimpses of quite a different Phillip Brooke. A man who pampered an old mare; a man who was a less than perfect father; a man whose heart had suffered a cruel wound at a tender age. Caroline found she liked this Phillip Brooke much better.

She thought for a time about the kiss she had received—rather, enjoyed with Phillip. She had never been kissed on the mouth before, a fact she had been secretly ashamed of at nearly four-and-twenty. Surely no proper miss should claim the experience, yet she felt ignorant when she saw twenty-year-olds like Iris Miller with children.

Caroline dressed, stopped to speak with her mother, then descended to find Phillip alone in the breakfast parlor. The remains of his meal had been cleared, and he sat with a cup of coffee and the London papers. He rose when she entered the room and sat again as she did.

"How is Lady Hargrave this morning?" he asked as the footman moved to serve her.

"She's much better, thank you. The congestion is nearly gone. She asked about you. She was distressed to hear you had gone out last night."

"So you told her about your little adventure?"

"Yes."

"And had she any comment on your behavior, or were her concerns all for me?"

"Unfortunately, she shares your opinion, Lord Brooke. She thinks I should not have gone." He raised one expressive brow but did not speak, and Caroline hurried on. "But she understands why I felt I must. She is not angry with me."

"Nor am I. I am pleased to hear your mother is improved. You leave for London in less than a week."

The footman soon finished serving Caroline. At her request, Phillip returned to his newspaper while she ate.

He read her a few items he thought might be of interest, and she listened attentively until her eyes found their way to his lips. She studied them. Could that really be the same mouth that had kissed her so passionately? It was firm, the lips full and well shaped.

He glanced up, and her gaze dropped to her plate. When he began reading again, her eyes immediately lifted. He must be very experienced at kissing, she thought. It's fortunate he has no memory of my effort in returning his kiss. No doubt he would have found it lacking.

Her eyes then moved to his hands, and she realized she had never looked at them before. They were attractive hands, square-palmed and long-fingered, the nails perfectly trimmed. A signet ring adorned the third finger of the right hand; the left was bare.

From her scrutiny of his hands her mind slipped back to the memory of his chest, the tightly curling black hair, the clearly defined muscles . . .

At that instant he spoke her name, and she started guiltily, upsetting her teacup and sending scalding liquid hurrying across the table toward him. He rose quickly and avoided injury, using the napkin at his elbow to stem the flow just as it reached the edge of the polished table.

Caroline was aware that she was stammering apologies.

"No harm done," he replied. "I'm sorry I startled you. You seem preoccupied this morning."

"I'm sorry. What were you saying?"

"I said the rioting of unemployed workers in the cities should not touch us here. We have more work than the men can do."

"Mm" was her only response.

Pushing back his chair, Phillip rose from the table. "If you will excuse me, I must join Matthew."

"Certainly, my lord. Don't let me keep you."

He frowned at her formality but left her there. Caroline sat, musing distractedly, while both her breakfast and her second cup of tea grew cold.

Chapter 10

CAROLINE RAN LIGHTLY down the main staircase of the Brooke residence in Curzon Street, her slippered feet making no sound on the carpet runner. A week ago she and her mother had made the short journey from Paxton to London in his lordship's well-sprung traveling chaise. They had been accompanied by Matthew Keating, two maids, a coachman, and two footmen, yet even this exalted mode of travel did not prepare Caroline for the elegance of Brooke's town house.

Decorated in shades of rose and blue, the bedchamber allotted Caroline was the most attractive she had ever seen. Dark rose-colored draperies and bed-hangings stood out against wall coverings of palest pink, while the carpeting depicted a delicate floral pattern in mingled pinks and blues. Two chairs covered in dark blue velvet waited invitingly near the fireplace. Southern-facing windows offered a charming view across Piccadilly to Green Park.

Throughout the house, handsome, richly decorated rooms created an almost shocking contrast to the drab, faded furnishings of Paxton Hall. Mirrors glistened, plush carpets cushioned each footfall, woodwork glowed with a well-oiled sheen. An army of servants saw that not a speck of dust lodged anywhere.

Having introduced the Hargraves to their hostess, Lady Winfield, Mr. Keating returned to Hertfordshire while Caroline and her mother spent the first three days after their arrival visiting with those of Lady Hargrave's friends who were at present in the city. Most hadn't seen her in years but were universally pleased to know she had come to town. In only a few days a large pile of invitations accumulated on the hall table.

At first anxious about meeting Lady Winfield, Lady Hargrave's fears were soon laid to rest. Henrietta Winfield was a slender matron near Lady Hargrave's own age who had been widowed only three years. She was friendly but not effusive and dressed modestly in the latest styles. When Lady Hargrave expressed surprise that she should choose to live in Bath, she explained that she had gone there to be near her mother.

"John and I never had children, and Mother is my only close living relative. But I was delighted to receive Phillip's letter. I haven't been to town in more than a year, and I am longing to visit the shops!"

So in addition to their social calls, Caroline and her mother accompanied Lady Winfield on numerous visits to the fashionable shops along Bond Street, daily adding to their rapidly growing wardrobes.

Caroline was in every way pleased with London, from the noisy city streets with hawkers touting their wares and carriages clattering over the cobbles, to the impressive mansions of Mayfair, housing the elite of England's aristocracy. In a few days she would meet some of them, perhaps speak with them—people she had previously only heard about, read about.

The single dark cloud overshadowing her pleasure was the knowledge that Lord Brooke was paying for everything. She had decided to keep careful tally of the money she and her mother spent. When Stephen was on his feet again, when the estate was profitable as they all knew it could be, she would repay Brooke, setting the record straight.

Caroline found her mother and Lady Winfield in the drawing room. "There is a letter from home in this afternoon's post," Lady Hargrave said. "Lord Brooke writes that William and Miles are safely off to school and the harvest is progressing well. He hopes we find everything here satisfactory and insists we inform his majordomo of any need we may have."

"I cannot imagine what he thinks we could need," Caroline replied. "There must be at least twenty servants in this house, each more determined than the next to please us. We have her ladyship to advise us, a carriage at our disposal, and more invitations than we can possibly accept. Shall we go to the Wainwrights' soiree tonight, Mama?"

"If you like. I think I should enjoy it. Augusta Wainwright is a dear old friend."

"Is Grace Bidwell attending, Caroline?" Lady Winfield asked. "I have noticed that you and she seem to have a lot in common."

"We do. Her father says she may accompany us if we decide to attend. How well do you know the Bidwells, Lady Winfield?" Caroline asked.

"Quite well. Lord Bidwell was one of my admirers in the days before I married. It's a great shame about his wife."

"Grace says it's been almost four years since her mother died."

Lady Hargrave folded Lord Brooke's letter and tucked it away in her reticule. "I am pleased to see that you and Grace have become friends so quickly. She's a charming girl."

Several hours later Lord Brooke's handsome town coach collected Grace Bidwell at her home, then rolled off through the gloomy London streets toward Wainwright House. It was a drive of only a few minutes; for Caroline it was much too short. It was ridiculous, but she was nervous as a girl of eighteen.

Grace Bidwell, still unmarried at two-and-twenty, had seen five London Seasons come and go. She easily recognized the cause of her friend's anxiety. "You mustn't be nervous, Caroline. You will be a great success, I promise you. Your gown is stunning."

Caroline did feel she looked her best. Her gown of blue-gray French silk fell in classic lines from a fashionably high waistline. Delicate cream-colored Brussels lace edged the short sleeves and low neckline. From her meager collection of jewelry she chose the single strand of pearls and matching earrings her father had given her on her eighteenth birthday. Ginny had braided her hair with long tendrils of artificial morning glory throughout.

Lady Hargrave privately thought she had never seen Caroline look lovelier. This evening marked for her ladyship the end of long frustrating years of waiting—years during which she had longed for the opportunity to introduce her daughter to society—years she had viewed as enemies, each one with its passing decreasing Caroline's chances of meeting and marrying an eligible gentleman. Now, finally, Caroline's time had come. She was in London, she was breathtakingly lovely, and she would have the chance her mother had prayed for.

Lady Hargrave shifted her regard from Caroline to consider her daughter's new friend. Remembering the late Lady Bidwell as an attractive woman, she found it puzzling that Grace should be so plain. With eyes too small and too closely spaced, a nose and chin too aristocratically sharp, and a mouth the most generous critic would call merely adequate, Grace Bidwell was not considered handsome.

Yet one's visual impression of mousy mediocrity was quickly displaced when the girl opened her mouth to speak. Spirit, humor, and animation combined with a pleasant voice to banish first impressions. The girl was poised, tastefully attired this evening in a gown of russet crepe, which enhanced both her excellent figure and the reddish highlights in her brown hair. When she spoke, she showed excellent sense.

As Grace and Caroline passed through the reception line and into the drawing room beyond, they had their first opportunity of the evening for private speech.

"I was amazed," Grace was saying, "when our butler said Lord Brooke's coach had arrived for me. You didn't tell me you knew him, or that you were staying with him."

"Lord Brooke is my trustee," Caroline answered simply. As her companion's eyes widened, she added, "At least, he is until next fall, when I attain the age of twenty-five."

"Is he in town?"

"No. He has spent the summer at our home in Hertfordshire, doing whatever it is trustees do. I think he does plan to come later, however, when the harvest is finished. Are you acquainted with him?"

"Yes, of course. When you have been on the town as long as I, you know most everyone."

"And what is your opinion of him?"

"I have always found him an amiable gentleman. Takes his seat in the Lords very seriously, I believe. He is well thought of, and though he is a great matrimonial catch, he seldom dangles after eligible girls. But surely if he spent the summer at your home, you must know all this?"

"I have had no opportunity to witness his society manners, Grace. I can tell you, however, that his 'at-home' manners can at times be less than satisfying."

They were interrupted before Grace could ask for any explanation of this curious comment.

"Caroline Hargrave!"

Hearing her name spoken from behind by a familiar voice, Caroline turned with a smile already on her lips for her good friend Gerald Layton. He was only a few steps away, closing quickly with both hands outstretched.

"Gerry! When did you get back?" She laid her forearms along his, then raised on her toes to give him the brief kiss on the cheek that had become the habit of friendship.

The muscles of the viscount's arms tensed instantly, easily holding her away. "No, no, my dear. Recall where you are. We cannot have kisses, sisterly or otherwise, in the public eye."

Caroline sank back onto her heels, releasing his arms. "I'm sorry, Gerry. I did forget for a moment where I was. I am so pleased to see a familiar face. Allow me to introduce my companion."

"I am already acquainted with her," he replied. "Good evening, Miss Bidwell."

"Lord Ashton," Grace returned, offering her hand.

"I returned home two days ago," the viscount said, supplying the answer to Caroline's earlier question. Then, to include Miss Bidwell he politely explained, "I have been traveling in Greece with my younger brother. Neither of us had been there before. It was quite exhilarating. I had no idea you were acquainted with the Bidwells, Caro."

"I wasn't," Caroline explained. She smiled at her new friend. "Grace and I only met earlier this week, but she has been a great help to me. I could never have found the courage to come tonight without her."

"What?" he asked. "One needs no courage for a party such as this. One needs only to feel the music and dance the night away."

"But this is my first London party, Gerry. I am so afraid I shall do something inexcusable."

"Nonsense. There is no difference between this gathering and the assemblies we attended in Hertford. It is merely larger."

"But there are sterner critics," Grace contributed. "And more watchful eyes, both admiring and jealous."

Ashton seemed to consider her comment for a moment, then grasped the arm of an acquaintance who chanced to be strolling by. "Harry, here is someone I should like you to meet. A neighbor of mine from the country, Miss Caroline Hargrave. This is Lord Beacon, Caro, a friend of mine—an excellent dancer, too."

The young blond lord was smiling at Caroline, clearly captivated, his tenor voice soft and inviting. "I should be honored if you would join me for the next set, Miss Hargrave." Since he accompanied this offer with an outstretched hand, Caroline laid her own in it and walked away with him.

"That was well done, my lord," Grace said. "She will soon find herself caught up in the excitement of the evening, and her anxieties will pass. Her manners are perfect. I cannot believe her capable of doing anything to offend."

"And what about you, Miss Bidwell? Will you dance tonight?"

"I think not, my lord. I am more accustomed to sitting—"

"With the dowagers and old maids," he finished. "What foolishness! You are younger than Caroline!"

As her cheeks flushed, he wondered what had prompted him to say something so personal. She would be perfectly within her rights to give him a set-down. He deserved it.

"I may be younger than she," Grace responded after a moment, "but after five Seasons I have earned the right to do as I please."

"You dislike dancing, then?"

The question caught her off guard. "No, certainly not. I think every girl loves to dance."

"Will you stand up with me?"

She gazed up into his face and read only sincerity there—no pity, no gallant gesture to dance with the wallflower, no effort to exert himself to be kind to her for Caroline's sake.

"I don't believe we have ever taken the floor together," he continued, uncertain whether they had or not.

"No, my lord, we have not," the young lady answered, absolutely certain of her reply. She could clearly remember every man she had ever danced with.

Grace took his arm, and they joined the other dancers. Before the set ended, Ashton secured the promise of a waltz with her later in the evening.

* * *

Caroline danced with so many partners that night that the next day she had difficulty separating the names from the faces.

"The Earl of Gresham was the portly man in the green-and-white striped waistcoat," she stated, pouring tea for her mother, Lady Winfield, and Grace in Lord Brooke's blue-and-silver morning room.

"No," Grace returned. "That was Baron Wells. Gresham is the tall, thin gentleman with the permanent dent in his cheek where his eyeglass rests."

"Oh, dear. You're right. I shall never keep them straight."

"You will, eventually," Lady Winfield assured her. "For now you need only remember the names of the ones you admire."

"The names of the *single* gentlemen you admire," Lady Hargrave amended. "Pay no heed to the fulsome compliments of married men, Caroline. No woman needs the problems a jealous wife can create, especially a woman comely enough to inspire jealousy on sight."

"Your mother is right, Caroline," Grace agreed. "You cannot afford to have certain leaders of society think you flirtatious or your behavior in any way unbecoming."

"Are they truly so powerful?"

"Indeed, they are. Should they take you in dislike, a word spoken here, a comment there, and you could find yourself quite ostracized."

"It seems very hypocritical to me," Caroline complained, "to have to toady to them just to earn their approval."

"Perhaps it is," Lady Hargrave said. "But it is the way of society, and it is all important, especially to an undowered girl."

So for the next month Caroline was a pattern card of propriety. Her behavior at all public gatherings was exemplary. Never without a partner for any dance, her admirers were many. When partnered with a married gentleman, she practiced modesty. For those whose excessive compliments failed to please, she affected great reserve. Only for those unattached gentlemen she admired—either for their appearance, their intelligence, or their manner—only for them did she exhibit any liveliness. She was experiencing for the first time the excitement of romance, the thrill of conquest.

Among the dowagers seated together at any social gathering, flattering comments were to be heard about the newest beauty.

"A very proper behaved gel," one would say.

"A great pity she has no fortune," another would add. "She would make an admirable duchess."

"With her looks and manner she should do well for herself without a portion," a third would reply.

So Caroline Hargrave was a social success. She had no title, no fortune, no high connections, yet she had managed to please the highest sticklers. For the first time she was being forced to deal with the heady stuff of male admiration. For the first time she began to think that marriage and a family were possibilities.

Caroline paused at the head of the stairs as the butler opened the front door to admit Lord Brooke, accompanied by a hearty gust of damp October wind. Phillip pulled his caped driving coat from his shoulders, deposited it with a hovering footman, then surrendered his hat and gloves. Turning about, he surveyed the numerous floral arrangements crowding the hall tables.

"Good God, Manners, what is all this? The place looks like a damned florist's shop."

"These have been sent to Miss Hargrave, my lord," the butler explained. "She was a great success at the Duchess of Devonshire's ball last evening."

"So it would seem," Brooke answered dryly. "Have some of them carried to other rooms," he ordered. "The fragrance in this space is overwhelming."

"Very good, my lord." Manners signaled to one of the footmen. "You may take those elsewhere. Leave these until Miss Hargrave has seen them."

It was as he turned toward the library that Phillip noticed Caroline. He sketched a bow as she hesitated a moment before starting down the stairs. Her descent gave him leisure to study her. She wore an apple-green-and-white striped morning gown. Caught under the breast by a wide green ribbon, the muslin fell in soft folds to brush the tops of green slippers. Short, puffed sleeves ended in matching ribbon, while her hair had been twisted into a simple Grecian knot.

He could easily believe she had taken the town by storm. If he were not her trustee, he might have been tempted to send her a floral tribute himself.

The observation was not all on his side. Caroline was amazed at how different he looked from the way she remembered him. She had spent the summer in his company and they had only been separated six weeks; yet she didn't recall his being so handsome, nor so tall. She didn't recollect his shoulders being so broad, nor his hair so uniformly black. Few of her London acquaintance could match him for sheer physical beauty, she realized.

Yet, she thought, "pretty is as pretty does" applied perfectly in this instance. In Caroline's judgment, Brooke's excellent physical attributes could not excuse his character faults. So she would not permit herself to admire the entrancing smile, the perfect teeth, the sensuous mouth, and inviting gray eyes. Reaching the floor, she took the hand he offered, forcing herself to ignore the scent of his cologne. It mingled with the faint odor of leather and horses, despite the influence of roses and other blooms adorning the entryway. It was a scent she had come unconsciously to associate with him.

"Caroline! I predicted you would be a success. You see, I was right!"

"I am not the only woman in London who receives flowers, my lord."

"Perhaps not. Yet I doubt many women can claim such a . . . multitude of admirers."

"We were not expecting you today," she said, eager to change the subject. "Have you brought Stephen?"

"I could not convince him to come. The harvest is in; it was as good as we had hoped. But there are some projects he wishes to oversee. I did not press him to leave them, for I knew he would be impatient here. He did agree to come in January when Parliament convenes. I think he intends to take his seat."

"I'm glad. Father never did."

"I see little similarity between Stephen and your father."

She regarded him with interest. "How well did you know my father, Lord Brooke?"

"Well enough to draw such a simple conclusion." Then, before she could respond, he continued. "This is not the best place to carry on a conversation. You will be anxious to write, thanking your admirers for these." His arm swept the room, indicating the flowers. "And I am standing here in all my dirt. I must hurry if I am to change in time for dinner. Do you go out tonight?"

"Yes, to Lady Castlereagh's."

"Perhaps I shall accompany you. Till dinner, then."

She nodded absently as he ascended the stairs. His presumption was typical, all of a part. She and her mother already had an escort for the evening. By the time she collected her wits enough to object, he was well up the stairway. She decided to wait; she could speak to him at dinner.

Chapter 11

WITH THE COMING of Lord Brooke to London, Caroline's enjoyment of the Season evaporated. A relative peace had existed between them since the night Iris Miller had given birth. But if Caroline had any hope the truce would last, she was soon to be disillusioned.

Caroline appeared for the evening in a sky blue gown shot with silver threads, the gown perfectly matching the blue of her eyes. Her fair hair, laced with silver ribbons, added several inches to her height. But it was not the color of her dress nor the arrangement of her hair that caught and held Phillip's attention. When Caroline entered the drawing room at her mother's side, it was the neckline of Caroline's gown that drew his eyes—the neckline and what it failed to conceal.

So startled was Caroline by his regard that she needed to summon every ounce of willpower to keep from raising her hands to cover herself. Fortunately, Viscount Ashton had already arrived, and she turned to him eagerly. In him she found the reassurance she sought. She saw only admiration in his eyes, with none of the disapproval she instinctively sensed in

Phillip. It restored her equilibrium, and she greeted Ashton with perhaps more feeling than she would have shown in other circumstances.

Phillip missed none of it. He noticed the slight flush on her pale cheeks as she turned to Ashton. He heard the warmth in her words of greeting. He noted how her hands clasped and held Ashton's overlong. Clearly there was an attachment there, one that appeared to be more than old friendship. Taking a moment to consider such an alliance, Phillip decided Caroline could do much worse. Ashton was young and handsome, well-heeled; from all Brooke had ever heard, he was an honorable man.

Yet later at the Castlereaghs', Phillip began to doubt his earlier impression that Caroline cherished a *tendre* for Viscount Ashton, for she seemed to have a veritable bevy of suitors. They clustered about her as bees round a blossom, and she smiled equally upon them all.

Ordinarily at his ease at such a gathering, Phillip found he was not enjoying the evening. With a great appreciation for music and exercise, he enjoyed dancing; yet tonight he had no desire for it. In the intervals he was usually prepared to enter into conversation on almost any topic, equally at home discussing politics or sport with the gentlemen, fashion or poetry with the ladies. Tonight he found the conversation insipid. Throughout the evening he kept a watchful eye upon Caroline, noting her behavior, not particularly surprised by her success.

Caroline's dance card for the evening filled rapidly. She fervently hoped all her dances would be claimed before Lord Brooke could request one. Then, perversely, with her card full and every dance promised, she wondered that he had not approached her. Clearly he had no intention of joining her throng of admirers. He was a leader, not a follower.

Caroline suspected he disapproved of her gown. His avoidance of her during the evening and his silence in the coach on the return trip strengthened the impression. It wasn't until the following morning when she was summoned to attend him in the library that she had verbal confirmation to support this belief.

Phillip indicated a comfortable chair near the fire, and Caroline seated herself while he remained standing, his hands clasped behind his back. "I am reluctant to read you a lecture when I have just arrived in town," he began. "But I have decided it is necessary if we are to avoid any repetition of last evening's . . . display."

Her eyes were wide; she was totally on the defensive. "Of what display do you speak, my lord?"

She steeled herself, waiting for his disparagement of her décolletage, but he surprised her. "I was not born yesterday, Caroline. Nor am I unaware of the current rage for dampening one's petticoats to make them cling to the body. Proper young ladies do not practice such artifice."

She could only stare at him. No one had ever made such a personal remark to her. Reluctant to participate in such an improper conversation, she nevertheless could not resist answering, "I did not dampen my petticoats, my lord. I wasn't wearing any!"

His only response was to elevate a mobile brow as she rose suddenly from her chair and swept past him to stand before a bay window hung with green velvet curtains tied back with golden cords and tassels.

"While we are making a catalog of my indiscretions, Lord Brooke, wouldn't you care to offer criticism of the neckline of my gown last night? Considering the length of time you stared at it, you surely must have formed some opinion."

If she had hoped to discompose him with this rejoinder, she missed the mark. His carefully schooled face showed no embarrassment as he answered coolly. "I would prefer to see you with a more modest neckline, but your gown was easily within the limits of what is acceptable. Concerning the petticoats, however," he continued, with irritating sangfroid, "I must insist you wear them in future, and that you resist the temptation to damp them when you do."

"How dare you speak so to me?" she asked, her voice quiet now, deceptively gentle. "You have no right."

"Quite true. Yet while you reside under my roof, your behavior reflects upon me. It is therefore necessary that you conduct yourself properly."

"So that no hint of scandal should attach to you?"

"Precisely. You would attract men were you garbed in sackcloth and ashes. There is no need for you to practice immodesty."

"And what of your immodesty, my lord? No true gentleman would speak to a lady as you have spoken to me today."

"A father might."

"You presume a great deal, Lord Brooke. My father is dead, and I recognize none other as holding his place in authority over me."

"Nor should you. Nevertheless, you would be wise to obey me in this instance." Her eyes flashed, but he forestalled her response. "From my observations last night, I conclude you are enjoying your sojourn in London. Disobey me, and you will find yourself returned to Paxton as fast as my strongest team can carry you."

"What power have you to interfere in a Season financed by my mother, sir?" she challenged.

"None. But if it were to become suddenly inconvenient for me to have you continue in this house, I fear you would find the cost of maintaining yourselves in London prohibitive."

He paused politely, giving her an opportunity to respond if she dared. When she remained silent, he continued casually. "I wholly approve, by the way, of your friendship with Grace Bidwell. As for your male admirers, most of them seem harmless enough. Severn is penniless, so you would do well to avoid him. I have no objections to Ashton, Chillingham, Wells, or Beacon; they are all quite eligible. I suggest you beware of Gresham, however. He has a fondness for dim, deserted gardens."

"No doubt I should thank you for this well-intentioned advice concerning my friends," Caroline replied, struggling to keep her temper in check. "But I will not! Hard as it may be for you to comprehend, I care not one jot for your opinion. A person need not have *your* stamp of approval in order for *me* to like them."

"Perhaps not. Yet should any of your male admirers consider matrimony, pray remember they must secure my approval if they wish to see any of your income before your twenty-fifth birthday."

Frustrated by the weakness of her position, Caroline refused to answer him. He turned away and moved to his desk, appearing to take an interest in several papers there. After a few moments he glanced up, seemingly surprised to find her still there. "Was there anything else?"

"*You* summoned *me*, my lord," she replied bitterly.

"So I did. And I am quite through, thank you. You may go."

She turned to leave and had nearly reached the door when he spoke again. "We go to the Mowbrays' tonight. They are particular friends of mine. Wear something blue."

Considering how badly her morning had gone, Caroline was greatly relieved when the evening started well. She chose a gown of navy silk trimmed in black lace. While it was one of her favorites, she had not worn it before, wishing to save it for a special occasion. Lord Brooke had desired her to wear blue; she would give him no cause for complaint. She resumed her petticoats, undampened. Just as she was stepping into her dress, her maid answered a knock at the door, returning with a small jewelry case in her hands.

"His lordship's valet has brought this, miss, with his compliments. He would be pleased if you would wear it tonight."

Caroline took the case from Ginny and opened it. Lying on a bed of black velvet was an exquisite sapphire pendant. Caroline caught her breath in surprise as Ginny exclaimed, "Oh, how lovely, Miss Caroline! Shall I put it on for you?"

"No," Caroline answered quickly. "I'm not sure I should. I must speak to his lordship first."

Ginny busied herself with the buttons that closed the back of Caroline's gown, while Caroline waited impatiently for her toilet to be complete.

Phillip was alone in the drawing room when Caroline entered. If she was indeed wearing her petticoats, he mused, they were undetectable. The sleek silk clung to her shapely hips, each step she took outlining her slender legs. He wondered if she was aware of how the dark material made her skin look paler, or how the black lace made her hair seem nearly white.

He saw she was not wearing the pendant, then noticed the case in her hands.

"It does not please you?"

"It's lovely, but I cannot accept—"

"It's not from me. It is a belated birthday gift from your mother. She asked me what gem I thought would suit you and charged me with purchasing something appropriate. There should have been a card."

Caroline saw now that there was indeed a card tucked neatly into the seam at the edge of the case.

"The pendant will go well with this dress," Phillip said as

he reached into the case and lifted it. Turning her back to him, Caroline stood still as he dealt with the delicate clasp, his fingers lightly brushing the satiny skin of her shoulders. When he had secured the clasp, he dropped his hands to her shoulders, turning her to face him.

She gazed up into his face, aware that his hands had stayed, not only resting there, but actually holding her. "You are very beautiful tonight, Caroline," he said. "And your beauty owes little to the sapphires or the gown."

"Thank you, my lord," she murmured.

"Must we always be at daggers drawn?" he asked, suddenly earnest. "Can we not find some way to form a lasting peace between us?"

"I don't know," she answered honestly. "We seem destined to be at odds, like opposite forces in the cosmos: light and darkness, fire and water, wind and calm."

"And can there be no meeting ground?" he persisted. "Surely there is always room for compromise."

"Not everyone is willing to compromise, Lord Brooke, for the very act of compromise whittles away at the edges of firm ideals, making them less than perfect."

"But there is no such thing as perfection in this world. Only dreamers seek it."

"Perhaps. Yet the world must have its dreamers," she insisted.

He frowned, then released her as Lady Hargrave crossed the hallway toward the drawing room doors. Caroline turned to her mother, her shoulders suddenly cold where Phillip's hands had been.

"Mama! What a lovely present! I can see you are determined to spoil me."

Recalling the nature of their conversation earlier in the evening, Caroline admitted to some surprise when Phillip made no effort during the Mowbrays' soiree to secure a dance. He stood for a goodly time in conversation with his host and hostess, then sometime later danced with several ladies. Caroline noticed that what Grace had said was true. He seemed to avoid unattached young ladies, choosing instead partners who were older, most of them married.

Caroline went in to supper with Grace, Viscount Ashton,

and Lord Beacon. The four were very much at ease with one another and were often seen together.

Seated near them, two tables away, were Lord Brooke and his supper companion. Caroline's gaze was first attracted to them when the woman laughed—a rich, sensuous sound. Caroline could recall seeing the lady before and thinking her exotic. Now, in company with his lordship, she found the woman's voluptuousness extravagant. Her black hair was as dark as Phillip's own. Their heads nearly touched as she leaned close to hear something he said.

"Gerry, who is the lady with Lord Brooke?" Caroline asked.

"The Countess de Villiers. She's a French aristocrat. Came over as a young girl during the Terror and stayed. They say she's on the catch for a rich husband."

"Really?" Caroline replied, her tone disapproving.

"Come now, Caro. Don't concern yourself for Brooke. He's been around the course a few times and can well look after himself."

Caroline tried not to think about the countess and Brooke, but later in the evening as she watched them dance together, her thoughts were so distracted that without thinking, she agreed to accompany the Earl of Gresham into the enclosed garden behind the house.

The evening was mild, for the day had been unseasonably warm. The cool air of the walled garden was refreshing after the closeness of the crowded salon, but Caroline soon regretted her impulsiveness. Lord Gresham gripped his quizzing-glass expertly between brow and cheek, fixing Caroline with a slightly myopic stare.

"You are looking quite lovely tonight, my dear," his lordship remarked, steering Caroline to a secluded bench near the vine-covered wall.

"I think, after all, it is a bit chilly, my lord," Caroline offered. "Perhaps we should go back—"

"Nonsense," he replied, taking hold of her arm. "I feel no chill. But perhaps the fire burning within me is responsible for that."

She gazed at him in amazement, shocked as much by the poetic attempt from such a stoic gentleman as by the sense of the words themselves. She was saved from having to respond, however, as Lord Brooke at that moment appeared.

"Excuse me, Gresham, but I should like a few words with Miss Hargrave."

Gresham's eyeglass slipped from its perch as he turned to confront Brooke. "Certainly, certainly, Brooke. I surely don't mean to monopolize her. Must get back for the next set in any case. You will excuse me, ma'am?"

"Certainly, my lord."

As Gresham sauntered away, Phillip offered a shawl to Caroline. "You came here rather unprepared, did you not?"

She took the unfamiliar garment and draped it round her shoulders, thankful for the warmth it offered, yet not willing to admit to cold. "It's not so bad. Quite a relief, actually, after the heat inside."

"I wasn't referring to the weather. I had the Earl of Gresham in mind."

"What do you mean?"

"I warned you about him, Caroline. And don't pretend you don't remember. You take a great risk when you willingly come to such a secluded spot with a man of his reputation."

"A great risk, indeed," she replied scornfully. "Exactly what terrible thing do you imagine could happen, my lord, within a few yards of more than a hundred people?"

"Any number of things might and could have happened."

"I am more than capable of handling Lord Gresham, sir."

"So I heard."

"What did you hear?" she demanded.

"I heard how willingly he agreed to return you to the house when you expressed a desire to do so."

"He would have in a moment," she contended.

"Are you so sure? How would you have loosed his hold on you if I had not appeared?" As he asked the question he took a firm grip on her arm in precisely the spot Gresham had held her.

"I would have asked him to release me, as I am now asking you, Lord Brooke."

"And what if he had paid no heed to your request, but had pulled you close against him, like this? What, then, would you have done?" With his hands locked tightly behind her, her body was closely molded to the entire length of his.

"No doubt I would have struggled against him." Even as she made an attempt to do so, she realized such an effort was wasted against the strength of the man now holding her prisoner.

"Almost any man could physically overpower you at will. A simple task." His voice was soft, mesmerizing. She could feel the soft thud of his heart, so close to hers. "And if Gresham had decided to kiss you, Caroline, how could you have stopped that?"

She raised her face to his then, not believing he would go so far to prove his point. But as their eyes met, she knew she had misjudged him. His lips parted slightly, then settled upon hers with the gentleness she remembered—the gentleness he had intended that first time for Victoria. Her own mouth welcomed his; she pressed even closer.

Then, as he realized how passionately she was responding, he broke away, thrusting her from him.

For one insane moment she thought, hoped, he would say something completely out of character, something kind. But after a moment he seemed to recollect himself. He stood silently, his face an inscrutable mask.

"I would not have let him kiss me," she declared finally, in defense of her actions. "I could have bitten him," she offered. "I could have screamed."

"I hope you will believe me now when I tell you not every man will do whatever you ask of him, whenever you ask it. Your actions speak more loudly than your words. When you agreed to come here with him, it was a form of consent for what was to follow. Can't you see that?"

When she failed to respond, he continued brutally, "It is to be hoped you have learned something from this simple demonstration. You are a fool if you think men can be controlled with words. Men are, by and large, ruled by passions. Words are a useless weapon against them."

"You are certainly excluding yourself from this invective, my lord."

"No, my dear, I am not. I am, sad to say, much like other men."

When he offered his arm, she took it without comment, and they returned to the house in silence.

Phillip sat behind his desk in the library while Lord Beacon slowly paced back and forth across the carpeted floor. For the past five minutes Beacon had been describing his situation and enumerating his expectations. Now he stopped his perambulation and turned to face his host.

"I know Miss Hargrave is of an age to decide for herself, but Ashton said you were her trustee. I thought it best to speak first with you."

"I appreciate the courtesy, Beacon. Are you sure you shouldn't like a glass of wine?"

"No, thank you. I wish only to know if you approve my suit."

Phillip smiled for the first time during the interview. Rising, he extended his hand to the younger gentleman. "I have no objection to the match, Beacon. Caroline is at home. If you should like to speak with her today, I will send her to you."

"Thank you, sir. You're very kind."

"Not at all. Please, pour yourself some wine and take a seat. I will find Miss Hargrave and send her immediately."

Phillip ascended the stairs and strolled down the hall to the morning room. He paused in the open doorway, his hand on the knob. Caroline was there, in company with her mother and Lady Winfield. "Good afternoon, ladies. A moment of your time, Caroline, if you please."

Caroline laid her embroidery frame aside. "Certainly, my lord. Excuse me, Mama, ma'am."

When she had joined him in the hallway, he said, "I have Lord Beacon in my library. He is most anxious to speak with you."

"About what?"

"His topic is one that commonly makes young men anxious, I believe."

As comprehension dawned, Caroline stopped and turned to face him. "He has made an offer?"

"Indeed, he has. A very handsome one. You are to be congratulated for bringing him up to scratch."

"But I had no intention . . . What have you told him?"

"I said I had no objection to his suit, and that he could speak to you whenever he wished. He wishes to speak now."

She turned away thoughtfully and continued down the hall. Assailed by a sudden suspicion, Phillip caught her arm, detaining her.

"You don't intend to refuse him?"

She met his gaze squarely, her chin high. "Yes, Lord Brooke, I do."

"But why?" he demanded. "The man is wealthy, intelligent, handsome, under thirty."

"I am aware of Lord Beacon's good qualities, my lord, but I have only known him a few weeks."

"I have known him for years, and I assure you he is all he seems. I warn you, Caroline, you are not likely to receive a better offer. Beacon is heir to an earldom and could look much higher for a wife. He does you great honor with this offer."

Caroline nodded and took a steadying breath. "I know he does. I will not keep him waiting."

As she moved down the hall, he kept pace beside her. "At least listen with an open mind to what he has to say," Phillip advised. "He expresses himself eloquently. You need not love a man when you marry him, Caroline. Those feelings can grow, and often do, with time."

Caroline paused at the top of the stairs. She hadn't wanted to mention love, certain he would scorn such consideration.

When she remained silent, Phillip spoke again. "Don't make light of his feelings for you. They alone are worth more than the sum of all his other qualities."

Phillip waited at the top of the stairs while Caroline descended alone. He then paced the gallery at the head of the stairway, keeping the front door in view. Within fifteen minutes Lord Beacon emerged from the library, collected his hat and coat from the footman, and left the house. He did not walk with the carefree step of a happy man. When Caroline did not appear, Phillip returned to the library, where he found her standing before the fire.

"You refused him," he stated flatly.

"Yes," she answered, without turning.

"I cannot conceive what you require in a man. He has every attribute a woman could want—"

"Please, don't berate me," she pleaded. "I believe I truly wounded him, and I feel bad."

Walking to her, he took her arm and turned her to face him. "You do care for him, then?"

"I like and admire him, I respect him—but I don't love him. Is it really so much to ask? You had love in your marriage. You loved Victoria and she you. Why have *you* never married again?" she challenged. "Isn't it because you never found another woman you could love as you loved her?"

"It's different for a man," he answered, deftly avoiding her question. "There is no need for me to marry again. I have an heir."

"Whereas I need to find a place for myself, so as not to be a burden to Stephen."

"Exactly."

"I believe I would rather be housekeeper to my brother and whatever wife he chooses than give myself in marriage to a man I do not love."

Chapter 12

"WE WILL BE leaving London in a few weeks," Grace remarked as she and Caroline walked from Hookham's Library to the coach awaiting them at the curb. "Has Lord Gresham spoken?"

"Yes," Caroline replied. "Yesterday. And Beacon the day before. They have both been properly refused."

"And what of Viscount Ashton?" Grace continued, rather tightly. "Surely he intends to ask for your hand as well."

"Gerry? Gerry has asked me half a dozen times and more, and has had as many refusals."

Grace turned shocked eyes to her friend as they climbed into the coach and settled across from each other against the dark blue squabs. "Surely you jest? Why should you refuse him?"

"Because I don't love him, Gracie, nor ever will."

"Oh" was all Miss Bidwell could reply, trying to comprehend how any female could not love the viscount, as handsome and gentle as he was.

Noticing her friend's confusion and seeming to think more explanation was necessary, Caroline added, "Gerry and I have been friends forever, but I'm afraid I can't offer him more than that."

Privately thinking that any gentleman who asked a woman to be his wife more than six times must be desperately in love, Grace resisted saying so. It was painful enough just thinking about it. Caroline was treating so cavalierly a love Grace would have given anything for. And the pain she felt was not for herself alone. She suffered for Ashton as well, knowing him to be the victim of unrequited love, knowing from personal experience how painful it could be. For Grace herself was desperately in love with Viscount Ashton and had been for several weeks.

Dropping Caroline in Curzon Street, Grace continued to her home, while Caroline entered the house to find the subject of her recent conversation awaiting her return in the morning room.

"Caro!" Ashton greeted her, coming forward to take her hands. "Can you spare me a few moments? I have come to seek your advice."

"I always have time for you, Gerry. How can I help?"

"Well . . ." he hesitated, "I'm not certain how to begin."

Suddenly suspicious, she asked, "You haven't come to make another proposal?"

"No. At least, not the one you think. You will be pleased to know I have given up on that. I can see which way the wind blows."

Becoming more puzzled with every word he spoke, she suggested, "You must be clearer, Gerry. I am not certain I follow you."

"The thing is, I'd like to . . . I thought I would . . . that is, if you think there is any chance of her accepting, I should like to offer for Grace."

Caroline's face lit instantly with surprise and a joy so genuine that Ashton was left in no doubt of her feelings.

"Oh, Gerry!" she exclaimed, taking both his hands and pulling him down onto the sofa beside her. "You care for her, then? I can't think you would offer otherwise."

He grinned appreciatively. She knew him so well. "Yes, I care for her. And I have you to thank for it. It was because of you that I came to be so often in her company, that I came to value her."

"Does she know how you feel? Have you said anything?"

"No, for strange as it may seem, I have only just come to see it myself. I had been making plans to remove to the country when it crossed my mind that it would be some time before I would see Grace again. The thought depressed me. I found myself trying to hit upon ways to see her during the winter. When I realized I was loath to leave her behind, I discovered I had formed a strong attachment without realizing it. I've spent the last four days thinking of little else. Now I have come to you, for I desperately need your advice. What should I do?"

"Are you such a simpleton, Gerry? You must go to her, of course, and propose."

"And if she refuses me?"

"I find it hard to believe she would. But if she does, it will not be the first time you have been rejected."

"No. But that fact alone doesn't make it any easier."

"Come now, Gerry. I believe you welcome rejection. Why else would you have persisted with me all these years?"

"I persisted because I hoped you would change your mind. But I will tell you this, Caro—and I don't think there is another soul I would confide in—I'm damned afraid to put it to the touch. I guess what I'm saying is that I should like some assurances from you first. Has she ever said anything to you about me?"

Caroline concentrated, searching her memory. "No. Nothing of a personal nature. She admires you, I know. She has often said she finds you considerate, dependable, a good friend."

He dismissed these compliments with a wave of the hand. "All women say such things. They show no special favor. I need something more concrete than that."

She shook her head. "I can't give you anything. I know she expected you to offer for me. She mentioned it today."

"That's not surprising. I have been sitting in your pocket for weeks."

"I explained to her that we are only friends. I'm sure she believed me. If you are uncertain of her feelings," Caroline suggested, "perhaps you should try to fix your interest with her before you make an offer."

"There is no time, for I must be home in a week. I'm not anxious to leave town with nothing said."

"Then you have answered your own question, Gerry. There is only one thing to do: Go to Grace, today, now, and don't consider the possibility that she may say no. Believe that she will say yes."

Caroline accompanied the viscount to the entryway, where they stood for a moment inside the great front doors.

"You are the best friend I have ever had, Caro," he said, "yet it seems our paths must diverge a bit today."

"Perhaps," she returned, "but only a bit. I wish you good fortune, Gerry."

"And I wish the same for you, Caro, always."

Then, before the shocked eyes of Lord Brooke's butler and two footmen, Viscount Ashton bent his head and kissed Miss Hargrave on the cheek. He had no regrets as he turned his back on his first love and marched off to do battle for his second.

Caroline stood for a moment near the door, then slowly turned to ascend the stairs. She did not look toward the library. Had she done so, she would have discovered that Brooke's servants had not been the only witnesses to the intimacy between herself and the viscount. The library doors, each an expanse of flawless mahogany nearly five feet wide, stood open to the fullest degree. Seated at his desk facing them, Phillip had a panoramic view of the entire entryway. His eyes had been drawn to the couple the moment they entered the hall. While he had been unable to hear anything they said, he had missed nothing else.

Grace Bidwell and her aunt and companion, Lady Kincaid, were reviewing the week's menus with the housekeeper when Lord Bidwell summoned his daughter to his study. She went to him immediately, entered the room without knocking, then stood transfixed upon the threshold when she saw her father was not alone.

"Ah, Grace," the older gentleman said. "Here you are. Come in, please, and sit with us."

Grace did as he asked, occupying a chair near the gentlemen as they reseated themselves and her father continued, "As you can see, I have Ashton with me. There was something he particularly wished to discuss with you."

He paused. When Ashton offered only a simple yes to fill the awkward silence, Lord Bidwell rose again.

"I shall leave the two of you to speak in private." Holding out his hand to the viscount, he added, "You know my feelings, Ashton. I leave the rest to you."

"Thank you, sir. Good day."

"Good day." With a brief nod to his daughter, Lord Bidwell departed, while a bewildered Grace was left to consider a clearly preoccupied viscount.

"What is it, my lord?" she asked. "Is something wrong? Has something happened to Caroline? I saw her only this morning."

"No, there is nothing amiss. Caro is well. I have come to speak with you on a private matter. I was hoping you might guess what."

"I've never been very good at guessing games, Lord Ashton. Perhaps you should simply tell me what it is," she suggested.

"Very well. I have already spoken to your father and he has given his consent. I have come to make an offer for your hand in marriage."

He watched her face closely but saw none of the reactions he had hoped to see. A warm smile of happiness would have pleased him most. A shy smile of pleasure would have been welcome as well, but he was offered neither of these. He watched instead as her cheeks grew pale and her eyes vacant.

"I think I have surprised you," he said simply.

"Yes, my lord," she finally managed.

Had Grace been a romantic, she could not have created a more idealistic scenario: Dashingly handsome, wealthy lord asks plain spinster to be his bride. It was the stuff of high romance. In real life it was unbearably painful. My God, she thought. He loves Caroline. Why is he asking for me?

She raised her eyes to find him anxiously awaiting some response from her. He was so handsome—she loved him so. She knew instantly she could never marry him knowing he loved another. She wished she could find the courage to ask why he wanted her, yet she was fairly certain she already knew. He wanted Caroline, and Caroline had made it clear she would never have him. He was of an age to want a wife . . .

"We have a great deal in common," he said suddenly.

breaking in on her thoughts. "We like the same things, laugh at the same things—"

He broke off, wanting to convince her but hampered by the troubled look she wore.

"I do not think of marriage, Lord Ashton," she said woodenly.

"You do not think of marriage," he repeated. "I'm not sure what you mean."

"Perhaps I should have said, I do not wish to marry."

That was certainly clear enough, he thought. He had heard it before, after all.

"I see. Is there any chance you might be brought to think of it? I would be willing to wait for an answer. Give you all the time you need to decide."

"I don't think it likely I will change my mind, my lord. You honor me by your proposal, but I must decline it."

She rose then and offered him her hand, knowing she could not withstand even one more minute in his presence.

Had she not been in such pain herself, perhaps she would have seen his, or even heard the disappointment in his voice. But she did not see it nor hear it.

The viscount left the Bidwell house in a black mood. Less than an hour later Caroline received a note, brought round by hand from Ashton's London residence.

Caro,
She said no—I'm leaving for the country. I'll see you in a few weeks.

Gerry

In the library, curled in a large armchair before the fire, Caroline sat with Canto III of Lord Byron's *Childe Harold's Pilgrimage*. Published the previous year, it had not yet come in her way; she was delighted to find a copy on Brooke's shelf. Outside the windows a steady drizzle fell through light fog. Caroline heard voices in the hall outside. They grew louder as they neared the library, then were in the room with her.

"Please, Harris," Brooke was saying. "I have no wish to discuss this. Forget the Hargrave loan. It need not concern you."

On the point of rising to expose herself to the gentlemen—for she was quite hidden from their view—Caroline hesitated.

"But, my lord, you employ me to look after your business interests. This loan is foolhardy. Had I known at the time that you intended to offer it, I would have strongly advised you against it."

Phillip was shuffling through papers on his desk, looking for what had brought him into the room. His solicitor persisted. "You will most likely lose those funds already invested, but if you would take my advice, you will withdraw from this situation immediately. At least then your losses would be minimized."

"Harris," Brooke said, his tone a study in practiced patience, "You are not the only lawyer this town holds, nor the only one capable of dealing with my affairs. If you wish to continue in my employ, you will listen to what I say and note it well. My loan to the Hargraves is a personal matter, not a business concern. If and when I decide to take any action in regard to it, I shall inform you. Until that time, I wish never to hear it mentioned again. Is that understood?"

"Yes, my lord," Harris answered, sounding not at all pleased.

"Ah, here is the inventory," Brooke said. "You must hurry if you hope to arrive at the bank before closing."

Their voices and their footsteps left the room and echoed away down the hall while Caroline sat still in her chair, her volume of poetry forgotten.

Caroline had decided that when next she met Grace, she would allow the other girl to bring up the subject of Ashton's proposal. But after they had been together more than an hour, Grace having made no mention of the viscount, Caroline felt she must say something. Their friendship demanded that she at least tell Grace she knew of it.

"Before Gerry left for Hertfordshire, he wrote me that you had refused his offer, Gracie."

"So he did tell you. I thought he may have. Yes, I refused him."

"I'm not sure I understand why," Caroline continued. "I thought you liked him?"

"I do. But I feel as you—liking is not enough to base a

362

marriage upon. I would rather not talk about it, Caroline, if you don't mind."

So Caroline let the subject drop, discovering there are some things too private for even the closest friends to share.

During the days following Phillip's rescue of Caroline from the Earl of Gresham in the garden, they had managed to get along surprisingly well. They attended the same functions nearly every evening, always accompanied by Lady Hargrave and often by Grace and Lady Winfield. Phillip never asked Caroline to dance with him; she had given up wondering whether he would.

The conversation she had heard between Brooke and his solicitor worried her, but she knew she could not raise the subject with Brooke. She would wait to discuss it with Stephen. Then, if necessary, they would face Brooke with it together.

As the Season rapidly declined, many families left town for the country. One particularly cold evening, Phillip and Caroline attended the opera with Grace and Lord Wells. After dropping Wells at his lodgings and Grace at her home, Phillip and Caroline continued alone.

"We leave town in less than a week," he said. "Was London everything you had hoped?"

"Yes. Everything and more. I had a wonderful time. I only wish you could have convinced Stephen to come. I think he would have liked it."

"No doubt he will come next year. Then you will have an opportunity to show him all the wonderful discoveries you have made here. Don't be too disappointed, though, if he fails to go into raptures over the art museums, or the riches of the libraries, or even a piece like the one we saw tonight. You and Stephen were not cut from the same cloth."

"I know. I would not expect him to admire the things I do. Yet it is impossible for me to imagine anyone being left unmoved by the opera."

"Some people are not impressed by a heroine who dies in her lover's arms, singing lustily the while."

Caroline smiled in the dimly lit interior of the coach. "The staging and acting is perhaps overdone. But the music, my lord. How can anyone be untouched by it? It has such power to affect the soul. I can think of nothing more inspirational than a beautiful piece of music."

"Ah, but perhaps you have never been in love? Love can be as moving, more so, if it is the right kind."

"The kind you felt for Victoria, and she for you."

"Yes. It is an irresistible force, and it carries all before it. It *also* stirs the soul in a way impossible to describe in words."

"It sounds wonderful," Caroline mused.

"It is. Wonderful, and priceless. And like all valuable things, hard to find and harder to hold."

As much as Caroline had enjoyed London, it was wonderful to be home again. When Stephen, Patience, and a barking Leo greeted her in the great hall, it was impossible to tell who— her brother, her sister, or her spaniel—was happiest to see her. After receiving a hug and kiss from Patience and a welcoming smile from Matthew Keating, Caroline linked arms with Stephen as they moved into the sitting room, Leo yapping noisily at her heels.

Lady Hargrave and Lord Brooke were welcomed as warmly, and for the next hour the sitting room hummed with happy voices. There was much to ask, much to tell, a great deal of catching up to do.

Caroline joined eagerly in the conversation until a question from Stephen and its answer from Phillip brought a sudden change of mood.

"When had you planned on leaving us, sir?"

"I must see Mr. Birmingham tomorrow afternoon. I thought I would leave the following morning. I wanted to see your mother and sister home safely, but there is no reason for me to stay longer."

As both Lady Hargrave and Patience expressed their regret that he must leave them, Caroline remained silent.

For some reason, until this moment she had not thought about his leaving. It was true that initially he had intended to stay only a few weeks. But when the weeks had turned into months, only she seemed to notice or care. Her family had been content to have him stay; her disapproval didn't seem to matter.

Now, after months of wishing him elsewhere, she found it unsettling to imagine him gone. She felt none of the joy, none of the relief, she thought she would feel when he finally left them in peace.

Caroline soon excused herself, saying she owed Leo a long walk, having deserted him for so many weeks. Pulling on a warm pelisse and fur-lined half boots, she ventured into the gusty wind of a gray afternoon. She took Leo on a leash but within a few yards of the house bent to free him from it. He scurried off, first in one direction, then another, scattering leaves wherever he ran.

Phillip caught up with her a short time later in the formal gardens behind the house. Low on the estate's priority list, the gardens had received little or no care for many years, yet Caroline found she preferred their unkempt state to their previous manicured one. Hedges once meticulously trimmed had been permitted to grow at will. Roses normally restricted to arbors and trellises grew wild, overrunning large areas. Plants and flowers bared of their leaves by the approach of winter reached desolate arms to a dreary sun. Their state perfectly suited her mood.

"I see you cannot share your family's regret at my leaving," Phillip said, falling into step beside her and bending to ruffle Leo's head as the dog came for a quick greeting and then was gone again, darting out of sight among the hedges.

Caroline wanted to deny his accusation, but there was a constriction in her chest, a tightness in her throat, and she could not answer him.

"I don't mean to tease you," he went on. "I know I have been a thorn in your flesh from the beginning. And though I know you will probably not believe me, I am sorry for it. Stephen doesn't need me anymore, so I doubt I will ever be back. Perhaps we will meet someday in town, if you decide to come again."

"I should like that," she managed.

"Good. There was one more thing, while I have you alone. . . . I lied to you once a long time ago, and it has weighed on my conscience since." She regarded him curiously, but said nothing. "The first day we met, you asked if I had come to the ridge before or after you had removed your stockings. I lied to save you embarrassment. I came before and I saw more than I should have. If an apology at this late date could change anything, I would offer one. But apologies can alter nothing between us now. We have come too far for that."

She was aware he was saying one thing and meaning

another, yet everything had grown so out of focus she couldn't pull it straight.

Caroline tried to remember her embarrassment that day. It had been horrifying to think he *may* have seen her legs. So much had happened since then. She had seen his naked chest, bathed it, been held against it. He had kissed her; she had kissed him. It didn't matter to her anymore that he had seen her legs; she couldn't believe it ever had.

"Think nothing of it, my lord. You were motivated by a gentlemanly regard for my feelings. I could not hold it against you."

" 'My lord,' still," he said. "It's hard to believe we have never even gotten past that." He raised his head and whistled shrilly for the dog. When Leo appeared, Phillip offered his arm to Caroline. "We should get back to the house. It's bitter. I shouldn't like you to take a chill."

Chapter 13

LATER THAT AFTERNOON Caroline found an opportunity to relate to Stephen the conversation she had overheard between Lord Brooke and his solicitor.

"What do you think it means, Stephen?"

"It simply verifies what I suspected at the outset."

"And what was that?"

"That Lord Brooke was the source of the mysterious mortgage he and Mr. Birmingham were able to secure."

"But why should he lend us money? He barely knew us then."

"He told Mother that Father saved his life in Spain."

"Ah, I see. So he feels he is repaying the debt by helping us."

"Perhaps. Since Mother told me about it, I have wondered if that debt was Father's reason for naming Lord Brooke trustee. With such a powerful obligation on his side, Brooke would be nearly forced to take an interest in us."

"You're probably right. But how much do you think we should let him do? Surely there is a limit to his debt."

"I doubt he would think so. I don't see how any man could hope to repay the gift of his life. No equivalent value exists."

"I hope you're not suggesting we make use of him all our lives, Stephen, simply because he owed our father a debt he cannot possibly pay."

"No. I'm not suggesting that at all. In fact, I feel he has done more than enough already. But if it's all the same to you, I would rather not tax him with this loan. Knowing him as I do now, I think it was something he truly wished to do. I do not want to offend him by seeming ungrateful or churlish."

"All right. I agree. We will leave things as they are, though I wonder if we will ever truly know what the relationship was between our father and our trustee. Did you ever come across any mention of Brooke in Father's papers?"

"I never took the time to look through his things," Stephen answered. "I couldn't see any reason. There was always so much work that needed doing. There still is. I imagine there could be something in his desk, or perhaps in the trunk where he kept his old letters and things. Mr. Birmingham gave me the keys months ago. I have them here, somewhere."

Crossing to the study desk, he extracted a cluster of mismatched keys from a narrow drawer and handed them to his sister. "You're welcome to dig through those old papers, Caro, if you think they could help solve the mystery. I doubt if you will find anything, but it can't hurt to look."

Early the following morning, while Stephen took his guardian about the estate to view the work done during his absence, Caroline put on one of her old gray gowns and made her way to her father's bedchamber at the far end of the east wing. Her mother still used the sitting room that joined the two bedchambers, so Caroline avoided it, going instead to the door connecting her father's chambers to the outside corridor. The door was locked, but the second of the two large keys she tried opened it.

The bedchamber was shrouded in Holland covers, its heavy draperies tightly closed over high leaded windows. Caroline opened all the draperies first, allowing as much sunlight as possible to penetrate the room.

She hadn't been in her father's room for more than eleven months, had spent little time there in recent years, yet it seemed very familiar, for she had often come here as a child. She remembered well the dark, ornately wainscoted walls with the gold-patterned paper above. Most of the paintings were gone, but one of her father and eight-year-old Stephen still hung above the fireplace. A King Charles spaniel sat at their feet—Leo's grandmother. On the wall to the left of the fireplace a large fifteenth-century tapestry remained. Caroline had spent hours studying it as a child. It was a busy design, filled with people, animals, and flowers. She had always admired it, for it seemed each time she looked at it, she would see some small thing she had never noticed before.

The massive bed, hung in black and gold brocade, looked exactly as it had the last time she had seen it—the day her father died. Sweeping the dustcover from her father's large oaken desk, she pulled a chair close and went to work with the keys Stephen had given her. Few of the drawers were locked, but even those that were yielded uninteresting things. She found various letters, notes, bills of sale, records of business transactions. There were some personal letters, none to anyone she knew. There were a few pieces of worthless jewelry, the pocket watch her father had worn, a war medal.

The trunk at the foot of the bed seemed a more likely place to find some mention of Brooke, for it contained memorabilia from Lord Hargrave's army years. On top were his uniforms, his sword, and pistols. Caroline lifted the pistols carefully, making a mental note to tell Stephen they were here. They were a fine pair, undoubtedly valuable. As she lifted the sword and scabbard, she found she was having difficulty seeing them clearly for her eyes suddenly clouded with tears. How well she could remember her handsome papa, dressed in his scarlet regimentals, his tasseled sash hanging just so, his dress sword—this very sword—swinging at his side. How different he had been when he died from the dashing soldier she remembered.

Brushing aside her tears with dusty fingers, she carefully lifted the uniforms and set them aside. In the bottom of the trunk she discovered a large strongbox; one of her keys opened it. It contained more letters, some of which were copies of letters he had written to the families of men who had died under his command. None of them mentioned Brooke. It was close to noon when she finished skimming through all the letters. In the very bottom of the strongbox she came upon a journal, kept by her father in his own hand. There was an entry for nearly every day during the years between 1800 and 1810. Finally she felt she may have hit upon something. Those years should coincide, she thought, with the years Lord Brooke spent in the army. Perhaps her father would have found the incident with Brooke worthy of mention in his journal. Setting the journal aside, she began replacing the articles she had removed from the trunk. She would take the journal away with her and read it carefully.

Having replaced the uniforms, sword, and pistols, she was about to close the lid when she noticed on its underside an unusual thickened area, bearing a small keyhole. Reaching for the key ring, she tried each key diligently but none would fit. The hole was too small for any of them. Next she tried a hairpin, but the lock had been too cleverly made to yield easily. Finally she gave up, reasoning that as old as the trunk was, the key for the compartment could have been lost decades ago. Chances were her father had never had the key and therefore never used the space. That would explain the absence of the key on a ring where every other necessary key had been.

Returning to the desk, she closed all the drawers, putting away the things she had disturbed. For a moment she studied the pocket watch she had found. She was unable to open the case, its latch resisting her efforts to spring it. The case itself was relatively plain, bearing on its back surface a delicate inscription: TO MY SON JOHN ON HIS TWENTY-FIRST BIRTHDAY, 2 MARCH, 1781.

"It was a gift from Grandfather to Father," Caroline said aloud. "Perhaps Stephen would like to have it."

Slipping the watch into her skirt pocket, she pulled the dustcover over the desk. Then, closing the draperies, leaving the room just as she had found it, she took the keys and the journal and returned to her own room.

After luncheon, having discovered from Stephen the approximate dates of Brooke's service under her father, Caroline returned to her room to continue her perusal of the journal. While Lord Brooke rode his mare into Hertford for a final meeting with Mr. Birmingham, Caroline began reading every entry for the years 1807 and 1808.

Finally, on November 16, 1808, Caroline discovered a reference to the event she was seeking. But what she found there solved no mystery but merely raised more questions. For on that day, her father had written:

Today was very nearly my last day on earth. Under heavy attack by the enemy, led by Bonaparte himself, we have been driven from Madrid. During an orderly retreat my company encountered an isolated pocket of French infantry with strength four times our own. Trapped in a crossfire, we had no choice but to gallop for cover. My horse was hit in the first volley. I managed to roll free unhurt and was fighting hand to hand when Captain Brooke came back for me. Fortunately the random firing had stopped, for we were in among their own men and they could not risk it. Brooke downed two of my opponents from horseback while I finished the third. Then, pulling me up behind him (my right arm was useless from a saber slash), Brooke galloped for the brigade. No other shot touched us, though any number passed close enough to stir our hair. The man is mad, but the best damned subordinate a brigade commander could wish for. He has more courage than any five men. I have this day recommended him for the regimental rank of major.

Just as Caroline was placing a scrap of ribbon in the journal to mark the place, the bell of the village church began to peal.

Rung on Sunday mornings, or for weddings and funerals, the bell was used as a means of mass communication only on rare occasions. The last time it had been rung with such abandon had been the day the village received news of the victory at Waterloo. The bell rang for no such joyous cause today.

Phillip's meeting with Mr. Birmingham took longer than he expected. When he rode through Welwyn in the early hours of the evening, the village was quiet, most of the shops having closed for the day. Smoke curled lazily from every chimney. Families were gathered indoors, for it was the dinner hour.

Phillip nudged the mare into a trot as he cleared the last of the cottages, then entered the heavy wood skirting the northern edge of the village. As his road wound up from the valley, the trees thinned, then ended. Before him lay the Welwyn Commons, rolling ahead for a mile and more, his own road visible at its high points, hiding in the dips between. But it was not the undulation of the road ahead that caught and held his attention. His eyes narrowed as he studied the horizon, first with interest, then with growing alarm. The evening air, so crystal-clear about him, was not so ahead. Clouding the sky to the east and cloaking the valley where Paxton lay was a heavy pall of smoke. He had seen enough crops laid waste, enough villages sacked and set ablaze, to recognize the evidence of a major fire.

He set spurs to the mare, holding her to a hard gallop for the remaining three miles of his journey. As he drew closer, he realized it could not be the Hall that was burning, for the source of the smoke was farther west. When he finally broke through the trees surrounding Paxton, it was to find nearly half the village gone. One entire side of the street was a smoking mass of rubble and smoldering timbers, while the opposite side remained untouched.

The church, half-timbered, wattle and daub, would need no whitewashing now. Its roof was gone, its massive timbers burned through. Without their support the walls had fallen inward, breaking loose from their stone foundation.

Where the cottages had been, all that remained were fire-places and chimneys silhouetted against the setting sun. Many of the villagers were moving about the ruins, quenching the last of the flames.

Phillip rode to one of the village men demanding, "What happened? How did it start?"

"No one seems certain, m'lord. We think perhaps it was the blacksmith's shop."

"Where is Lord Hargrave?"

"The family has gone back to the house. There was nothing more they could do. We have the fires under control, and all who lost homes have found shelter for the night."

Without another word, Phillip wheeled the mare toward the Hall. He found Stephen, Matthew, Lady Hargrave, and Patience in the salon. All four looked as if they had indeed spent the afternoon fighting a fire, their faces smudged with soot, their clothing damp and soiled. Patience was pouring tea at the table before the sofa. Near the fire, Lady Hargrave, with Matthew's assistance, was wrapping Stephen's hands in long lengths of cotton lint.

"How badly are you hurt?" Phillip asked, cutting through any necessity for greeting.

Stephen shrugged off his concern. "It's nothing. Blistered only."

"He didn't even realize he had burned himself until we got back here," Matthew said, reaching past Lady Hargrave's shoulder to cut the excess from a knot she had just tied.

"Someone in the village told me it started in the blacksmith's shop. Is that true?" Phillip asked.

"We think so," Matthew said. "However it started, it traveled with the speed of the wind, jumping from rooftop to rooftop. By the time we arrived, every house on the east side of the street was ablaze. We couldn't do anything for the cottages except be sure everyone got out. We tried to keep it from spreading."

"We put as much water as possible on the church," Stephen continued, "hoping to spare it. We didn't succeed."

"I saw," Phillip said. "Was there any loss of life?"

There was a pause as Stephen glanced at Matthew, then his mother, before answering. "Walter and Iris Miller lost their son—the baby Caroline helped deliver. Everyone else is safe."

Phillip had been holding his breath while he waited for someone to answer his question. He let it out suddenly. "How? Their cottage is set apart from the other houses in the village."

"We had been working a long time, trying to keep the church wet," Matthew offered. "When it caught anyway, we felt defeated and stood there, watching it. The wind was fierce, whipping flames high into the air. Some small piece of the roof was evidently carried as far as the Miller cottage. Like you, we had thought it far enough to be safe. The baby was sleeping inside while both parents helped in the village. By the time someone noticed the roof afire, it was too late. Stephen got there first and tried to go in, but the roof was already coming down. He burned himself when one of the rafters collapsed and he instinctively raised his hands to protect his head. We pulled him away; there was nothing anyone could do."

"Where's Caroline?" Phillip asked.

"In the library," Lady Hargrave answered. "We tried to comfort her. She said she preferred to be alone."

As Phillip turned toward the hall, Patience asked, "Lord Brooke, should you like a cup of tea? Perhaps you could take one to Caro, too."

He smiled at her, moving to take the tray and the two cups of tea it held. "Thank you, Patience. That's a good idea."

He left the room with the tray. They listened to the slap of his booted feet against the stone floor of the hall, then the soft opening and closing of the library door.

The library was dark, and Phillip hesitated, allowing his eyes to adjust to the dimness. There were no candles lit. The draperies of one window were open, but the rapidly approaching twilight offered little illumination; the fire had burned so low that the room was chilled. Setting the tea tray on a small table near the sofa, Phillip crossed the carpeted floor to the fire. The dry logs he laid on the glowing coal bed were welcomed, orange tongues of flame leaping up to embrace them.

Caroline was standing at the window in the dim light of the fading day. She had not looked up at his entrance and even now seemed not to notice him.

"Patience has sent you a cup of tea," he said quietly. "Should you care for it?"

She turned to face him. "The baby is dead."

"I know. Stephen told me." He closed the space between them. It was impossible in the uncertain light to see her face, but it wasn't hard for him to imagine how she was suffering. He opened his arms to her, offering a refuge if she wanted it. She walked straight into them, and he closed them tightly, holding her close.

"It was terrible," she sobbed into his coat. "No one saw the fire until it was too late. Stephen tried, but when he opened the cottage door, everything inside was in flames. Iris was beside me. We were standing in the plowed-up vegetable garden, in the dirt—we hadn't even noticed. When the beam fell on Stephen, she screamed and she kept on screaming. She was on her knees in the dirt crying 'My baby, my baby' over and over again. I could do nothing. I couldn't help her; I couldn't speak. I could only stare at the flames. And all I saw when I looked at them was his face—his precious, smiling face—"

"Don't do this. Don't torture yourself," he said. He gave her his handkerchief and she wiped her eyes, but she was unable to compose herself. He continued to hold her, his hands moving in a gentle massage up and down her back, his chin resting gently in her hair. It held the strong odor of wood smoke, yet beneath it the subtle scent of lavender. His lips brushed her hair once, then again. They found her temple and lingered there. He took her face in his hands, tipping her head back, wanting to read her expression but finding it impossible. His next kiss tasted her eyebrow. When she closed her eyes, he kissed them both several times before he took her lips. She responded instantly, bringing her hands to his neck and pulling him closer.

His mouth played over hers teasingly, hungrily, as if he was relishing something long denied. She responded instinctively, knowing little of the art but willing to follow his lead. Then, reluctantly, he broke away. Taking her hand, he led her to the fire.

"Your tea is cold, and so am I," he said. "Could we light some candles? I should like to see you."

When she offered no objection, he lit half a dozen candles near the sofa, then added several more logs to the growing fire. "I'm hungry. You?"

"No. But go ahead; have Webber bring you something."

He rang for the butler and a short time later a collation of bread, cheese, cold sliced meat, wine, and a fresh pot of tea arrived. He ate little, she less; he poured her a cup of tea, himself a glass of burgundy.

In the better light he noticed that her face, like those of the others, was smudged with soot. The hem of her gray gown was darkened by dampness and ash. He filled her teacup again, then set his food aside.

"I believe this is the first time in my life I have ever poured a cup of tea," he said thoughtfully.

She tried to smile, but her preoccupation with the tragedy of the day made it a pitiful thing.

"Come here," he said suddenly. "Come closer."

She obeyed him, moving closer on the sofa until the space of two feet or more was closed to a few inches. He put an arm about her and pulled her closer still, till her head rested against his shoulder.

"You understand how I feel about the baby, don't you?" she asked.

"Yes, I do."

"It was this way for you with Victoria, wasn't it? The horrible loss. The sense of waste. The feeling that there should have been something you could do, coupled with the knowledge that there was nothing . . . I wish you weren't leaving in the morning," she added incongruously.

"I'm not. There is no pressing reason for me to go. Stephen will need me now."

She pushed herself a little away from him, regarding him seriously. "When you kissed me earlier—why did you?"

He considered a moment before answering. "Kissing is a—closeness. It makes you feel as if you are a part of someone else. It shuts out loneliness and the associated feelings of being alone, standing alone."

"Did you enjoy it?"

"Of course I enjoyed it. But I don't want to talk about it. I would much rather do it again."

And he did. He kissed her lips, her neck, her shoulders, kissed her till her senses numbed and her thinking blurred. His hands explored her body and she permitted it, knowing he was not delirious this time but fully cognizant of his actions. After a few minutes he desisted, but he kept an arm about her, pinning her close to his side.

They talked long into the night, and when they quit the library near midnight, the salon was dark and deserted. "Everyone has gone to bed," Caroline remarked.

"Yes. And so must we. There will be much to do tomorrow."

They separated at the top of the stairs, their rooms being in opposite wings. "I'll see you in the morning" was all Phillip said before continuing down the hall to his own room.

Chapter 14

THE FOLLOWING MORNING the men rose early. Volunteers arriving from Welwyn, Styles, and the outlying farms of several surrounding estates formed crews to begin cleanup of the fire-ravaged village. Viscount Ashton had come himself with more than forty of his tenants and neighboring freeholders. Ultimately they would begin the slow process of rebuilding.

After luncheon, when Stephen and Matthew returned to their work in Paxton, Phillip stayed behind to speak with Caroline. She had spent the morning at the rectory with her mother, formulating plans to help the families left homeless by the fire.

Phillip led her to the library, where he felt relatively certain they would not be disturbed.

"We must talk," he said as the door clicked closed behind him.

"Yes, certainly. What is it?" she asked, crossing the room to stand before the fire, its warmth most welcome on a crisp November day.

"We need to talk about last night."

"Oh," she said, taken aback. "Do we?"

"Are you forgetting what happened here?"

"Of course not," she replied, taking a seat on the sofa they had occupied the previous evening. "I suppose you have been thinking the worst possible things about me. You may not believe this after the way I acted, but I have never done anything like that before."

"I know that," he answered simply, seating himself near her.

"Yes . . . well . . . I don't know why I behaved so. I think it must have been the situation. I was in shock; I still am. When death steps up to take a front seat in your life, everything else is thrown out of balance somehow. Perhaps it was as you said—I needed the closeness, something to keep me from feeling so desperately alone. If I shocked you, I'm sorry."

"What kind of foolishness is this?" he asked. "I wasn't shocked and I certainly don't want an apology. It was I who kissed you, not the reverse. Understand me! I don't regret it. Yet I am fully aware of how inappropriate my behavior was, and I am prepared to right that wrong. I think you will find my offer beneficial, both to you and to Stephen."

"And what offer is that, my lord?" she asked, all at sea.

He frowned. "You haven't the vaguest notion of what happened in this room last night, do you?" he asked, exasperated.

"Surely, I do. I remember everything!"

"Yet you clearly do not comprehend the significance. We spent five hours alone here. We made a private commitment that needs to be honored publicly." When her features remained puzzled, his frustration mounted. "If I must spell it out for you, then I will. My behavior last evening was compromising in the extreme. I am asking you, Caroline, to become my wife!"

As his point finally came home, Caroline's eyes widened and her mouth fell open slightly, much as it had the day by the stream, when he had marched through the water for her.

"You feel you must offer for me because we kissed?" she asked. "That's ridiculous! If every woman felt compelled to marry the first man she kissed, half the women in the country would be wed at sixteen! Besides, as you said, what we did was private. If no one knows what happened between us, how can there be any question of compromise?"

"Your mother knows how long we were here alone. Stephen knows, and Matthew."

"But you are my trustee," she offered. "My family can have no objection to our being alone together. We have often been so."

"But don't you see? That only makes it that much worse. I had no right to take advantage of the opportunity my trusteeship offered me. Believe me, if your mother knew what had transpired here last evening, she would strongly disapprove. So would Stephen. I believe they would expect nothing less than the offer I have made."

"Then I think it would be best if neither of us told them

about it," she said soberly, "for I have no desire to be your wife."

"Is the thought of marriage to me so repulsive, then?"

"Not repulsive, no. But I have already told you that when I wed, if I do, I should like to be in love." She saw his shallow smile, fleeting though it was. "You may laugh at me if you like, my lord. I don't care if my notions seem romantic or impractical to you." She plunged on, trying to ignore his unsettling, steady regard. "In addition to a mutual love and respect, I should like for my husband and me to be compatible, 'well suited,' as everyone is so fond of saying. Marriage to you would be a continuous battleground."

"I don't agree that we are so poorly suited," he argued, "and I have found that a battleground can sometimes be an exhilarating place."

"Well, I should not like it," she persisted. "Nor should I like to be wed to a man who tells less than the whole truth, and who will not believe me when I speak the truth to him."

"Those are strong accusations," he replied sternly, all trace of his earlier smile disappearing.

"I do not make them without foundation, Lord Brooke."

"When did I refuse to believe what you said to me?" he demanded.

"When I told you my mother's jewelry was worthless."

"Was it?"

"Yes."

"I believe you."

"But you wouldn't believe me then," she complained, "when I tried to keep you from expending money on my behalf, money I shall now have to repay."

He made an impatient gesture. "The money is nothing. I don't want it back."

"Next you will say it is the least you can do, considering you owe my father your life."

"Your mother shouldn't have told you about that."

"She didn't. Stephen did. But it won't wash anymore, my lord, for I have discovered my father's journal among his personal possessions. There is a very interesting entry for November 16, 1808. It seems that in my father's recollections of that day, the boot was on the other leg. Surely you remember? It was the day you went back for my father after his horse was shot. By the way, did you ever receive the majority for which he recommended you?"

"Yes."

"Well, Major Brooke, it seems the effort you expended to rescue your colonel was well spent. It yielded you an advanced rank then, and it has blessed you now with an impecunious baron and his indigent dependents. What madness possessed my father that he should place an additional burden upon you when he already owed you so much?"

"I don't know why he did it. I probably never will. When I was first informed of the trusteeship, I was bewildered, then incensed."

"That's why you dealt only with Mr. Birmingham, and never came to see us."

"Yes. Then I spoke to Ashton and he suggested I stop to meet you. He aroused my curiosity, so I did. I'm not sure why I decided to stay. Maybe I was bored. Maybe I saw a challenge here. Maybe I was intrigued by you. Whatever the reason—perhaps it was a bit of all three—I stayed, and I became involved. Now I could no more easily walk away from all of you than I could have left your father behind that day."

"You deceived us about the mortgage."

"How can you know about that?"

"I was in your library in London the day you and your solicitor came in searching for some papers. You were there a few moments only, yet you spoke of the loan and I heard."

"I never lied to Stephen. I told him I had managed to secure additional funds. He never asked if I was the source."

"You are splitting hairs now, my lord. Lie or simple deceit—they are two sides of the same coin."

"Surely you must see why I did it. He would never have accepted my help otherwise. And believe me, he needed it. Your family would have been able to continue here six months, perhaps a year, but no longer. Would you have preferred that? To have had your home sold from under you?"

"No, of course not. I didn't realize the situation had become that serious. Or perhaps I did, but was refusing to admit it."

"Did you tell Stephen what you overheard?" he asked.

"Yes, I did. He suspected something of the sort all along, but he was willing to accept it since he felt it was your way of fulfilling your obligation to our father. I doubt he'll feel the same when he has seen the journal."

"I suppose you must show it to him?"

"Yes, sir, I must. I would never keep such information from him. We will pay back the loan eventually."

"You may redeem it instantly if you agree to marry me. The loan would become history. And I would be more than willing to further aid my brother-in-law in his financial difficulties. His losses from the fire yesterday will easily nullify this whole year's work. To rebuild the lost cottages, he'll need every penny he made on the harvest and more."

There was a long, uncomfortable pause before she responded. "Stephen would not want me to compromise my happiness to secure his financial position."

"I know he wouldn't. It was unfair of me to make the suggestion, for you have already refused my offer in no uncertain terms, have you not?"

"Indeed I have, sir. But I should like to thank you for it. It is by far the most flattering offer I have had. If I were inclined to accept it, at least there would not be the necessity to seek my trustee's approval."

He answered her teasing smile with one of his own. "You're never at a loss, are you?"

"Not often."

He rose then, taking her hands and pulling her to her feet. "I will speak with Stephen about the loan. I am certain we can arrive at some mutually agreeable arrangement. On the matter of your Season, however—the clothes for you, your mother, and Patience—on that matter I do not intend to compromise. It was a gift, and I will not accept any repayment."

"When you talk with Stephen, you will tell him the truth about that day in Spain?" she asked.

"Yes. I haven't liked the deception, but I saw no way to avoid it."

"I should like to thank you, my lord," she said, suddenly serious, "for what you did that day. Your brave action gave us eight years with our father that we would not have had otherwise. While some of those years were painful, I would never have chosen to do without them. My father was two very different men, you see. When he was gambling, he could not think or care about anything else; but at other times he was a

380

wonderful father, a giving, warmhearted person. I loved him very much."

"I am sure you did. And I can understand why. He was an admirable man in many ways."

"I must go to the rectory now, my lord; my mother is expecting me."

"Come along, then. I'm going that way. I will drive you."

That evening Phillip told Stephen the truth about the rescue in Spain and the source of the money. They agreed between them that Stephen would pay it back as he was able. Phillip prevailed in the matter of the cost of the Little Season.

"There was something else I wished to discuss with you, Phillip," Stephen said. "I received a letter today from Miles. He has asked if William may accompany him here for the winter vacation."

"I can guess why. I told William I planned to be at Southwell in December. Clearly he prefers to be where I am not. I hope he won't be too disappointed when he finds me here."

"I don't think he intends to slight you, Phillip. It's just that he and Miles have become friends. When he has known you longer—"

"He has known me nearly as long as you have."

"Yes. But it's different with your own father. I never got on with mine. He and I always seemed to be butting heads. He assumed I would want some army experience; it was the last thing I wanted. He had little interest in agriculture, while I was often concerned for our people. He never seemed to care that his weakness for gambling was affecting many others besides himself; I despised him for that. Caro tried more than once to convince me his gambling was an illness, something he couldn't control, but I never believed it. I still don't. It always seemed to me a man could change if he truly wished to."

"Perhaps *you* could," Phillip conceded. "But each man is different. It could be your father didn't have the strengths you do."

Stephen shrugged. "In any case, I don't think you need worry about William," he assured his guardian. "I don't mean to put you to the blush by saying this, but one day William will come to realize what a fine man his father is. Years from now he will look back and wonder how there could ever have been any estrangement between you."

"I hope you may be right, Stephen. If I could one day be as close to him as I feel to you, I would be content."

The next weeks passed busily for everyone on the estate, yet Phillip noticed that although Caroline kept busy, her spirits remained low. Seeing Iris Miller nearly every day was a constant reminder of the baby's loss. He thought Caroline looked poorly, as if she were not sleeping well. There were dark circles beneath her eyes. He was not imagining she had lost weight.

Searching for some means to raise her spirits, he hit upon the perfect solution. Surely a visit from her friend Grace Bidwell would cheer her. To that end he requested that Lady Hargrave write the Bidwells, inviting them to visit Paxton Hall.

Miss Bidwell read the invitation with mixed feelings. She had no desire to be near Lord Ashton, yet it was hard to resist the opportunity to see Caroline again, especially when Lady Hargrave wrote that Caroline was in poor spirits. So during the second week in December, Miss Bidwell, her father, and her aunt traveled into Hertfordshire. Lord Bidwell found the shooting at Paxton Hall exceptional; Lady Kincaid lent herself to Lady Hargrave's many projects with enthusiasm; Caroline and Grace renewed their friendship as if they had never been apart.

Lady Hargrave, with no knowledge of the offer made by Ashton to Grace, invited the viscount to dinner at the Hall four days after the Bidwell's arrival. Determined not to let Gerry's disappointment over his rejected suit throw a damper on the evening, Caroline kept the conversation light and lively, making certain everyone was included.

Ashton recounted how a newly acquired horse had thrown him that afternoon. "I was almost forced to refuse this invitation tonight," he said. "I thought it likely I would be unable to sit through dinner." He glanced about the room casually. "I say, Stephen, you wouldn't happen to have a soft cushion handy."

Smiling, Stephen shook his head. "Sorry, old man, I fear you must suffer. At least you didn't break anything—like that time with old Blossom."

Caroline laughed aloud, and Lord Bidwell demanded they share the joke.

"Well, I have a mare," Caroline explained. "She is the gentlest creature in nature. We all learned to ride on her. One day Stephen said he thought Blossom so gentle that he wouldn't be surprised if she would take three riders without complaint. Gerry, to outdo Stephen, said he felt she would probably accept a burden of four. Stephen couldn't swallow that; he disagreed, and a wager ensued. Clearly, the only way to see who was right, and who would win, was to put four riders on Blossom. So we did.

"Gerry, Stephen, Miles, and I all climbed onto her back. She just stood there, calm as you please. Gerry was mentally counting his winnings when the mare took two steps, reconsidered her passive behavior, and promptly pitched us all into the weeds. We were laughing so hard it was a full five minutes before we realized Gerry had broken his arm. To this day he won't ride double on a horse."

The story was greeted with smiles and laughter all round the table, though Phillip, glancing at Miss Bidwell, thought her smile more sad than amused. The following day he came upon her quite by chance as he passed through the long gallery on his way to the salon. As he entered the room, she drew closer to the draperies of a large bay window. He had the impression she was hoping not to be noticed. But as he had seen her, common courtesy demanded he acknowledge her presence. He moved to stand behind her, his gaze sharing her view from the window. "There is usually a fine prospect from here," he said, "but on a gray day such as this, it is somewhat less than appealing."

When she did not turn or speak in response, he reached to take her shoulder and gently turned her to face him. Nothing unmanned him so much as a woman's tears. "What is it, Miss Bidwell? Why do I find you so?"

"Pay me no mind, Lord Brooke," she said, taking the handkerchief he offered and dabbing her wet cheeks. "I am a silly, overemotional fool."

"Nonsense. You are no such thing. Tell me what troubles you."

"I made the wrong decision when I agreed to come here. I thought I could cope. I cannot. You see, I have committed the

383

folly of admiring someone who does not return my regard. It is more painful than I imagined it would be."

"Ashton?"

She looked her surprise. "Yes. How did you know?"

"A calculated guess. If it were me," he smiled, "I doubt we would be having this conversation. Since you have only known them a few days, I cannot think it would be Stephen or Matthew. Therefore, Ashton is the obvious choice. Are you so certain your case is hopeless?"

"Yes," she replied simply, "for he is in love with Caroline."

Chapter 15

PHILLIP KNEW CAROLINE was strongly attracted to Ashton, and he suspected that attraction had been Caroline's reason for rejecting both Lord Beacon's proposal and his own. That Ashton should admire Caroline as well did not surprise him. He only wondered why the viscount hadn't taken any action to make the relationship permanent.

During the following days, Phillip closely studied Caroline and Ashton when they were together. What he observed led him to doubt the veracity of Miss Bidwell's disclosure. Caroline and Ashton were indeed close, but it seemed to be the closeness of well-established friendship; Phillip detected no loverlike passion between them.

If Ashton exhibited that emotion at all, Phillip thought, it seemed to be directed at Miss Bidwell, not Caroline. It was for Grace that Ashton's eyes scanned a room upon first entering it. It was when speaking with her that he chose each word carefully, that he appeared tense and ill at ease—uncommon behavior for a man of his experience.

Phillip's thoughts were distracted from Ashton when Miles and William arrived several days later. Their coach swung onto the drive just as Phillip was returning from Welwyn. He gave his horse to one of the grooms and pulled open the coach door himself.

"And here we have the scholars, home from their adventures," he said. "Are the walls of Eton still standing?"

"They are, sir, but just barely." Miles smiled, taking his guardian's hand warmly.

William followed closely behind, his face expressionless as he descended from the coach.

"I daresay you didn't expect to see me here still, William," Phillip said to his son.

William took the hand his father offered. "I hope you didn't misunderstand about my wanting to come here," he said. "It seemed such a dreary prospect to spend the time at Southwell."

"It would have been even drearier for me, had I been there alone," Phillip responded. William's eyes dropped as Phillip continued immediately. "However, I am here. You are here. And I daresay we are about to experience one of the most interesting Christmasses ever. This family is many things, but I have yet to find it dreary."

Two evenings later, when Phillip went in search of William, he had difficulty finding him. Coming upon Matthew in the library, he asked if he had seen the boy.

"I believe he and Miles went into Welwyn."

"At this time of night?"

"There is cockfighting at the tavern near the crossroads. They intended to ask Stephen if they could go."

"And he permitted it?"

"I don't know. But if you can't find them, perhaps he did."

Phillip left the room abruptly. He found Stephen in the salon and beckoned him into the hall.

"Did you give William and Miles permission to attend a cockfight in Welwyn?"

Hearing the patent disapproval in Phillip's voice, Stephen answered hesitantly. "Yes, but only after we carefully considered it."

"We?"

"Caro and I. They came to me first and I sought her advice."

"And together you decided to permit boys of that age to attend something as barbarous as a cockfight?" Phillip asked scathingly. "Tell me this. What was your first, instinctive response when they told you what they wished to do?"

"To deny permission."

"Then why didn't you?" Phillip demanded. "Why did you involve your sister?"

"Because I'm not as good at dealing with Miles as she is. I often consult her."

"You should have trusted your instincts this time, Stephen, for they were exactly right. Now I shall have to ride into Welwyn and bring those boys home. I had not planned on a long, cold ride this evening."

"Phillip, before you go after them, I think you should speak with Caroline."

"Ah, no. As angry as I am at this moment, I should most likely strangle her if she came within reach."

"Here is your opportunity, then, Lord Brooke," Caroline said, as she came from the salon into the hall. "But first let me know what it is I have done to anger you."

"The cockfight," Stephen said simply.

"I thought it must be that," she said. "Mama wants you, Stephen. Lord Brooke and I can finish this discussion alone."

As Stephen returned to the salon, Caroline crossed the hall to the morning room and passed through its open doors. Phillip followed stiffly, put off as much by her attitude as by her assumption he would follow. Welcoming the opportunity for privacy, however, he closed the doors tightly behind them.

"I take it you disapprove of Miles and William going tonight," she said.

"You take it correctly, ma'am."

"I'm sorry to hear that. I think it was best to let them go. I still do."

"In future, I would appreciate your leaving such decisions to Stephen."

"Stephen was planning to refuse his permission. That would have been a mistake."

"Indeed?"

"Yes. And if you agree with him, I believe you would have been wrong as well."

"No doubt you base this opinion upon your vast experience of cockfighting."

"Not at all. I have no experience of cockfighting, other than what I have heard. I base my opinion on a lifetime of knowing Miles. There is a slight chance I could be wrong about William, but I don't think so."

"You seem to be missing the point," he answered sharply. "You should never have been consulted in this matter, and I will warn Stephen to avoid such situations in future."

Hurt by both his tone and his manner, she continued evenly, "Stephen often consults me where Miles is concerned. He is my responsibility—"

"He is *not* your responsibility! He is mine. My ward, my responsibility. Decisions such as the one made tonight are mine to make, perhaps Stephen's—never yours."

Caroline stood before the drawn draperies, her back straight, her hands clenched tightly at her sides, her glance locked with his even as tears stung her eyes. How could she have allowed herself to unbend toward this man? Had she really kissed him and enjoyed it? She must have been out of her mind! His ward, his decision, his responsibility. Everything his. All the epithets that came to mind—selfish, self-centered, egotistical—seemed far too weak to express her feelings.

"Don't speak to me of responsibilities," she said at last, her voice not quite steady. "I have always known what mine are. I have loved my brothers and sister and cared for them all my life. I will not stop now, simply because you hold a piece of paper that claims what is mine for yourself.

"You have played at being a father now—how long is it?— six months?" she continued. "From what I've seen, you're not doing such a good job. If you are so fond of responsibility, why have you spent the last fourteen years avoiding your own children? I have always been here for my brothers. You were never there for William or his sister. You are an insufferable hypocrite, a blight on my existence."

She was already moving across the room as she uttered the last sentence. She flung open the doors and stormed off down the hall.

Phillip made no attempt to follow her, nor to recall the boys. He had nearly forgotten them in light of the scene that had just taken place.

As it happened, not more than five minutes later William and Miles returned of their own accord. Phillip watched them pass the door of the morning room on their way to the salon. They did not notice him, nor did he call out to them. He had no desire to discuss their evening's exploits.

Phillip entertained very strong feelings about Caroline's interference in this matter. As was his custom, he had told her plainly what displeased him, but he had not anticipated her impassioned reaction. He could see now he had been too harsh. Discounting her influence with and power over her siblings, he had attacked a position she was clearly determined to defend. His assault had wounded her, so she had struck back naturally, instinctively, at his weakest point, making little of his abilities and much of his shortcomings as a father.

When they met during the following days, Caroline refused to speak to him unless it was absolutely unavoidable. Since she made no effort to hide her anger from the others, it was soon apparent to everyone that something was very wrong. Miles was distraught.

"You have argued with Phillip over our going to the cock-fights, haven't you?"

"I have argued with Phillip, Miles, but the subject of our argument is not the issue. We disagree on nearly everything. We cannot get on. It's that simple."

When Stephen spoke with her privately, he was more specific. "Phillip didn't agree with your reasons for letting the boys go?"

"He never heard my reasons. He has no interest in them. His only concern is to keep me in my place. Women have no business making decisions that are the prerogative of men. My God, Stephen, how I loathe him!"

Stephen didn't know what to say. To have his beloved sister speak so of a man he held in affection was distressing. "If I had for one instant supposed this situation would lead to such bitterness, I would have denied Miles permission instantly," he said.

"I have told this to Miles, Stephen, and I shall tell you, too. The cockfight had little to do with it. If it hadn't been that, it would have been something else. Lord Brooke and I have never truly agreed on anything. I doubt we ever will. I'm tired of trying to understand him, and I pray he will soon leave us. Until then I hope to see as little of him as possible. I must go now; Patience is waiting."

"Caro, one moment. I found something when I managed to open the case of Father's watch. There was a small key inside. Here it is," he added, fishing it from his waistcoat pocket. "Do you know what it fits?"

She took it with interest. It was tiny and intricately made. "I think I know where it might work. I'll let you know."

If Stephen found his sister sullen and moody of late, he found his guardian no less so. The work on the cottages was progressing well, yet Phillip seemed uninterested. He was often preoccupied and inclined to shift more and more responsibility to Stephen. Then, one afternoon, as he and Stephen were riding home from the village, he spoke of the day he and Caroline had argued.

"I realize it's late in the day for explanations, Stephen, but I should like to know your sister's rationale for allowing the boys to attend the cockfight."

Stephen held himself in great part to blame for the disharmony between his sister and guardian; therefore he welcomed this opportunity to clear the air.

"It seems some of their friends at school had recently been to a cockfight and were bragging of what a great lark it had been. You know boys. Those two got it into their heads they should like to see one. They found out from the grooms about the one at Welwyn and came to me.

"At first, as I told you, I was inclined to forbid it, but Caro convinced me we should let them go. They were so keen—she knew they would think us unfair to deny them such a simple thing. She also felt the best way for them to judge the cruelty of the sport would be to witness it themselves. She believed, as I did, that they would not stay long once they realized just how *unsporting* it was. And she was right. She sent your head groom along to watch over them and bring them home when they had seen enough. He reported that they didn't even care to stay to the end of the first contest. Caro also thought if we denied permission, they might be tempted to disobey us and sneak off on their own. Caro didn't want to risk that. Honesty is a strong bond among us. We would not happily see it broken."

Phillip took a slow, deep breath, then let it out in a rush.

"She was right. When you explain it so, it seems simple enough for a child to comprehend."

"Your reaction was not an unnatural one," Stephen assured him. "We all seek to protect those we love from anything that would shock or distress them."

"Perhaps. Still, I handled the situation badly. Perhaps I am deceiving myself when I think I can attempt being a father at this late date. Caroline's right. I don't know the first thing about fatherhood. Then I compound my stupidity by criticizing her for doing exactly the right thing. I don't blame her for refusing to speak to me."

Phillip pulled his horse to a standstill, gazing at the Hall across the meadow ahead. "It's time I go home," he said suddenly, unexpectedly. "You don't need me now. You must have wondered why I stayed on these past weeks. I stayed because of her. I am in love with your sister, Stephen."

Chapter 16

IF PHILLIP EXPECTED to surprise his ward with this declaration, he was mistaken. "I have thought perhaps you were," Stephen replied. "I'm not sure it will serve."

Phillip nearly laughed at Stephen's delicacy. "That's an understatement, lad. She won't even speak to me. How do you manage it? Getting along so well? I've never heard the two of you exchange a cross word. I find it nothing short of miraculous. My feelings are so strong that I get this mistaken impression I can say anything to her. Then I manage to wound her unforgivably. Fourteen years ago I lost a woman I loved. I never expected to feel this way again. The amazing thing is, they are as different as two women could possibly be. Victoria was shy, biddable, meek; your sister is none of those things."

"You are not the same person you were fourteen years ago."

"Oh, but I am. Basically I am. I can't say why I feel as I

do. I only know I need her as I need . . . air. Perhaps in the end she will marry Ashton after all. I suppose that would be best."

"Gerry? Gerry doesn't want Caroline. He is in love with Grace Bidwell."

"What makes you think so?"

"He told me himself."

"Well, it seems the fool has failed to inform the lady of his sentiments. Grace told me he is enamored of your sister."

"What? That's impossible. Gerry said he offered for Miss Bidwell while they were still in London."

"He may have offered, but he failed to declare his love. Or perhaps he did and she disbelieved him. In any case she believes Ashton to be in love with Caroline."

Phillip put his horse in motion again and they moved toward the stables. "As much as I shall miss you all, I will make plans to leave by the end of the week. I will take Matthew and Claude with me. I cannot do without them. I imagine William will prefer to stay here, and I don't see that I have any right to object."

Having decided to be gone from Paxton, there were several things Phillip needed to accomplish before he could depart. They included speaking with Ashton and with William.

Early the following morning he rode to Ashton's estate. He was shown to the breakfast parlor, where he found the viscount finishing his meal.

"Brooke! Will you have something?"

"I have already eaten, thank you."

"Some coffee, then?"

Phillip nodded and a footman moved to pour him a cup.

"What brings you here at this hour? I would have been leaving soon for Paxton."

"I know. I wanted to talk with you privately. I thought this would be the best place." He glanced at the footman standing behind the viscount's chair.

"That will be all, Wilkinson," Ashton said. "I will ring if we need anything."

When the footman was gone, Phillip settled back in his chair, his coffee untouched. "I may be totally off the mark, and if I am, tell me so and send me about my business. I make it a rule never to involve myself in the private affairs of others, but in this case I have decided to make an exception. I find myself in possession of several facts that may interest you. As I am leaving Hertfordshire in two days' time, I felt I should speak with you before I go. Stephen told me yesterday that you had asked Miss Bidwell to be your wife. Is this true?"

"Yes. She refused me."

"Are you aware she believes you to be in love with Caroline Hargrave?"

The viscount's eyes widened in astonishment. "Why do you say that?"

"She told me so herself. I came upon her one day in great distress. When I pressed her, she admitted she cared for you but felt her case was hopeless since you loved Caroline."

"Then, when she rejected me, she did so because she thought I didn't care for her."

"Apparently, unless she had some other reason. Did you not share your feelings with her on the day you proposed?"

"No. I intended to, but she refused my offer so quickly I never had the opportunity. It is difficult to make a declaration of love when the lady has already said no."

"I understand. But the lady said no because she was suffering under a misapprehension—one you can easily disabuse her of. If you are willing to tell her how you feel, I believe you will find her response everything you hope for."

Having imparted this valuable information to Ashton, Phillip felt every inch the hypocrite Caroline had accused him of being. He had been in love with her for months, yet had found it impossible to expose his feelings. Their rivalry had become so strong that he knew if he bared his soul to her, she would have ultimate power over him. So he was biding his time, hoping in some unguarded moment she would give a hint of her feelings for him. He thought she had done so that night in the library, yet her rejection of his proposal proved otherwise.

Later that morning Viscount Ashton called at Paxton Hall and invited Miss Bidwell to go driving with him. When she tried to refuse the invitation, he insisted. Returning to the house nearly an hour later, their glowing countenances and linked arms told Phillip all he needed to know about how the viscount's mission had fared.

* * *

Early in the afternoon Phillip found an opportunity to speak with William. They went to the library, instructing the footman outside to see they were not disturbed. Phillip offered his son a glass of wine, which William declined. Phillip then suggested they sit near the fire, where they could be comfortable.

"I am leaving for Southwell Friday morning," Phillip began. "As I do not plan to return here and it may be some time before we meet again, I thought it important we discuss several things. A few days after you arrived here, I received a letter from your aunt Helen. In it she spoke of you. She said you had been asking her questions—questions about me. If you still have questions, William, I am willing to answer them now."

William said nothing, but stared into the dancing flames of the fire as if hypnotized.

"I have your aunt's letter here," Phillip continued, drawing it from his pocket. "Perhaps you would like to read it." He handed it to his son and waited while William read it through. When William still failed to speak, Phillip asked, "Did you ever read any of my letters to you?"

"No. I saved them all. There were at least twelve every year, sometimes more. I wasn't interested in anything you had to say, because you weren't interested in me."

"But I was. I cherished the letters I received from Beth. She always mentioned you, so I never felt completely cut off."

"I didn't know she wrote about me," William answered. "I never wondered what she said to you. I didn't care. About a year ago, I don't know why, I started reading your letters. I started with the first one and read clear through to the last. When I finished, I felt I had a good impression of you—as a man—as a person. All those earlier years I had been despising a *thing*—a father. Now I felt there was a real person there to resent, to hate, if you will. I wanted to know more about you. I worried that since I carried your blood, I might grow to be like you—a man who couldn't care, a man who didn't love his children, maybe hadn't even loved his wife."

"I loved your mother more than life itself," Phillip said quietly. "When she died, a part of me—the part that cherished her, the part that had been joined to her by our marriage vows, the part that had with her created you and your sister—that part of me died with her. I was not a whole person then,

William. I had been torn into tiny pieces, and I couldn't function. I couldn't be what you and your sister needed. I was so young—Stephen's age. My parents were dead. I had no one who could share the pain with me. I wanted someone to hold me while I cried, but there was no one. When your aunt Helen came, I only knew I had to be gone. I asked her if she would take you and your sister and she agreed readily, gladly. I joined the army. I went abroad and stayed away.

"It was more than five years before I came back, and I only did so then because Helen wrote that George had been posted to India. She insisted I come to discuss the future of my children. When I arrived home and saw you with them, it was obvious you loved them as much as they loved you. I knew instantly I could not take you from them. To me you were two dark-headed five year olds; to your aunt and uncle, you were everything. Having given you up and left you so long, I felt I had no right to take you back.

"That I was never a father to you has been the cause for a great deal of regret in my life. Victoria would have wished me—would have expected me to love her children. And I do. But I made a decision in a moment of pain that once made could not be unmade. No life is ever perfect, William. No one makes all the right choices. The best we can hope for is to live up to the choices we make. Helen has chosen this time to give you back to me. I'm sure she knows how much it means to me to have you here. You're my only son, William. They say a son is a man's greatest pride. You are certainly mine."

Phillip turned his eyes from William to the fire, his voice growing quieter, subtly charged with emotion. "You and your sister came into my life at great cost; the cost of your mother's life. When I was younger, there were many times when I thought the cost too dear, when I felt cheated. But life isn't fair; as I grew older, I accepted that. We must play with the cards we are dealt, and not waste valuable time thinking about how things might have been."

William had come into the room filled with anxiety, a father-and-son talk not something he cared to take part in. He watched his father carefully. He had just been given simple answers to what he had always considered complex questions. Amazingly, he found himself accepting them at face value. His father was making perfect sense, and he found he wanted more than anything to believe him. Phillip's face, unknown to him for so many years, had become very familiar now. As he watched that expressive face, silently, thoughtfully staring into the fire, he found that all trace of resentment had left him. In its place he was discovering an array of new emotions. Admiration, respect, and pride were there, newborn feelings that were lifting him, bonding him tightly to this man who was his father. Yet mingled with those were others: regret for the years that had been forever lost to them, belated grief for the loss of a mother he had never known, fears that the path ahead would be neither smooth nor painless. Of all his father had said to him, he picked up one thought.

"You said you are leaving Friday and will not be back?"

"Yes. My work here is done. It's time I was home again."

"Then I should like to come with you, if you don't mind. I have some vacation left. I suppose it can't hurt for me to become acquainted with Southwell."

Phillip smiled, his gloomy mood lifting perceptibly. "No. I don't suppose it could."

That same afternoon, while Phillip and William spoke in the library, Caroline took the small key Stephen had given her and made her way to her father's bedchamber. She didn't bother opening the draperies but lit a branch of candles instead and carried it to the trunk at the foot of the bed. She unlocked the trunk, then carefully tried the key on the locked compartment attached to the underside of the lid. At first it resisted her efforts but finally yielded with a click as the panel slipped aside. The compartment was small. There was only one piece of paper inside, folded but unsealed and unaddressed.

Puzzled, Caroline wondered why her father had locked it away. For whom was it intended? Whatever her father's intent, she had found it.

She opened it carefully, spreading out the single sheet closely written in her father's neat hand. It was dated scarcely a week before his death. It was addressed to Lord Brooke, clearly meant for him, but for some reason never posted. She should have folded it then and given it to Brooke. But having come this far she found she could not keep her eyes from reading on.

November 17, 1816

Major Brooke—
I am dying. No doubt it will come as a shock to you to hear from me after all these years. Yet this week, when the doctor told me I had only days left, I thought of you and that other time I came this close to death. I had always hoped to find some way to repay you for what you did that day, but the opportunity never arose. It was only today I hit upon what may be a solution. I have spoken with my solicitor and have appointed you trustee of my estate, guardian to my minor children. You may laugh at my presumption and refuse the job, which would not surprise me, yet I hope you will at least visit my home and meet my family before you make a decision.

These last years of my life have not been prudent ones. Since I left the army, my life has been without direction. I have squandered the money left me by my father, I have mortgaged this property heavily, and though I have settled my personal debts, there is little left for my family.

I do, however, have one thing of value, one priceless gem. If you come to Paxton, you will meet my Caroline. You will find no finer girl in all the realm. She is so like you— single-minded, spirited, courageous, defensive of the rights of others, loyal, loving, and strong-hearted. If you should meet Caroline and admire her, you may take her with my blessing as payment of the great debt I owe you. So highly do I value my girl that I will feel the debt well and fairly paid by her. To know you are tied through marriage to my family will also set my mind at ease concerning Stephen, my beloved wife, and my babies, Miles and Patience.

I don't know what waits for me as I pass beyond this life, but if it is possible for me to look back, then I will watch with interest to see if my little plan succeeds.

There was no more, no signature. The letter seemed unfinished, as if he had locked it away intending to continue another day and had never found the opportunity. Clearly he had meant to send it.

Caroline laced her fingers together tightly, her father's scrawl blurring before her eyes. Dear, dear, Papa. She could hear him saying every word. He wrote just as he spoke. He had named Lord Brooke trustee as part of a matchmaking scheme! How ludicrous! He had thought she and Phillip were alike, while they were as different as any two people could be!

Suddenly aware she had grown cold sitting there, Caroline closed the trunk, leaving the key in the lock. Blowing out the candles, she left the room, taking her father's letter with her.

When she got to her own room, she found Grace waiting there, full to bursting with news of her engagement.

"I refused him because I thought him in love with you," she told Caroline.

"You goose. Gerry would never offer for one woman while he was in love with another. If you thought that, you have a great deal to learn about him."

"I know I do, and I cannot wait to start. He has invited us to stay at the Castle. Would you mind?"

"No. I think it's a wonderful idea. Your aunt and father will like Gerry's mama. Everyone does. She's the sweetest creature imaginable. And just think—when you are married we will be neighbors. I couldn't be happier for both of you." She gave her friend a warm hug before they parted to dress for dinner.

The Bidwell party left the next day after breakfast to make the short journey to the Castle. When the Hargraves gathered for luncheon, Phillip announced his intention to leave the following morning.

"I never intended to stay this long. I have been neglecting my own property. Matthew and I must go."

"And I'm going with them," William added. "I'll spend what's left of this holiday at Southwell."

"We shall miss you," Lady Hargrave said, sorry to see them go but pleased that William should wish to accompany his father.

Stephen and Miles both added appropriate comments, while Caroline's silence created an uncomfortable void, which Matthew hurried to fill.

"Mrs. Ribbon will certainly miss Claude. She told me only yesterday how pleased she was to have him rule the kitchen, for he takes all the decisions upon himself. She says she willingly allows him the praise when he prepares an excellent dish, for he also wins his lordship's displeasure when a particular offering isn't acceptable."

"Am I so exacting, Matthew?" Phillip asked.

"Absolutely," Stephen confirmed. "Don't you remember the soup you sent back yesterday because you thought it too thick?"

"But it was too thick," Phillip defended. "Didn't you find it so?"

Stephen only laughed, and Matthew was about to comment when Caroline suddenly rose from her seat, forcing the men to rise as well. "Please, please sit," she apologized. "I find I'm not hungry. If you will excuse me."

As she laid down her napkin, Phillip did the same, using the presence of the others to force her into the conversation she had been avoiding for the past several days. "I should like to speak with you a moment."

"Perhaps later, my lord," she suggested.

"I won't keep you long." He moved to the morning room door and held it for her.

She hesitated, all eyes upon her, then without a word moved past him. She heard Phillip excusing himself to the others before he joined her, closing the door for privacy.

"I have been hoping for a chance to speak with you, but you are avoiding me," he began.

"We have nothing to say to each other, my lord."

"I wish to apologize," he went on. "I was wrong about the cockfight; you were right. Stephen explained everything. I'm sorry. I hope you can forgive me."

She could only stare at him, saying nothing. Finally she turned and walked away.

His brows rose; he spoke to her back. "I have offended beyond forgiveness?"

She turned about, her hands clasped before her as she wrung them uneasily. "It's not that. It seems so senseless to be alternately at odds, then making peace. I don't like it, never knowing where I stand with you. Never knowing when you speak, if it will be approval or disapproval that showers down upon me. I had a governess once whom I feared for the same reason. I never knew what to expect from her. It was unsettling. It was one of the happiest days of my childhood when my mother dismissed her."

He swallowed uncomfortably. "Then tomorrow should be a happy day for you as well. I was hoping that before I left we could clear away this last misunderstanding. I have convinced myself you will forgive me if I can make you believe I am truly sorry." Walking to her, he took her hands, holding them in his.

As always when he touched her, her resistance crumbled.

"I won't leave while you're angry with me," he persisted.

"I'm not angry."

"You forgive me, then?"

"Yes."

"I knew you would. We always make our peace in the end, don't we?" He was greatly relieved she had forgiven him, for he was afraid he had gone too far this time. Convinced he knew her reasons, he was on the verge of declaring himself. It should be easy enough to say—I love you. I don't want to leave. The words were actually forming themselves on his lips when she spoke again.

"I forgive you, Phillip, but I think it's best you're leaving. The truces between us never last. It would be only a matter of time before we argued again."

Feeling like a ship that had been driven before a gale and was now in an instant becalmed, he dropped her hands suddenly and turned away. He realized he had been holding his breath and released it slowly. "Well, then," he said, struggling for an even tone. "I suppose there is little more to say. We will leave early in the morning."

"I am pleased William is going with you. Was it his choice?"

"Yes."

"I thought so. He seemed eager when he mentioned it. You've reached an understanding, then?"

"It seems we have."

"Good. I'm glad. While we're apologizing, I should like to beg your pardon for the cruel things I said that night. I spoke in anger and what I said wasn't true. You have done well with William, not pressuring him, giving him time to make his own decisions. Don't doubt yourself because of what I said."

"You spoke more truth than you realize, but your apology is accepted." Phillip had sought the interview but now felt he needed to be free of it. "I won't keep you longer. I promised to be brief."

"I will see you at dinner, my lord."

He only nodded as she turned to leave. After she had gone he stayed on some time, going back in his mind over all the conversations they had had, thinking if he had said or done things differently, perhaps their meeting today would have had a different ending.

Chapter 17

LORD BROOKE, HIS secretary, his son, his chef, and a number of servants left the following morning to begin the long drive into Nottinghamshire. The morning was cold and clear. Stephen and Miles walked with their departing guests to the carriage and waited on the steps as the coach rolled away.

Standing alone at a window in the long gallery, Caroline had an excellent view of the departing company. She watched the carriages move slowly down the drive, disturbing the thin layer of frost that had settled overnight. Lord Brooke was finally leaving her life. She felt immense relief, as if a great weight had been lifted from her shoulders. She could relax now, be herself again. Things could return to the way they had been before he had ridden into their lives and changed everything.

Yet as days passed, then weeks, Caroline found that things did not return to normal. Her friend Gerry, with whom she and Stephen had often spent many hours of the winter, was engaged to be married. He had little time for them now. Patience spent most of her time with her governess; Miles had returned to Eton; Lady Hargrave busied herself with housekeeping and charity work, fussed over each of her children in turn, but was often away from home.

No longer living in straitened circumstances, Caroline found there was less for her to do. She turned her hand to many projects but soon lost interest. She took Leo for long walks, indulging in solitary periods of melancholy reflection. She was vaguely aware of a general feeling of discontent, but she was at a loss to discover its root.

In January Stephen prepared to leave for London, intending to be present for the opening of Parliament. He had been invited to stay with Phillip in Curzon Street.

"You're sure you won't come?" Stephen pleaded as he and Caroline shared an afternoon tea in the library. "You said you wanted to show me the sights, and the Season will be starting before long. Gerry and Grace will be there."

"Yes. And so will Lord Brooke."

"You stayed at his house once before," Stephen argued. "I will never understand this animosity you bear him, Caro. He has always been good to us."

"It's not animosity, precisely. I would simply rather not be where he is. We always come to blows sooner or later. It's never pleasant when we do."

"There were times when he was staying with us that I actually thought you admired him."

Caroline considered this. "Mmm. There are some things I admire about him," she admitted. "He asked me to marry him once."

"I'm not surprised. I know how he feels about you."

"What do you mean, you know how he feels?"

"He told me he was in love with you. Surely, if he offered, he told you as well."

"He asked me to marry him. He said nothing of love. Stephen, you must be mistaken. He can . . . he cannot be in love . . . not with me . . . I . . ."

"I hope I haven't betrayed a confidence," Stephen mused. "I'm sorry I said anything." He doubted whether his sister heard him, for she had turned away and walked from the room. She called Leo to her in the hall, and a few moments later Stephen heard the outside door close behind her.

Stephen left Paxton two days later. He and his sister had not discussed Phillip again.

Stephen enjoyed London far more than he had expected. He found the House of Lords to be an experience more unique than any he had ever known. At times dismally attended, at other times packed to overflowing, the speeches were occasionally petty, sometimes brilliant. But whether the discussion was too noisy to hear or too silly to listen to, one thing was abundantly clear—he had a great deal to learn.

Stephen wrote Caroline often, Phillip's name regularly appearing in his letters. At first it annoyed Caroline to see it, but as time passed, she began looking for any mention of him and felt deprived when it wasn't there.

Not a day went by that she didn't think of what Stephen had told her before he left. Had Stephen misunderstood? Perhaps Phillip had simply said he admired her and Stephen had assumed the rest. Or had there been more to Phillip's marriage proposal than met the eye? Did he have another reason for asking aside from the one he offered—that he had compromised her?

There were too many questions and no answers. Yet no matter how she tried, she found it impossible to believe Phillip loved her. It was true he had kissed her, but she was not naive enough to believe that men only kissed where they loved. If his feelings had been so strong, why hadn't he spoken of them?

Then, after long periods of speculation about his feelings, she would turn to an examination of her own. Yet even there, where she had all the answers, none of them made the least sense.

March was unseasonably warm; April cold and wet. As May drew nearer, Stephen came home full of ideas for the planting season and the summer beyond. That same afternoon Caroline took the letter she had found in her father's trunk, folded it, sealed it, then asked Stephen to frank it and post it to Lord Brooke in London. She told herself she was sending it to fulfill a wish of her father's, for he had surely intended Brooke to have it. In truth she was sending it to see if it would raise enough curiosity to bring his lordship back to Paxton.

May arrived and with it warmer weather, yet no sign of Lord Brooke. Caroline traveled into Oxfordshire to see Grace and Gerry wed. The crops were planted. Miles came home from school. Caroline and her mother were once again sewing infant clothing for Iris Miller, for she was expecting another child in the fall.

On a warm sunny day in June, a day bearing a striking resemblance to the day she had first met her trustee, Caroline walked to the stream after luncheon. It looked exactly as it had

402

that day a year ago, not a single thing changed, yet she knew everything else in her life had changed and would never be the same again. Leo dashed about her skirts as she made her way to the edge of the water. Caroline raised her eyes to the ridge where she had first seen Phillip. The beeches were there, growing widely spaced yet spreading their limbs to mingle above. Two squirrels chased each other through the branches at breakneck speed, but there was no handsome rider on a shiny bay mare.

Caroline sat to take off her shoes and stockings. She would wade to her rock today and bask in the sun and enjoy the blue sky. She pulled off her bonnet and tossed it aside, knowing she would be encouraging freckles, but not caring. No sooner had she removed her first shoe than Leo snatched it and scampered off.

"Oh, no, you don't, sir!" she exclaimed. "Bring it back this instant!" Fortunately for her feet, considering the length of the walk home, he obeyed and she breathed a sigh of relief. She praised him for his obedience, then tucked both her shoes and stockings out of reach in the crotch of a tree, in case his good manners were to be short-lived.

Caroline hitched up the skirts of her pale blue muslin gown. The water was cold, but she stepped through it quickly, then climbed onto her flat rock. It had been thoroughly warmed for her by the sun, and she thought she knew how a lizard or snake must feel when they found just such a spot to bask.

It was Leo who first noticed the rider approaching from downstream. He had been hard at work digging a rabbit from its burrow, but the arrival of a rider was of more interest to him. He set up a continuous yapping, straining his eyes steadily to the south. Perceiving a chestnut horse, Caroline decided Stephen had come to offer her a ride home. But as the rider drew closer she discovered it was not Stephen. She made no effort to leave her rock, but sat with her knees drawn up to her chest, her arms wrapped about them, her bare feet flat on the rock with her toes peeping from beneath the hem of her gown.

Phillip rode his horse to the bank directly opposite Caroline and brought him to a complete stop before he spoke. He wore a coat of blue superfine, buckskin breeches, and top boots. His linen reflected the sun with dazzling whiteness.

"Have you any other occupation in June," he asked, "or do you always spend it there?"

She would have preferred to offer some quick rejoinder, something clever, but she found herself tongue-tied.

Dismounting, Phillip took a step toward the water. "We seem to be involved in a déjà vu, Miss Hargrave. Shall I come for you again?"

She rose quickly, gathered her skirts, and stepped into the water. "That will not be necessary, Lord Brooke. It is rather senseless for me to hide what you have already seen."

He smiled. "I agree. And I should dislike spoiling these boots."

She took the hand he offered to pull her from the water onto the grassy bank, but when he showed no inclination to release hers, she moved toward his horse. Their hands fell apart.

"You have a different horse," she commented. "Where is your lovely bay?"

"I have put her to the stud this year. I thought she might like to try motherhood."

"It is your intention, no doubt, to reproduce those wonderful legs she has."

"Exactly. And she will, too. Fine bone runs solidly in her bloodline. Where are your shoes?"

She pointed and he retrieved them but kept them from her as he asked, "Who sent me the letter, Caroline? You, or Stephen?"

"I did. He hasn't read it. I found it among my father's things some time ago. I should have given it to you then. It was directed to you, and I'm sure he intended you to have it."

"Have you read it?"

"It wasn't sealed when I found it. I don't think it was ever finished."

"Have you read it?"

"Yes. I couldn't resist. There had always been that mysterious question as to why my father appointed you trustee."

"But there is no question now?"

"No. He clearly hoped to pay his debt with me."

"And what would you say if I told you I am willing to settle for the payment your father suggested?" He gave her no time to answer but quite deliberately tossed her shoes aside, reached for her hand, and drew her closer. "I much prefer this dress to

404

the one you were wearing the first time we met. Your hair is lovely—such a rare color. It was the first thing I noticed that day."

Her brows wrinkled, questioning. "Was it?"

"Yes. I remember wondering how long it would be, how it would look were it loose." Before she even realized what he was about, he had pulled several pins from her hair. As it cascaded down, other pins spun away and the hair was soon free, hanging to her waist in pale waves.

"My lord—" she began to object, but he silenced her instantly.

"No. Say nothing—nothing at all." His left hand tangled itself in her hair as his right caught her waist. She tried for a moment to pull away, but her resistance evaporated as he gathered her tightly against him and his lips settled over her. He offered her no quarter, and she wanted none. She had learned by now what he expected from her, and she returned his kiss with a passion equal to his own.

After one kiss he backed off, holding her at arm's length. "That is quite a welcome from someone who was eager to see me gone."

She backed away, then collected her shoes and stockings and sat to put them on. He turned away instantly. Walking to where his horse was grazing on the fresh spring grass, Phillip led him to a tree and tethered him. Caroline was finishing as he returned; he took her hand to draw her to her feet but loosed it immediately when she stood.

"When did you find the letter, Caroline?"

"Just before you left Paxton last winter. The day Gerry and Grace became engaged."

"Why didn't you give it to me then?"

"Because I didn't know, then, how you felt about me."

His eyes widened, his brows rising in surprise. "And you do now?" He sounded doubtful.

"Yes. Stephen told me."

"When?"

"In January."

He seemed to digest this for a few moments before he continued.

"Why did you wait until this spring to send the letter? You must have known it would bring me back."

"I hoped it would. I've missed you."

He smiled then, taking her face in his hands and forcing her to look at him. "Missed me? The blight on your existence?"

She looked genuinely shocked. "I never said that! Did I?"

He nodded, his eyes twinkling. "Yes. I am afraid you did, my love. And alas, it is only one in a long list of horrible names you have called me during the past year."

"If I did, it was only because I was greatly provoked," she fired at him.

"Oh, no. I will not let you start a row with me now, when I am about to collect from your father. Are you truly willing to settle this debt for him?"

"I am. If you'll have me."

"You already know I want you. I *did* ask once before," he pointed out.

"You only asked then because you felt obligated."

"No. I asked then for the same reason I am asking now. Because I love you. For all the things your father mentioned and a dozen others besides. But heed this, Caroline! I am not eager to lay my love at any woman's feet, for it is quite fragile, you know. I don't think I could bear to have it scorned or trodden upon. So before I ask, and before you answer, I should like to know—"

"You should like to know how I feel," she interrupted. "I never knew until you went away how much I needed you. Even through all the arguments and disagreements, you had added a dimension to my life that I feel lost without. I love you, Phillip. There is no joy in my life without you."

He kissed her again, then held her away. "Very well, Miss Hargrave, since I have your father's permission in writing and since I am certain your trustee will not object, I take leave to ask you to become my wife." He raised his eyes to the meadow beyond her shoulder and added, "If you mean to accept me, ma'am, I think you should do so quickly. For unless I miss my guess, we are about to be descended upon by your younger brother and my son."

"William is here?"

"Yes. I brought him with me. Didn't I say so?"

"No."

"It's beside the point in any event. Will you have me to husband, or will you not?"

"Yes, please."

"Good. That's settled, then."

"You know we will probably have the occasional disagreement, Phillip," she added, wanting to be totally honest with him.

"I would be disappointed if we didn't."

"And I suppose there may be those times when I do things of which you disapprove."

"I would think twice before I did them, were I you," he warned.

"And I should like to have children, Phillip, despite the risk."

"I know. And I would never deny them to you, though I can't promise I won't fuss over you like a hen with one chick."

"You won't mind starting over with a whole new family?"

"No. Not if it's what you want. Besides, I missed most of it the first time around."

She smiled at him through misty eyes and rose on her tiptoes for his kiss.

As the riders drew closer, Phillip and Caroline separated unwillingly.

"Seeing William reminds me, Caroline, that I need your advice. Beth is arriving from India in less than a month. I haven't the least notion how to deal with a fifteen-year-old daughter."